within

ben scott craig

within

ben scott craig

First Print And eBook Edition: May 2012

Copyright © 2012 Ben Scott Craig

Learn More At withinanovel.com
Follow At twitter.com/bscwriter

ISBN-13: 978-0615643281
ISBN-10: 0615643280

part one
UNDER COVER OF DARKNESS

CHAPTER ONE

It wasn't that Andy Stone wanted to die. He was just more conscious of death lately. As he walked along the sidewalk leading to the *Denver Journal*, he realized that a shift of his body two feet would send him careening into oncoming traffic. Only two steps to the right and the bus charging at him would end his life. Just like that, the tension would release.

Despite these thoughts, he knew he wasn't anywhere close to the edge. Those two feet could have been twenty. Perhaps it was the phone call he was anticipating; perhaps it was his newspaper's grim future. The thought of death was creeping into his life.

Andy walked into the glass-encased entry of the *Denver Journal*. The second-floor elevator light was illuminated. He hastily smacked the already-glowing button a few more times. His phone buzzed to life. Andy's hand trembled just slightly as he reached into his pocket. He was desperately waiting for a call from his father. Whether the call would bring encouraging news, or whether he would need to board a plane immediately, he needed to know. Even bad news was better than the uncertainty. He recognized the number, but it wasn't his dad.

"Lucas. What's up?" Andy asked his fellow reporter.

Lucas asked, "Did you hear?"

"No."

"About the public relations guy, John, from The Leadership Project," Lucas explained. His words weren't clearly enunciated.

"Public relations," Andy scoffed. His slender frame paced back and forth in front of the elevator door. "I've never heard a more deceptive euphemism. Hit man would be more accurate. What about him?"

"He's been calling the paper nonstop, trying to find the reporter doing an undercover story about their leadership course," Lucas answered.

"What?" Andy begged. He stopped pacing. "How does he know? I've been planning this investigation for months. Nobody knew anything. And they find out *now*?"

"Forget about that for a second," Lucas replied. "Where are you?"

"Downstairs. Stupid elevator's jammed on the second floor again."

"You're downstairs?" Lucas asked.

"Yeah."

"Andy, he's coming here now."

"What?"

"If he sees you, the story's over."

Andy scanned the parking lot. Sporadic cars dotted the spaces. Thin clumps of densely packed snow were melting. It was a mild day in March. Tributaries of water flowed out of the small mounds of snow, over the pale concrete, and into the budding grass. Spring was coming. A silver Ford sedan whipped into the parking lot and abruptly came to a stop at a reckless angle over two spots. A younger man with neatly-combed, brown hair and a pressed blue shirt climbed out of the car.

"Oh, no..." Andy whispered into the phone.

"What is it?"

"I think he's here." Andy squinted. "That's him."

Lucas whispered back, "Get out of there."

"I'm coming up."

Andy waved his identification card in front of a scanner next to a thick gray door. A light flashed from red to green. He pulled open the door and climbed the metal stairs, skipping steps along the way. His long, toned quads still burned from an epic day of snowboarding a few days before – a foot of new snow, open powder fields and steep cornice drops, graceful turns etched into a blank canvas like a form of snowboarding calligraphy. He loved the holy cathedral of the Rocky Mountains.

Andy ran into the newsroom. He passed stacks of abandoned promo materials once destined for the old music editor. Campaign signs from an indicted state representative were scattered around another empty cube. As he searched the vast room for Lucas Smith, he passed the arts and entertainment reporter who collected small figurines. Hundreds of trolls, elves and army soldiers encircled her chair, as if they were all sitting in an arena and she was the main attraction. A core of reporters and their cluttered desks remained in the middle of the newsroom, but empty desks were rapidly expanding inward. The occupied desks shrank into a circle in an Alamo-like last stand.

"He's coming up," Lucas said. He was a large, light-skinned black man with blue eyes that gave away his white father. He was a gifted journalist who had worked for several years at the *Washington Post*. He had been a correspondent in Israel, Baghdad, Paris and London.

"What do I do?" Andy pleaded to his friend and mentor. "If this guy sees me, he'll recognize me at the seminar today. The story's toast."

"Get out of here." Lucas pointed to the next level of administrative desks and an adjacent restroom. "Go into the bathroom. I'll deal with him."

Andy rushed into the bathroom. As he leaned next to two sinks, he caught his breath. Bright blue cakes rested inside three white urinals. Hand towels were piled over the top of the garbage bin. A daily cleaning crew was a luxury the newspaper could no longer afford. Andy slapped some water on his face. He scanned his reflection in the broad mirror above the sinks. His crystal blue eyes illuminated from the intense sunlight penetrating through the skylights above. Most people first noticed his eyes. His hair was somewhat long, expertly disheveled. He had a slender build. His face displayed angular, attractive lines with a round nose and childlike cheeks that belied his age. He had just turned thirty.

Andy hid inside the back stall. He sat on the edge of the toilet. Through a small window, he could see the city and mountains to the west. The front door of the bathroom swung open. Andy's breaths shortened. He pulled his feet closer to the base of the toilet.

"Don't worry, Andy. It's just me," a familiar voice said. It was the graphic designer who sat near Andy's desk.

Andy asked, "Is he still out there?"

"Yeah, that guy's nuts."

"I know," Andy agreed.

"Stay put for a little longer."

Andy peered through the small window. The urban center of Colorado, known as the Front Range, had been booming for the last decade and a half. But the wave had finally crashed, and its growth was receding from its peak. Two cities anchored the Front Range – Denver and Boulder. Sharp, distinct rock formations known as the Flatirons rose to the northwest. At the base of these mountains was Boulder. It was a city full of unique brilliance and innovation, but also disturbingly isolated. It seemed like everyone in Boulder discovered within the last ten years that they were allergic to gluten. Denver was different. More blue collar, less money. More people ate bread. The city had an industrial background. It was still a hub for technology and innovation, but to a lesser extent than Boulder. Denver was more diverse in race and income.

The bathroom door swung open again.

"He's gone," Lucas announced. The sound of his voice bounced around the white ceramic tiles.

"You sure?" Andy asked. He quietly exited the back stall.

Lucas answered, "Yeah, positive. Reception is watching the entrance closely. Even if he comes back, you'll know."

Andy hurried over to his desk. He grabbed his computer bag and stuffed his laptop inside. "I've got to get out of here."

"You're still going to do the story?" Lucas asked.

"Yeah."

"Is it worth it?"

"Lucas, they barely clear me to do any stories," Andy said. He jammed some papers into his bag. "I've been planning this one for months. I have to go. Today is everything. It's when they do all of the controversial techniques."

"There will be other stories," Lucas said. He reached for Andy's arm.

"Honestly, I'm not so sure how many more stories there will be...for me." Andy stopped for a moment and scanned the newsroom. One editor was watching his frantic movements through inquisitive eyes. He continued, "Editors are already walking away from me right now. I've promised this provocative investigation of a psychologically dangerous leadership course. I have to deliver. There's no choice." Although Andy had been reporting for a few years with the newspaper, there just wasn't enough money to keep his salaried position. He was demoted to freelance status a few months ago. He started bartending again to pay the bills.

"What's the deal with this place again?" Lucas asked. "Some sort of leadership training?"

Andy explained, "The Leadership Project is an international corporation. Everybody there calls it 'TLP.' The majority of its money comes from seminars and courses. They claim to be a personal improvement organization. Making people's lives better." Andy zipped up his computer bag and slung it over his shoulder. "They hold this super-intensive, closed-door course. They promise more happiness, success, and all that stuff."

"That doesn't sound so bad," Lucas said. His curious eyes narrowed behind wire-rimmed glasses.

"Their technique is psychologically reckless. The first day was brutal, and supposedly the worst is still today. It's the last day of the leadership course, and I have no idea what the hell I'm going to see."

Andy looked at him with vacant eyes. "The whole thing is just bothering me. The psychological attack is intense. It's hard to resist, Lucas. No story has affected me like this."

"That's not like you, my friend."

"I know," Andy said.

"Any other news?" Lucas asked. "Have you talked to your father yet?"

"Not yet. I'm in a bit of a fragile state right now." His eyes welled up. "This crazy Friday isn't helping anything. I'm doing this leadership course, then I have to work tonight at the bar."

"Andy, listen..."

"I can't, Lucas. I've got to go," Andy said.

Andy rushed toward the entrance. He checked his phone again. His tear-filled eyes appeared to beg the phone for an answer to his growing concern – a call from his dad telling him that his mother was going to be fine. It had none.

The second day of The Leadership Project was about to begin. Andy sat on the far side from the door, halfway back in a sea of chairs. A single chair rested on the stage. The room was filling up. About 150 people with white nametags and notebooks were buzzing. TLP had grown into a lucrative, international company. The majority of its revenue came from self-improvement courses that it held throughout the world. They had been banned in some countries for techniques some experts believed bordered on brainwashing. Further courses were also offered, and most of the participants were required to volunteer time with the organization.

The forum leader, Marcus Langford, entered like a prominent world leader. TLP volunteers in white button-up shirts flocked to shake his hand. Langford was a tall man with black hair and silver highlights. His eyes were black and vacuous, as if all matter might be sucked into them. It was simply hard to look away from him. Some people just had greater gravitational pull. Andy remembered meeting famous politicians and athletes. They were just people, but something about them drew all of the energy and attention toward them. They appeared to bend the fabric of space-time toward their intense energy.

Marcus Langford confidently ascended the stage. As he rose above them, the people applauded. They applauded nothing in particular. Langford held a slender black leather binder and reading glasses that he carefully placed onto the podium next to the chair. He looked around the room with his arms raised. "Please, please, I haven't done anything yet," he said, laughing.

He looked back at the volunteers and confidently announced with a powerful voice, "They ain't seen nothing yet, have they."

The people cheered. The room was thick with anticipation – like a campaign rally for a candidate with rising poll numbers. Andy clapped and looked down at Langford's feet. He fought the urge to look into his eyes. *Gravitational pull.* Andy watched patiently. This story was perfect for him. It had multiple moving parts, a compelling central character, and a controversial practice. It wasn't exactly his typical health care feature story, but it was about mental and psychological manipulation. Not much of a stretch.

Day two officially began. Rules were established. The leader dictated all action. He encouraged free discussion, but shot down anyone bold enough to challenge him. Langford sold the program. He promised happiness, authenticity, richer relationships and success beyond their wildest dreams.

The first session of the day-two course was called Devotion. Audience members were asked to walk up to a solitary microphone next to the stage. The first volunteer was Elaine, a forty-five-year-old, single, administrative assistant at an insurance company. "My boyfriend says that I'm always unhappy. He's always putting me down."

"So dump him. Fuck him. Are you so insecure that you can't live alone? That you have to have someone propping you up?" Langford barked.

Elaine seemed afraid to look at him, as though she were looking directly into the sun. She asked, "I'm sorry?"

Langford asked, "Why are you sorry? You've been sorry all your life. Everything about you says you're sorry."

Elaine shriveled. Her glasses reflected the glaring fluorescent lights from the ceiling. "I don't. I don't know what to say."

"Then don't say anything. You speak with intention here," his voice bellowed. His movements, down to the way he adjusted in his chair, were sharp and precise. Langford folded his strong hands and squeezed them together. Every movement was intimidating. He continued, "Your words have meaning. You are clouded by your own insecurities. To the point where you don't realize that your boyfriend is preoccupied with his own insecurities. Wake up, Elaine! Stop being such a whiny bitch!"

"Why would you say that?" Elaine's shoulders hunched over. She reluctantly looked up at Langford with brief glances.

"Because you're weak," Langford announced. "Let me ask you something, Elaine. Why are you here?"

"I just wanted to..." Elaine trailed off. Her hollow voice shivered.

"Forget what you wanted. Why are you here!" Langford demanded.

"Because. I don't know."

Langford looked up at the crowd and sarcastically announced, "Brilliance in the room tonight."

The conversation continued for almost twenty-five minutes. The audience watched as Elaine unveiled her deepest thoughts and emotions, then Marcus Langford tore them down. He had a contrary view for everything. He found weaknesses and squeezed. The words he chose, the posture he carried, everything about the situation established him as the answer to her problems. She was left with an empty shell to hopelessly flounder until The Leadership Project gave her the answers.

The hours dragged on. The room reverberated with the changing tides of Langford's voice. He would start slowly, quietly and compassionately when a new person came up to the microphone. He hinted that this time would be different. The berating was over. Marcus Langford listened to their fears, concerns and wishes. He encouraged them to be honest. He insisted that others likely felt the same way in the crowd. Then he would unpredictably shift and tear them apart.

"You're a selfish bitch."

"You would rather no one made love to your son but you."

Every line was an attempt to shock, and a desire to jar the confessors loose. Marcus Langford had a hypnotic control over the audience. Even during the worst parts, not a single person walked out. The only noise that cut through the silence was the sharp declarations made by Langford, the shaking voice of the confessor or the occasional cough. The force to stay became so great that Andy wondered if he could even leave if he desired. After six hours, seventeen people had unveiled the deepest parts of themselves, and Marcus Langford tore them apart. It was a hypnotizing power.

Andy constantly checked his phone for new messages. Nothing. His suppressed feelings were boiling to the surface. The techniques of Marcus Langford began to take effect. Andy began to feel hollow inside.

After a couple more confused participants drifted back to their seats, Langford pointed over to Andy. "You. You're next."

Andy's chest pounded. His body burned with rapid metabolic intensity. He tried to appear calm on the outside. As he walked to the microphone, he expressed a sarcastic smile to the glassy-eyed people in the front row. Andy walked up to the microphone like a threatened lion seeking to protect his cubs. He was dizzy with the thoughts of his mom.

Langford watched Andy shuffle to the front. "Next up, what's your name?"

Andy recalled the fake name he had been using during TLP orientations. "Ah…John," Andy said, lifting the microphone to his dry mouth.

"Don't be shy, John. You're the next contestant." Langford twisted his thick neck in a stretching motion as he asked, "What brings you here today, John?"

"I just would like to be more confident." He spoke a rehearsed facade.

Langford laughed and leaned back in his throne-like swivel chair. "You're a pansy, huh?" Andy noticed Marcus Langford's rolled-up, starched sleeves and thick, dark arm hairs.

"I'm a what?" Andy asked. His uncertain tone came sharply into focus. His blue eyes burned into Langford's.

"Pansy," Langford said with a laugh.

Anger was fueled by the pain and uncertainty of his mom. "You know what, screw this. You know what my problem is? It's people like you."

The statement got Langford's attention. He sat up and retorted, "People like me, or people like everybody."

Andy snapped back, "Fuck your word games."

"You won't speak like that to me, John."

"Fuck your word games," Andy repeated louder. His mouth blatantly enunciated every syllable. "I see what you're doing here. I see your game of mind manipulation. You're breaking us down and destroying our sense of self so that we'll be dependent on you. Just like David Koresh. You're going to put us all in white robes and make us drink Kool-Aid."

Langford rose from his chair and stood over Andy. He spoke surprisingly softly, "Let's focus on you here. This is my room. You will not speak to me like this. I'll have you up here all day."

Andy retorted, "You have no power over me, Langford."

"You think you're strong, huh?" Langford asked.

9

Andy said, "I wasn't finished."

Langford dropped down to eye level with Andy. The leader's eyes burned into him. "You finish when I say, not you."

Andy continued, "I wasn't finished! You are the enemy of all things good. You know why?"

"All right, let's hear it." Langford leaned backwards, apparently willing to allow this clear violation of protocol to wake the room up.

"You're the enemy because you're trying to rob us of our awareness. You're trying to make us empty inside so we're dependent upon you and your stupid program. Your message is that none of us should trust ourselves, that we're wrong, that we suck without you. You're committing the cardinal sin of all existence – to rob other people of their power and awareness. You're a fucking cancer, and I think it's appalling." Andy kicked a chair out of his way as he headed for the door.

"Where are you going? I'm not done with you yet. You get to speak and then I don't get to. Stop him!" Marcus Langford pointed above the crowd to the volunteers. One of the bigger white-collar, Kool-Aid drinkers grabbed Andy's arm.

Andy still couldn't believe what he had said. The lines kept replaying in his mind. He just wanted to get out of there. He wasn't himself. "Get out of my way." His eyes focused on one of the volunteers blocking his path.

For a moment he was stopped by a younger man with neatly-combed brown hair. John, the public relations hit man, stood in front of the door. "Good luck with your story," he stated. His arms were crossed.

Andy walked past him.

John said, "You know, if you felt this way about our leadership course, maybe you shouldn't be telling this story. Not exactly objective. Ever think about that? I think it's time to let it go, don't you?"

Andy mumbled, "I don't know what you're talking about."

"Yeah, right," John barked.

Andy's mind raced. He had never injected himself into a story before. He walked briskly to his car, and sped away. He got off at the next exit, pulled into the dark corner of a Party City Outlet Store parking lot, and cried.

The sun descended below the snow-capped peaks to the west. The planks were cold. They creaked reluctantly with the weight of footsteps. Andy and his fellow bartender, Justin, had prepped the bar below for the night's concert. He found temporary comfort in the predictable ritual of working behind a bar. Mary's Tavern expected about 300 people this evening. The building was a music venue throughout the year and a rooftop party deck when the weather got milder. The two bartenders had climbed the back stairs and walked onto the dormant rooftop for a break. Collapsed umbrellas and plastic chairs were stacked on the wooden walkways between two tiki bars.

Andy walked away from his friend for a minute, raised his phone to his ear, and desperately whispered, "Dad, I was just wondering if there's any news. Is your phone on? Please call me back whenever you know anything. *Please.* I love you, Dad."

The city was thawing. Rooftops dripped. Cold water pooled all around creating glossy mirrors and a hint of a parallel city in reflection. Across the street at Coors Field, workers in purple golf shirts marched back and forth on the terraces. The whitecaps on the mountains were receding back into their peaks. The blue awning of another rooftop bar across the alley sagged and bobbed aimlessly, like a sailboat precariously anchored in a harbor.

The deck was eerily still. Justin lit up a cigarette and offered one to Andy. Andy held up his hand in polite refusal, although this day made him crave vices.

"It's strange to see our rooftop so dead," Andy said. His breath rose in a rapidly dispersing fog.

Justin agreed, "It is." He was a shorter guy, packed with energy. His other job was jumping with newbie skydivers with a camera on his helmet. He had done over five hundred jumps. He had a chin beard that knifed down to the ground like a frozen icicle of hair. He looked tired.

"You all right, Justin?" Andy asked.

He changed the subject and asked, "Quite a show tonight, huh?"

"Jacobs the Great," Andy said.

Lily Jacobs wrote a song about Andy called "False-Hearted." There wasn't a lot of room for misinterpretation. It was about a guy who portrayed himself as spiritual and appeared to search for meaning, but he was just trying to meet lots of women. This image was far from the truth. Andy rarely ever met or advanced on anyone in his bar. He had encounters with two girls during the entire year, a server named Jenna and a bar regular named Amy. They happened to be a week apart. And they happened to meet at a small party and both talked about the guy they had just met by the name of Andy. They happened to have a friend who loved

11

to wedge herself into the affairs of others. She was the singer and songwriter named Lily Jacobs.

A week after the incidents, Lily pulled Andy away from the rooftop bar and presented the two distraught women along the back walkway. He would never forget Lily's rage combined with satisfaction. She was out for blood. Lily screamed and pointed at his crotch. A lot. Andy twisted his left leg over his right to protect himself from the threat of scrawny limbs in violent, unpredictable motion. The situation made him feel terrible. Since the incident, he deflected all advances from the bar.

"Lily Jacobs." Andy shook his head.

For the next few hours, Andy poured drinks with his phone set to vibrate in his pocket. He played the role of bartender with ease. Even though it bothered him to be back, he appreciated the time-honored ritual of bartending. Yes, he served poison. Yes, it killed brain cells. He understood this. He recognized the hypocrisy and sometimes it even bothered him. But more than any hypocrisy was the purpose he respected. He fully recognized the need to forget about life and find a temporary escape from the sometimes-harsh realities. Watering holes served this purpose on every corner of the planet. Andy listened more than anything. He heard about how bad Republicans were, how bad Democrats were, how Atheists could be so ignorant, how Fundamentalists could be so dumb, how kids these days didn't care about anything, how older generations were closed-minded and just thought the world was going to hell and feared young people. It didn't matter what they said. It didn't matter how they said it. Andy listened to them.

As the clock struck eleven, the place was packed, and the opening act, Lily Jacobs, was wrapping up her set with a song called "False Hearted."

"This goes out to my friend at the bar." She pointed at Andy and held her accusatory hand, waiting for him to acknowledge it.

"Andy, take a bow for the audience. Everyone, give Andy a hand for being the inspiration for this song."

Andy continued to plunge dirty pint glasses into a foamy sink. "When will she ever let it go?" He could feel the whole room focusing on him. He waited it out.

"Is that song about you?" A young woman leaned over the bar. She wore a pink tank top. Her skin was the orange complexion that could only come from some sort of spray tan. She reached for Andy's arm.

"Kind of." He deliberately pulled his arm away.

"Wanna do a shot with me?" She smiled and searched for a sign of interest.

Andy looked up from his glassware, "Thanks, but I'm going to take it easy tonight. He poured her a shot. It was the house shot for the night. Fruity and sweet, with the crappiest vodka the bar could buy. "On me."

"Aww, that's so sweet of you."

"Have fun," Andy said as he retreated.

Lily Jacobs clutched the microphone and peered through short clumps of bleached-blond hair at the bar.

I could have seen it coming,
But how was I to know,
How much you said you cared,
How quick you let me go.
A week of loving you,
Till I found out there was another,
The thoughtful man you projected,
Turned out to dive asunder.
How could I have been such a fool?

Andy hid next to the sound booth. He sipped a clear plastic cup of water.

"Great song, huh, Andy?" Chuck the sound guy asked.

"You know about this too?"

"Everybody knows," another server said to Andy. She was utterly disinterested.

"Man."

Chuck gazed out to the stage and said, "She keeps pointing at you."

"Whatever. It's been a year. How guilty do I have to feel?" Andy asked.

"I wouldn't worry too much about it," Chuck said, shaking his head. "I mean, 'turned out to dive asunder?' I don't think you'll be immortalized by this song."

Chuck climbed back to his perch and gazed down at the vast soundboard in front of him. Andy liked Chuck. He was old school. He toured with some jam bands from Boulder on occasion. He wore skinny black jeans and a black denim shirt. His dark hair and eyes, and

13

intimidatingly-bushy goatee gave a misleading first impression. He was a peaceful, understated, thoughtful guy. He rarely stuck around after the live acts were finished. If he did linger, it was under the single yellow light of the soundboard. Late one summer night as the rest of the staff was drinking rum on the roof, Chuck shared his philosophy with Andy. Although he just looked like a guy passively standing in front of a board, he was a composer who conducted a symphony through megahertz and decibels. Always shifting, always moving. In this soundboard Chuck saw life. He saw an endless series of dials that needed attention and adjustment. Just when he thought one was perfectly balanced, another one fell out of tune. It was a dance in a world of spectrum. Chuck saw his work as a romantic dance, an art in itself, an expression of awareness during sacred moments of musical creation.

Day after day, cycles of patrons walked up to the bar, ordered drinks and faded into the background. Hundreds of them. Through the years, thousands. And then one night, one person is completely different. She emerged out of the crowd at the end of the bar. Her smile and energy magnetically drew Andy's attention, and his chest thumped, even at the distant sight of her. Andy continued to nod as he made drinks for a couple of guys talking to him. They wore pressed business-casual attire with their sleeves deliberately rolled up. He was pouring them a couple of vodka tonics. On the second drink, his eyes drifted back to the lovely woman at the end of the bar. She laughed and joked with a couple of friends. Andy looked hypnotized. He missed the second glass and poured vodka onto the bar top. It trickled off the other side. Tonic gurgled from the soda gun into the second glass. It was overflowing.

The two guys yelled in unison, "Whoa, whoa!"

Andy returned to them. "Yeah, twelve dollars."

The taller guy debated. "This one's all tonic."

Andy poured half into a pint glass and filled it with a ridiculous amount of booze. "That better?" Andy's eyes locked onto him with a repressed tension. It was rising to the surface now.

"That's just fine man. No problem."

"Twelve." Andy stated, flatly.

"Here's twenty. Keep it."

Andy closed his eyes for a moment as he turned to the register. The rush of emotions of this day was taking a toll. He kept looking at the end of the bar for his strange new woman. He waited for a glance, anything.

Then she looked. Her gaze became a welcome oasis from the pain that otherwise defined the last twenty-four hours waiting for one particular phone call. She looked at Andy with a curiously familiar compassion and acceptance. On this night, Andy needed her look. He needed someone to assure him that everything would be fine. And he felt this when they locked eyes.

She leaned on the bar and motioned to him.

She said, "I promised I wouldn't drink tonight."

Andy replied, "A wise man once told me that there's nothing wrong with a little escapism every once in a while." Lines like this usually elicited condescending looks from flirtatious women. It was a survival mechanism to a statement many of them didn't totally get.

"But what am I running from?" Andy's head tilted ever so slightly. He tried to repress a smile. His eyes squinted with cautious amusement.

"So what brings you here?" Andy asked, trying to mask the rush of energy he felt in his chest.

She explained, "I'm staying with a friend down the street. She dragged me out tonight."

"Where are you from?"

"San Francisco," she said.

Normally this answer would be a deal-breaker. But not tonight, not with her. "Well, I'm glad you're here."

Emma said without hesitation, "I'm glad too."

Others waved money at Andy and pleaded for drinks. His fellow bartender, Justin, was struggling to keep up with orders at the other end of the bar. Andy couldn't see any of this. He was lost. Andy and Emma talked for a few more precious stolen moments. She spoke with intelligence and poise. She spoke with a broad smile, and they locked eyes for intoxicating seconds.

He said, "I'm Andy."

"Nice to meet you, Andy. I'm Emma" Her voice, her smell rang through him like a tuning fork, as if he had only heard the perfect tone a moment ago.

Andy leaned over the bar the next time she came back for a drink. They exchanged a few words. He was smashing his phone in his pocket. He pulled it out and laid it in the corner under the bar. He inhaled the entrancing scent of her skin where her neck met her shoulders.

She moved to the end of the bar where she could watch him work, and where he could see her. Her high cut shirt showed off just the hint of a tight midriff. They shared glances. Her smile was intoxicating, broad and genuine. She mentioned working for a cosmetic company. Rows of drinkers flashed money, but he couldn't see them.

In between rows of drinks and drunken banter, Andy returned to the corner to speak with Emma. Her energetic friends dragged her from one group of guys to the next. Meanwhile, buried in a corner under the bar, Andy's phone repeatedly buzzed. No one noticed.

During a special encore by the headlining band, Andy retreated from the bar. He squeezed through the crowd until he found Emma. He gently touched her shoulder and interrupted her conversation. She smiled brightly at his presence.

"Can I talk to you for a second?" He asked.

"Yeah," she answered, somewhat breathless.

"I know you live in San Francisco. And I really don't do this a lot."

Just then, Lily Jacobs yelled from the bar, "Don't trust him!"

"Please don't listen to her. She's crazy," Andy insisted.

"I could tell on stage," Emma said, seemingly unaffected.

"Listen. I want to talk to you again. I want to see you again. Can I call you some time?" The question sat suspended in terrible, thrilling uncertainty for a moment.

"Sure, do you have a pen?"

Andy reached into his pocket with widening eyes. He pulled out a pen and a small piece of printer paper. She was the most beautiful woman he had ever seen. She possessed a delicate mixture of a strong body and voluptuous curves. Her face seemed more comfortable smiling than not. He could already see she was funny, kind, and masking a vast intelligence. He wasn't in love, but he knew he wanted nothing more than to fall in love with her. Her smile lit up the room. She was a drug, and he wanted more.

Justin called over shaking his head, "Andy, I'm a little buried over here."

"Crap." Andy gently reached for her hand. "I really look forward to talking to you again."

"Me too." She squeezed back. Andy felt her grip tighten. He had always been self-conscious about his small, frail fingers, but the thought quickly vanished as he looked into her eyes.

"I'll call you." Andy held up the piece of paper.

He bailed out Justin who was drowning in a sea of drink orders. By the time Andy looked back in the corner for Emma, she was gone.

Under the bar top, Andy saw his abandoned phone. After he helped Justin with the final wave of drink orders, he grabbed it. He had missed six calls. He walked into the dank alley behind the bar. He called his dad. His breaths were rushed and rigid as he waited for his father to answer. Trash was scattered along the ground. Potholes were filled with black dumpster water. Snow flurries descended upon the dirty landscape and were swallowed by the dark puddles. Snowflakes fell from the heavens and melted on his warm face. They fell from miles above down to the precise coordinates on the tip of his nose. The flakes were always destined to land there.

"Hey, Andy," his father answered. He was wide-awake even though it was well past midnight. His father's voice hinted that something was wrong, just by the tone. His father liked to joke. He enjoyed some freedom in his dialogue, but there was no hint of humor or desire for multiple meaning. He could sense this in just two words.

"Well, you know Mom went in for her scans. She was feeling really sick. They found something." Immediately the word "something" conjured up the vision of a giant ball of cancer in his mother's body, reaching its pale white tentacles into her vulnerable organs. "Her cancer has spread."

"Yeah?" Andy's voice softened. He was a kid again, thirteen at basketball practice. All of the years of cancer and all of the calls, they all came back to him. He thought of his mother and how scared she must have been. He wanted to talk to her. "Where is it?"

"It's in her lymph nodes. They have to run some more tests," his father said with a sigh. It was the tired sigh of the head of a household, the man who took care of things, the father who always made Andy feel safe as a child. It was a voice that had faced his wife's death before, but this time it sounded different.

"What does that mean?"

"It's not good, Andy." His father's voice sounded hollow. It had little force behind it, as if he gently released the sound of the words into the receiver and wanted them to hit his son's ears with minimal pain.

"I think you should come home. We don't know how much time she has." Those words had never left his father's mouth before.

Andy's eyes welled up. "I'll leave tonight, now."

"You can catch a flight tomorrow morning."

"I'm going to the airport now."

17

Andy told Justin and left. As he raced home to grab a few things, his dad told him more. His mother had advanced cancer. It was her third bout and this time it had spread from her lymph nodes to her bones and lungs. His mother had been given a death sentence. It was the diagnosis that the family had always dreaded.

CHAPTER TWO

Thick flakes fell onto the windshield of Andy's rental car. They disintegrated into drops of water on the warm glass. The sleet accumulated in semi-circles at the base of the windshield where the wipers couldn't reach. Andy gazed out at Anytown, U.S.A. He passed the usual suspects – Chili's, Old Navy, Best Buy, Home Depot, Hooters and Barnes & Noble. He thought about people buying the same baby back ribs all over the country. An Old Navy billboard near the actual store showed a family in varied colors of cardigan sweaters. "Happiness is an Old Navy cardigan." This was America now. Life was layered upon an imaginary world of advertising that sold images of beautiful people of mixed races celebrating love and friendship. Products were no longer sold for function; they were sold by emotions. This layer of advertising had become so thick on the East Side of Rockford that it was difficult to tell where the world of advertising ended and actual life began. A friend once told Andy that, in business, sales was the lie you hoped would come true. Marketing was just the lie.

Rockford was eerily still on the West Side. A warehouse the size of an airplane hangar still displayed the ancient signs "shipping" and "receiving," but the cracked concrete and sprouting weeds suggested that a semi hadn't backed into the loading docks in decades. Andy turned onto Main Street. A yellow sign for the Alamo Club announced "Exotic Dancers" and just below it read "Dancers Wanted." As he headed further west, sporadic figures crouched over bar tops and the pale blue glow of television screens were the only signs of life. He drove by the old Essex factory. It was once a hub of production for heavy machinery. It looked gutted and barren. The Rockford Covenant Hospital sign glowed brightly through the dark orange of the streetlights. Hasty tracks cut through the slush from cars rushing to get to the emergency room. Andy carved out another pair of tracks as he slid into an open parking spot and rushed inside.

The number five in 415 dangled on its side on his mother's hospital room door. He knew it was the right room when he saw the patient folder hanging next to the door. The folder was thick. At the top, he saw the name Sarah Stone. The only evidence of movement in the room was the flickering glow from the television screen. He stood at the foot of the bed looking up at his mother. An IV lazily dangled from a silver rod. A cart was parked next to her with an electronic device that looked like an old Apple computer. It counted her heartbeats and registered them with steady beeps.

His mother lay on her back. Various clear lines were plugged into her body. Her breaths were tough and strained like she was sucking oxygen through a clogged straw. Her body looked deflated under the clean white bed sheets. Her skin was pale. It was the wrong tint on a scale of gray instead of tan. It had no pigment, no red from the blood, no resulting orange hue. Her arms appeared frail and weak. Her blotchy hands looked as though her heart could barely pump enough blood to her extremities. Her face looked like a ghostly reflection of her former self.

Andy hugged his mom. She began to cough as he squeezed his shoulder against her head. "Oh, sorry, sorry."

In the silence of the room, her eyes strained open. She slowly turned to her son. She wasn't sad or embarrassed. It was worse than that. She wasn't nervous or concerned. Any one of these emotions would have appeased him. She was calm. Despite her shell of a body, her clear hazel eyes hadn't dulled at all. She looked at him with a serene acceptance, like a spirit watching over her son from the dead. It was the worst emotion Andy could have possibly seen from his beloved mother. *Surrender.*

"Hi, Mom." His voice shook. He felt like an unsure teenager again. Once again, he was susceptible to the flows of the currents and the gusts of the wind.

"Hi, Andy," her hoarse voice whispered with the hint of a squeak. Her vocal cords had been paralyzed from the illness. "How are you, my son?" She spoke with a forced casual tone, as if Andy had just returned from an errand.

Andy squinted his eyes with concern. "How are you feeling?"

She said, "Oh, I'm okay."

"Okay," he replied. His hand clutched the metal railing on the side of the bed. "Are they telling you what's wrong?"

Her left leg flexed in what seemed like involuntary movement. "Not yet. Don't know. Let's not worry about it right now. How are you doing?"

Andy spoke softly, "Hey, you don't have to do this. Not this time."

"What?" She asked.

"Shield us. Protect us. We're older now," Andy insisted. The words sounded rehearsed.

"I'm not trying to shield you. I'm not hiding," his mother hastily said.

"We're here for you. I know you guarded Jamie and me from cancer before, but you don't have to shield your boys anymore. No matter how bad it gets. No matter what happens. That's why you have kids, Mom. So we can help you through this."

His mother reached her frail hand over to him. She missed it, touching forearms instead. "Thanks." The movement looked like a major effort. She asked, "How was your flight?"

"I want to talk about *you*." Andy insisted. "What are the doctors saying?"

His mother flatly stated, "There's nothing for me here after the surgery."

Andy pleaded, "Nothing for you here? This is a hospital. Where else would you go? Back to the Bahamas?"

"Not enough energy."

Andy asked, "That alternative doctor again in Mexico?"

"No."

"What are you going to do?" He asked her.

"I don't know," she said as she gazed passed her son and out the window. "But I know the answers aren't here. I've been in and out of these conventional hospitals for years, and they all do the same thing. Drug you, poison you. Doesn't matter who you are, what type of cancer, doesn't matter. They're like protocol robots. They do what the clinical trials say so they won't get sued. If I've learned nothing else after dealing with cancer treatment for the last whatever-many years, it's that these guys aren't close to a breakthrough. And I'm so tired of dealing with them. In fact, I'm worried they're just ensuring that we all..."

"It's okay, Mom. You don't have to censor yourself with me."

His mother continued, "That they're just ensuring that we all fucking die."

Andy said, "Definitely not censored."

"Sorry," she forced out in a particularly hoarse tone.

"I love you."

She turned to Andy. She didn't raise her voice. In fact, her voice lowered and softened. She looked into her son's blue eyes and said, "I'm tired of talking about me, about my status. I don't want to talk about it right now. Do you understand? Dad can tell you everything. He'll be back soon." Her chest jolted back to life with another harsh inhale. "How was the flight?"

Andy looked out the window. "Not bad. It was calm; sky was clear."

"How were you?" She asked as she expertly checked her IV pouch that hung above her. Even with advanced cancer, she acted like a nurse.

"My heart pounds at every little hint of turbulence. Hands sweat like crazy," Andy explained.

She asked, "Did you drink?"

Andy smiled. It was a guilty smile. "A little. Not like normal." He added, "A guy tried to convert me on the plane."

"Really?" His mother perked up.

"He sat next to me. Kept talking about how much he loved the Grateful Dead, while a small book of psalms and a pocket Bible kept mysteriously sliding closer to my tray table."

The left side of her mouth rose expressing a half-smile, "That happens to you a lot still, doesn't it?"

"Yeah. I don't know why."

She said, "I do, my son. They all sense something special about you. But they think you're lost. They can't understand what someone like you believes."

"What *do* I believe?" Andy joked.

"You believe in the search, that life is an incomplete search. And it's supposed to be incomplete. These people who try to convert you, they mistake your willingness to live in the uncertainty as being lost. They want to show you the answer, but there aren't easy answers, not for us," she explained. "They sense something special within you."

Andy raised his left eyebrow. He shook his head. "Thanks, Mom. You might be a bit biased."

She asked with rising interest, "What have you been thinking about lately?"

"About what?" Andy wondered. A nurse walked in. His mother gave her a slight nod of approval. The nurse checked a couple of the lines that led to his mother's wrist. She pressed a couple buttons and checked a plastic bag dangling just below the bed.

His mother continued, "About life."

The nurse grabbed another round, plastic bag from a supply basket and pulled off the crinkly wrapping.

22

Andy insisted, "Mom, it doesn't feel right to just sit here and talk about me. I want to know how you are."

She said, "I'm tired of talking about me, sweetie. Don't you understand?"

"I guess I do."

"Don't you know how much I love hearing how your minds work? It's the beauty of children. They keep moving forward, looking ahead, dreaming of new places. Why not talk about life? What better time than now? I miss hearing your thoughts." She hesitated before she concluded, "I could be gone tomorrow, Buzz. I could be gone in a week." His mother had used the nickname "Buzz" for as long as he could remember. It began when he used to have a buzzed haircut.

Andy leaned closer to his mom. As the nurse left, she dumped the used bag into an orange biohazard bin near the front door. "It all started with you. We pursue our truth in different ways, but the search for meaning came from you."

She smiled.

Andy looked around the room. His eyes stopped at the device next to her bed. "The closest thing I can call a religion is explained on your heart rate monitor. With every pulse, life bursts into existence. And with every flat line, it hangs suspended until..."

Andy stopped as he heard her breaths become long and pronounced. Within moments she went from alert to sleeping. Andy also realized that the nod she gave to the nurse was for more pain medication. It knocked her right out.

As he stepped out of the room, he saw his father emerge at the other end of the hallway. One of the fluorescent lights flickered just in front of his dad. Andy's father was a tall man with broad shoulders and curly black hair. His shoulders were uncharacteristically slumped over. He usually walked with a quiet professionalism that hinted at his successful career as a financial adviser. His dad was very funny and thoughtful. He possessed a jovial personality that often masked his intimidating presence.

He carried a brown leather overnight bag and an oversized bottle of water. He was wearing his glasses. A stack of books and his favorite pillow were wedged under his armpit. He dropped his overnight bag and wrapped one arm around his son.

"How are you doing, Dad?" Andy asked. His father had trouble keeping his head up.

"It's not good, Bubba. Not good." His father's voice cracked through the statement. For some reason he had nicknamed Andy "Bubba" since his early childhood. Andy could never recall the origins of the name.

Andy hugged him. He asked, "Is she going to be OK?"

His father pulled off his round, wire-rimmed glasses and wiped them on his green and gray flannel shirt. "We don't know right now. We just don't know."

"How bad is it?" Andy asked his father. He turned away from his dad in nervous anticipation. He looked like he was nervously waiting for half-lit fireworks to shoot into the air.

His father pulled the door closed and took a couple steps down the hallway, just in case his wife was listening. "The cancer has spread – to her liver, her small intestines, her large intestines, her bones, fluid in her lungs. Her liver is at risk of failing. She has several infections. Her breathing is getting worse because of the fluid in her lungs."

"Jesus." Andy dropped to the ground. He threw his hands over his eyes. His father sat down next to him.

His dad explained, "She was having trouble with her digestion. So they put in this tube a few months ago, which you know. But yesterday she wasn't feeling well, which was why I called earlier. They decided to have another surgery. And that's when they found everything."

"What?" Andy asked. He placed his palms on the cool floor tiles.

"Tumors everywhere," his father explained. "The doctor said that it looked like a bomb exploded in her small intestines."

"What?" Andy asked. His voice rippled with erupting emotion.

"Tumors everywhere," his father said, repeating the statement like a mantra one had to recite in order to fully believe. "In so many organs, it's easier to say which ones don't have tumors, than do."

Andy stared blankly at the ground, unable to fully grasp the information he was receiving.

His father continued, "They had surgery to remove two-thirds of her small intestines, and that's most concerning. She had trouble absorbing nutrients before. I don't know how that's going to work now."

Andy asked, "What about the other tumors?"

"That's what we'll talk about tomorrow. There's a large tumor in her liver. Did she tell you any of this?"

"She didn't want to talk about it. She said you would tell me everything, Dad," Andy explained.

His father exhaled loudly and nodded. "I can understand. It's been a flurry of doctors and discussions in the last twenty-four hours."

Andy looked into his eyes as he asked, "Is she going to die?"

"I don't know. Nobody knows. She is definitely standing at another fork in the road, and one road leads away from us, Bub."

"I just can't believe it."

His father insisted, "She's still got some fight left though. Your mother is one tough woman. And as long as that fire to live burns inside of her, you never know."

"Yeah," Andy agreed.

An attractive younger lady helped an old woman who looked like her grandmother down the hall. She smiled at Andy. His blue eyes focused sharply on her seductive curves.

His father said with a slight chuckle, "She's been tough on these doctors."

"Really?" Andy asked.

He continued to track the woman walking away from him. She reminded him of Emma. He wanted to talk to her again.

"Yeah," he answered. "You know how she feels about another round of chemo and radiation."

Andy asked, "So why did you come here?"

"No choice. Yesterday was bad. Probably the worst day I've ever had with Mom. We had to get to an emergency room quickly."

"Yeah."

"Your mom and I both thought it might be the end."

"I'm sorry, Dad." Andy reached for his shoulder.

As he fought back tears, his father said, "But it's not the end. We're still here today, and that's a good thing. The focus now is to build up her strength and figure out the next step. I'm glad you're here."

"Me too." Andy asked about his brother, "Where's Jamie?"

"Don't know. I think his phone's dead. I need your help with that," his father said somewhat sternly.

Andy asked, "He doesn't know what happened? How is that possible?"

"No. I could use your help tracking him down," his father stated.

"Okay."

The two embraced in the half-hug kind of way that men often did. Andy shook his head on his father's broad shoulder.

Andy said, "I need some time before I see her again." His voice shook. "I'll be back in a few minutes."

"I'll be here," his father answered with resolve.

The stroll was brief. Every hospital room was difficult for Andy to pass. Every cough, every wastebasket with a biohazard symbol, and every administrator scribbling on a clipboard reminded him why hospitals had always scared him. Something was lurking in those dark rooms. It was a force that was bigger than him and his mother. It was more powerful than any one person. In the world outside of the hospital, the force was easier to ignore. But in these long hallways, there was no running from it.

The hospital grew quiet as his father fell asleep on the cot. His baritone snores were strangely soothing to Andy. He curled his lanky body on the chair and looked at his mother out of the corner of his eye. He could barely recognize her. Tears fell onto the fluffy comforter that engulfed him.

Beyond his mother's ailing body, Andy once again focused on the heart rate monitor. It registered every precious thump of her heart, moment after moment. The flat line pulsed, pulsed back to life. One point became two, even several. Within these two points was the spectrum of experience that was life. The thumping beat of the heart was the point where life began.

For Andy, this was the place of life – within two points. Take this single heart beat and layer billions more and the spectrum became more complex, gray and uncertain. In a world full of life and action, absolution was an elusive state. It was the search for the flat line, the constant line in the pulse of life. By definition, it wasn't there. Maybe someday, but not now, not here.

A constant state of uncertainty had its side effects: attachment to things, people, places; identification with sports teams, celebrities, nations. Andy felt the ever-rising desire to grab onto something solid and seemingly stable in a place that offered anything but stability. The awesome force of uncertainty was always lurking and threatening. It was the very fabric of human existence.

As Andy maneuvered to find a more comfortable position, large lumps in the pockets of his jeans encumbered him. He reached into his pockets and unloaded handfuls of evidence from the last 24 hours: airport receipts, various clumps of cash, several snack wrappers and a piece of paper neatly folded at the bottom of his left pocket. He remembered the angel named Emma. He wanted to call her right now, but he thought he should wait. He wondered how he was going to tell her about the move and why he didn't say anything. He wondered if she would be scared away, or whether she felt the same excitement that he did. He remembered her stunning beauty as he unfolded the paper. It was scuffed and ripped, looking as though it had been sent to America over the Pacific Ocean in a leaky bottle from China. The tattered paper was his only connection to her. His heart pounded. His fingers shook. He prayed for a legible number as he thought about his drunken state on the plane. His clammy hands had been shoved into his pockets dozens of times during the flight. Her name was still legible. He could barely read the area code, but the rest of the number was gone.

CHAPTER THREE

Andy Stone's eyes stung as he slowly opened them the next morning. He forgot to take out his contacts last night. Sleeping with them resulted in dry, crusty eyes. Nevertheless, the room was bright with life and bouquets from well-wishers. As he looked out at his mother's body, his vision was blurry. He watched rays of gold and red light stream over his mother's body. Her chest glowed with an elusive pulsing greenish hue. He couldn't tell if he was really seeing this or if his crusty contacts were playing tricks on him. The woman standing over her only complicated the question. Lisa was a very close friend of the family. She had worked in finance at the same hospital as his mother. She was also an energy healer. His mother continued to lie still on the bed. A serene smile lifted her wilted face.

Andy asked Lisa, "What are you doing?"

She took deep breaths and focused on his mother's chest.

"A little house cleaning. How are you?" She threw a brief wave Andy's way.

Ten minutes later, three doctors walked in. A short, round Indian man walked in first. A lanky, balding man of a much paler complexion walked in second. Finally, a woman with incredibly straight hair and rectangular glasses followed. She had furrowed eyebrows and piercing eyes. As Andy's contacts cleared up, the streaming visions of light faded away. Lisa's hands continued to trace the length of his mother's body. Andy's father followed the doctors into the room from his morning errand to get newspapers and breakfast. Andy watched as his mother's expression shifted from serenity to anger.

The furrowed doctor barked at Lisa, "She shouldn't be doing that here."

Andy's mother asked with a smirk, "Doing what?"

"Whatever she's doing," the furrowed doctor insisted.

His mother snapped back, "You don't believe she's doing anything, so don't worry about it."

"I'm not interested in debating this with you. She can't work on you in this hospital room."

His mother insisted, "She's fine. By the way, she's an energy healer. A Reiki healer. She's working on my chakras, my energy centers. But I'm sure you don't really care about that."

Lisa pulled back, seemingly unwilling to take on the fight. "I can just."

His mother stated, "You're fine."

"Sarah, let's just talk here for a bit," the lanky, balding doctor requested.

Just as she was about to respond, Andy's father grabbed her hand. The motion had an immediate calming effect. She stopped and listened.

The round, Indian doctor calmly said, "Your surgery was a success. We cleared out most of the malignancies in your intestines. The procedure accomplished all that we hoped it would. But we have some complications moving forward, Mrs. Stone. Our biggest concern is the tumor in your liver. It would require another aggressive round of treatment. We could try another round of chemo. Of course, we would need to build up your strength before we administered any more medicine."

"Poison," Andy's mother said. Her arms were tightly folded, her eyes narrowed.

"Mom," Andy stated. He looked at her with wide, frustrated eyes.

The lanky, balding doctor asked, "I'm sorry, Sarah?"

She continued, "Poison. It's poison. Call it what it is. Poison."

He insisted, "Well, chemotherapy is your best option right now. I understand how this feels."

"What do you understand?" She lashed out.

The doctor adjusted his oval glasses and gazed down at his lap. He explained, "I lost my wife two years ago. Believe me; I know how difficult this can be. I went through it. It's an insidious, stubborn disease. It must be fought with everything we have at our disposal. And, yes, we must fight it with some very...strong treatments."

Andy's mother shook her head. Her neck was so tense that her head barely moved. "Treatments," she said with a diminishing sarcasm. She looked at the sympathetic doctor and said, "I've been a nurse for over twenty-five years. This is the third time I've had cancer. Be honest with me doctor, don't you think there's got to be a better way than this to treat the disease? Can't we do better than *this*?"

The short Indian man looked like a Buddha doctor. His soothing voice and tranquil presence only added to the Buddha vibe. He was clearly sent in to deal with the tougher cancer cases. He said, "We go by hard research and..."

Sarah reached for his hand. It was the only gesture of affection she had left. "I'm not trying to make you out to be the bad guy here."

"No, no."

"I know you're doing everything you can. I know that. And I understand that the statistics say my best option is more chemo. But when you imagine thirty years from now, do you really think we're still going to blast the body with radiation and chemo to kill cancer?"

Buddha doctor responded, "Perhaps."

Andy calmly squeezed his mother's leg. Just by his touch he hoped to sooth her rising anger. She jerked it away from him.

His mother said, "Or do you think it's possible that we could find a better way, that the better way could be out there right now, dying for us to find it, perhaps incorporating all knowledge of health and healing. Not just this hospital's narrow, lawsuit-paranoid, drug-company-dominated treatment."

The Indian doctor looked at her with sympathetic eyes. The serious doctor with incredibly straight hair in the back of the room saw this and interrupted, "Sarah, this is a difficult time."

"Yes, we've been over that," Andy's mother retorted. She didn't even bother to turn toward her. She merely threw a brief glance her way.

"And we will get you on a regiment of medications to try to build up your strength." She handed Andy's father a flyer.

On the cover was an elderly woman in a wheelchair. She had a clear plastic tube running across her face and under her nose. It was an oxygen tube. A golden retriever and blond child played in the lush green grass at her feet. The message was clear. *Die comfortably.*

The serious doctor in her slim white coat explained, "Sarah, we recommend looking into home health care as well." She said these words without a hint of emotion.

"Hospice?" His mother pleaded. The word made her body recoil. She stopped talking as her eyes shimmered with tears. She tightened her lips and shook her head, peering into the off-white ceiling tiles above.

The doctors walked out as the Buddha doctor turned and said, "We'll be in touch with you guys. I'll check back in a couple of hours."

Andy walked over to his mother. He stood between her and the doctors.

His father said, "Thanks for the information, doctors. We appreciate it."

She looked at the flyer. "Hospice."

His father said, "We can talk about the options."

"Hospice is a death sentence," she said to her beloved husband.

"You know they go by the statistics. It's the best thing they know how to do. The goal right now is to do everything we can to regain your strength. Forget the hospice thing. Forget it. We don't know what's going to happen. Neither do they. They know the chances. If you want to try something else, we can explore other options. The choice of what to do next is completely yours, Sarah. Whatever you want to do. If this is the end, this is the end."

"Do you think this is it? Do you think I'm going to die, Bob?" She looked at her husband. She looked for a sign. She had asked her husband this question several times before. The answer was always the same.

"No, I don't think this is it," Andy's father stated. He had always answered the same. "What do you think?" He asked his wife.

She shook her head. It was a sign. She still had some fight left. The faint glimmer of light had not extinguished within her. Even at this overwhelming hour, she wasn't ready to let go.

The rest of the day was uneventful. Occasional visitors, discussions about what to do next, short errands and lots of sitting. Andy read the *Chicago Tribune* from cover to cover.

As the world outside the broad window grew dark and the hospital once again became quiet, Andy's father convinced him to go home for the night.

As he hugged his mother, she whispered, "Where's Jamie?"

"We haven't heard from him."

"What?"

"Don't worry, Mom. I'll find him."

Andy walked out with a quickening pace. He needed a shower. He hadn't changed clothes in almost two days. Hospitals gave him an uneasy feeling in his chest. As he peered into one hospital room, he remembered why. A family crowded around an elderly man lying motionless on a bed. Two children were hugging by the front door. Their father gazed out the window as a nurse felt the old man's arm for a hint of a pulse. *Flat line.*

The most difficult part of cancer was the reality that existed within the halls of this hospital. Andy could feel it every time he came here. Death could take his mother at any moment. This was the reason why Tibetan Monks were known to flip their drinking cups upside down every night. It was a reminder that they were not in ultimate control.

Andy thought of all of the messengers who claimed to have the answers to the ultimate questions of life and death. These prophets told us to love our neighbors, do unto others, and live in the moment with awareness. They claimed the answer to life was to forgive and have compassion for those less fortunate. Andy knew the image of this utopian person – a prophet-like being who walked the Earth with consciousness, principles and love. This imaginary person had been illustrated by any guru with an audience or a blank page since the dawn of time.

If so many knew this ideal human, why did we fail to live up to this myth? This question was the one that all of the mystics, prophets and gurus had failed to address. It consumed Andy. And this was the great blunder of the prophets. They showed the ideal without understanding that the deck was stacked against it. They claimed that we all had the potential to walk the planet as Christ-like, enlightened beings free of the attraction to escapism and attachment. But did we? Andy wasn't so sure. Did they fully understand the scope and difficulty of a human life predicated upon uncertainty?

In this hospital, death was the shape that the uncertainty manifested for Andy. The framework of uncertainty was not only manifested in death, but also the concepts of right and wrong, and every fundamental building block of thought, judgment and reason. Andy Stone was defined in relation to others. He was defined by whom he attracted and whom he opposed. This overwhelming, yet invigorating uncertainty was the reason why Andy had failed – like every other person he had ever known – to live up to the utopian ideal of myth and allegory.

Jobs, homes, friends and enemies were more arbitrary frames of comparison. They were all opportunities to create the illusion of stability. The force of uncertainty remained underneath it all. Life was a constant balancing act between opposing tensions. Uncertainty was a force that provided no resolution to the debates over whether we had souls, whether there was heaven, whether there was a God, whether Israelis were more justified than Palestinians, whether Coke was better than Pepsi. The absolute answer to the most important questions in human existence was that *we didn't know.*

Religion preyed on the framework of uncertainty.

So did Atheists.

So did Coca-Cola billboards.

Movie endings appealed to the desire to escape from it.

As did anyone preaching one answer to the debate over God and the afterlife above another as absolute, unquestionable truth.

This was Andy's ideology. He believed in the religion of uncertainty. He may have been the only one. The challenge for him was to live within the uncertainty, have the bravery to respect its awesome power, and resist the seductive forces seeking to break the delicate balance. He had to fight the urges to judge, attach and escape.

In his mother's situation, Andy could feel these life forces at work. Underneath it all was the uncertainty of his mother's outcome. She could die. She could live for another week or miraculously for another year. He didn't know. This was the framework. These were the rules. Reacting to this uncertainty was his mind, desperately looking for a conclusion like a heat-seeking missile. It was a force within him that wanted absolution to the situation. Was she going to die soon or recover? No one knew for sure, but the mind wanted a conclusion. So the battle ensued. On one side, the powerful urge to conclude, to judge, to decide, to seek out a fixed point and live relative to it. The answer was to live without conclusion with his mother and live each moment with her. Everyone knew this. It was what the utopian would do with his sick mother.

He tried to escape these thoughts constantly, and he fought the magnetic pulls to conclude. It was the place that every guru had found. But they had failed to articulate the forces trying to pull us away from this space, and failed to provide the reason why everyone Andy had ever known in his real life had failed to live up to this unrealistic ideal.

CHAPTER FOUR

Jamie Stone tried to remember the name of the trendy art gallery. *Rise, shine, sin.* It was some one-syllable name. He stood politely smiling behind Michael Donald, the famous glassblower. This night was all for Michael. He had risen to elite status in the glassblowing world. A massive half-circle of news media, buyers and fans threw out random questions at him. Cameras flashed. Various digital devices recorded. The prominent artist discussed his latest collection and his long overdue art opening. Besides a line of people that stretched around the block, the opening had attracted three Chicago news trucks. Twenty-four sculptures stood on various blocks and pedestals throughout the gallery. They twisted and reached for the ceiling.

Jamie stood with four other artists. They stood in a row just behind Michael. Jamie folded his strong, precise hands in front of his waist. He stood still. His eyes burned with passion. He had short brown hair and scruffy cheeks that distracted from a slightly receding hairline. His pale complexion was accentuated under the white gallery lighting. He stood with an athletic, yet hunched-over posture. As he stood surveying the crowd, he looked somewhat annoyed. But a spark in his light brown eyes hinted at a man with great humor and livelihood. Jamie Stone brought energy to the world around him.

The spacious gallery seamlessly flowed into a trendy night club. It was located in the converted warehouse neighborhood of Chicago known as the West Loop. This neighborhood was home to many of the most promising restaurants, trendy clubs and hip shops in the city. If you were to win a cooking reality show, you probably opened a restaurant here.

A man at the front of the semi-circle with blond highlights and a voice recorder barked at Michael Donald, "Describe this series of glass sculptures for us."

"I was riding a wave during this series. I just went with it. And I wanted to take this one a little less serious. I didn't want to make a statement about war or repression, whatever." Michael answered the audience with emphatic hand gestures and facial twitches. With his designer jeans and circular-rimmed red glasses, he looked the way an artist should look. He was a slender man of medium height with surprisingly broad shoulders. His pale gray eyes were a perfect accessory to the gray scale gallery.

He continued, "Glass can be fun, and humorous, senseless and whimsical. Free of all of the tired categories and definitions." His arms made circular motions in the air. He tried to suppress a smile that rose from deep within. It bubbled to the surface as a broad grin.

Michael Donald did something that had always plagued Jamie. Somehow Michael was able to detach from the deeply personal act of creation and market his glass pieces. He was a salesman. He spoke of his work as if he had never been emotionally involved in it, as if it were a faceless commodity that he was dispassionately trying to move off the shelves. And move sculptures he did.

"What is it about this series that has everyone buzzing?" A round woman with heavy makeup and thick curls asked, her pen waving in the air.

Michael turned to her with his arms comfortably folded in front of his waist. "I think that sometimes we can be bogged down by art as representation and commentary. Sometimes you just like something. You can't exactly explain why or break it down. You just like it. That's the feeling I went for with these. It was fun. And these pieces will be rays of sunshine and levity wherever they reside."

Jamie still wondered if the latest Donald series was a joke. It was a group of pieces that looked like deflated jars with glass vines twisting and rising several feet toward the ceiling.

Michael scanned the crowd and announced, "So, please. Eat, drink, and enjoy the night. And for once, let's not ask why. Keep the brain out of it." He laughed. His hands motioned for the people to scatter. They dispersed, as if his hands had some sort of magical power to manipulate them.

Jamie walked over to a dark corner of the gallery, where three glass pieces stood alone. They were vessels of Jamie's creation. He had been agonizing over them for weeks. Jamie's sculptures were tall bowls that looked like fancy flower holders. They were beautiful and symmetrical. Although they were clearly created by a talented professional, they were easy to ignore. They had no magnetic pull.

Fifteen minutes later Michael Donald walked over. He was joined by a middle-aged woman with short hair, square glasses, and a black computer bag that gave away her occupation as a writer or blogger.

Michael turned to her and said, "I'd like you to meet a wonderful glassblower in his own right, Jamie Stone."

Jamie smiled awkwardly. "Hello."

"He's a brilliant artist, and he shows incredible promise for the future," Michael exclaimed.

Jamie thought about that word he'd been hearing for almost a decade. *Promise.* Eventually promise had to transform into something. Otherwise, promise became something else, something tragic. Michael and the blogger waited for Jamie to take over the conversation and describe his work, but he didn't.

The blogger said, "I've read about your work, Jamie. It's very nice to meet you. Are these yours?" She pointed to the three sculptures.

Jamie replied, "They are." The words sounded defensive.

"Very cool," she answered, trying to defuse the tension. She turned to his vessels and asked, "Can you describe these pieces for me? They're lovely shapes."

"My work has to mean something. I'm not just interested in making pretty things. If I need to explain it, then we haven't made a connection. What does it mean?" Jamie asked himself. "I was thinking about a lot of subjects when I made these. I can't just sit here and tell you that I was thinking about the struggle for freedom over oppression. Description kills the piece. Words cloud the meaning. I was dealing with a lot of topics when I made these."

"Okay?" She asked. The second syllable rose in the tone of a confused question.

"I mean, we can talk about them. But my sculptures mean more than some catchy selling points." Jamie's statements were abrupt. "They mean more than that."

"Very good. Well, they're lovely pieces." The blogger breezed over the hollow statement. She changed the subject. "Have you two been working together? What exactly is your connection?"

Michael hesitated at the question. His desire to bolster Jamie was receding with his concern for his own reputation.

Jamie interceded, "I was working with Mr. Donald on this collection."

"Oh, an assistant." She smiled.

Jamie let out a loud exhale and answered, "Sure, assistant."

Michael gently touched his shoulder. "I couldn't have done this without people like Jamie."

"Oh, Michael, you're so humble."

Jamie's face turned a pale shade of red.

She turned away from Jamie and asked, "Can you describe this series?"

Jamie looked at his three pieces that stood on square white pedestals. They looked lonely. He was about to describe his work when the reporter asked, "What do you think Michael wanted us to see in his pieces?"

"Oh, *Michael's* pieces." Jamie looked over at the rows of deflated jars surrounded by inexplicably ecstatic onlookers. He forced a smile and said, "It was fun. Michael is a very easy-going, approachable artist. But there's also a depth about him that makes everything he touches fascinating. These sculptures are just another wonderful point on the long line of unique and inspired work. I'm very glad that I could be a part of it."

"Well, thank you." The reporter smiled and wandered back to the crowds around Michael's collection. She picked out a man and woman in formal evening attire and held up her microphone.

Jamie stood by his work. He stood alone in a quiet corner of the gallery sipping a clear plastic cup of water. He looked outside the broad windows at Randolph Street. A biker with Jesus-like hair and a thick brown beard to match rode past. The biker had tattoos on his calves and a fixed-gear bike beneath his deliberately tattered Levis. Jamie listened to the buzz around Michael Donald's pieces. He looked at his own sculptures as an abusive parent would at his disappointing children. He felt about three feet tall.

"Are these yours?" A shorter woman in her mid-twenties asked Jamie. She had smooth olive skin and soft brown eyes.

Jamie could barely look at her. He was so frustrated, but still couldn't repress a subtle smile when he locked eyes with her. "Yeah, I did these," he answered.

"Very balanced. You're a gifted glassblower."

Jamie smiled. It was probably the nicest thing anyone could have said. "Symmetry has consumed me lately. Not easy to do." It was the first true thing he could remember saying all night. Jamie had become convinced that most glassblowers were obsessed with symmetry. Glass looked easy to make completely balanced. But mastery of creating uniform shapes took years, even a lifetime.

She reached her soft hands out to his arm. "Clearly you've been doing this for a long time." Her movements were smooth, calm and caring, as if she were an expert handler dealing with an agitated, venomous snake.

Jamie answered, "Thanks."

"I'm Mya."

"Hi. Jamie."

"How long have you been blowing glass?" Her chest rose and fell with slow, calming breaths.

"Since I was about eighteen," Jamie answered as his eyes hastily scanned the gallery. "Over ten years." He contemplated the timeline. "Yeah, that's right. Almost eleven years of glass. I'm twenty-nine."

Mya asked, "Any brothers or sisters?"

"One brother, Andy. He turned thirty last year," Jamie replied.

"Are you involved in a lot of openings?" Mya asked.

"Not lately. I used to. When I got out of college, I sold a lot of work. But lately..." Jamie trailed off. He stared at the ground. Mya took a step closer, apparently sensing his distress.

Mya asked, "Doing other stuff?"

Jamie anxiously looked around the gallery. "Well, yeah. Teaching and working for other artists."

Mya turned toward the crowd of people. Jamie noticed her alluring curves. She asked, "Like him?"

"Yeah." Jamie scanned the bustling gallery. "This show's mostly about him. He gives his artists a few spots. It's nice of him."

Her phone chirped in her large purse. She reached for it and shut off the ringer. She did all of this without breaking eye contact with Jamie. Normally, a woman so interested would seem a bit creepy to Jamie, but she wasn't. She was different. "Well, I like your work," Mya said.

"Thanks. I kind of cranked them out at the last minute." Perhaps it was the lack of interest in his work; perhaps the concern for his mother. For whatever reason, he opened up to her. "To tell you the truth, Mya. I've been blocked."

"Like writer's block?"

"Yeah."

"I'm sorry."

Jamie explained, "I've been doing work for other glassblowers for a while now. I haven't created anything on my own that was any good in a long time. Nothing that I was really excited about."

Mya looked at him with a carefully seductive smile. "I have to tell you, this isn't the greatest way to attract someone."

Jamie couldn't tell whether she was referring to the sculptures or asking her out. "Yeah, I guess not." He asked, "How about you? What brings you here tonight?"

"I moved from Southern California about a month ago. I used to do a lot of sculptures. Ceramics," Mya explained. "I'm working full time as a nurse, but I want to get back into it. Anyway, I live in the lofts across the street. I love glass. So I slipped in."

"I like California," Jamie said. He tried to see this wonderful woman in front of him, but his head was clouded.

"Me too."

Jamie asked, "Why did you leave?" He continued to fidget. Most people within a ten-foot radius of him would feel scattered and nervous. Mya didn't seem affected.

"School, job. The usual."

Jamie awkwardly cut off the conversation, "Well, thanks for coming. It's been a long day. I think I might grab a drink." He nodded toward the bar. It almost looked like he was inviting her over.

Jamie Stone slouched at the dark end of the bar. He was surrounded by plasma televisions displaying nothing but ambient screen savers. Slate tile walls were illuminated from below, and sheets of water descended from the ceiling and hugged the tile as they fell to the floor. Servers walked by with styled hair, piercings and tattoos. He watched the media, art buyers and fellow artists pack the shiny new lounge.

No one cared about Jamie tonight. He was the ghostwriter, the man who didn't exist, the one that no one wanted to acknowledge. The buyers were happy to pretend Michael created all of the sculptures with his elegant hands and soft gray eyes. This illusion was evident by the fact that twenty of the twenty-four pieces were already sold. Not one glass piece sold for less than ten thousand dollars. These numbers sank Jamie lower on the bar stool, further into the corner, and deeper into a bottle of Jack Daniels.

An hour later, Mya walked up to him. "You mind if I sit?" She softly, suggestively touched his arm.

"Sure," he answered. Jamie motioned to the open stool next to him and looked back down at his glass of whiskey. When he swirled the cubes, he could see the fluid moving. It looked like a chemical, like the drink was laced with gasoline or cooking oil.

Mya said, "He sure has sold a lot of pieces." Mya motioned to the bartender. "Mojito, please."

Jamie blurted, "You know, he only made three or four of those."

Mya replied, "Really?"

"Lots of big artists do that," Jamie explained. He paused for a moment and looked around to see if anyone was listening. No one seemed to notice. "They dream of unique and thought-provoking shapes, expand them into a full series, create a bunch of hype, and employ starving, yet talented glassblowers to actually make the series."

"Guys like you?" Mya asked. She carefully sipped her drink. Light pink lip-gloss stuck to the top of the black straw.

Jamie looked at her somewhat annoyed at the question. "You got it." He waved his glass above his head. "At this point, he's really just the head of a glass factory."

He noticed her loosely fitting scarf and stylish denim jacket. She was delicately feminine, yet powerfully grounded to some planetary force that made her seem impenetrable to the mercurial thunderstorm that was Jamie Stone on this particular evening.

Mya said, "I have to say, I don't totally get these pieces."

"I *made* them and I don't understand them," Jamie said. He dropped a listless finger into his drink.

She asked, "You don't?"

"I mean, I understand what he was trying to do. I get it. But I think what you mean – and I agree with you – is that it's hard to understand why this collection is getting so much hype."

"Yeah," Mya agreed. She pulled a thick mint leaf from her tongue and laid it next to her glass on the white napkin.

"You have to understand that he's an incredible salesman. I was never able to sell my work like that. Michael does it like he's selling...a vacuum cleaner. There are wonderful artists out there. Musicians, painters and sculptors who you'll never know. They don't understand how to do this, how to create massive hype and buzz around their work. To be a professional, to create art for money, the buzz is half the work for guys like Michael. Actually, more than half. Michael Donald makes it easy for all of these people to embrace him, to fill their pages with stories about him."

"What's wrong with that?" Mya asked.

40

Jamie raised his eyebrow and leaned into Mya. "Nothing. Really. It just feels a little dishonest to the art. It's dishonest to the pure act of creation."

"I guess so."

The two of them sat together in silence for a few sips.

Finally, Jamie turned to Mya once again and leaned even closer. Although his voice had quieted to a whisper, he bluntly said, "To tell you the truth, Mya, I'm also jealous because he just made a ton of money. And I can't sell a piece for the life of me right now. That might be a part of my issues with this opening too...if I'm being honest with you."

"I'm sorry you're stuck, Jamie."

Jamie leaned over to her and touched her arm. He said, "I never tell anyone this, but being blocked is like being dead. I hate it. This is all that matters to me. Professionally. I'll never be a banker or lawyer. This is it. It's all that I am. That feeling of creating something truly new. It's all that matters."

Jamie spilled a little whiskey on the bar as he attempted to lift the glass to his mouth. "Sorry, I'm a bit of a mess tonight. Lots of stuff going on."

"Something else?" Mya asked.

"My family." His eyes welled up.

"Do you want to talk about it, Jamie?" The sound of her saying his name bothered him for some reason. He almost felt a need to fight his growing attraction.

"There's not much to really discuss right now." Jamie drooped over the bar top. He looked up at her through slightly melodramatic eyes. "I'm a wreck tonight."

Mya smiled. "It's fine. I like listening to you. You're not like these other guys." She pointed to a group of men in dress shirts. She carefully squeezed his hand resting on the bar.

He slowly pulled his hand away from her. "I don't want to offend you, but if you know what's good for you, if you have any sense at all, you won't be interested in a guy like me. You have no idea what you're getting into. Those guys over there. That's what you want. You don't want me. I am not a simple man. I'm a huge headache for a nice woman like you."

"Okay," she said, curiously unaffected by Jamie's rant. She pulled another mint leaf from her wide mouth and full lips. A small pile of mint leaves began to accumulate next to her drink.

"Look, I'm sorry. You're a lovely woman, Mya. Thank you for keeping me company. It's just been a bad day. I need to get out of here."

He brushed by her, left his drink at the bar, and walked outside. He wanted a pack of cigarettes. He didn't even really smoke. There was something about drinking whiskey at a one-syllable bar that made him want to smoke. Plowed mounds of densely packed slush and ice lined the street. They were the last evidence of a particularly harsh Chicago winter. The mounds had been melting all day, creating a dense fog. It was so thick that Jamie couldn't see the streetlights. Ghostly headlights of sporadic cars materialized through the haze and then vanished behind him. A man and woman seemed to form before his eyes on the foggy sidewalk. Behind him, they were quickly enveloped in the mist.

Jamie sat outside the one-syllable night club, puffed a smoke, and watched the world in silence. He thought about his mother as he sucked in a carcinogen. He had to call her. As he rested his head against the red bricks of the building, he could feel the thump, thump of dance music from inside. He watched as more people materialized into view and vanished in a cloud of white vapor. He peeked in at his three sculptures one more time. There was nobody within thirty feet of them. No sale. Nothing. Jamie pulled out another smoke.

The thin, metal outer door of the gallery swung open and Mya walked out. She looked over at Jamie with a polite smile. It was the look of a woman who had been shot down and didn't want to cause any more pain.

Jamie walked over to her. "Listen, I'm sorry I was a jerk back there. Sometimes these openings can be a little rough for me. I had no right to be that way. I've just been kind of stuck lately. It's tough to be around other openings right now."

She assured him, "Don't worry about earlier. I should have left you alone."

"No, you were being nice." He had been so wrapped up in his thoughts before that he failed to notice how beautiful she was. She had long, thick brown curls and seductive oval eyes. Her tan, olive-tinted complexion gave away the fact that her family was from Argentina.

"It's been kind of a rough night, huh?" She asked as she buttoned up her jacket and fluffed her scarf. They walked back over to the bench. Jamie plopped down.

Jamie laughed. "Yeah. It hasn't been my best. I just wanted to get out of there." He paused and glanced over at Mya. "And I'm worried about my mom."

Mya fell onto the bench next to him. "Your mother?"

"That's my family issue that I mentioned before I rudely ran away from you. She went into the hospital today. Complications or something." Jamie squinted his eyes and looked up at an orange streetlight. "I can't even really think about it right now. I'm still waiting on a call." A thin strand of cigarette smoke rose from Jamie's mouth.

"Is she sick?"

"She's had cancer before," Jamie answered. "So we're all worried."

"I'm so sorry."

Jamie explained, "Not knowing is the toughest. She's already been to the hospital a few times this year. It's always just small stuff. There's no reason to think it will be any different this time. Still, it's worrying me."

Mya calmly stood up and looked back at Jamie. "I'll leave you alone."

Jamie tossed his cigarette on the ground and reached for her arm. "No. I'm tired of worrying about it. I want to think about something else. There's nothing I can do right now."

"Okay."

Jamie looked up at her with a smile and asked, "You want to grab a drink?"

"Sure." She smiled. Her smile was cooling to Jamie; her sweet demeanor was somehow lessening the burning pain. They walked together into the misty Chicago night. It ended many hours later at her place, between sheets that smelled like citrus oils and an alarm clock that forgot it was Sunday.

Jamie opened his eyes at six in the morning. He had no hangover, no pain. He went to the bathroom and stood looking at himself in the mirror for a moment, while washing his hands. He looked at himself differently this morning, and he chuckled at his reflection. He grabbed a glass of water and headed back to the bedroom.

Mya rustled. Her thick black curls were neatly tucked underneath her head. She was beautiful. She rolled over and gazed into Jamie's eyes. She had a serene smile rising below her half-opened eyes. "Sleep, sleep," she whispered through a contented moan.

"I will. Just thirsty." Jamie leaned over and kissed her. He felt like they had been sharing a bed for years.

Her breaths soon became longer and more pronounced. She was sleeping again.

Jamie lay on the bed. He felt a wave of calm from Mya's presence. He inhaled, exhaled, and let go. His eyes relaxed, and he fell into a calm meditative state. Life had become a dizzying sprint through mindless schedules and rituals, but not this morning. As he gazed at the speckled white ceiling above, he allowed thoughts to casually drift in and out of his awareness.

Then it happened. Jamie Stone saw sculptures that he had never fathomed before. It began some place deep within. It was the place that all artists knew. It was a place more precise than the broad, elusive concept of consciousness. It was deeper than the mind or the heart. Where an instant before there was nothing, a grain of light came into being. Pure creation was Immaculate Conception. It intoxicated an artist. Art was a big bang of creation. One point of overwhelmingly concentrated energy exploded and manifested into the physical world.

He lay awake in bed next to Mya. He saw stunning, unique shapes and began to dream of the process of creating them. They weren't like anyone else. They were Jamie Stone. They were his fingerprints, and they could only be his.

Mya was still sound asleep as he carefully placed a folded piece of paper next to her serene face and quietly walked out.

Jamie rolled a black garbage can over to an old apartment building in the Bronzeville neighborhood. A woman walking her dog stopped and watched him with skepticism.

Jamie looked over at her while standing on the garbage can and explained, "It's okay. I need to talk to a friend. Really."

He knocked on a bedroom window several times and whispered, "John. John, wake up! John." The woman continued to stare. She pulled out a cell phone.

"What do you want, Jamie?"

"I need to get into the studio."

"Are you drunk?"

Jamie paused for a moment and contemplated the question. "I don't think so."

The woman walking her dog gradually meandered away. John rolled over to his desk and grabbed a ring of keys. "Just make sure you lock up when you're done. I'm not coming in till Monday."

"I might still be there."

"Did you get something?" John asked with a clarity that came from his excitement for his friend.

Jamie smiled.

Thirty minutes later, Jamie popped open the latch to the InDesign Glass Studios. The studio was just west of Humboldt Park. It was at the end of a block-long brick building that housed an auto repair shop, antique dealer, and a couple of other curiously ambiguous businesses. He sucked in a deep breath of dust from the storage room and the subtle smell of burning newspaper. He turned off his phone and peeled away his jacket. He knew others would eventually begin to filter in, and he wanted to remember this.

He walked out to the first glassblowing station. The station had an old wooden table next to a bench. Two skinny, level metal arms reached out from the bench. They looked like arm rests that were all metal and too wide. The bench faced a furnace. Its bright heat could be seen through a round opening where glass creations were constantly inserted to maintain proper heat. The furnace burned a neon orange hue, as he imagined the surface of the sun would look. He sat for a moment on the bench. The ventilation system hummed above him. He arranged his tools on the adjacent table. Charred clumps of blackened beeswax had accumulated on its surface. The wax was used to keep some of the metal tools lubricated. Jamie carefully arranged his tools on the table. He imagined the sequence of actions he had to take in order to create the sculpture. Glassblowing was a chess game. He always had to be thinking several moves ahead. He re-arranged a few metal tools accordingly, plopping unnecessary ones into a five-gallon bucket behind the table.

He walked over to the center of the room. In the middle of the furnaces was a thick cask full of molten glass. He grabbed a four-foot blow rod from the dozens lying next to the cask. The sculptures he wanted to create required two layers of glass. First, he dipped the blow rod into the molten glass. He pulled out glass the size of a large orange. Jamie molded the inner glass cylinder into a slender oval. Then he coated it with stripes of powdered glass, like a tiger print. Once the striped inner glass cylinder was symmetrical and heated to the appropriate temperature, Jamie could add the second layer of clear glass. He dipped the blow rod into the cask of glowing liquid. His chest pounded with excitement. He pulled out a glowing oval of molten glass about the size of a cantaloupe. He rested both ends of the blow rod on the metal arms of the glassblowing station. He rotated the rod back and forth, back and forth with a gentle rhythm. Jamie watched the connection between the blow rod and the glowing glass.

It was the umbilical cord. This connection was everything. It kept the piece alive and he only had a thin window of temperature variance. Too cold and the glass would crack. Too hot and the piece would droop toward the ground. This was the act of glassblowing. It was a constant balance between two extremes. As the piece temporarily cooled, he could see the subtle stripes. He sat back down at the bench, reached for a folded, charred clump of newspaper. He held the newspaper under the glowing oval and rotated the glass back and forth. Steam rose from the living sculpture. Ashes flaked off the newspaper. The glass gradually dimmed to a deep amber color, and smoothed to a perfectly symmetrical oval. The tiger print design became visible in the dimming glass. He stood in the middle of the room, pointing the glass down toward the ground holding the end of the metal blow rod up by his face. He began swinging the glass back and forth – like a ride at a carnival. As he whipped the piece from one side to the other, it lengthened, growing longer and skinnier. Jamie laid his creation over a curved steel miniature ramp. As he laid the piece on the ramp, the glass molded to the curved steel. It looked like a giant, concave glass larva. He grabbed a blow torch and heated the whole piece. "Now for the fun part," he mumbled. He grabbed two cork paddles. They were the size of a car buffer. Jamie rubbed them over the glass, flattening the piece dramatically. It looked like a beautiful tiger-striped blade of grass about four feet long. It was time to detach the glass from the rod. He grabbed a pointed metal tool. Jamie dipped it in water and dug the points into the end of the blow rod. Then he tapped the rod. The piece cleanly broke away. He quickly moved the piece into the kiln where it would slowly cool down overnight. And hopefully not crack.

During his third piece, three fellow glassblowers entered the studio. They mumbled and joked with each other. All three stopped in their tracks as they watched Jamie move around the studio in an effortless simplicity. For years, Jamie trudged through his glass creations. But today he moved with such stunning grace and efficiency that the other artists stopped speaking, pulled up three chairs, and watched in silence.

Twenty minutes later, a slender sculptor with cut-off jeans and hair that sprouted toward the sky like a party favor simply stated, "Wow."

It would be like this for the next day. Teachers and students came for classes and stayed to watch the graceful dance of Jamie Stone and his living sculptures. The chubby studio owner and other artists regularly stopped whatever they were doing, pulled up a chair and watched.

Glassblowing was an intricate ballet. But it took place in an environment that resembled the shop of a medieval silversmith or ironworker instead of a modern studio. Over the next day, Jamie became obsessed with the process of manifesting the sculptures. Glass was a living, flowing medium. It allowed only a brief window of temperature and structural integrity where it could be manifested into something truly beautiful. Grace in glassblowing only came through repetition, and the measured dispersal of the deep well of passion that now burned within Jamie.

Besides a brief nap on a tattered couch in his storage area, Jamie worked nonstop. By Monday evening, his hands ached. His forearms were crusty from exposure to the intense heat. People were constantly watching him. Some hung around for hours. He had run out of room in the kiln. Others were complaining. As he slid yet another glowing orb of glass into the furnace, he squinted his eyes in an effort to refocus. He shook his head fighting the impending fatigue. Glass production was like an endurance sport. It was a long period of sustained focus and exertion.

Rap pumped from a dusty boom box. Jamie bobbed his head.

"Brother!" Jamie heard the statement but didn't think it could be directed at him.

"Jamie!"

Jamie turned to see someone walking toward him with his arms raised. "Andy?"

Andy asked, "What's going on? We've been trying to get a hold of you for the last two days."

"Why are you here?" Jamie asked, his latest glass piece sagged toward the ground and spilled onto the concrete below.

"Let's talk," Andy said softly.

The brothers walked outside. Cars whizzed by a stop sign that seemed like only a suggestion for Chicago drivers.

"Why are you here?" Jamie looked through bloodshot eyes. His strong frame slouched with mounting fatigue. He desperately searched his brother's expression for an answer.

Andy looked down to the ground. He didn't need to say anything.

"She's sick again," Jamie whispered to his brother. "Mom." Jamie fell to the ground much as his brother had done.

Andy asked, "Why was your phone off?"

Jamie held his hand up to his mouth. He stared through glassy eyes intensely into the world in front of him. "It died. I forgot about it. I've just been working in the studio nonstop. I forgot. I can't believe I forgot." He looked up at Andy and asked, "Cancer again?"

"Yeah, but it spread."

"Where?"

"A lot of places. Come on. Let's go home."

"What's going to happen?" Jamie asked.

Andy helped his brother up and said, "Don't know. We need to get back there. Mom's been asking about you."

Andy raced his brother back to Rockford. Jamie slept the whole way.

Andy and his father watched from the doorway. Jamie carefully entered the hospital room. Tears streamed down his face. His mother remained asleep, her breaths straining for oxygen. Jamie pulled an old hospital recliner next to her bed. He looked at the windowsill where two rows of flowers were packed together. Jamie climbed onto the recliner, leaned his upper body onto the hospital bed, and knelt down next to his mother. He laid his head next to hers.

By Thursday afternoon, Jamie and Andy had barely been outside. Two close calls failed to tear their mother from her grip on the precarious ledge of life. There was a weight pulling her now. She was dangling over a great abyss. Andy was worried that she was about to let go. She didn't even need to jump, just stop fighting the force pulling her down. This battle wasn't clear to the average person looking at her, but Andy could see it. She was clawing into the ledge. Her fingers were slipping lower and lower. Her friends, her family and her doctors could only do so much. Ultimately, she was alone in this battle. No one else knew her body or how much it could take. For twenty years she had been fighting the gravity of cancer. Some years it didn't pull as hard. Other years it felt like her legs were coated with concrete. Andy knew that she was tired. He knew that she was beginning to let go.

On Tuesday afternoon, she complained about knifing pain in her abdomen. She stopped drinking fluid. She was incoherent. The doctors gave her more drugs. She stopped twitching in pain and eventually fell asleep. After a three-hour nap, she awoke and seemed better. Wednesday night was worse. A nurse negotiated her way through the two brothers sleeping on cots and studied the monitors next to the bed. She was doing her routine rounds. But something on one of the monitors kept her in the room. Andy had gotten used to the ritual of the nurses. This time was different. After a few minutes, a second nurse entered, then a third.

Finally, two doctors walked into the room and flipped on the lights. Andy looked over at his mom. A thin stream of blood dripped down from her mouth. They rushed her back to an operating room where the doctors cut open her chest once again. She was having liver and stomach complications. It was a concern, but apparently not life-threatening. Two hours later, she was back in her room. Although she had yet another surgery, it was largely considered a false alarm.

Thursday was a good day. All signs were stable and her mood improved. Andy's parents seemed to be inspired by the good news. In the afternoon, their father walked the boys out of the room. "Why don't you guys get out of here for the evening? She's doing better. I'll call you if anything changes." After some refusals, the boys left. They finally came to rest at a bar downtown. They caught up with each other in the awkward, semi-sentimental way that brothers often did.

Jamie told his brother, "I met someone."

"You did?" Andy motioned to the bartender for another round.

"Yeah, there's something about this one, bro," Jamie said, as he held the hourglass-shaped beer glass in his hands. He ran his hands expertly over its shallow curves. Andy couldn't tell if he was thinking about glassblowing or the girl he met. Jamie said, "Something about her."

Andy laughed and said, "I met somebody too."

"Really?" Jamie asked. "You like her?"

"A lot," Andy said. Despite these words, a vacant stare washed over his face. He looked blankly at the window behind the bar.

"We're just two lucky guys," Jamie said. He looked at the large beer vats through the broad window. He wondered if Andy saw something in the brewery that suddenly made him sad.

"Where did you meet her?" Jamie asked, sensing complications.

"Denver." Andy looked at his brother with concern. "Actually, she lives in San Francisco."

"And?"

"I really liked her, man. But I made a mistake," Andy said.

"What?"

"I lost her number," Andy explained. "She wrote it down on a piece of paper and it got smudged on the flight."

"Can't read it?"

"No. It's gone. I have no idea how to get a hold of her." Andy picked at an indentation in the glossy wooden bar top. "I only saw her for a night, but she was the coolest girl I've ever met. How could the world work like that? How could I not at least get a chance with her?"

Jamie pulled out his iPhone.

"I thought you couldn't stand people with iPhones."

"I know, I know, but they're so cool. I couldn't hold out any longer."

Jamie asked his brother, "What's her name?"

"Emma."

"Last name?" Jamie looked up from his phone.

Andy squinted as he took another gulp of his amber-colored ale. "Don't know."

"Where does she work?" Jamie asked. His questions became more abrupt. He was losing patience with his brother.

"Neutrogena." Andy nodded with relative certainty.

Jamie searched "Emma Neutrogena California." "That's not going to work. What else do you know about her?"

Andy squirmed in his chair as he nervously looked around. "This feels a little weird to me."

"We're just doing some innocent Google searches."

Andy recalled, "Oh, she played soccer at school in California. I think it was called Davis, UC-Davis?"

"Now you're talking."

He searched the key words and found a picture. And they found out her last name and finally discovered an email address, and maybe a work number.

"There you go."

"I can't do that. She'll think I'm some kind of stalker."

"It took like two seconds to figure it out. You already know she wanted to talk to you again. Who cares? Like she hasn't Google stalked you. You know she has."

"Yeah, but nobody admits to Google stalking. I would have to admit to it."

"I don't see many other options."

Jamie rose from his bar stool. He tapped his brother on the shoulder. "I gotta pee, brother."

Andy walked outside, dialed the number he found for Emma, and hovered his thumb over the call button, but he couldn't do it. He figured a message to her work email would be better. He could explain everything.

Andy and Jamie walked back into the hospital Friday morning. Sunlight drenched the halls from checkered skylights. The building was stuffy, as if the ventilation system hadn't anticipated such an unseasonably warm day. Nurses in the front office chatted and laughed as the boys walked past. A cleaning crew parked their supply cart next to room 416. Jamie knocked on the door. He peeked in. The flowers were gone. Their cots were missing. Andy had to look back at the room number. But when he saw the same dangling five in 415, he knew it was the right room. Andy felt like he had been punched in the chest. His mother was gone.

.

CHAPTER FIVE

Two hours later, Andy and Jamie Stone stormed into the Blake Cancer Treatment Center in Madison, Wisconsin. The only contact they got from their father was a text message. It gave them this address and a room number, along with the line, "Doing okay. Hope you guys had a good night." Jamie marched in first, his eyes burning red. Andy followed staring at his phone.

A receptionist called, "Excuse me!"

Andy barked back, "We're looking for our mom."

"You must be the Stone boys. If you wait just a moment..."

They ignored her and opened the frosted glass door beyond the waiting room.

The receptionist yelled, "You can't go back there!"

They raced past one room. "Harmony!" Jamie announced back to his brother.

"No."

Jamie looked up at the name of another patient room. He said, "Tranquility!"

"That's not it. We're looking for Serenity."

As they looked around, Jamie pleaded, "Where the hell is Serenity?"

"Serenity!" Andy said, as he pointed to a closed patient room with a natural calligraphy stencil that read, "Serenity."

Jamie swung the door open to see his mother resting comfortably on a hospital bed. He fell to the ground, lying sprawled out on the floor. He looked up at the ceiling and spoke with the tone of a lecturing parent, "How many times do we have to go over this? How did you think we were going to react to that empty bed?"

It was a lecture they had given their parents regularly for years. Their parents had always been extremely hands-off with them. They were the anti-disciplinarians. They provided for them and cared for them, but let the brothers make their own decisions. Their parents regularly forgot to call on birthdays and missed numerous orientations and graduations. Jamie and Andy never minded. It allowed them to follow their dreams, albeit foolishly at times. They were so hands-off that they would sometimes forget to contact their children during critical events, like escaping from a local hospital.

Andy echoed, "I can't believe you did this without telling us."

"How...by any stretch of the imagination..." Jamie said as he sat up.

Their mother raised her narrow hand and both boys reluctantly stopped barking.

She said, "I was dead back there. That would have been it for me. That hospice flyer is a ticket to death. Once you accept that, once hope for life goes away, you will die. This was very scary for your father. If something happened to me, he would be blamed. Don't blame your father. If you have a problem, it's with me. I was worried that anyone we told would try to stop us."

"Even us?" Andy asked. He noticed something different about his mother. She still looked weak and fragile. In fact, her skin had lost even more of its pigment. But she was more alert than he had seen her in years. Her eyes were wide open; her left hand was anxiously tapping the metal frame of the hospital bed.

His mother explained, "Especially you two." A small fountain next to her bed muddled away the brief windows of silence. Andy noticed green plants facing his mother on the windowsill.

"Why would we try to stop you?" Jamie asked.

"Because you love me, because you want me to live. You would have thought this move was crazy. And the decision to leave was already made and it was mine to make. We got up here late last night." Something had returned to their mother's face that had been missing. She expressed a childlike innocence.

Jamie asked his father, "How did Rockford Covenant Hospital let you just leave like that?"

His dad raised his eyebrows and reached for his wife. "They didn't. We made a break for it."

Andy asked, "You broke out?" He looked at his mother. She nodded with a deviant smirk.

"I pushed your mother down the halls in her hospital robe," his father said, clutching his mother's arm under a fleece blanket. "We raced her wheelchair out of the hospital, skidding through the slushy parking lot."

"What about all of the IV lines and monitors?" Andy asked. He sat down next to the window. He smelled herbs. Rosemary and sage were sprouting in a small potter next to him. The room was vibrant with sunlight and vegetation.

Their mother scoffed. "It's just a port. I can remove that stuff in my sleep."

"Did these guys know you were coming?" Jamie asked.

Their father answered, "Yeah. They were kind of expecting us. Apparently, your mom isn't the first cancer patient to make a break for this place in the middle of treatment."

"I still don't understand why you guys didn't call when you got here?" Andy asked. His voice grew calm and composed again.

"We had some complications this morning. It took all of your father's energy." Their mother began coughing. It was a deep cough. It originated where fluid in her lungs had accumulated. Over the last week, just his mother's cough alone made Andy feel overwhelmed. It was a suffocating and permanent cough. Andy worried she was going to suffocate every time she reached her brittle fist to her mouth. She carefully drank some water.

"Why didn't we take her here before?" Andy cautiously asked his father. He noticed pastel painted canvases on the wall just behind his father.

"Because we hear lots of claims. Lots of people recommend places. They all claim to be different," his father explained. His eyes looked red and irritated. His black, wavy hair was frazzled. "It's hard to know the truth."

"Well, there's actually another part of the story," his mother said. "We didn't really know about this place. It was a mystery to me." She spoke with a bewildering alertness.

"How did you find out about it?" Andy asked.

His father asked, "You remember your mom's friend Diana?"

"Yeah."

"Her husband was treated here last year. Diana visited your mom in the hospital two weeks ago," his father said, as he ran his hand through his tangled hair. Andy noticed a growing population of gray hairs on his head, multiplying daily. "She told us about this place. She also told us the only way to get in was to be recommended by another patient. She said it was revolutionary, like nothing she had ever seen before."

Jamie asked, "Why is it so secretive? If the treatment is so much better, why aren't they screaming from the highest Madison mountain top?"

"You would think so, but for some reason, this place is extremely private," their father said. "I don't know." He shrugged.

"Don't know," their mother echoed. She turned to Andy and said, "Maybe that's something you can help us with, my reporter son."

Their father continued, "After the last meeting with the Rockford doctors, we decided we had nothing to lose. Your mom didn't have much of a chance there. We just needed to make sure that insurance would cover the new doctor. This place is a little tricky when it comes to coverage."

"We thought you were dead. A phone call, guys, just a phone call," Jamie said. He shook his head, but his piercing eyes managed to stay focused on his mother.

His mother pointed at him. It was a gesture to drop it, a gesture normally directed at young children. She looked serious, but there was the hint of a smile.

Their father said, "Go take a look around. It's incredible."

"You're not going to sneak away to another hospital while we're looking around, are you?" Jamie joked.

His mother threw a pillow at him with curious strength.

Andy and Jamie walked past contorting sculptures that filled indentations along the hallway. Large, beautiful photos and paintings crowded the walls. Jamie's phone rang and he drifted into a nearby corner. He answered with his soft I'm-talking-to-a-lady-friend voice. Andy sheepishly returned to the waiting room where the boys had just made a scene. Comfortable lounge chairs, tall plants and modern lighting filled the spacious waiting area. It looked more like the entrance to an amazing spa than a doctor's office. Dark slate tiles checkered the floor. Multicolored wood paneling lined the walls. New age music with an ambient harp echoed through the building.

Andy walked up to the receptionist. She looked up at him above her reading glasses. She was in her forties. She was slender with lively short brown dreadlocks that jaunted away her head. Her eyes gave away her intelligence and wit. Andy got the feeling that she kind of ran the office, which was reinforced by the title on a small sign affixed to the corner of her desk, "Edna Hodge. Office Manager."

She hung up the phone and looked up at him. Andy said, "Sorry to barge in like that. We just worried that..."

She lifted her hand. "Everyone here understands. Just don't do it again." She enunciated with authority.

"Deal." Andy rested his arms on top of the counter above her reception desk. He asked, "This place is different, huh?"

She peered at Andy. "Come with me." She looked at another woman behind the reception area and said, "Deb, I'm going on break. Maybe I can talk some sense into this boy."

They walked outside to a garden patio. It was a glass-enclosed patio in the winter. The space looked like a science fiction greenhouse. Many of the glass walls and panels looked detachable for the warmer months. Leafless vines wove through a wooden frame above a sunken lounge area where one patient sat alone with her eyes closed. She sat on a large patio couch. It had a dark brown, wicker frame and thin, tan cushions that matched furniture scattered over multiple levels of the patio. Slate tiles intertwined with gardens, wildflowers, and flowing water. It was a place where a patient could envision returning to health.

Andy and Edna sat at a table in a secluded corner. Edna held a giant mug with both hands. She lifted the steaming fluid up to her mouth and blew on it, apparently waiting for Andy to say something. He did. "By the way, my name is Andy." He reached out his hand.

"Edna."

"Thanks for talking to me." He felt like a reporter again as he uttered this line.

"So what exactly is it that you would like to know, Andy Stone?"

Andy looked around as he asked, "What's going on here?"

"What do you mean?"

Someone opened the door from the kitchen that led to the patio. Steam spilled out of the door and blurred a few glass ceiling panels. Andy snapped back to his conversation. "Why is this place different? How do you treat patients differently?"

Edna leaned back on her wicker chair. "That is a complex question. I cannot give you the specifics. But I can tell you that the cancer treatment at the hospital your mother left is like the typewriter. You've just walked into the age of computers."

Andy reached for a pitcher of water on the table and poured himself a glass. He thought about how much he missed interviewing people. Many people Andy interviewed didn't get to just sit down and talk about the big picture of their lives and their work very often. Interviews often helped the interviewee gain perspective.

"A typewriter during the dawn of computers? The Blake Center is *that* different?"

"Ever heard of Plato's *Allegory of the Cave*?" Edna carefully examined Andy's face for any recognition.

"Huh?"

Edna smiled and looked up at the bare vines dangling above her. "You've never heard the *Allegory of the Cave*?"

"No.

"Imagine a row of people sitting in a cave. It gradually descends from its entrance. The people are looking at the back wall of the cave. Their arms and legs are chained. They can't turn their heads." Edna sat cross-legged on the chair with a stiff neck to illustrate their posture. "All they can see is the back wall. Behind them is a large, perpetually-burning fire just outside of the cave. People pass by the fire, casting shadows on the back wall of the cave. Can you picture this?" She asked Andy. "The people chained to the ground only see the shadows on the wall, illusions of reality. All they have ever known are the shadows projected on the back wall by these people who pass by the fire. To them, the shadows are real objects, not projections of people. It's their reality, and it's incomplete. Science and medicine constantly discover that their previous reality was an imperfect projection of a more accurate truth. Some discoveries are dramatic, others are small. No aspect of modern science is more trapped in the cave than cancer treatment."

Edna sipped her cup of tea and checked her watch. When she drank, the massive mug seemed to swallow her petite face. "When your mother walked into the Blake Center, she broke out of the cave. You guys may not realize it yet, but you will. Our society's understanding of cancer is tragically incomplete. Despite all of the benefit concerts and football players wearing pink ribbons, cancer and its treatment have been practically stagnant for thirty years. Conventional cancer care is the illusion of healing, like shadows on the wall."

"That different?" Andy questioned.

"C'mon, I'll take you back to your mom," she said with a rising hint of humor in her voice. She let out a dramatic groan as she rose. "Back to the grindstone."

They walked past a sign near the test kitchen that read, "No sugar beyond this point."

"Sugar?" Andy whispered to Edna. He tapped her arm like they were old friends.

She explained, "You don't know the connection between sugar and cancer? Sugar to cancer is like gasoline on a fire. Cancer feeds on sugar.

Very few doctors out there have even made this connection. You could go back to drinking monster-sized sodas all day long, as far as they're concerned. But here, there's no sugar. Do you know how PET scans work?" She asked.

"No."

"Literally radioactive glucose is injected into the body. Of course, glucose is a sugar compound. This glucose latches onto any cancerous cells in the body. Then the scan can detect where the radioactive glucose has accumulated. Even in our scans, we see the truth. Sugar is like a magnet to cancer. Do you know how much our sugar consumption has increased in the last five decades?"

"Like gas on the fire, huh?"

"But what do I know? I'm just an administrative assistant." She laughed as she sat behind her desk. She opened a binder and put her reading glasses back on. They rested precariously close to the bottom of her nose. Edna pointed to her watch and motioned for Andy to return to Serenity.

He quietly asked her, "I know you have to work, but one more question. If this place is the Holy Grail of cancer treatment, why do you keep it such a secret?"

She replied, "That is a question I cannot answer, not today. Hopefully someday soon."

Andy raised his hands. "I didn't mean to..."

"Don't worry, Andy. It's fine." She motioned for him to go away once again.

"Thank you. It's been a disorienting twenty-four hours."

"I bet," she said as she answered the phone. As Andy waved goodbye, he noticed Edna point emphatically over at a man walking into the communal room.

Andy whispered, "Is that him?"

She nodded.

Andy stood just outside of his mother's room and watched him. The doctor spoke with one of the nurses. They went over a few charts and documents. He was turned from Andy. He could only see the back of his head. His hair was carefully combed back. He was wearing a dark sport coat and gray pants that hung somewhat loosely from his body.

A woman in a turquoise shawl walked up to him and patiently waited as he talked to a few nurses. The woman had short brown hair. She appeared to be returning after some sort of treatment. Her limbs were thin, but strong. She had bulging veins that Andy could see, even though he was across the communal room. Blake finally saw the woman out of his peripheral vision.

"Maggie," Doctor Blake said with a deep, soothing tone. He extended his arms.

She looked up at the doctor. Tears streamed down her face. She hugged him. Staff members walked away. No words were exchanged. As Andy finally walked into Serenity, the woman in turquoise was still sobbing and laughing. She was a mess – a vibrant, elated, energized mess.

Andy was anticipating the door to swing open so much that he felt he might jump when it actually did. After a few minutes of uneasy anticipation, a hollow knock cut through the silence, and the door cracked opened. In the doorway, stood Doctor Richard Blake.

"Hello, Stone family."

He was sixty-two but looked in his early fifties. He had a neatly manicured beard, youthful skin and jet-black hair. He expressed a compassionate smile. It was the perfect expression for a doctor dealing with cancer patients. His soft smile hinted at a man with great perspective and genuine empathy. But his eyes were his most striking feature. As he turned around to greet Andy, Blake's dark eyes commanded his attention. They weren't black in the terms of the absence of color, but black like the night sky. They were black with depth, black with clarity, and black with centuries of wisdom. Andy believed the color black was often misrepresented. Although it was regularly connected to death and depression, black could be a beautiful color with bewildering depth and majesty. Blake's eyes felt like a black hole in the fabric of space-time. He had great gravitational pull – like a charismatic politician or the ringleader of The Leadership Project. But unlike Marcus Langford, Andy felt empowered by the presence of Richard Blake.

Andy no longer questioned his parents' move under the cover of darkness.

Richard Blake greeted everyone in the room. He grabbed a chair and sat facing Andy's mother. He placed his clipboard on a table and leaned forward. He focused on his new patient. She was wrapped in blankets on the bed. She held up her withering body with sheer adrenaline. Andy tried not to attach to the rising level of hope in the room.

"Hello, Sarah."

"Hi." Her slight hands clutched onto a white sheet that was covering most of her body. Her eyebrows rose with childlike hope.

"We haven't received your charts from the other doctors yet," he said softly. "They said you made an unapproved escape under the cover of darkness."

Doctor Blake looked around the room with a calm, fatherly authority. The Stones looked like disciplined puppies. Everyone stopped breathing.

Blake smiled, "I would have done the same thing in your situation. Don't worry. We're talking to your insurance company right now. Everything's going to be fine."

And exhale.

"We're in a race against time, Sarah. A race to bring your body back into control of its environment. Right now cancer has taken over, but together we can bring you back to health. You may have previously felt like you were alone in this fight. Your immune system was overrun, and you didn't feel like your previous doctors were helping you return to health. But we're sending in reinforcements. We will be taking on cancer in a variety of ways. Together, our unique combination of treatments creates a synergistic effect in your body. Hopefully, we can bring your body back into balance. For the first few months, some of these changes may be unsettling, but I can assure you that everything we will do is vitally important to your recovery."

Jamie whispered to his brother, "First few *months*?"

Blake turned again to their mother. "But most importantly, you," he said. "This cancer will not kill you. I know this will take some time, but Sarah, any healing that can happen here, must start within you. I understand the fear that's attached to this disease, and your fear is understandable. But you must overcome this fear. You must believe that cancer will not kill you."

"Okay," Sarah said. Tears dropped from her eyes and streamed down her cheeks.

Andy realized he hadn't seen his mom cry in a decade. In five minutes, this man had managed to crack her seemingly impervious shell. His dad cried all the time; just put on the movie *Field of Dreams*.

"We'll begin immediately. We have a room for you at St. James this week. You'll spend the first night here. I'm asking another doctor, Jennifer, to come in and begin the supplements. You will also meet a reflexologist who will work with your feet. Then you can rest, and we'll go from there."

Doctor Blake looked around the room as he calmly rolled a pen back and forth between his thumb and fingers. The simple motion was soothing for Andy to watch – like the doctor had stress relief balls rotating in his palm. "Do you all have any questions for me?" Blake asked.

The boys both looked at their mother. They waited for the usual flurry of questions. She sat contently shaking her head. The brothers were bewildered.

Their father asked, "What are the supplements?"

Blake answered, "A combination of vital nutrients that your body has needed for a long time. Given primarily intravenously."

Andy carefully prodded, "What are they?"

"It's our own secret recipe. The nurses call it liquid gold. It's a unique combination of vitamins and minerals that have proven to help our patients recover. Basically, highly concentrated plant-based supplements from the most beneficial sources found all over the world. Seaweed supplements common in Japan and rich in minerals. Anti-oxidants from fruiting plants found in tropical environments. We have also found that the complex combination of amino acids in carrots help to reverse the disease."

"Carrots?" Andy asked. His brow furrowed with confusion.

Blake answered, "Not carrots alone. You will receive all of these nutrients in highly concentrated doses through the liquid gold in a way your body has never experienced before." He stopped. A nurse entered with a tray full of colorful serums and vitamins. He continued, "We'll start you on the supplements, nutrition, guided imagery, homeopathy and customized injections. Perhaps we will need additional treatment like chemotherapy, but that would be a last resort."

The boys all nodded blankly.

After a moment of silence, their mother asked, "Injections of what?"

"We'll discuss that later," Blake insisted.

She prodded, "Chemo?"

"No." Blake politely smiled and picked up his clipboard.

"Stem cells?"

"No. I'll explain it you later, Sarah. Before we administer them," he assured her, then quickly continued, "Once your strength returns, we will incorporate more treatments. And we will find the unique formula that works for your body and your cancer."

Andy asked, "Unique formula?"

"No two forms of the disease are the same," Blake said. He walked over to the blooming sage plants next to the window. "No two treatments are the same. Every patient that comes to this center receives a unique combination of care from our vast toolbox of possible remedies. For instance, we have found that some patients experience a great reduction in side effects from chemo when it is administered in the middle of the night. Some react better mid-morning. Although we hardly ever administer chemo anymore, the theme of personalization permeates everything we do here. This idea of personalized care is probably a departure from what you're used to hearing."

"No shit!" Their mother squeaked. Doctor Blake laughed.

"Can you give us any idea of how long you think we have?" Andy's father requested. "The other doctors said two months."

Blake smiled, "I can't give you that answer. I can never give anyone a definite answer for survival. My job is to keep you alive as long as possible."

Jamie looked up and said, "But you said the first few months."

"Let's start with this week. We'll go from there," Blake explained. "I don't want to give you an unrealistic time span, Sarah. You have advanced cancer. The situation is very serious. And there are no guarantees dealing with this disease. I'm sure all of you understand this. But hope for years and years. Maintain hope in your mother, in your wife. It's the most important aspect of any healing. Some may call this false hope. I hear the claim that my treatment gives terminal patients false hope. I never make guarantees. No one knows their own lifespan, but I believe that hope is a driving force for well-being and quality of life, no matter how long we live. Those who worry about false hope are those who have lost it. Believe in my treatment, Sarah, and we will do everything we can to extend your life as long as possible."

Jamie and Andy nodded casually. They had heard these lines from hopeful, but unsuccessful doctors in the past.

Blake saw their reaction and turned away from the family as he asked them, "You see that woman over there?"

Andy turned around to see the same slender woman wrapped in a turquoise shawl who hugged the doctor earlier.

Andy's father asked, "Yeah?"

"She was given two months to live. Diagnosed with stage-four lymphoma."

They watched as she marched around the office, scanning the magazines. Her hair was short, but thick and brown. She had a tropical-colored braid in her hair with beads at the bottom. She walked with a seemingly recent confidence, like a paraplegic with brand new legs.

Jamie said, "That's impressive."

Blake stood up and said as he left, "The diagnosis was five years ago."

Jamie stayed with his mother while his father and brother found a hotel. His dad needed a break. Jamie sat patiently next to his mom. Her breaths were still strained. Water continued to trickle down a miniature waterfall on a white round table next to his mother's bed. Nurses came in and out. They checked her vitals and monitored the clear bag, which contained the mysterious golden fluid. It was about halfway gone. Jamie thought about the much-needed nutrients seeping into his mother's system. They talked for a while, but his mother's eyes gradually grew heavy. She fell into an uneasy sleep, occasionally waking in a disoriented state. Glass shapes continued to materialize in Jamie's mind. Various glass pieces expanded and contorted in his vision. He felt a growing need to remember all of the beautiful shapes. Jamie thought about his last encounter. He thought about the Argentinean nurse, and how he felt waking up in her bed.

His mother began coughing and Jamie rushed to her side. "You all right?"

She reached for a plastic cup of water. She tried to take a sip, then looked at the cup and shook it. The straw made a hollow rattling sound.

Jamie reached out. "Want some more water?" He grabbed the cup from his mother's blotchy hands. He felt a pain in his chest as he noticed how unhealthy her skin looked.

His mother pointed to the door. "Just go into the kitchen."

Jamie asked, "What's up with that kitchen? Can we go in there?"

"Of course! It's a teaching kitchen. They show you recipes and food that works for the Blake diet."

Jamie muttered as he walked outside, "Blake diet?"

Jamie felt like an imposter as he pulled the glass door open and tiptoed into the kitchen. He could smell the spice of fresh herbs and the slight burn of citrus. The kitchen looked like the set of a television cooking show. Large baskets of root vegetables, squash and fruit crowded one of the counter tops. Jamie had trouble finding the sink in the darkness.

He opened the fridge. Pale light permeated the silent kitchen. He saw leafy vegetables in a produce drawer. Orange, maroon, red and green juices were lined up along the top shelf. The colors were so vibrant, Jamie almost thought he was looking at jars of paint. He scanned the room. He saw clear glass cylinders packed with beans, rice and grains. He could smell an intoxicating medley of rosemary, garlic and citrus. The kitchen was full of life. He finally noticed a water dispenser and filled his mother's cup. The water slowly trickled out as he stared into the glowing refrigerator. He continued to imagine glass sculptures. He couldn't tell if it was the thrill of being unblocked or being around so much death, but everything felt amplified. His eyes fixated on a bowl of pale brown dough. He grabbed a chunk and patted down the rest.

He carefully walked back into Serenity with a cup of water and a ball of dough. "Here's your water, Mom," Jamie said.

"Thanks, Jamie," she said with hurried breaths. After a series of intense gulps, she laid her head back on the pillow and looked up at the ceiling. She smacked her lips as she watched her son.

Jamie laid the ball of malleable dough onto a shaky coffee table. He grabbed a small portion, closed his eyes and his hands replicated what he saw in the form of the dough. He imagined the feel of the metal blow rod; he thought about the dance with the glass.

Jamie's mother smiled as she watched him mold lumps of dough into elegant shapes. "You're in the zone again."

"How do you always know, Mom? It's been three years. How would you know that?" He squeezed the dough back into a ball.

Her legs flexed and relaxed under the blankets. "You're my baby boy, Jamie. You're not as tough for your mother to figure out as you'd like to think. You've found one of those creative windows."

"Yes, finally." Jamie tossed a ball of dough up toward the ceiling. It spun until it hit the off-white ceiling tiles, then fell back into his agile, capable hands. The dough made a subtle smacking noise every time he caught it.

His mother looked at her son and said, "I always knew you would."

"Thanks, Mom," Jamie answered.

The conversation came slowly. It was divided by awkward breaks of prolonged silence. After days in hospital rooms together, topics became exhausted.

"What's on your mind, Jamie?" His mother asked. She slowly reached for the cup of water. She took careful, steady sips like someone lost at sea sucking down their last ration of drinking water.

"I don't know," Jamie said quietly. He had always been nervous about philosophizing with his mother. She pontificated with Andy all the time, but Jamie always felt insecure about these conversations. Jamie sat up in his chair. His thick arms flexed as he leaned forward. A rectangular silver watch with a thick, black leather band wrapped around his left wrist.

Jamie held up the ball of dough in the light. "Waiting for windows of creation as an artist can be painful. You're totally focused on it, wondering what you can do to force something that can't be forced. All the time when you're not in the zone, questions creep in." He paused as a nurse came into the room and checked the monitors. As she closed the door behind her, Jamie continued, "Like I said, Mom, questions were creeping in. Am I any good? Will I ever create anything worthwhile again? Should I be working a regular job like the ocean of people I see walking to the train station every day to work in the Loop? Are they happy? Is that the answer?" Jamie looked at his mother with wide eyes. "These creative windows are all that matters to me, but it's temporary. I hope this window lasts a long time."

His mother reached for his thick forearm. "I have a feeling it will."

"It may not last forever, and I don't know if these pieces will sell or not, but it's the creative windows that matter, not the destination. The destination is death." Jamie looked at his mother with a repressed smile. "Wait till you see what I'm making now, Mom."

He laid his head on her bed. She combed his hair with her hand. Her brittle fingers ran over her son's short hair.

His mother said, "You need to get back."

"Not right now. I'm not leaving."

His mother stopped massaging his head for a moment and said, "Try not to talk too much about death around your mother right now."

"Sorry. I get carried away sometimes."

As the time neared midnight, Andy lightly knocked on the door. "You ready for a shift change?"

"Sure," Jamie answered.

Andy quickly fell asleep on a blue recliner next to his mother.

A half an hour later, he awoke to the crack of the door opening. A young doctor walked into the room. She was wide-awake with energy that felt nuclear-powered.

"My name is Doctor Mitchell." She extended her hand to Andy. "You can call me Jennifer."

"Andy Stone."

She turned to his mother and asked, "Sarah, I'm just going to do some tests and take your blood pressure. Okay?" She was younger, probably in her early thirties. She had an unflappable demeanor. She wore a classic white doctor's coat. She had a compact, solid build. Her hair was straight and medium length. "Don't mind me, Sarah. You can keep sleeping if you want."

Andy's mother opened her eyes and watched the new doctor perform her tasks. She was evaluating the doctor in the naked way that kids often did with adults they just met. She always watched new doctors or nurses as they performed basic medical tasks on her, assessing their competence.

Jennifer turned to Andy. "I heard about you guys sneaking up here in the middle of the night, huh?"

"Actually, it was their plan. My brother and I weren't exactly kept in the loop about the great escape. But now that we're here, I can see why," he stated with a slight hint of flirtation.

She didn't react. He changed the subject. "How long have you been working here?"

"Three years."

"You like it?"

"Like is not the word." She wrote a few notes on a white clipboard as she checked the machine next to his mother. Andy noticed that her burgundy undershirt matched highlights in her flat shoes. He didn't think it was a coincidence. His mother had fallen asleep again. She was snoring. Apparently, Jennifer passed his mother's basic medical aptitude assessment.

"It really is that different," Andy agreed. "I've never seen any place like it. Totally focused on healing."

"It's very different," she said. Andy believed she was holding back a wealth of information.

Andy looked around and said, "You see it done the same way so many times. The same cancer care in conventional hospitals. You get used to vending machines everywhere with candy and chips. Vacuous, bland hospital rooms. Sterile glass jars. Rubber gloves. You watch overweight nurses waddle outside to smoke a cigarette in between sips of diet soda."

He looked up at the vibrant painting on the wall behind Jennifer. "And you start to believe that it's the only way. This is how cancer care has to be. You believe it's right because the vast majority has accepted the old hospital model forever, which creates a powerful momentum. Then you walk into this place. And you realize that it doesn't have to be that way, that your instincts about conventional hospitals were right. My mom's instincts were right."

Jennifer rolled back his mother's blanket and exposed her stomach. She said, "I used to travel to hospitals all over the country and you believe that this is the way. See malady, kill malady. See malady, kill malady." She peeled back a bandage and examined his mother's abdomen. She continued, "They care very little about the cause of the disease. Just eradicate the tumor."

Something on his mother's stomach caught Jennifer's attention. As she examined it more closely, Andy continued. "It happened to our mom. The answer wasn't at Rockford Covenant Hospital. Not for cancer. And she knew it in her heart, at her core. And no one could tell her different. So, in between her bouts with cancer, she desperately searched for another way. She looked for something that rang true. A place that felt different. She searched and she searched. She traveled to a remote retreat in Mexico. They gave her an organic diet; she meditated and did yoga. But it was too far from the advances of modern medicine. It wasn't the answer. Then she traveled to a supposed groundbreaking doctor in the Bahamas, which turned out to be a dead end. Nothing about his treatment turned out to be groundbreaking. Wrong again. She searched and searched. She began counseling and helping people diagnosed with cancer. She became a specialist. Through her decades of work as a nurse, her knowledge of conventional treatment and her vast knowledge of alternative therapies, she searched for the answer."

Jennifer finally pulled the blankets back over Andy's mother.

Andy said, "Then this morning we walked into the Blake Treatment Center on the outskirts of Madison, Wisconsin. My mother finally found you. I believe this is the place that she knew was out there, that she was desperately seeking. And here we are. And I hope it's not too late. Because I couldn't imagine the sense in that."

She wrote a few more meticulous notes on her clipboard. Andy could make out the word "stable."

"What's going on here?" He asked as he looked into her deep hazel eyes. They were surrounded by light freckles.

Her right eyebrow mischievously rose. "What do you mean?"

"I mean, what is going on here?"

"Some things I can tell you about and some I cannot," Jennifer stated. "Your mother mentioned something earlier about you being a journalist?"

"At the moment, freelancer. Which is another way to say unemployed reporter," Andy explained.

Jennifer looked at him with a widened eye. She asked, "Is everything I tell you going to show up in story some day?"

"Not if you don't want it to. We can say all of this is off the record, confidential," Andy explained. Andy spoke carefully and deliberately. His blue eyes focused casually on the doctor. "Listen, I'm very aware that you don't want to give too much information about this place. I know you can get into trouble for saying too much. But I promise you, I won't repeat anything you say. I won't write a story about it. My mother is dying, and I just want to know what's happening here." Perhaps it was the fatigue or the surrender to his mother's death, but Andy spoke with conviction. He said, "Look, we were expecting her to live for two more months." Jennifer looked surprised by this comment. Andy pleaded, "What's happening here?" He felt like he was playing poker, holding the hand of his life, and trying not to make any sudden movements. He showed no signs of fear or excitement. To look at Andy, one would believe they were discussing the weather forecast, not a potentially revolutionary cancer care. It was a skill reporters needed.

"Anonymous, off the record..." Jennifer looked outside of the room. The communal room was completely silent.

"Deal." Andy held up his hands and then calmly lowered them. "Never to be repeated to anyone ever again. I'm just a son who's worried about his mother."

"Most of this is cleared to talk about anyway. I may have to gloss over a few things." She took off her jacket and sat back in her chair. "It's first important to understand the cancer cell. Cancer is a disorder at the cellular level. Our body is full of specialized cells that grow, divide, serve a specific function, and eventually die. Liver cells, respiratory cells, blood cells. Healthy cells work in harmony with their environment. If they are damaged or mutated, they either repair themselves, shut down, or they die. Healthy cell function is controlled by an incredibly complex series of switches, rules and signals contained within our cellular genetic makeup. The DNA is the instruction manual and the switchboard. I like to think of it as the control panel of an airplane cockpit."

Andy thought about his friend working the soundboard back in Colorado. He pictured him constantly adjusting a vast array of knobs and dials – the intricate dance in a scale of gray. Apparently, the rules were the same at the cellular level. It was a dance in the spectrum within.

"A simple liver cell incorporates a beautiful symphony of genetic signals working in harmony with the biochemical, respiratory and circulatory functions of the body. The life of a simple cell requires genetic switches. They regulate cellular growth and function. Our DNA is the foundation. It keeps the system functioning in this tenuous equilibrium. What more scientists are asking these days isn't, 'Why do we get cancer?' But, 'How is it that we don't get cancer more often?'"

A strange creaking noise interrupted her. "Excuse me for a second." Jennifer carefully peered outside of the room. Her long, slender, floral skirt ended at a well-defined calf. "I swear this place is haunted," she said as she sat back down. "A cancer cell is a mutated or damaged cell. That's it. It's a cell whose function and DNA have been altered or damaged. A great example of damaged cells is when you lie out in the sun for too long."

Andy said, "Sun burn."

"Yes, technically these are precancerous cells. They no longer function properly. A healthy, functioning body can normally mitigate the damage and return the body to health. But when the body is weakened, cancer takes over the system. It convinces the body that it deserves oxygen and nutrients. Once cancer cells spread, they're most lethal."

Andy looked at his mom. She took a particularly long gap before her next inhale. His eyes strained as he waited for a sign of life. Finally, her chest rose and expanded, and her son took a breath as well.

Jennifer continued, "Cancer basically controls the system within. It creates its own miniature, separate circulatory system and tricks the body into providing it with the fuel it needs to grow. Unlike normal human cells, a skin cell or a liver cell, cancer cells grow exponentially. They grow for the sake of growth. They have no function but to multiply indefinitely. They trick the body into thinking this model is good for the system as a whole. When in fact, it only benefits the tumor. At the expense of all of the specialized, balanced cells that serve a function, stay closely connected to their neighboring cells, and adhere to the delicate equilibrium of a healthy human body. Cancer destroys the balance."

She excused herself for a moment and checked on another patient. Andy could hear her knock gently on the next room. Andy reached his slender arm over the bed. He rubbed his hand across his mother's forehead. His fingers ran through random regions of thin hair. She still felt cold as she often did, but she slept with a contented grin.

Moments later Jennifer returned and said, "We're going to let that patient sleep. Where were we?" She requested.

"Blake's treatment," Andy said with great focus. His words failed to mask his rising fascination.

She looked around the room. "Right. Three phases. During Phase One, we basically shut down all cancer cells." She breezed over this statement.

"What?"

Jennifer glanced at the door once again. Her sharp eyes quickly scanned the environment. She looked hesitant to speak. She eventually continued, "Doctor Blake has found something new. Something I cannot get into specifically. But it works like an emergency kill switch. Think of metastasized cancer as a complex, random electrical grid throughout your mother's body. We temporarily cut off the electricity. The cancer cells shut down. They don't die, but they don't multiply. They become severely weakened and susceptible to other treatment."

Andy asked her, "You've found something that shuts off cancer cells?" He enunciated very clearly.

"Yes."

"What makes them shut off?" He asked as he let out a quiet laugh of disbelief. "Does anyone else use this mysterious technique?"

"I can't tell you what it is. And no, there's no one doing what we're doing. We can only shut it off temporarily – like briefly cutting off oxygen to a fire. This kill switch alone isn't the answer. It just buys us time. Once we flip off the switch, we aggressively work to strengthen the body and the immune system. We only have a slim window to do this before the cancer cells return to full function."

"How long?"

"Months. Four to eight months, generally. Depends on how severe the case is." Jennifer saw Andy try to fit his mother into this timeline. "Next is Phase Two. A complex combination of supplements, intense treatments, physical therapies, and psychological therapies working in conjunction to give the body strength in this brief time when cancer recedes." She picked at her neatly manicured fingernails.

70

"What therapies?" He asked.

"It all varies. Everyone gets liquid gold. Reflexology, homeopathy, hyperthermia."

"Hyperthermia?" Andy muttered to himself.

She added, "We rarely ever use chemotherapy. When we do utilize chemotherapy, we don't use the most popular chemo. The one from Plaxin Pharmaceuticals."

"Why not?"

"It's extremely toxic. Causes lots of side effects. It's the chemo drug most widely used by cancer doctors today. We have a better chemo."

"Can you do that? Just not use the regular chemo? Won't Plaxin have some issues with that?" Andy asked. He twisted in his chair.

Jennifer ignored his question. "Phase Three may seem a little boring, but it's the most vital. It's a complete change of diet and lifestyle. Just as the amount of processed foods in our diet can overwhelm the system and facilitate disease, so too can healthy food have an incredibly synergistic effect on the body. It's basically an organic, plant, bean and grain diet. And the effects of these super foods on the body is truly amazing."

"Diet?" Andy anxiously picked at his a fingernail as he asked.

Jennifer reached for Andy's jittery hands. She looked him in the eyes as she took a deep inhale then exhale. She could sense his concern for his mother. Anxiety was difficult to control for many family members with a loved one clinging to the ledge of the great precipice. She continued, "Let me explain something to you. Going back to the cancer cell. Cancer cells are mutated cells. The cells have been damaged or altered. How does this happen? We're seeing an increase in cancer. In other words, we are seeing an increase in genetic mutations. This increase has correlated with the mutations in our environment."

Andy asked, "What do you mean?"

"Unfortunately, the stuff that mutates or damages our cells is everywhere. We come in contact with it every day," Jennifer answered as she looked around the room. She rubbed Andy's fleece jacket between her fingers. "Formaldehyde in clothing. Carbon monoxide in red meat. Pesticides in strawberries. Fire retardant in carpets. Genetically modified grains that have had thousands of years of genetic perfection recklessly altered by people who barely understand the complexities of tampering with genetics. This all creates mutations."

Andy echoed, "Creating cancer."

Jennifer answered, "Indirectly, yes. It's not that hard to figure out. We believe that many of the man-made mutations in our food and our environment are creating mutations at a cellular level. Harmful chemicals and compounds are making their way into our bodies and damaging our cells." She got up and checked the IV bag of liquid gold hanging from a slim metal rod. It was almost empty. "We have developed a tangible number. It's called the Blake Number."

Andy echoed, "The Blake Number?" He ran his hands through his hair. He felt tired. For a second, he thought about where he would sleep. He twisted his body in an effort to find a decent position.

Jennifer asked, "Have you ever heard of a regression equation?"

"Yeah, I think so. Is that the long equation? It takes multiple variables and attaches a percentage or a relative weight to each factor? You get a single, final number at the end." Andy thought about a college class long ago.

"Exactly. We use this equation to get the Blake Number. We have a broad equation that includes many major factors that either advance or reverse cancer." Andy fought the urge to yawn after she began talking about equations. Jennifer watched this act. She finally continued, "We've found that several hormones found in red meat can increase the risk of mutated cells. Patients receive a highly alkalizing diet. We believe that the modern diet has become so acidic that the body must work extremely hard to maintain normal PH levels, thus inhibiting its ability to fight tumors. These are just two of hundreds of elements in the equation. The equation also incorporates various remedies that are known to help cancer patients. No patient's equation is the same because no patient's treatment is the same. But we know that an intensive, personalized combination of anti-cancer nutrition and treatment, along with a dramatic reduction in carcinogen intake, can greatly tilt the scales toward recovery for many patients. After we measure all of these factors, cancer-causing and anti-cancer, out comes a single number. The Blake Number. Below a certain point and we know that it's very difficult for cancer to grow and thrive. Excuse me for a minute." She marched out the door. Moments later she returned. As she unwrapped another bag of liquid gold, she said, "That's our treatment in a nutshell. Kind of a big nutshell."

"And this works for all cancer patients?"

"Doctor Blake's mainly working with people with very advanced cancer right now." Jennifer calmly shook her head. She pressed down on a white clamp attached to the tube that fed the IV to his mother's arm. She stood up and grabbed some supplies from a nearby cabinet.

"Why is that?"

"Because terminal patients are the only ones allowed to receive experimental treatment." She made a quoting gesture with her fingers as she said "experimental."

"What?"

As Jennifer pulled rubber gloves over her hands, she explained, "No more liability. When you're viewed as a terminal patient, no experimental treatment is risky. You don't see malpractice lawsuits made by patients who are given only a few months to live. With the lack of liability, comes great freedom to treat terminal patients completely unconstrained by conventional medicine and lawyers." She unhooked a plastic tube from his mother's wrist and thoroughly swabbed the end of it with a square pad. The dense aroma of rubbing alcohol filled the air. "Cancer treatment for the individual. That's what we say. That's what's needed. You can't get away with that anywhere else. Any difference in treatment suggests to the lawyers that the doctor did something wrong. It's only here – under the veil of the terminal cancer diagnosis – that we're allowed to treat patients in the way that best fits them."

Jennifer carefully squeezed the new, full bag of IV fluid. She unclamped the white piece of plastic. Yellow fluid came streaming down the clear tube. She continued, "Out there is a word called protocol. Protocol is the cancer treatment standard. Any deviation from protocol opens a doctor up to litigation. Even the fact that we recommend more garlic to one patient could be seen as inconsistent and we could be liable. The exact thing that these people need – a doctor who treats each person differently – is what doctors cannot do. I feel bad for doctors now, their hands are tied in many, many situations, and that's the problem. Each body, each cancer is different. But with conventional care, they must all be treated the same."

She efficiently stripped her rubber gloves and dropped them into a garbage bin. She explained, "Cancer is a completely unique disease. There will never be a magic pill that will cure it. If you want to be cured, the care must be comprehensive. Nutrition, alternative therapies, as well as mainstream ones. Conventional cancer treatment alone isn't the answer. It never will be. In the future, all cancer will be treated comprehensively, holistically, even though I don't like that word."

She sat back down, her hands propped rigidly on her knees. Andy could sense her frustration. She explained, "But if they would ever let him treat early cancer, if they would ever let more patients go to Doctor Blake, and..."

Andy asked, "So what are you saying?"

"I'm saying that the Blake treatment works. We have found great success in treating terminal patients, and we know that cancer almost always goes into remission when the Blake Number is low, except for the worst of…" Jennifer paused as she looked at Andy's mother. "It's likely, and I'm trusting you to keep this private, but it is very likely that the Blake treatment would be even easier to administer in patients with non-terminal cancer. It could greatly reduce the chances that cancer was to overtake them down the road."

"What are you saying?" He emphasized the question. He felt an almost overwhelming shot of adrenaline. He could barely believe what he was hearing.

Jennifer reached for his hand and leaned toward him. Her hazel eyes were beaming with energy, as if she had been dying to tell someone. "Between you and me, I'm telling you that Richard Blake may have found a way to reverse cancer."

CHAPTER SIX

Ashley Markum licked the tip of her finger and scratched off a faint white smudge on her favorite black dress. She straightened her shoulders, tilted her head to the right and assessed herself in the bathroom mirror. She was shaped like a majestic blond sculpture. She had the soft brown eyes of a woman many years younger than she. She wore a flowing black dress. It was sheer and fitting. It maintained the delicate balance of feminine beauty and the professional appearance required of an executive. Almost daily, people told her she looked like a well-known model named Elaine Irwin who was better known for her former husband's last name. She expressed a curious combination of wisdom and youth. Her face created double takes, sometimes prompting tourists to request a picture with her. They assumed she was famous, and would ask who she was only after the picture was taken.

Ashley looked at herself in the mirror. She looked beyond her beauty, as if this were a minor detail in her composition as a person, which it was. Her eyes unveiled an ancient wisdom and intuition, a motherly energy that made friends and family seek her out in times of pain and desperate need. Something about her presence made people respectful of her space. She seemed to be protected by an invisible shield, perhaps conjured by some elusive spirits and beings from another realm, beings directed to protect her through the tumultuous waters of her life.

She heard a knock at the door. The front double doors of her suite were cracked open. A younger man cautiously entered the common area.

Ashley walked up to him. "Hello, nice to meet you."

"I'm Charlie."

"Charlie, Ashley Markum." She reached out her hand. Ashley towered above him. She was well over six feet tall in her heals.

"So, where do you want to do this?" The twenty-something man with bushy hair asked, as he stripped his bag off his shoulder.

Ashley pointed. "Table is good." A round table stood in the middle of the living room. It was close to the double doors that opened up to the hotel hallway. The doors were still swung wide open. She motioned for Charlie to sit down. Her movements were poised, professional, yet comforting and familiar. Ashley filled a glass with water from the sink. The water came out frothy and white. It eventually became clear. She checked her phone. She asked, "Would you like something to drink? Coke? Water?"

Charlie replied, "No, that's fine. Thank you. Give me just a moment and I'll be ready," he said as he reached into his bag.

"Yeah, of course."

Charlie asked, "So what brings you to Las Vegas?"

"Annual meetings in conjunction with a small genetic research convention," she explained.

Ashley walked over to the wall on the far side of the suite. A white curtain enveloped the glass panels behind it. As she pressed a button that made the linen curtains retreat to the edges of the windows, the city of Las Vegas emerged in front of her.

She asked, "Do you ever get used to living here?" She spoke with a subtle force. The volume of her voice wasn't particularly loud, but her words seemed to amplify through the room. Her natural blond hair curved down to her tan porcelain shoulders and back. She leaned on the broad window, against the backdrop of Las Vegas neon.

"I think I'm getting used to living here." As Charlie caught a quick glance of her standing at the windows, he had to check her age again. She seemed to defy physics. He revisited his notes. Ashley Markum. Forty-three. Plaxin Pharmaceuticals VP of Finance and Development for North America. Top of class University of Chicago MBA. When researching Ashley Markum before this interview, he read descriptions like "prodigy" and "analysis that bordered on clairvoyance."

Charlie snapped out of his notes and continued, "I don't know if anyone is completely accustomed to this city. It can be kind of surreal. But there are a lot of nice neighborhoods in the valley. Far away from all of this stuff. At least farther away. The short answer is, no, you don't ever quite get used to living here. I'm from North Carolina originally. I have a daughter. My wife and I are worried about her growing up in the Sin City. Do you have kids?" Just as he asked, he felt he made a mistake.

Ashley looked down at the Strip. The question made her chest hurt.

"Nope. No children," she said. It sounded more like a statement of reality than choice.

Charlie quickly retreated from the question. He nervously shifted in his over-starched black shirt. He said, "I like these hotel rooms."

"You have one kid?" Ashley asked, unaffected by the previous comment.

"Yup. Just my little girl. A year and a half."

"Oh, that's a great age. Is she talking?" Ashley smiled and asked.

"A lot. It still blows my mind that they can just start putting words together." His mouth contorted to various shapes as he spoke, seemingly imitating his daughter. "It seems so obvious, but when you observe it day-after-day, in your own house, it's mind-blowing." He pointed to the recorders on the table. "Okay, I'm all set here. You don't mind if I record, do you?"

"Not at all." Most people in Ashley's position would have declined an interview with an obscure Nevada health care blogger, but she did as many as she could. She felt that big pharma had become misunderstood and demonized.

"Let's get started. I'm sure you have a busy weekend here." He checked the recorder to make sure it was registering the conversation. He placed it back on the table as he watched the digital equalizer pulse with the sound of his own voice.

"Great."

"Ashley, briefly describe the drug creation process if you could," Charlie said with pronounced inflections. "There is a lot of misinformation out there about how quickly drugs are being approved."

Ashley nodded, "Fast tracking."

"Exactly. I was wondering if you could speak to this and provide some perspective about just how long it takes and how careful you are in approving a drug. Because a growing perception seems to be that big pharma can ram untested drugs recklessly through the system in a matter of months."

Ashley took a sip of water. "Most pre-development begins through licensing agreements with independent biotech companies, large research firms, sometimes we work with academia. These are the people who are constantly dreaming of new ways to cure disease. They find an ailment and look for a medicine."

Through hundreds of interviews, she had a great talent for explaining the company, not saying anything damaging, yet providing interesting information. Ashley had always marveled at the way politicians gave such bad interviews. They always looked stiff, desperately trying to control every word that left their mouths. They were afraid to offend, and they never said anything of significance.

"Can you be more specific?" Charlie asked as he carefully directed his digital recorder closer to her.

Ashley leaned forward and settled into her answer. "Sure. Our bodies are made up of an astounding variety of proteins. These proteins provide many countless functions in the body. Some proteins malfunction or damage the body. Our researchers often look to isolate the central protein causing a specific problem. For instance, say they find a certain protein that is excessively found in people with prostate cancer."

Charlie said, "The troublemaker protein."

"Exactly." Ashley twisted in an effort to stretch her back. She had been working deep into the night, sitting at the same chair. She drank about a gallon of coffee. Cups were piled into the nearby garbage can. At one point, she had so many color-coded spreadsheets opened that her laptop locked up. She continued, "This is phase one. Target discovery. In other words, we have found a target substance in the body that may be responsible for a malady."

"Okay," Charlie answered as he frantically scribbled notes.

"Using our example, prostate cancer. We have discovered a certain curious protein that accumulates more in a sick prostate than a healthy prostate. This protein has some relationship with the disease. Largely through computer modeling, we can find substances that will interact with this protein in some way. Most won't. Once we've found the ones that interact, we can find the substances that create the *desired* effect on the protein. In the case of prostate cancer, it's to reduce the number of these specific proteins that we have isolated as the primary troublemakers. Out of the three hundred thousand compounds initially tested, say a couple thousand will show promise."

Charlie asked, "How do scientists discover these compounds?"

Ashley explained. "Basically, three ways – isolating them in organic matter, creating them chemically, or simulating them on a computer." She watched the digital recorder by her folded hands. A digital display pulsed with every word she spoke. Her words created a powerful ripple effect that echoed out in all directions. This stationary device happened to capture the ripples passing through.

Charlie asked, "Computer?"

She smiled. "This is where the majority of our early testing occurs. Advanced computer simulation."

"Like science fiction."

"Yeah, but it's reality. Through better computer modeling in the future, we hope to make the drug pipeline dramatically more efficient," Ashley explained. "In the very beginning of development, scientists test hundreds of thousands of compounds that may affect the isolated, troublemaker protein. *Hundreds of thousands.* Most of this early testing is still done with the independent firms. Once we discover compounds that create the desired effect, we begin testing in the real world. Plaxin will usually take over the development process at this point. The first experiments are performed in test tubes. Next we test with animals. Finally, the drug is ready for clinical trials, when the drug is first administered to actual sick patients. Initial doses are extremely low, eventually rising in dosage as the drug is deemed safe and stable. The clinical process alone takes at least four years. These trials are the majority of the cost of bringing a new drug to the marketplace. Hundreds of millions of dollars. The trials take place all over the globe in a variety of medical facilities. It's an incredibly complex logistical and informational challenge. After fifteen years and over a billion dollars, out of the hundreds of thousands of compounds initially tested, one drug makes it to the marketplace. Just one. And a drug company has about seven years before its patent expires to make back its sunk costs."

Charlie asked, "Do you believe there's a misconception about drug development?"

"I think so. The idea that we would hurry a drug to market before we were sure it was stable and effective is unrealistic. Frankly, we believe that the FDA's approval process needs a careful examination. It's outdated. Drug discovery is rapidly moving forward, and so far the FDA – like many regulatory agencies – has struggled to keep up. Many issues need to be addressed. The more reckless we are with the development process, the more at risk we are of litigation down the road. From a business standpoint, that just makes no sense. From a moral standpoint, it would be appalling. Every company has risks associated with new products. Toyota never knows for sure if their brakes aren't going to fail. But they test and they test. They do everything they can to be certain that the car is safe. That's what we do. I can assure you that the medicines brought to patients by Plaxin have gone through the most rigorous testing and research of anything else that a human can purchase or consume. Most of the drugs reaching patients today entered the development pipeline during the Clinton administration."

"Development costs are certainly enormous. How do you feel about Plaxin's marketing strategies?" Male reporters always asked female executives how they felt.

Ashley explained, "We have a very short window to recoup substantial expenses. It's a necessary part of the business. We need people to be aware of our products. We're a publicly traded company, and we take our responsibility to our shareholders very seriously. The same as Coke or Target or Ford." Ashley expressed a subtle smile. She wasn't expecting this soft-spoken reporter to ask such pointed questions.

Charlie prodded, "I understand that, but is it really ethical to market prescription medication to end-consumers who are in no position to diagnose themselves? Is it wrong to make ads that tell consumers to ask their doctor?"

"The doctor is still in charge. The ads are more about creating awareness." For the first time in the interview, her answers became more abrupt.

"I can tell you what I've said in many interviews. Health care and prescription medication are complicated subjects with no simple solution. It's a balance between free market innovation and socialized medicine. I truly believe that the free market drives innovation. It benefits consumers. Yes, we use marketing to create awareness. But we also open our laboratories and research facilities to causes that are not ideal for our bottom line, but may be greatly beneficial." Ashley once again spoke with patience and confidence. "We're working with foundations in Central America to combat Malaria. And a group in India working on a cheap, stable Polio vaccine. We'll lose money on all of these projects, but we do them. We don't do this because we have to. We do it because it's in our core values, but we're still a business. We must still act like a publicly traded company. I believe that there is a balance where we can all benefit."

Charlie hesitated for a moment, seemingly thrown off by such candor. He had to scan his notes for his next question. "So what's the future of the development process?"

"Getting more efficient with our testing. Effective and comprehensive computer simulation will save precious time and money. We would prefer to bring fewer, more promising drugs to the costly clinical phase."

"The majority of Plaxin's portfolio is cancer treatment."

Ashley answered, "That's right."

Charlie scanned his notes. "I saw that your chemotherapy drug accounts for about one third of all of your revenue."

"31.6%. Approximately." Ashley smiled, as the number 31.582 appeared in her mind.

"You seem to be at the forefront of new cancer treatment. Without giving too much away. What's next for Plaxin? What are the challenges?"

"Cancer is extremely complex. At the same time, it's deceptively simple. I believe we must understand cancer's biology better. We're just beginning to understand the genetic and biochemical implications of the disease. This all varies, whether we're talking about liver cancer or breast cancer. Our geneticists and scientists are making great strides in understanding the disease."

"Can you expand on that? What are you looking into?"

Ashley Markum thought of the Blake Center. Her eyes beamed with excitement. "I can't talk about that right now. Cancer is our focus. It's the disease that keeps us all up at night, seeking an answer to this ailment that affects so many people."

The elevator door opened to the faint smell of smoke. The air was cool with the slight whisper of humidity from the Bellagio Gardens. As Ashley crossed the hotel entrance, she focused on Dale Chihuly's bouquet of hand-blown glass flowers. They looked like a fantasy garden of glossy blossoms on the ceiling. Ashley Markum walked through the gardens. Three army soldiers had a man snap their photo. One boy chased his sister around the rectangular paths. Ashley gracefully swung to the side as they passed.

The casino floor of the Bellagio hummed with energy. Slots flashed. A crowd surrounding a jammed craps table cheered in unison. It made Ashley twitch with desire. She loved craps. She never thought she would like gambling until she walked up to a craps table at the Sahara Casino long ago. She rolled for forty-five minutes. She loved it because it defied the laws of man. Everybody won in unison.

She watched a sea of legs trudge on the ornate Bellagio tiles in front of her. Tourists with red Nebraska hoodies and hats, a family with two hyperactive children, a bachelor party of twenty-somethings all wearing light blue designer shirts and pressed jeans. Behind all of them was Ashley Markum. She walked alone, strolling at her own pace. Her steps echoed throughout her surroundings. As a boat created a wake over water, Ashley shaped the currents all around her. The atmosphere warped and collapsed into her energy.

Dozens of people lined a walkway and waited to be allowed into an exclusive nightclub just beyond the craps tables. They were waiting to enter the front area of the club. Ashley was headed to a private party deep in the exclusive rooms of the nightclub. Ashley approached the velvet rope wondering if she would need to explain herself. With a slight nod from the doorman and a reach for the silver clip, she knew there was no need. She walked into the club. No one in line complained.

Ashley Markum sat at the end of the exclusive bar. Amber lights illuminated flowing white curtains that rose to the vaulted ceiling. A woman in an orange tank top darted behind the bar with a shaker in one hand and a bottle of Grey Goose in the other. Ashley was early. One of Plaxin's genetic research subsidiaries was hosting a cocktail party. She recognized a handful of people. The bar was still sparse. People steadily flowed in. Some wore nametags. They carried folders and computer bags. Half of the time, they were looking at the glowing screens of various iDevices.

She sat with her slender legs crossed and casually sipped a martini. Subtle flavors of ginger, agave, and lime danced in her mouth. Ashley looked at her reflection in the mirror behind the bar. She checked her phone and realized that it hadn't beeped, buzzed, rang or chirped for a good half hour. New personal record. She whipped her thick locks of blond hair to one side. She scanned the planner on her phone. She took a deep breath as she contemplated another whirlwind week ahead. She continued to look behind her. More people populated the lower level of the banquet room. They began filling up the rounded booths on the second level. The booths overlooked a dramatic view of the Strip. Finally, Mike Landis, Plaxin's CEO appeared in the growing sea of blue suits and nametags. He looked like a massive earthquake could flatten the entire city, and Mike would still be standing there.

Mike walked up to the bar a few groups away from Ashley. He stood far enough that no one would suspect anything, but close enough to look at her. He ordered a club soda. Ashley quickly stole a glance. On the plane into Vegas, she read a magazine with a clothing ad that displayed a vibrant, well-manicured Sean Connery on the back cover. Mike had always reminded her of a younger version of Sean Connery, only slightly less attractive. *Slightly.* He was in his sixties with stylish peppered hair. He still glowed with great energy and magnetism. He emitted a confidence much different from other men. He didn't wear it on his shoulder. He didn't need to. When Ashley realized Mike was looking at her with a faint recognition, she gave a polite smile and turned toward the front quickly. But she knew he was still looking. She always knew when men were still looking. She looked back at him. Her blond bangs fell over her bright brown eyes. The two held the look for a few moments. She tried to fight it, but she couldn't look away. He smiled in the way that a dog did after misbehaving. The rush of memories returned. She remembered being with him, and how many women he had treated just like her. Rumors swirled that Mike had already selected his next conquest in the company. She finally turned away. Her heart pounded. Even now, at the abrupt decline of a whirlwind romance, it pounded at the sight of him.

Ashley also noticed the way other employees greeted Mike Landis. They tried to avoid direct eye contact. Even when they did lock eyes, they would humbly acknowledge him and carefully shake his hand. Ashley watched the slow, steady movements of the people who approached Mike, as if they were in the presence of predatory beast waiting to pounce. They acted the way people would as they met a violent dictator. Mike Landis was becoming more reckless in his personal life. His marriage had officially ended a year ago, rumors swirled that his former wife was spiraling into full-blown alcoholism. Despite his potent confidence, Mike had become different since the separation with his wife. He was more paranoid, more defensive.

"Ashley," a warm voice stated behind her.

She spun around with great enthusiasm. "Tanji!"

Tanji had a broad smile on his face. He was always smiling. Tanji was originally from Japan. His first name was actually Tanjiro. His father owned a successful restaurant supply company and put Tanji through school. He moved to America and continued his schooling at Carnegie Melon. He eventually married a nice lady from Idaho who looked like she was coming down with a cold every time Ashley met her. He was a shorter man with flowing dark hair, like he had just been riding a motorcycle. His default expression was a welcoming, convivial smile. His jovial personality made many underestimate has brilliance. He created a genetic research company in Southern California. His specialty was early in the drug development pipeline, long before the clinical trials, when scientists could dream of new ways of combating the afflictions that haunted humanity. Tanji joined Plaxin's management team ten years ago. He quickly rose to head of all Research and Pre-Clinical Development in North America. He had been a critical advocate for the genetic mapping of cancer. He never stopped dreaming of new ways to fight the disease. He had also become a close adviser and confidant for Ashley.

Ashley stood up and led him over to the corner. "Tanji. We need to talk. Not here." She spoke abruptly.

Tanji failed to mask his concern. He motioned toward the exit. "Let's go outside."

Ashley insisted, "Not together, not together. Meet me around the right corner outside of the main entrance in fifteen minutes."

Ashley sat alone at the end of a stone bench. Groups of tourists marched up and down the walkway. She could see them through some shrubs. The muted sound of water cannons rhythmically thumped in the distance. The Bellagio's landmark fountains were performing their regular dance. Crowds of people cheered. Constant camera flashes cut through the secluded darkness. Ashley listened to the sound of water flowing nearby. Cabs whirled away from the entrance. Men in suits directed the constant traffic. Ashley leaned back and squinted as she peered into the night sky. As she searched for a star in the darkness above, she laughed at herself. She was looking for a faint glimmer of light while sitting in the middle of the neon blowtorch of the Las Vegas Strip. *No stars here.*

Tanji emerged from around the corner. His eyes locked onto Ashley's. "What's going on?" He sat next to her. His uniquely pale skin gave away his Japanese heritage.

Ashley looked back up at the evening sky. "I've been thinking a lot lately."

"About what?" Tanji asked.

"About chemotherapy. Our chemotherapy." She shook her head. Her symmetrical collarbones steadily rose and fall with her breaths. She turned to Tanji and said, "I told you my uncle was really sick last summer."

Tanji replied, "Yeah, I think I remember that. He lived in Wisconsin. Had cancer, right?" He had always been known throughout Plaxin for his astounding memory. Tanji could retain details from the most casual of conversations.

"Lung cancer. Never smoked a cigarette in his life. But that's not the point. I spent time with him up there. I stayed at his lake house for a weekend," Ashley explained. "Spent the mornings on the water with the family; spent the nights in his hospital room. They gave him chemo. Our chemo. Oncologists had been going bi-weekly for the previous two months before I got there." A light breeze ran up the sheer ruffles of her black dress.

"Two months?" Tanji asked, somewhat surprised.

"Two months of chemo."

"And I watched a man about to die. I listened to the doctors tell him that the chemo would buy him weeks, a couple months tops. Ten thousand dollars a pop. Do the math. He had complications. The usual. Vomiting, nausea, infections. He was weak and ill." Ashley wiped a faint tear from her right eye. Tanji gently touched her shoulder. She continued, "Near the end, he got much worse. The doctors, the family, everyone said that the cancer was taking hold. They assumed that cancer was doing all of this, but I knew the truth. Because I know the labs. Cancer was doing some of it, but our chemo wasn't helping his body either. I watched as my uncle shriveled into nothing. Part of his pain, part of his struggle was because of the drug that I brought to the market."

"Ashley," Tanji said. He spoke with a fatherly voice that calmed his friend.

"I'm not saying that it wasn't the best thing for those doctors to do. It was the best treatment option. But sitting in that hospital, watching our drug poison and weaken his already battered body, I found a new mission. I felt a rising sense that there had to be a better way to treat this disease. *There has to be a better way*, Tanji." Ashley wiped her eye one more time and continued with a renewed composure. "I promised to find treatments that helped people when I took this position at Plaxin, but it hasn't been that way with our cancer treatment. More like drug self-preservation than drug discovery. So I've been searching for another way, looking for something different, more experimental to test in the pipeline."

"Why are you telling me this now?" Tanji frowned with concern.

"I found someone. Actually, he came to me. A doctor. As I was searching for a new cancer treatment, a doctor working with terminal patients showed up in my office three months ago. The doctor found out about me from my dad's best friend. The doctor that treated him, Doctor Richard Blake, told me his vision, and he said he needed my help. He needed someone he could trust working for a reputable cancer drug company. Doctor Blake came to me with a potentially groundbreaking treatment. We've been meeting and talking for the last few months. I guess to build up his trust in me. He was hesitant to hand over his clinical data." Ashley paused for a moment. "Until now. He finally gave me hundreds of pages of data from decades of clinical work. He also promised to send his mysterious treatments to a trusted researcher of my choosing for further testing. Tanji, I need you to research his cancer center and its unique treatment."

"Why now?" Tanji asked. He was skeptical. "Why didn't you tell me this back in Chicago?"

Ashley explained, "A couple reasons. First, Doctor Blake didn't give me anything to use until a few days ago. Before this week, I knew nothing about his treatment or his research data. I only heard testimonials, which I must say were quite convincing. But I think he trusts me now. He knows I'm going to keep the research in a tight circle." She held up two fingers. "The second reason is that the only person I could trust to do this research is you, Tanji. I know you just finished some major pre-clinicals just before this conference. I knew I had to catch you before you were bombarded with more projects, which usually happens to you at these conferences."

"It's already happening," Tanji said, shaking his head. "So this cancer treatment. Do you want something officially in the Plaxin pipeline? Or is this a secret?" Tanji asked. He abruptly stood up, nervously walked toward the main lobby, and peered around the corner.

When he returned, Ashley answered, "For now, secret. Keep it quiet. A low-profile subsidiary would be best. Perhaps one of our small research facilities up by Minneapolis. Somewhere that goes unnoticed until we're ready to go public. And possibly put something into the official development pipeline later."

Tanji shook his head. He didn't understand why she was being so secretive. "Why this place in particular?"

Ashley looked around before she whispered, "I believe he's reversing cancer in terminal patients."

"Another one of these? Ashley. We hear miracle doctor claims almost weekly."

"This one's different, Tanji. What he did with my dad's friend is unbelievable. He believes the doctor's treatment center is revolutionary."

Tanji asked, "What's it called?" His long black hair had a particularly wild rooster-like quality. It seemed to get wilder as the night progressed.

"The Blake Cancer Treatment Center."

"Okay." Tanji asked, "What's he using? Chemo?"

A teenage couple emerged from around the corner. They sparked cigarettes with a creepy giddiness. As they noticed Ashley and Tanji on the bench, they quickly turned around and walked away.

"What is this miracle doctor using? Is he using our chemo?" Tanji repeated.

Ashley whispered, "No. Most of the time it's something else. Enzyme injections."

The statement caught his attention. "What enzyme?"

She reached under the bench and handed him a binder about five inches thick. That's for you to find out. He claims he's taken the treatment as far as he can, and he needs us."

"He needs us?" Tanji asked. His skepticism was noted in the emphasis of every word in the question.

Ashley grabbed his hands and said, "Check it out. Please, Tanji."

Tanji shook his head. "You realize the implications of devoting resources to a place like this. Mike Landis will..."

Ashley stood up, grabbed a plastic gift shop bag from under her seat. She grabbed the Blake binder and shoved it in the bag. "Mike Landis doesn't need to know."

Tanji reached for the bag. "Ashley, I've always trusted you. I've always believed in you, but..."

"Believe in me now, my friend. Believe me when I tell you that something amazing is happening," she said with a rising energy in her voice. Her energy had always been contagious. "I know there are claims about these miracle doctors all of the time, but see this one for yourself. Go talk to him. Richard Blake. This one could be different. Get that binder to your room. I'll see you back downstairs."

Ashley began to walk away as Tanji said, "One last thing. This raises so many questions. Our cancer revenue streams. Have you..."

She nodded and turned to him. "I know the questions you want to ask. Please don't ask them, not yet. I'm asking you as a friend. I trust you more than anyone in the company. That's why I came to you with this, and I know that you're like me. Even when the revenue stream isn't totally clear, you want to find cures. Doctor Blake believes we can work with him, and I agree."

"Okay. I'll look into it, Ashley. But if this thing goes south."

Ashley nodded. She spoke with conviction and a rising sense of peace, "It's on me."

As the night grew later and the dance floor became crowded, Ashley Markum stood in front of a span of concave windows. She stood alone at the edge of the elevated lounge. It provided dramatic views of the Las

Vegas lights outside and the dance floor down below. Ashley leaned against the glass and sipped another martini. She looked back at the nightclub. She was content to sip her drink alone. The club was packed. She looked out over the Strip. It looked like a breathing organism of capitalism suspended in this moment just for her. It was difficult to tell if the new construction was advancing or had been abandoned. She thought the same could be said for this country right now. Were we growing still, or were we standing at the edge of a steep decline? Were we advancing or were others about to leave us in their wakes? She had been arguing for years that this rate of growth and acceleration was unsustainable. Something eventually would have to give.

She gazed out onto the replicas of Paris, New York, the Pyramids, Caesar's Palace, and she imagined all of society reaching this point. There was one thought that she couldn't escape. *Acceleration.* As much as any place in the world, she could see it in Las Vegas. We moved so fast now. Our minds danced from one distraction to the next, to the point where we had grown accustomed to being an instant society. Anything we wanted was accessible in a heartbeat. *Faster, faster, faster.* In this great acceleration, she felt like some of the good things in life were lost, although she wasn't sure what. Men stood on the sidewalks smacking cards in their hands that promised sexual satisfaction. Slot machines glowed, spun and beeped at every push of a button. Las Vegas was like a giant bug zapper that could be seen from space. And houseflies flew in from all over the country.

In the middle of a desert, a city grew from a whisper into an international icon in a matter of decades, all of it churning, climbing, growing and speeding up to this suspended moment for the eyes of Ashley Markum. She saw it clearly and wondered what, if anything, one person could do against the momentum of all things, against the runaway train of our society speeding faster and faster down a hill. And the big question was whether or not there was a cliff at the end of the tracks. Of course, no one knew this answer, and that was the difficulty of life. We never knew for sure. We never knew what was too fast or too slow, too little or too much.

She didn't believe in any of that end of the world stuff. But if the end really was nigh, she thought it would definitely look something like this. The end of civilization would strike at the end of the great acceleration – like an engine running in the red for too long. Everything seemed fine until the engine finally gave out. This was the engine of

Earth. There were no other engines by which to compare. It was accelerating beyond our wildest dreams. Everything was heating up.

"Nice view." Mike Landis walked up to the window.

Ashley noticed a distinct reduction in volume from the people on the floor. She felt like they were all watching them.

"It's a nice view," she reluctantly agreed.

Mike walked over to her. His presence made Ashley lean back and take an awkward sip of her drink. Her eyes desperately tried to fix onto something outside of his line of sight. It didn't work.

She looked at him. "Something you wanted to talk about?"

He whispered, "Please come see me again. Tonight. I know things have been bad between us lately, but be with me tonight."

"I can't." She gazed back at the panoramic view of the Strip. She said with tempered anger, "This has to be over."

Mike spoke softly in her ear, "Just come to my room. I need to see you again. I miss you."

Ashley shook her head. Her eyes reflected the neon blues and reds outside of the window. "I can't do this anymore."

Mike pleaded, "Why?"

"For lots of reasons, you already know." She tilted her head toward him.

Two men in black suits called over to Mike. He said, "I should get back." As he walked past her, he paused next to her ear. "I'm in Penthouse Suite 12. North Tower, if you want."

Ashley didn't move. She didn't react. She just kept looking outside.

She finished her drink and joined a group of friends. Most of whom she had promised to teach how to play craps. She finally led them out of the nightclub and onto the casino floor. After a brief conga line at the cash machine, she led a group of five friends from Plaxin and a handful of others from subsidiary companies out to the tables. She walked up to three dealers standing with their arms behind their backs around a massive oval of green felt. The table had a solitary gambler.

Two hours later, Ashley sipped from a straw as another deceptively strong drink had vanished. She recognized a dozen faces from the company or the convention all leaning over the table. They threw out chips with rising confidence.

"Hard eight," her friend Joanie from accounting called to the dealer. He placed her chips on the dice that indicated a pair of fours had to be rolled.

Ashley whispered to a young newlywed couple standing next to her. They were placing the minimum bets and chatting with Ashley. She explained, "The woman rolling is a craps virgin. She rolled for a while the first time."

The newlywed husband asked, "How do you guys know each other?"

Ashley said, "Here for a genetic research convention. Kind of small, but really interesting for someone like me. I do development for a drug company."

The chips were flying. It was one of those nights at a craps table. Everyone passing by wanted to be a part of it. Rows of onlookers pressed the players closer to the felt. Ashley looked at two rows of casino chips. She had been stuffing black hundred dollar chips into her purse for a while. She had already broken even, just by the chips she had stashed.

Joanie hit her first number. Five. The table erupted. Dealers hovered around, dropping stacks of chips in front of each player.

The newlywed wife quietly asked Ashley, "How long have you guys been playing?"

She looked up toward the perimeter of the casino floor for a moment. "I forgot there are no clocks in here. Probably two, three hours. Who knows?"

Joanie rolled again. Seven. Everyone got paid even money for their pass line bet. She rolled again. Six. Point was established. Ashley dropped a black chip on every number. Joanie hit a ten.

The dealer flashed two black chips at Ashley and asked, "Press it?"

She asked the newlyweds, "Should I leave it out there?"

They looked at each other. The husband said, "I don't know that's a lot of money."

Ashley motioned for the chips. She slid them to one side of her top row of blacks. Joanie rolled for another thirty minutes of pure gambling bliss.

Finally, Joanie hit a seven. And the dealers grabbed all of the chips from the table. Everyone clapped. Ashley smiled at her friend and pointed to her stack of chips.

In the passing time between the next roller and the next drink, the voice of Mike Landis echoed inside of her head. The casino floor seemed distant.

Most of her friends said goodbye and cashed in. Ashley remained for two cold rollers. The table deflated. The crowd dispersed. As the newlyweds were leaving, Ashley reached in front of her and grabbed two massive cylinders of black chips. She handed them to the newlywed bride.

"Take them. Consider it a wedding present."

"No, we can't. There's no way." The bride held up her tan hands.

Ashley explained to the bright-eyed couple, "I just really want you to have these. Look." She showed them the inside of her purse, littered with chips. "It's been an amazing night. If I keep all of this, I'll buy some expensive, lavish bag or dress that I don't need. It will make my night to give you guys a wedding gift. Please, let me do this for you."

The couple looked at each other and shrugged. The groom hesitantly said, "If you really want us to..."

"I do," she said with a blissful smile. She handed them two thousand dollars in chips. They exchanged emails and promised to stay in touch.

Ashley walked into the elevator blinded by adrenaline, booze, and the pleasure of her good deed. She stood pressed next to the bronze door. It couldn't rise fast enough. She felt a euphoric tingling in her head that could only come from a craps table and an unknown number of cocktails. She walked through the hallway as fast as she could while counting the rising room numbers until she reached Penthouse Suite 12. Nice suites always had low numbers. She quietly knocked on the door of Mike Landis and saw the white light of the peephole go dark as he walked toward it. She loved the anticipation of waiting outside of the room in the silence of the hall. The locks popped open. Ashley peeked through the crack in the door with a smile. Her blond hair fell down to her right side.

They didn't speak. In the vast living room of his penthouse suite, Mike Landis stripped off her clothes. They forgot about their issues. Ashley forgot about her rising disdain for him. She was still drawn to him. In front of the Las Vegas skyline, Ashley gave herself to Mike Landis.

Ashley awoke the next morning, naked and cold, tangled in a bundle of sheets on the couch. She felt a potent satisfaction from the night of reckless passion. And she awoke to the pain of her rational consciousness returning after a long break. She looked around the room. There was no sign of Mike anywhere.

"What did I do?" She whispered to herself, as a scolding parent would to a child.

Before she could figure out where he went, or whether he had already checked out, she headed for the door. She grabbed her dress bunched on the floor. Windows of the previous night returned. She remembered his raw passion, his intoxicating presence. She fought these feelings. She slipped on her shoes, grabbed her purse next to the front door, and vanished down the hall. She took the next flight back to Chicago.

..
CHAPTER SEVEN

Jamie Stone dug a wooden paddle into a glowing orange orb of molten glass. The glass studio was uncharacteristically cool on this mild, breezy Friday afternoon. The studio would soon be baking during the summer months ahead. As he rotated the orb with his right hand, it molded into a cone shape. His left hand gripped the paddle. His hands were strong and precise. The world around him melted away, as it had for months. He still hadn't scheduled an art opening. He was beginning to believe he would unveil his new series at the massive SOFA show on Navy Pier after Thanksgiving. Jamie didn't think about that. All he could see was the living, transforming glass in front of him. He wore a thermal sleeve that covered his left arm. It shielded his skin from the intense heat of the sculpture.

Mya sat behind the workstation. She watched her boyfriend at work. A duffel bag sat next to her chair. Her thick brown curls splayed over a bunched scarf. She watched Jamie with a suppressed amazement. She tried not to distract him during his studio time, but tonight was different. Andy, Jamie and Mya were meeting at the studio and driving to Rockford. They were going to take Andy's mother to her treatment in Madison the next morning.

Andy had been taking his mother every week, and growing more comfortable with the staff, especially Jennifer. She was guiding Andy through the process with his mother and telling him everything she could about the Blake Center. Doctor Blake remained an enigmatic figure for Andy, only occasionally stopping by the room to administer injections and provide basic updates.

Jamie worked with a partner today. She leaned down next to the tip of the blow rod. Jamie rolled it back and forth on the metal arms of the workstation.

Jamie requested, "Blow now please."

His partner filled her cheeks with air and pushed one intense burst of air into the hollow rod. Jamie watched intently as the bubble of air expanded in his glowing glass.

"One more please," he stated with a polite assertiveness. "That's good."

The air bubble expanded inside the orange glowing orb. After reattaching the piece to another rod from the top, Jamie inserted the orb back into the furnace. When he finally pulled it out, it was so bright that it looked ready to spontaneously burst into flames. He brought it back to the workstation. He rotated the piece feverishly as it drooped toward the floor.

"You ready?" He asked his blow partner.

She nodded with a deep breath. Jamie brought the piece over to a long metal sheet that spanned six feet on the floor. He grabbed a pair of medieval looking pliers, grabbed the top of the glowing glass and pulled. A long, slender cylinder of glass extended out from the sculpture as Jamie pulled. He laid the piece on the metal.

"Holy shit," he said to his assistant. He wiped the sweat from his brow. "I think we did it."

"It's amazing," his assistant agreed.

Just as Jamie negotiated the piece into the kiln to cool down, Andy walked into the studio. The metal front door clapped shut behind him. "Did I miss it?" He asked his brother.

"Just finished," Jamie said as he wiped his neck with an old red towel.

"You ready?" Andy asked.

"Got to clean up," Jamie answered. He looked around the studio intensely. "I need a little time."

Andy asked, "Can I take a look at your storage area?"

"Go ahead. Be careful in there. Don't knock anything over."

Andy raised his arms and said, "Brother! You know me better than that."

Mya and Andy meandered through the front halls. Mya pushed open a thick steel door that opened to a vast warehouse space. Sections were cordoned off for different artists. A man with long, frizzy black hair sat in an old office chair at the center of the common space in the middle of the warehouse. A garage door opened to the outside world. He sat smoking a cigarette, staring at a metal sculpture. He seemed baffled by its presence. Green grass striped the landscape beyond the garage door. The city was awakening to summer. Few settings compared to summertime in Chicago.

Mya asked, "Have you seen his storage space here lately?"

Andy said, "No, but I keep hearing things about it."

Mya motioned to Jamie's storage area. She slid a key into the padlock.

"It's locked?" Andy asked. "It was never locked before. Is this all new? I don't even remember there being walls."

Mya nodded. "He cleaned it, reorganized and put up walls. It's basically a locked storage space now."

She popped open the door, and Andy walked in. He remembered his brother's old storage space. It was a small corner of the studio. Most of the regular artists who worked there had a similar little storage section. It was dusty and dark. Abandoned glass pieces littered sporadic tables. It looked more like the space of an old tradesman or repairman than that of an artist. But all of the old pieces were gone. Oblong vessels with extended tips stood in neat rows on white tables. Their elegant shapes and vibrant, bewildering patterns made Andy smile. Rows of sculptures that looked like long blades of grass from a forest setting in a sci-fi movie were mostly bubble wrapped and lined up along the back wall.

"What happened to all the old stuff?" Andy asked Mya.

"Jamie got rid of it all. He said he didn't need it anymore."

As Andy knelt closer to one of the vessels, he whispered, "I can see why."

"Pretty amazing, huh?" Mya asked Andy. Her warm olive skin clashed with the lack of earth tones in the storage space – like a warm flower in the middle of a sterile gallery. She asked, "Did you ever think your brother would make something like this?"

Andy shook his head. "I knew he was capable of it. We all did, but to imagine pieces like this and to actually make them are two very different things."

Andy could still hear his brother cleaning. Metal tools plopped into plastic buckets. Chunks of glass tumbled in front of a broom across the concrete floor. Andy turned to Mya. "I'm sorry. I feel like I'm ignoring you. How are you doing? Jamie says your job is going really well."

"It's going great, actually. Almost too great. I'm doing my dream job, working labor and delivery at Prentice downtown."

"Delivering babies."

"I love it."

Andy said, "You know, that's what my mom used to do."

Mya nodded as she looked closer at one of Jamie's oversized blades of glass. "Jamie told me."

Andy said, "She always called it a truly noble profession to be a nurse delivering babies."

"Well, I agree. I love my job! How about you? I heard you're bartending and doing investigative work again."

Andy picked up a broken piece of glass. He answered, "The first part of that is true. I did finally get a gig bartending in Lincoln Park. But as far as reporting, I've been kind of stuck. Newspapers have laid off so many good reporters that they're going to take their own people as freelancers before they take me. It's been slow going. I'm not going to lie. It's been tough. But I've had a few stories published lately. So I'm hopeful."

Jamie walked in and looked at his collection with a tortured smile. "Let's go."

The next morning at his parents' house, Andy Stone awoke to the blinds lightly tapping the old wooden window frame in his old bedroom. They shifted and clinked together in a metallic way like a slinky. It was early. As he squinted at the eastern sky, he could only see faint bands of dull pastels. The sun wasn't even up yet. Andy's crusty mouth made him rise from the bed. He walked downstairs. The old carpet stairs flexed from the weight of his steps. Tropical fruit replicas were stacked in a ceramic bowl on the dining room table. The fruit was part of a Key West theme that permeated the house. Photos of the Florida Keys hung from the walls; a vivid acrylic painting of a tropical Key West bay hung in the living room. Andy's parents went to Key West every year. They stayed in a lush Victorian resort for a month in the winter. The timeshare began as a week, but his mother continued to expand the vacation time as she neared sixty. Andy looked at a picture of his parents on the famous Duval Street in Key West. His mother smiled blissfully in the tropical sun. He wondered if she would ever see the island again.

The floorboards in the kitchen creaked and moaned at the weight of someone walking on them at such an early hour. A stained-glass window leading to the sunroom glowed from the faintest hint of dawn. The woods behind the house still looked dark and ominous. Through an opened kitchen window, Andy heard crickets chirping in the back yard. Birds sang rhythmic morning songs. Fresh herbs and spices saturated the kitchen air with a potent bouquet. Despite numerous signs of life, the house felt different to him. It felt deflated. It was an empty shell with only faint echoes of past life. Orange bottles full of medication lined the counter. They were accompanied by a variety of medical supplies. The cold, sterile medical equipment felt like an imposter in his house that had always been full of warmth and spirit. It was a reminder that cancer had penetrated these walls. Not even the strength of this family, with its love and hope, could keep cancer out.

Water dripped from the kitchen faucet onto the steel sink making a tap, tap, tap sound. Each drop hit the metallic surface and soaked in the light from a floodlight outside. The tiny orbs of water exploded into dozens of smaller ones that lit up like little translucent beads and scattered in all directions across the bottom of the sink and then faded away on the perimeter. As his head moved ever so slightly, the drops disappeared. He moved his head back into position and they glowed again.

His father's tan leather briefcase rested on the kitchen island. Throughout Andy's childhood, his father always put on a suit and went to work. He could still remember the smell of his dad's shaving cream and the sound of him swishing his razor in the bathroom sink. His father wore newly dry-cleaned gray suits, lightly starched shirts, and the striped ties of a measured man in finance. In the morning, his father's black dress shoes clomped on the hardwood floor with purpose and meaning. Andy could picture him filling up his silver travel coffee mug. A newer version of the same travel mug stood next to the tan briefcase. His father worked six days a week all of the time. He never complained and always had time for his kids.

Andy's father, as with many sons, was his hero. Andy went to college and got a degree in business then told his dad he was going out West to be a journalist and snowboard bum. His dad never pressured Andy to follow in his career, not once, not even a subtle comment. Although he supported his son completely, Andy had always felt lesser than a man in a suit. Real men went out and worked in the real world. This insecurity was self-imposed.

After a couple more hours of sporadic sleep, Andy and his brother drove their mother to the Blake Center. Mya came along at the insistence of the brothers. They raced up Interstate 90. They slowed for the last tollbooth in Illinois. The toll was seventy-five cents.

Andy felt nothing jingling in his pockets. "Crap, do you have any change?" He asked his brother.

"Only hundreds."

"Hundreds?"

Jamie explained, "I just got paid."

"What are you selling now, cocaine?"

Jamie reached for the ashtray. It was stuck and finally opened with a jarring motion. A few pennies flew out into the space of the car and ran for cover like reclusive insects launched from their hiding places. On Jamie's forearm was a new tattoo. It was a small, abstract yin yang. The tattoo was only a faintly different color than his skin. The lines were distinct where the two spirals ran parallel to each other and seemed to dissolve at the edges of the circle. Andy had never seen ink like it.

"So we don't have any change?" Andy asked.

Andy reached for the pennies on the floor. "Watch this." He threw them into the toll basket. It was seventy-two cents short.

"What are you doing?"

"See the cameras? You act confused. You act like you put in the right amount of money and the machine didn't read it. When they review the tape, it'll create enough of a question that they won't ticket me."

Andy threw up his hands in confusion, assuming that a video camera was capturing every gesture and would be scrutinized by a team of toll booth officials as they debated whether to give the confused motorist in the video a ticket or whether it was a mechanical malfunction. Finally, he dramatically waved his arms at the toll machine with a frustrated shake of his head and drove away.

"You're an idiot." Jamie laughed.

The shape of the yin yang danced in Andy's head as they passed the rolling green farmlands of southern Wisconsin. He eased his foot off the gas as he remembered he was driving a car with an Illinois plate into Wisconsin. A recent study showed that Wisconsin police were much more likely to ticket Illinois drivers than their own. It was a fact that people from Illinois had always suspected.

As everyone else in the car drifted to sleep, Andy thought about the yin yang. In the shape of the faint yin yang burned onto Jamie's wrist was a lost meaning. This symbol may have represented balance, cause and effect and harmony to some, but Andy saw something much more profound and central to his life. The yin yang represented the big bang, the creation of the planets, human beings, and everything to come after us. In this ancient symbol was the birth of two out of one. In this place – where one became two, and three, and four – we debated the existence of God and the meaning of the creation of our universe. Scientists collected data. Prophets and philosophers pontificated. Regardless of what anyone believed, Andy felt we could agree that the birth of our universe was both miraculous and magnificent. Whether the scientists or the prophets were right, the birth of the physical was sacred because it gave us life, and all of the joy and crap that came with it.

Good and bad, happy and sad, hot and cold, none of these were absolutes. They were manifestations of the great split embossed on Jamie's arm. None could exist without the other. None would ever be complete without incorporation of the other. We were separate, incomplete and flawed.

Andy felt that it wasn't only eastern religion that understood this profound significance of the great split. It was also Christianity. The tale of the Garden of Eden was based on the splitting of one entity into two. Good and evil were not merely a set of moral coordinates, but rather the illustration of a vast spectrum between two extremes. Life began in this space within. In the birth of man, was the birth of relative existence.

"Love your hair, Sarah. You're in Harmony today," Edna said from her reception desk. Outside of the broad windows, the sky was gray. A spring storm was rumbling into Madison. Rain trickled down the tall glass panels. "Hey boys." She waved to Andy and Jamie. Mya followed with a smile. Edna returned to her conversation with a curious man leaning against the front desk. He had chocolate black skin and towered well over six feet. He was built like a diesel truck. He looked at Andy with a sharp gaze. Andy felt like he was there for something other than cancer treatment. He almost looked like he was doing security.

"I know. Long day." Their mother waved back toward the front desk. She was growing accustomed to the routine.

The brothers accompanied their mother back to the room. She seemed annoyed that her sons were helping and walked ahead of them. She clutched her left hip and slowed as she neared her room. Jamie rushed ahead to help her. She whipped around and said, "Jamie, I can do this. Back off." Jamie looked back at his brother and Mya with a rising smile.

After they settled into the room, everyone was asked to leave for a few minutes as they changed their mother into a gown.

Mya grabbed her purse. "I'm going to grab us some food. See you boys in a bit."

The brothers stood outside of the room awkwardly straining for subjects to fill the silence. Jamie finally asked, "Whatever happened to that girl from San Francisco?"

Andy explained, "I don't think she was too excited about the Google stalking. She didn't know how I got her work number, then email. I talked to her once over the phone, but it was strange. Something was wrong. I almost felt like she was afraid to talk to me."

"Really? You don't think she has a boyfriend, do you?"

"Don't know." Andy sighed. "It hurts, though. I really liked this girl. Thought it was going to work out, somehow. It sucks."

Jamie crossed his arms over his chest. He shook his head with resolve. "After losing her number, there weren't a lot of options left for you."

"I know," Andy said. "It's just too bad it turned out that way."

"That was it? One awkward phone call and that was the end of it. Bro, I know you better than that. You don't just give up."

Andy looked at his brother with wide eyes. Jamie asked, "Oh no, what did you do?"

"I broke the cardinal rule of dating," Andy said.

Jamie looked at his brother as a disappointed father would and repeated, "What did you do?"

"I left a really long email and I kind of told her everything."

Jamie shook his head. "Bro."

Andy explained, "I know. But it was honest. I just told her that I really felt we had a connection, and I really enjoyed our conversation. I told her about mom and the move. I told her how I felt when I met her. I explained how easy it was to search for her email and that I didn't want to scare her. If there was ever a chance we could meet again, don't rule me out. Leave that window open because I hadn't met anyone like her."

"And?"

"I haven't heard anything."

"Well, you never know," Jamie said. He slapped his brother on the shoulder. Jamie's lips were tucked into his mouth with concern. "I'm going to check on our mother."

"I'm going to run to the bathroom real quick," Andy said. His brother looked at him with intuitive skepticism in his narrowing eyes.

Andy walked away. The conversation put Emma squarely back in his mind. He walked out to the patio. Rain water continued to trickle down the glass patio roof. Specks of green buds emerged in the trees outside. Summer was near. Andy pulled out his phone. He looked around. When he realized he was alone, he dialed Emma's number. It went straight to voice mail.

Andy paused for a few moments, then spoke, "Emma, it's Andy. Look, this is the last time I'll call you. I just wanted to be sure that you saw the email I sent you. It explains everything. Please, just read the email. I know that I've broken like every rule of meeting someone and dating, but I hope you can look past all of that. Okay, goodbye, Emma."

He ended the call. Waves of regret drenched his mind. He meandered back inside.

Richard Blake was standing outside of his mother's room when Andy returned. Blake looked up from a chart. White pages were curled up over the top of the clipboard like a cresting wave of diagnostic information.

Blake turned and asked, "How's it going Andy?" The wave of papers crashed back to the clipboard as Blake lowered it to his side.

Andy felt uneasy about such undivided attention directed his way. "Good," he answered.

"Great!" Blake responded. "If you have a moment today, I'd like to talk to you in private."

"Sure." Andy's mind raced.

"Meet me in my office in an hour."

"Okay."

Blake said, "Your mother's doing pretty well."

"Yeah, we've had some steady improvement lately," Andy agreed. "She's getting some strength back. Her signature feisty personality is returning."

A look of skepticism formed on Blake's face as he asked, "Did it ever leave?"

"Now that you mention it, no."

As Blake walked into Harmony, Jennifer walked out. She nodded at Andy. Andy and Jennifer had spoken a lot during the last several weeks. She waved to Andy's mother. "Goodbye, Sarah. See you in a bit."

Andy reached for her arm. "Hey, Jennifer. What's up? How's she doing?"

She pulled Andy into an empty room. She closed the door and motioned for him to sit. She checked her watch as she explained, "The injections took. At the moment, your mother is in complete remission. But as I said before, this is an illusion. It's temporary. It's like the eye of the hurricane. Everything looks good, but the storm will be back."

"The eye of the storm," Andy echoed.

Jennifer said, "Yes, to use the same metaphor. We need to repair your mother's boat before she sets sail in the storm again."

"So this is phase two?" Andy asked.

"Exactly. Every anti-cancer therapy, medicine, food and supplement known to man. We'll give your mom everything. Because the storm will return," Jennifer said. Her voice lowered as she continued, "And your mom must be as strong as possible to survive. Make no mistake, Andy, the coming months are everything. We're in a battle for your mother's life. The first phase went well, but we're far from safety. Much rougher waters lie ahead."

"What can we do for her?" Andy stood up, sensing she had to leave. She was usually in constant motion whenever Andy visited.

She flashed a compassionate smile. "Everything you're doing now. Support her. Be there for her. But also enable the therapies that we recommend. Make sure she follows our recommendations precisely. Whether it's the Blake diet or receiving reflexology three times a week. It all matters. It all factors into the Blake Number."

"I'm sure you're busy. But thank you for being honest with me. It makes things much easier when I know what's going on."

"No problem," she said as she whisked out of the room. Her heels clomped with authority down the hall. It almost sounded like she was running.

Fifty-eight minutes later, Andy carefully peeked into the office of Richard Blake.

"Come in," a strong voice announced from inside. Blake sat behind a broad dark wooden desk. Books were lined along the two adjacent walls. The room smelled like sandalwood. His large ears flared out from his head. His chiseled face gave way to trenches of expanding wrinkles. His black hair was combed straight back. Besides the man in front of him, Andy didn't notice much else. He was so nervous and excited to talk to the elusive and mysterious doctor.

Blake said, "Jennifer's been telling me a lot about you. She said you might be the person I've been looking for."

"You're looking for someone?" Andy asked. He noticed a thin, manila file at Blake's fingertips. "I don't know if I like the sound of that."

Blake looked at him with his arresting black eyes. "I knew you were a journalist, but I researched you. You've done stories in health care. Investigative pieces. You're a very good reporter."

"Thanks," Andy answered.

"Well..."

Andy asked, "What?"

"You aren't curious about this place?" Blake raised his arms. His large hands and slender fingers rose toward the ceiling. "You aren't curious about our treatment?"

Andy looked away from Blake and answered, "More than anything. But I'm not about to rock the boat. My mother is doing better, thanks to your treatment. I hardly think this is a good time to start kicking up any dust."

Blake slid the folder toward Andy. "Well, maybe it's time."

"What do you mean?"

Blake answered, "I've been looking for someone. Someone I could trust. Someone who could learn about my process and tell my story. In case anything happened to this place, or happened to me."

Andy looked around. The statement made him uneasy. "If something happened to you?"

Blake closed his door and pulled his chair up to Andy. "I know you and Jennifer have been talking. A lot. You must be piecing this all together. What this place is. What it could mean to other cancer patients. Cancer is a big business. A lot of people stand to lose, people who would fight to maintain the status quo when it comes to cancer treatment. When the time is right, I may ask you to tell my story."

"You...what?" Andy asked. He ran his hands through his sandy hair. It spiked in various angles toward the ceiling.

Blake continued, unfettered by Andy's confusion. "In the meantime, I want you to spend some time with me. I want you to learn about this place."

Andy shook his head. He leaned back in his chair. "You've been doing this for over thirty years. Why now? Why have you been so private before and now you want to change it?"

Blake stood up. He walked over to the window. His broad shoulders eclipsed one of the window panels. He explained, "This center has been a place of hope and healing for many years. I've had no choice but to remain hidden from the mainstream until now. There's no further I can go on my own. I don't want to create a healing program in secret for a select few. I want this treatment to be available to the masses. I've decided that it's time to come out of hiding. But with this exposure, comes great risk. I'm afraid I may have failed to fully grasp these risks."

"Why don't you tell everyone?" Andy asked. "Scream it from the highest mountain."

"I can't. Not yet."

"Why not?" Andy pleaded with a subtle shake of his head.

He handed him the folder on his desk. Andy stared at it with intense curiosity. As Richard Blake walked out of the room, he looked back at Andy and said, "The treatment that I use. It isn't exactly...legal."

CHAPTER EIGHT

Sarah Stone's first diagnosis of breast cancer came at the age of forty, after her first mammogram. She was working as a manager in the labor and delivery unit where she had worked as staff nurse for many years. She knew everyone well, understood the work inside and out, and felt responsible for everything. Whether a nurse had missed charting a vital sign, or supplies weren't delivered on time, or the floors were scuffed, she felt that it was her job to fix. She volunteered for hospital committees and enthusiastically supported administrative initiatives. She worked long hours and was involved in every decision made on the unit.

This job came at a good time for Sarah personally. She had two great teenage sons. Her husband, Robert, whom she met in college and married soon after, had traded his big curly hair and teaching degree for a suit and tie and a very successful career as a stockbroker. Sarah was comfortable and content with her life. She saw no need to change any part of it, ever.

Her family practitioner had been pushing her for a while to have a mammogram. She didn't think it was necessary, but agreed eventually. It never occurred to her that there would be anything wrong. She had no risk factors for breast cancer and no family history. When microcalcifications appeared on the mammogram, she wasn't worried at all. The doctor told her that 80% of these were benign when biopsied. There was no reason to believe she wouldn't be part of the 80%. The area was less than half an inch, much too small to be felt, so she would need needle localization biopsy, where a radiologist inserted a needle into the breast to point out the location of the cells to the surgeon, who then removed them for analysis. It was an outpatient procedure that shouldn't be too painful or involved. As she had experienced three C-sections, she wasn't concerned about a little procedure on her breast.

The biopsy proved to be more involved than anticipated. The area was deep in her breast, near the chest wall. It ended up taking six tries and almost two hours to get the needle placed correctly. At least three of the needle placements were extremely painful, feeling as though they were sticking her in the chest or lung. She told the radiologist that it hurt to breathe, but he said it wasn't possible that the needle had gone in that deep. Finally, the needle was placed correctly and she went into surgery. Her first hint that something was wrong came when the surgeon returned to recovery after the procedure. He assured her that everything had gone well, but he was evasive about what he thought it was. She knew that no doctor would tell a patient definitively, but surgeons saw cancer cells every day, and they knew what they saw.

When he didn't volunteer an observation, Sarah pressed him for his impression. "I don't know what it is," he told her, but he wouldn't look at her, and he didn't repeat any reassuring statistics about most of these being benign. Sarah shook off her doubts. There was no way she could have cancer.

When the surgeon called three days later, she was at work. He told her that the biopsy was positive for breast cancer, a slow-growing, intraductal variety. He was quite matter-of-fact, and told her that she needed to schedule more surgery as quickly as possible. Although she could opt for a mastectomy, he felt that a lumpectomy with follow-up radiation would take care of it, provided that samples of lymph nodes proved to be negative. If they found cancer in the lymph nodes, then they would have to consider chemotherapy. Sarah asked if she should see an oncologist, and he told her that the surgery came first, so that the oncologist knew the extent of the disease, and could plan treatment.

Sarah was shocked. Even though she should have at least considered the possibility that it would be cancer, she hadn't. She didn't know anyone her age diagnosed with breast cancer. She sat in her office trying to figure out what to do next. She couldn't even pretend to think about anything else, so she told the unit secretary what happened, knowing that everyone on the unit would soon find out, and left to go home. She didn't remember telling her husband, but she quickly had her emotions under control. Everyone she talked to, including her mother, wasn't worried about her survival. The consensus was that she was lucky it was caught early, and treatment was very effective for small, localized cancers such as hers. Her mother-in-law had a similar breast cancer some years before and opted for a mastectomy and chemotherapy. Sarah hadn't paid much attention to what her mother-in-law went through, but when Sarah told her about her own cancer, she told Sarah she had three positive lymph nodes. Although treatment was no fun, she had gotten through it. There was no recurrence in her other breast. So Sarah never considered that she might die, even if she had some positive lymph nodes. She would need more surgery and six weeks of radiation, but she could have the radiation at the hospital while she was working. She was tough, and she felt sure she could handle any treatment without disrupting her life.

The only disturbing comment came from a friend on the East Coast, who was a radiologist. Sarah called her because she was the only other woman she knew her age who had been diagnosed with breast cancer. She had a very aggressive cancer in both breasts and had a double mastectomy with a bone marrow transplant. She was the only one who wasn't sure about the lumpectomy and radiation plan. She pointed out that you were still left with quite a bit of breast tissue after a lumpectomy where the cancer could return. Sarah could not imagine that she could be so unlucky to have cancer come back, when she felt she shouldn't have even gotten it in the first place. Besides, her cancer was small and slow-growing, not aggressive like her friend's had been. "Well," she said, "if you do decide to have radiation, be sure to get your regular mammograms in that breast." When Sarah asked why, her friend said, "We see a lot of cancers coming back in the radiated breast in the first two years." How could that be? Why would they recommend a treatment to prevent cancer that increased the chances of it coming back? Her friend must be wrong, she thought.

When you worked in health care, especially in a hospital, you felt very confident that you knew the "best" doctors. Even if you didn't work in that area, you knew who to ask to make sure you got the most progressive oncologist or the most skilled surgeon. Nurses talked to other nurses candidly about doctors, in a way that they would never share with the public. So Sarah knew which doctors to choose to take care of her problem. She had the lumpectomy – again outpatient. Since her lymph nodes came back negative, it looked like the radiation plan was still reasonable. There was plenty of clear breast tissue around the cancer, so the surgeon was confident that he had gotten it all. She didn't think to question why she was being radiated if there was no more cancer.

As soon as her lumpectomy site had healed, Sarah was scheduled to begin radiation. The radiation oncology department was in the basement of the hospital. She could just walk downstairs, have her treatment and be back in the office within an hour. On her first visit, the radiation oncologist told her decisively, "I don't know what you've heard, but you will have no side effects from this radiation. Radiation for breast cancer is limited to the breast, which is on the outside of the body, and we don't have to radiate any other organs to accomplish our goal. You may have heard about radiation side effects, but those are associated with other cancers, such as prostate, where we have to go through more tissue to get to the organ involved. You won't have any of those problems." That sounded good to her, consistent with the idea that this cancer was a relatively minor problem that was easily taken care of with the best technology.

The radiation didn't hurt, and she didn't notice any problems until her second week of treatment. She started noticing that she was more tired than usual, and she felt like she was coming down with the flu, except it never materialized. Since she had been told that she would have no side effects, she didn't associate these symptoms with the radiation. But when she was getting ready for bed one night, she saw that her breast was red and hot, as if it had been sunburned. Could radiation cause this? It seemed logical. She scheduled a visit to the radiation oncologist before her next treatment. At the appointment, the doctor explained, "Your symptoms are not due to the radiation." When she showed him her reddened breast, he said, "That is not from the radiation. You must have a wound infection in the lumpectomy site." Sarah felt like an idiot. She was a nurse, used to checking wounds for signs of infection.

Sarah went back to the surgeon for an evaluation. She hoped he wouldn't have to do more surgery, or put her in the hospital on IV antibiotics. She was getting tired of all this. The surgeon took one look at her breast and said, "This wound isn't infected. The red area is exactly between the markers they're using for radiation. This is a radiation burn." She asked him to call the radiation oncologist to try to come to some conclusion between them. She heard him arguing with the radiation oncologist on the phone in the hall. When the surgeon returned he told her, with a wry smile, he said, "Well, the radiation oncologist still insists that this is not due to the radiation, but he feels you should take a week off treatment to recover." Although she didn't understand why they couldn't decide what the problem was, taking time off seemed like a reasonable plan.

After a week of treatment, she was feeling well again and the redness in her breast had subsided. But at the end of another week of treatment, she could feel the same symptoms coming back, the feeling she eventually knew to be a result of the radiation. Since she felt sure there was no point in telling the doctor about it again, she decided to see what she could do to help herself. Although she had never taken any supplements and didn't know anything about natural healing methods, she went to a health food store for the first time in her life. Sarah learned that health food store employees were not allowed to give you advice, because that would mean that they were claiming that supplements treated disease, a claim that couldn't be made legally in this country. But the sales person showed her a book that listed supplements used for different conditions. Under the heading "Radiation", there were seven or eight herbal supplements listed. Sarah bought all of them and started taking them that night. By morning she felt almost back to normal, and didn't have any more problems through the end of her treatment.

During the last week of treatment, she had a scheduled appointment with the radiation oncologist. She had been anticipating this meeting. The supplements really helped her, and she thought the radiation oncologist with a waiting room full of radiation patients would be interested in ways to help his patients feel better. When he came into the room, he asked her, "How's your energy level?" Why ask that, she wondered, when he had made such a point of assuring her that radiation wouldn't have any side effects? It seemed like the perfect opening, though, so she replied, "It's been much better since I started taking some supplements from the health food store." She expected him to ask her which supplements, or maybe to ask her to share them with his nurse. Instead, he patted her on the shoulder and said, "I think it's important that you believe something works." *Asshole.*

After her course of radiation was completed, she went back to the oncologist for a final evaluation. He suggested that she might want to participate in a study of a new drug for the prevention of breast cancer. He explained that it was an estrogen-blocking drug that showed promise to decrease recurrence in estrogen-receptor-positive cancers such as hers. But Sarah knew she was poor study material. She didn't like to take medicines, especially if she didn't know if she was taking medicine or a sugar pill, and she didn't think she would be compliant, which was one of Sarah's least favorite words. She told him she would rather wait for the results of the study and take it once it was proven. There was a distinct change in the oncologist's attitude when she declined his offer. He was obviously displeased that she had formed her own opinions and quickly dismissed her from his office, telling her that there was no need for further appointments. Fine, she thought, she was never going to have to deal with an oncologist again, anyway.

Sarah had successfully completed her treatment, obediently following the established protocols. While there were some disturbing aspects and some things that hadn't made sense, nothing had seriously shaken her basic faith in conventional medicine. Although she had positive results from the supplements, she didn't continue to learn about them, thinking that this had been an interesting, but isolated incident, not necessary to pursue now that she was healthy again. She felt that cancer was something she "got", not related to anything she was doing. Sarah broke what would later become an important rule for her when dealing with cancer. She remained content in her current situation. She didn't change anything.

Two years later, the cancer returned. It had spread. Located around the area where she had received radiation.

Twelve years after that, it had spread to her bones.

part two
THE KILL SWITCH

CHAPTER NINE

Waves lapped to shore. On a cool Friday morning in July, Ashley Markum stared into the gray water. She wore a black wetsuit and bright blue swim cap. She could only see the faint specks of two other swimmers in the distance. No lifeguards were on duty yet. To her right the sun began to burn through the eastern sky. It hovered just above the Lake Michigan horizon. To her left stood the towering steel and glass buildings of the Chicago skyline. The newly dawned sun painted the glass panels of the high-rises a metallic orange. The sky above her glowed with maroon, orange and blue pastels. Clouds floated above, capturing the light and reflecting it. The clouds looked like blossoming galaxies in the far reaches of space.

The world felt new and bright. Ashley looked up to the sky and she whispered, "Give me strength." She touched her chest and repeated, "Please give me strength." She heard the steady words of her father, "Touch your heart. Be yourself. Tell the truth."

It was the final day of a week-long budget review with the heads of the company. Ashley and a woman named Martha Solis ran the North American Development office. Although the office appeared to be a cohesive unit, Ashley and Martha essentially ran separate businesses. Martha Solis recently unveiled to upper management that her business had a thirty million dollar budget gap. One of Martha's most trusted financial analysts demanded close control of the budget. The analyst grossly overspent. What once was a small problem, grew with the depressed economy. Then the analyst's father died, and he had a mental breakdown, and the business fell apart. He lied to Martha and hid expenditures in the future. By the time Martha uncovered the deception, it was too late.

Ashley had been out of town the whole week, but she was in regular contact with Martha, trying to work through the problem. Ashley ran licensing for North America. She was in charge of finding external researchers, companies and scientists. Ashley was a venture capitalist for researchers studying new drugs. That was it. It was really that simple. Some groups were as small as five. Others were massive biotechs. But this was the momentum of the company now. It was outsourcing more of the pre-clinical process. Martha Solis worked with the in-house researchers. Labs operated by Plaxin. It was a dying part of the business. Her budget had been slashed, her staff hacked.

Despite being completely separate from the catastrophe, Ashley was in danger of being lumped with it. Same office, same region. Martha and a few others were subtly trying to connect Ashley's business with theirs. Perhaps to mitigate their own personal exposure and damage. It was a mild act of betrayal from a woman who Ashley had supported and guided. It was the reason why she couldn't sleep. And the reason why she craved an early swim at Ohio Street Beach.

Even with a wetsuit, the temperature was jolting. Her hands and head quickly numbed as she cut through the calm waters on this July morning in Lake Michigan. Ashley's freestyle stroke was graceful and smooth. She remembered not to fight the water. *Flow with the water.* Her arms sliced into the lake. Her legs churned the slightest froth as she kicked just under the surface. She glided through the water, effortlessly knifing forward. In this sustained motion, she found meditation and clarity. She extended her arms with each stroke and pulled the water in front of her, shaping it and leaving a vacuous wake behind her. She swam along the cement wall for twenty minutes, passing buoys and trying not to look at the rocky, seaweed bottom of the lake. She eventually looped around a tall buoy and headed back toward the beach. She stroked steadily and quickly, looking up at runners and bikers on the paved path just above her.

Finally, her slender hands swept the sandy bottom as it raced upward to shore. She stopped, flipped over and floated on her back, looking up at the pastel sky above, and listening to the hum of cars whipping past on Lake Shore Drive. She closed her eyes and said, "Please give me strength for this day."

She emerged from the water like a siren coated with a slick black wetsuit. As she ascended to the beach, a man in tattered clothing was standing in the middle of the sand. He held a bottle wrapped in a brown paper bag. He wobbled with a disturbing regularity. As Ashley walked past, he looked up and caught a glimpse of her. As she emerged from the cool morning water, he fell to the ground. Her presence alone seemed to be too much for him to handle. He pressed the back of his head against the sand and looked up at the sky with a jolting cough.

Two hours later, Ashley walked down Michigan Avenue. She moved with speed and grace, almost gliding more than walking. She rushed past the rows of stores that lined Michigan Avenue. Drowsy employees with stylish clothing and iced coffees walked into the empty stores. Lights flickered on. Displays were dragged to the front. She regularly walked to the Plaxin office just south of the Chicago River. Her mind raced with numbers. As she walked over the river, the honeycomb metal grate of the drawbridge dug into her shoes.

The Plaxin North American Development office perched fifteen stories above State Street. It was an urban enclave somewhat secluded from Plaxin's headquarters in the northwest suburbs. It was two blocks south of the Chicago River. The office was filled with tension. All week executives swarmed in from Plaxin's suburban headquarters and drilled down to the line-by-line reality of Martha's budget. Four days of scrutiny had defused some of the tension. Martha found about fourteen million that had been missing in the numbers. The last day was mainly supposed to be dedicated to Ashley's business.

Ashley Markum wore a gray suit. The designer suit coat cut off just above her gently curving hips. It had narrow lapels and long sleeves covering her slender arms. It was an elegant balance of style and authority. A thin black belt encircled her slim waist. A sheer skirt stretched from her waist down just below her knees where it slightly flared outward. She wore black leggings and white Nike running shoes for the walk to her office. Her blond hair waved back and forth in controlled undulation with every step. Her phone chirped.

"Hey," Ashley answered.

Martha asked, "Did you get those Q2 forecast numbers in yet?"

"Not yet. I worked till midnight, but couldn't finish them."

Ashley's job had become anything but orderly. Changes were constant. From cost and revenue standpoints, a budget was a living, moving, shifting number. It lived in the middle of her best and worst scenarios. It was a juggling act. At any time, she could make a mistake that could derail her entire career. Her job wasn't the stable position of a powerful executive that one might imagine. It was a high-wire act of uncertainty and chaos. She imagined this was the same way her superiors felt. Not as rulers on high of a powerful drug company, but people put in charge of the livelihoods and families of thousands of employees. They didn't see themselves as an evil pharmaceutical company. Perhaps she was naive, but she thought they were just people trying to navigate a company through dangerous waters. Where one bad drug or one unknown side effect could be the end of the company.

Plaxin was in trouble. Lackluster sales, marked by an invasion of generics, were pulling down the balance sheet. Martha's budget gap was an untimely bomb. Ashley had nothing to hide with her own numbers. She was 98% to her forecast. But there was another problem. All of her development projects would be examined. She feared they could find her secret projects. Mainly, they could figure out that she had devoted funds to the Blake Center without any viable potential drug. If they were to discover Blake now, it would be shut down.

Ashley peered into an adjacent office to hers. It had been empty from recent layoffs. But this morning it was alive.

"John." Ashley said. John McKenzie was the VP of Finance, next in line after the CFO. He normally worked at the Plaxin headquarters, but spent the week sorting through Martha's overspent budget. He held up his hand as he finished a conversation.

He walked around the desk and gave her a hug. "Ashley." His brown eyes bulged slightly. He spoke with a mix between a Scottish and British accent. His uniformly spiky hair made him look somewhat younger than he actually was. His green and gray tie had already been loosened. His white sleeves were rolled up to his forearms. His blue pants were strangely baggy and made him look much heftier than he actually was. John was uniquely adept at numbers. He was one of the few people in the company who could fully grasp Ashley's complex analysis and poignant insights.

"Hey, John," she said with a relieved sigh.

John asked, "How was the trip? Southern California, right?"

"It was good. But I've got to tell you, John, I'm a little nervous," Ashley said without her usual, forceful inflection. "Mike is coming today. Should I be worried?"

"Ashley, you're fine. They're going to check out your numbers to be thorough, but it'll be quick. There are still a lot of questions with Martha's business. How are you, Ashley?"

Ashley stood up and led John across the hall into her own office. Her Nike running shoes were replaced by black heels. She towered over John. She explained, "Well, it's been a little bumpy lately." She closed the door behind her. Ashley sat tall, but relaxed on her gently curved office chair. She folded her slim hands in front of her face. Her hands looked like finely-tuned instruments especially built for the modern world of keyboards and touch screens.

He said, "A little bumpy for everyone." John flopped down on one of the chairs in front of Ashley's desk. "How did this happen?"

"I don't know. It's a mess. Martha's main analyst had a personal breakdown. He got overwhelmed and kind of took the business down with him," Ashley explained.

"I'm beginning to understand that. Was it malicious?" John asked.

"That's the question a lot of people are asking now. It doesn't matter really. He's long gone and what's done is done," she said. Ashley spoke with contagious poise and confidence, despite the whirlwind happening in the office. There were always storms in upper management. It was the way everyone handled the storms that mattered.

John's phone buzzed inside his black suit pocket. He checked the message with raised eyebrows as he said, "I just don't understand how it got to this point. Thirty million overspent. Well, about half that now, but still. That's never happened anywhere in this company."

Ashley spoke candidly to her friend, "John, what did they expect? Think of the amount of revenue that comes out of her pipeline, yet her staff has been cut down to six. Think about that for a second. How tiny of an issue it is to hire some more people in the big picture of things. The days of cutting flabby middle management are over. Pretty much everyone in our organization is absolutely essential at this point. These people are online till one in the morning. Juggling a mess of stuff." She poured some loose tea into a coffee press filled with steaming water and swirled it around.

John agreed, "It's like that everywhere now. We're cut to the bone."

She rubbed her hands over her angelic, luminous cheekbones. She whispered with anger, "Two more people. Two more people on the budget and this problem wouldn't have happened. We saved two hundred thousand in salaries to lose $16 million. What sense does that make? They cut all of these people, and they're surprised that things don't get done as quickly, as orderly. When will it be enough cost-cutting?" The ground tea leaves spun around in the coffee press as they emanated wisps of brown fluid in the clear water.

"Apparently, it's never enough." John adjusted his coat as he checked behind him to see if anyone else was visible.

Ashley pressed the lever and strained her tea. "We always need to do more with less. Even when it's *less* with less. And now there's a massive budget shortfall. Because Martha's people didn't do their jobs? Or because Landis eradicated their entire budget staff. What did he think would happen? And now we think the remaining skeleton of a staff is the problem. These people have no lives. They barely see their kids. Their marriages are strained. But it's not enough. It will never be enough."

John agreed, "Grow for the sake of growth."

Ashley and John stared into the coffee press as the pigment from the tea leaves rose in the clear fluid. Ashley asked, "How can a cancerous company ever hope to cure cancer? That's my question to you."

"I don't know."

"We've had some declines, but we're still very healthy. Give these teams enough people. In the big picture, these are tiny drops in the bucket. And we need to clean up the chain of command. This budget shortfall was a complex labyrinth of self-preservation, fear and hasty information," Ashley said as she booted up her computer. "It's just never enough. Until profits are up every quarter forever. In a recession, in prosperity. Doesn't matter. Have to go up. All the time. It will never end. And I fear that constant pressure, that short-term vision will be our demise."

The intensity of the discussion caused both of them seeking another topic. Ashley said, "The way the tea diffuses in the coffee press. It reminds me of something." Plumes of tea-pigmented fluid rose and bubbled through the clear water like mystical clouds of gas.

Ashley pulled a large touch screen tablet computer out of her case.

"What is that?" John asked as he slid closer to the desk.

Ashley smiled as she placed the large tablet on its stand. It displayed a strange world of shapes floating in space. She explained, "Computer simulations from the Genserve research facility out in La Jolla. They just gave me this little toy."

"You're actually watching pre-development compound simulations?" John shook his head. "The technology in these research firms baffles me."

"Yeah. I know. A virtual world created by powerful software. They're playing with this new application that lets you tap into their simulations."

John looked closer at the screen and said, "Like the Matrix."

"It's just a tiny cross-section, an aesthetic representation of the thousands of simulations that are happening all of the time. But it's still pretty amazing to see."

The broad screen displayed a mystical, three-dimensional scene. Ashley held up her screen. Blazing magenta round balls that represented molecules were connected to each other in malleable strands. The strands formed compounds that looked like orbs attached to tree branches, or the models of molecules found in high school chemistry class. Brightly colored compounds drifted around in three-dimensional space. An ethereal mist surrounded these compounds. The setting looked like galaxies far away where stars were born within a bewildering milky mist of energy and potential. This was the place that very few people ever saw. It was the place of chemical wizardry.

The virtual compounds floated in a netherworld. Other compounds materialized on the screen and bumped into them. Some connected to each other; others just glanced off and drifted away into the vacuous imaginary space in the distance. It was the first step in drug development. Virtual proteins and compounds were created, then a simulation program brought them together. In this computer, they were observed to see if they interacted with each other. If they did, they could move on to the next phase. And the effects were as real as the table on which Ashley's computer rested.

As the vivid screen continued to display a bewildering virtual world on the desk, John changed the subject. "People are starting to talk about you now, Ashley."

Ashley asked, "What do you mean?"

"Your speech about a new direction in the national meeting last month. About re-inventing and re-imagining our role in health care," John said. He spoke in a tone that suggested none of this would be news to Ashley. "Lots of people are talking about it. Your new vision for the company is gaining some powerful allies."

"I know. I've talked to a lot of people lately. From research, from the board. All over. It's a message that seems to resonate with most people at Plaxin."

Ashley sipped her tea and asked, "How is Mike? I haven't talked to him since his ex-wife died."

"Honestly, I don't know."

Ophelia Landis never recovered from her divorce with Mike. Depression and alcohol enveloped her life. Five weeks ago, Ophelia ran her silver Mercedes CL Coupe into a concrete barrier. She was going eighty at the time of the collision, and she died instantly. Although it hadn't been confirmed, it was widely believe that she was highly intoxicated at the time of the crash. Mike took two weeks off, and returned to work as if nothing had happened. But cracks were beginning to show.

John explained, "He's been very scattered, unpredictable lately. I tried to get him to take some time off, but he won't do it. Worried that a leave of absence will lead to his permanent replacement."

John stood up to return to his temporary office. Ashley asked, "What about my budget review? Do you want to go over everything? Even the smaller development projects?"

John answered, "Let's go with everything for now." The statement brought more pain in Ashley's chest. All she could think of was Richard Blake. He sought Plaxin because they were the cancer treatment experts and they were right down the road from him. Now, she feared Mike Landis would find out about the little center, realize the potential risks it posed, and squash it before anyone knew. Her slender body stiffened with nervous anticipation. Morning construction didn't help her tension. As she organized her documents, a jackhammer cut through the concrete street below with an incessant bap, bap, bap, bap.

Twenty minutes later, Mike Landis arrived. Ashley didn't see him come in. She could just feel it. The way employees acted and moved was different. They were mice in a field while a hawk hovered above. Ashley hesitated as she held up her hand to knock on the south conference room door. Low rumbles of agreement gave way to a much different tone. She could see the black briefcase of Mike Landis resting on the broad, oval conference table. She listened to Mike from outside the door. Her heart pounded.

Mike barked into the phone, "You make it happen, Jack. I don't want to hear about that. This one has to go through. Phase three clinicals or not. It has to go through."

Ashley heard more muffled words from the other side of the conversation.

Mike erupted, "Hey, I brought you here to make miracles happen, not to tell me why it couldn't be done. Don't tell me to calm down! Don't you ever tell me to fucking calm down. You do it! Or I'll find someone who will."

Ashley knocked just before Mike whipped open the door. Her hand was still clenched up in the air. They locked eyes. No one around them would notice, but she did. Their connection was still electric. She was still drawn to him. She fought the urges.

Mike stated, "Ashley."

"Hello, Mike."

He peered beyond the beautiful Ashley Markum. "Is Martha ready yet?"

"I'm sure she'll be right in." Ashley felt almost insignificant in his presence.

"Tell her to get in here," he ordered. His eyes blazed. He rushed past her.

Ashley turned and said, "Mike."

"Yeah?" He asked with a curious innocence.

She said, "I'm sorry about Ophelia. I can't imagine what you must be going through right now."

"Thank you. It's okay. Just get those numbers ready. We'll begin whenever Martha gets here." He talked right around Ashley's words. His detachment scared her. He didn't look the same, didn't walk the same.

Martha finally came in with stacks of papers. Her hands trembled. "Little too much coffee lately," she mumbled. The noise of the distant jackhammer rattled through the office. Ashley sat in the chair next to her. A file listing all of her pre-clinicals was wedged underneath her tense arm, like she didn't want to release it. For the next eight hours, they carefully examined the budget. John found another three million of the lost funds. Her overspent budget was looking much better. Mike said very little. He listened and occasionally left to answer a call. By the end of the day, Martha Solis trudged out of the office exhausted and somewhat relieved. She reflected a faint hope that she might keep her job. John and Mike briefly scanned Ashley's numbers, but did so mainly symbolically. The Blake Center was safe for now. Development would continue. John rushed out of the office to catch his family for dinner in the suburbs.

By seven at night, the office was empty. Most of the rooms were dark. The steady hum of the city streets began to subside. Ashley temporarily sat alone in the conference room. She tried to call Richard Blake. Blake knew what was happening. He didn't answer. She hung up the phone as she heard the front door swing open. Mike Landis returned to the conference room with a black plastic bag. He opened a slender box inside and pulled out a bottle of scotch that had been aged for twelve years in oak sherry barrels.

Mike said, "Not the greatest, but it will do."

"Is Martha safe?" Ashley asked.

"Ashley, I don't even know if I'm safe. How can I guarantee that? She is for today. I want to help her. I want to right the ship, but that's a heck of a lot to overspend. It ain't good, but we'll see." Ashley felt like he was softening his words, perhaps being calmed by her presence.

He poured some scotch into her glass. "Just a little," she insisted.

Mike peeled off his tie, loosened his collar, and leaned back in his chair. He said, "You caused a bit of a stir lately. With your talk of a new direction."

"I know," Ashley acknowledged. She took a small sip.

"People are starting to believe in your ideas. You're protected from up on high." Mike was referring to a few board members who had been preaching the same mission.

Mike lifted his glass of scotch from the middle of the table. It appeared resistant to his hand, even stuck, as if the table and the drinking glass weren't ready to part ways. Mike lifted the drink. Ashley gazed down at the ring of condensation left from his glass. The water ring was contiguous except for a single spot that was disconnected. It almost looked like the connection point for a compound, something that one might see in the thousands of computer simulations for new drugs. Mike was focused on the ring of water on the pristine table as well. He touched his finger in the middle of the ring and slid it through the opening of the ring.

Mike held up his hands and looked at his palms. He explained, "I got a palm reading almost as a joke the last time Ophelia and I went on a cruise. The palm reader described success in my career, good health. The usual. Then I asked her about my lifeline. I'd always been curious about it."

He showed Ashley. His lifeline jolted out from the edge of his hand, curved down toward his wrist and curiously split in the middle of his palm. The lifeline ended halfway down and branched off into little tributaries as a river would at its shallow mouth before it opened into a large body of water. An independent set of branches formed just below and to the right of this one and continued down to the bottom of his hand.

Mike downed some more scotch and filled the glass again. "I've always been told that I have a very unique lifeline."

"That's interesting." Ashley leaned closer and grabbed his hand. Mike never broke his stoic focus on his hand, but he carefully inhaled Ashley's intoxicating perfume.

He explained, "My lifeline is split in two. There's a curious gap in the middle, like this broken ring of condensation. I always wanted to know what it meant." He briefly glanced up at her face. Her eyes remained focused on his hand. He remembered her rare combination of beauty and strength that drew him to her.

Ashley looked up at him. Her eyes glistened like translucent gemstones. She asked, "Did you ask the palm reader?"

"I remembered to ask her as I was walking away. She said she didn't know and hastily looked away." Mike stared down at his hand. He could feel Ashley studying his face. He fought the urge to lock eyes with her.

"That's strange, Mike," Ashley said as she deliberately placed his strong, opened hand back on the armrest.

Mike swirled his drink. "I've always wondered why a stranger would feel so compelled to lie to me about something like that. But now it seems to make sense. The split is a tragedy, the split in my lifeline is a time when my life is jolted. And the life that I know now is very much different."

"I'm so sorry about Ophelia, Mike."

He looked surprised by the comment. "Don't worry about me. I'm doing pretty well, considering."

"You know you can talk to people about it."

"That's all we need right now," he said with a sarcastic laugh. "CEO Mike Landis is getting psychological treatment." He said this as if he were reading a breaking news story.

"I'm worried about you, Mike."

"I can handle this." He slid his chair closer to Ashley and leaned his head into her hands.

Ashley touched his head.

"Tell me about these ideas of yours. About the new direction that everyone is talking about." Mike grabbed her hand and moved it back and forth on his head, seemingly hoping the momentum would coerce her into massaging him. It worked.

Mike lowered his head. His shoulders fell with relaxation. He said, "Everyone is turning against me, Ashley."

"No they're not."

He said softly, "And you're a part of it." He straightened up in his chair. His eyes narrowed and glazed over.

Ashley paused for a moment. "Mike. Don't blame me. Many people have come to the same conclusions about the company."

He asked, "What conclusions?"

Ashley spoke with quiet conviction as she explained, "It's time for a new direction. That isn't a shot at you. You could be one of the biggest advocates for this. Most of this discussion is about cancer, our disease of expertise. The current treatments aren't good enough. Cancer isn't like any other disease. And the answer won't come from just isolating proteins and simulating compounds. It's time to look at it in new ways. In our hearts, we all know this. But we're afraid to do anything about it because we're afraid of losing that revenue stream. Companies die because they're afraid of losing outdated revenue streams. Cancer treatment needs a revolution. You can feel it. Everybody can feel it. We can be a part of this revolution. We can lead it, but we have to change."

"You're rejecting the scientific process. The process that has brought countless remedies to countless people." Mike shook his head. His neck strained with tension. "What do you want me to do, Ashley? You're rejecting a research and development process that has brought civilization out of the dark ages."

"I'm not rejecting our process, only urging the expansion of it. It's been successful for many illnesses," Ashley said. She itched the inside of her neck where her gray suit coat had been rubbing all day. "Our researchers have helped millions of people live longer, more fulfilling lives. But isolating single proteins and specific compounds isn't sufficient for cancer care. It's time to open up to new possibilities. It's time."

Mike shook his head.

Ashley rose and said, "I need to go to the bathroom."

Mike looked into the empty space of the room. He stared at the blank wall as the wheels turned inside. Suddenly, Ashley's phone hummed to life on the conference table. Mike tried to ignore it, but it buzzed toward his hand. He flipped it around and checked the phone number.

Mike Landis whispered to himself, "Doctor Richard Blake." He looked at the area code. 608. "Is that Wisconsin?" He wondered quietly. He held the phone up to his ear. "Hello?"

The other end was silent. A voice finally replied, "I must have dialed the wrong number. Sorry." The call ended.

He quickly slid the phone back over to its original spot, wondering why a doctor would call Ashley now.

Before he could give it any more thought, Ashley returned and asked, "How are you doing?"

"I'm doing well. Glad we're done with the budget."

"No, Mike, I mean how are you?" Ashley asked. "With what happened to your ex-wife."

"Tell to you the truth, sometimes I feel fine. Other days, I just feel empty inside. Like there's a big hole in my chest where my heart used to be." He took a forced sip of scotch. "There's so much to deal with. I've been running from it for so long. I don't know where to start. Then sometimes I just feel empty." Mike downed the rest of his booze and leaned closer.

He said, "Enough of this. Come back with me, Ashley."

"Where?" She asked as she nervously laughed.

"To a hotel. I want to be with you again. Let's forget about all this tonight."

"No, Mike. That's over."

He abruptly stood up and grabbed his stuff.

Mike's tone shifted. "Don't think I don't see the angles here. All of this talk. Think about all of the people who work at our company. Great change means great risk. What you're suggesting is very risky. People, families depend on this company for their livelihoods. All of this talk of a new direction, rethinking cancer treatment, adopting a more holistic approach; it all has consequences that ripple throughout the company. Consequences that I'm afraid you don't fully understand."

"I will not be on the wrong side of this. I will not sacrifice what I believe is right," Ashley said. "Ever again."

Mike peered into Ashley's eyes. She suddenly felt a wave of fear as she realized they were the only two people left on the entire floor. Mike grabbed his coat and said, "If I happen to get stabbed in the foreseeable future, I suspect that your lovely hand will not be far from the blade." She looked at him with a reassuring smile as he said, "Goodbye, Ashley."

CHAPTER TEN

"You ready?" Richard Blake turned to Andy and asked.

"I think so."

It was Saturday at the Blake Center. The summer sunlight filled the patient rooms and spilled into the halls. Andy followed Richard Blake with a notepad in one hand and a tape recorder in the other. A camera dangled from his neck. His usually randomly spiked hair was calm on top of his head. Andy's blue eyes illuminated from the penetrating sunlight. His mother was receiving her weekly treatment. It was going to be a long day. During the doctor's morning rounds, Andy was to shadow him.

Blake knocked on the door of Tranquility. His large, tan ears flared out from his youthful face. His dark skin contrasted with an ensemble of khaki dress pants and a recently pressed white shirt. His hair was combed back in the usual uniform rows of black strands.

They entered the room. A family with bronze skin and large brown eyes looked upset. They sat around their father. He was straining to sit up on the hospital bed. His skin was a much sicklier, paler hue than his wife. She held his hand tightly. His three daughters surrounded him. The whole family looked deflated, as if an air valve had been depressed in each of them. Their shoulders and heads collectively slumped. They looked scared and lost.

Blake walked toward the father and asked, "Luis?"

"Yes," he said with extra emphasis on the end of the word.

Blake walked over to the bed and pressed a button. The back of the bed rose behind Luis. Blake pulled up a chair. He asked, "Better?"

"Yes, thank you," Luis quietly replied.

Blake focused all his attention on the patient. Luis' oldest daughter stood behind him. She had short brown hair and a steady gaze. She placed her hands on her father's shoulder like a protective angel.

Blake looked down at his notes and asked, "You guys know Elsa, huh?" Elsa was one of the nurses at the center.

The mother answered, "Yes. She's my sister-in-law."

Blake replied, "Elsa's great. We're very lucky to have her here. I don't know what you've heard about the center, but I like to give an introduction."

Luis answered, "Elsa, she told us a lot. I really hope you will treat me." His voice shuttered with nervous energy. His eyes regularly shifted down and away from the doctor. The family was filled with fear. They looked like a heard of antelope afraid of some unseen pride of lions that could pounce at any moment.

Blake scanned his chart. His strong hands gently thumbed through pages of cancer treatment history. Finally, he placed it to the side. He leaned back in his chair and crossed his legs. "Luis, we will help you. You don't have to be afraid anymore."

The mother asked, "What about our insurance?"

Blake looked over at his chart. "You guys will be covered. This is a good insurance company. We work with them all of the time."

One of the daughters, a skinnier girl with eyes hiding behind chunks of bangs, wiped tears away from hopeful eyes.

Blake continued, "You have been diagnosed with prostate cancer. Middle-grade prostate cancer. I assume you're familiar with the PSA test by now."

"Yes."

"We will take all of these tests again. Just to make sure everything is accurate," Blake said. "Tell me, Luis, what do you do for a living?"

Luis answered, "I work in a factory." He rubbed his thumb and fingers together. His hands looked strong and rough.

"What do you do?"

"Industrial painting."

"Painting," Blake answered. He didn't shake his head or sound upset, but just the echo of the word indicated a problem. "Painters can be at a higher risk for prostate cancer. Many of the chemicals in paints, coatings and cleaners are carcinogens. Are you still painting?"

"I was." He looked at his wife with concern.

"We'll deal with that later," Blake answered in his calming way. He was always trying to dispel fear, which seemed to be constantly threatening cancer patients. It always wanted to rise up and attack. Blake sensed the rising fear in the room. And somehow, just by the momentum of his energy, he made everyone believe.

Blake continued, "You have middle-grade prostate cancer. We're going to take you off chemotherapy for now. We'll take blood today.

Wait for the results of the tests and go from there. I can assure you, Luis, your prostate cancer is not growing fast. It's very treatable. One of the most important issues for you is nutrition. Prostate cancer is linked with diets high in fat and red meat. Pretty much any food that comes from an animal living on land."

The family laughed. "Dad loves the steaks."

Blake nodded. "Prostate cancer is much lower in Japanese men. We believe that has a lot to do with their plant-based and ocean-based diet. Between tests, you will meet with our nutritionists who will help you change your diet."

The mother asked, "What can he eat?" She stubbornly shook her head.

"Don't worry, they'll explain everything. In short, you will be on a highly plant-based diet. Grains, legumes, some fruit. Occasional seafood."

His wife looked concerned.

Blake saw her reaction and sternly responded, "These aren't just suggestions. Changing his food will save his life. It's that simple. Can you do that?"

Luis said, "Yes."

"Good. Let's get started. I'm glad you guys found us. I think Elsa comes in later."

"She does."

The two younger sisters stood up as Blake prepared to leave the room. They shook his hand, but couldn't suppress their relief. They both hugged him. Their dad laughed.

Andy followed behind Blake as he glided through the halls. Andy wore a collared shirt with short sleeves and bright stripes. Slim khaki pants covered his long legs. He could see a faint spot of sweat soaking through the middle of his shirt. Part of the sweat came from the heat, but he was also nervous and excited to be following the doctor.

Andy held up his recorder as he followed the doctor through corridors and office. As the doctor walked, he spoke, "We stand at a certain point in a constantly advancing timeline of medical discovery." Blake performed a whirlwind of tasks between patients. He signed documents, confirmed requests and discussed his schedule with Edna. He continued, "Cancer treatment is way behind. It's the greatest mystery. Finding a way to reverse cancer has been the mythical quest of the last half century. Chemotherapy does not cure cancer. Neither does radiation.

These are the only solutions we've had in fighting cancer. We eradicate all cells in the area. We do unseen damage to the body and create an environment that often makes cancer more likely to resurface later in life. These treatments were never cures. They were incomplete stopgaps during a vast dead zone of discovery. That time is over."

Blake explained, "There are many different treatments that we use here. Unfortunately, FDA approval is hopelessly arduous and outdated. And it heavily favors the expensive, exhausting drug development process of the big drug companies. Natural remedies that help patients don't stand a chance if they can't be patented. So all of the energy and resources pour into conventional medicine. Cancer foundations and charities literally rake in hundreds of millions of dollars a year. I have no doubt that the people supporting and running those massive nonprofits have the best intentions. But they're stuck in the old way of thinking, the conventional way. Where does that money go? It should be going everywhere, to *any* possible remedy for cancer. *Anything that benefits cancer patients, regardless of profitability.* Even if these remedies cannot be patented. In fact, especially if they can't be patented. We have so many new treatments that could help cancer patients today. Luis is a candidate for one of our newest treatments. Hyperthermia."

"What's hyperthermia?"

Blake asked, "Have you ever heard of the Lance Armstrong Effect?"

Andy answered, "Like when he enters a bike race, he wins it."

"Good guess, but not what I'm looking for," Blake answered. "Let's step outside for a second."

He led Andy out to the side of the parking lot. Although it wasn't even noon yet, the temperature was already looming near ninety with the signature blinding Midwestern humidity.

As Andy turned his recorder back on, Blake continued, "The Lance Armstrong Effect has been most recently described and studied by a group of magnificent doctors at Johns Hopkins University. Lance Armstrong had advanced testicular cancer. It had spread to many major organs throughout his body. Metastasized, advanced stage cancer is normally terminal, but of course, we all know the story. Lance Armstrong went on to win multiple Tour de Frances after having cancer."

Andy asked, "Okay?" He stood with the doctor under the blazing morning sun. The horizon was distorted from the heat.

"Testicular cancer had spread throughout his body, but testicular cancer is highly treatable and vastly less deadly than other cancers." Blake paused. He waited for a couple of men in golf shirts to pass them. He asked, "Any idea why?"

"The cancer has to travel farther to get to other organs in the body? I don't know. You're the doctor here," Andy said, anxiously gazing at the air conditioned lobby.

"Not a bad guess. The answer lies with the cancer's source," Blake explained. Ignoring Andy's childlike gestures to go inside.

Andy joked, "The key is in the balls?" He wasn't sure this was appropriate, but he couldn't let it go.

"Yes," Blake answered deadpan. *Probably not appropriate.*

"Testicular tumors rarely kill patients. Metastasized testicular cancer is uncommonly weak compared to other forms," Blake explained. He grabbed a white handkerchief from his back pocket. Andy didn't think anybody still used handkerchiefs.

"Why is testicular cancer more treatable?" Andy asked.

Blake patiently dabbed his forehead. He continued, "Testicular cancer exists at a temperature much lower than the rest of the body. When these cells spread, they weaken from the slight temperature increases, going from the testicles to the rest of the body. The cells weaken to the point that they are much easier to treat."

"So testicular cancer can't survive excess heat?" Andy leaned over and took dramatic, panting breaths. He said, "I don't know if *I* can handle this excessive heat." He looked up at Blake through eyes that had to squint from the sun's penetrating rays. "Can we go inside?"

"No, not yet. This is extremely confidential, Andy," Blake insisted. He held up his hands and continued, "It turns out other cancer types weaken when exposed to excess heat. Testicular is just the one that we discovered first because it is born at a lower temperature."

"So, the slightest rise in temperature weakens testicular cancer because," Andy paused. He didn't how to phrase the statement. "Because the sac is well below the normal body temperature."

"Correct. In fact, this treatment of heating tumors to weaken them is commonly used in many non-conventional treatment centers today, including ours. It's called hyperthermia – applying either localized heat to a malignant region, or giving the patient a controlled, general hyperthermia treatment. Sound familiar?"

Andy finally stood up. He looked confused. "Not really."

Blake said with a smile, "We're giving patients controlled fevers."

"Fevers?"

Blake motioned back into the treatment center. He explained, "To weaken cancer cells. It turns out that controlled fevers, either localized or general, can sometimes weaken the cells and often make supplemental treatment more effective. The magical, natural defense mechanism of the body. Turns out it may help to reverse cancer. The body knows what to do."

Andy asked, "You're giving people fevers?" He felt a chilling rush of artificial air as they walked back through a side door.

Blake insisted, "Fevers are part of the equation, not the whole thing."

"Fevers." Andy laughed.

Doctor Blake knocked on the door of the room called Hope. He turned to Andy and said, "You can record with Gloria. She's cool."

Gloria stood up with outstretched arms. "Well, look who it is!" She had a full head of auburn-tinted hair. She was in her fifties and didn't look like she had ever been sick. She was dressed in business casual attire. She expressed a vibrant alertness that was energizing. Gloria had fire.

Blake asked, "How are you, Gloria?"

"I'm doing well, Doctor Blake. Doing well."

"How's New York?"

"It's great," Gloria replied with a sense of contentment. She turned to Andy. "Who's this guy?"

Blake answered, "Oh, I hope you don't mind. This is Andy Stone." Andy reached out his hand. "He's a journalist, and his mother is a patient of mine. He's been following me around for the last few months. Learning about this place, about my treatment."

"Great! It's about time somebody figured out what this great wizard is doing behind the curtains." Gloria moved her hands around a giant imaginary crystal ball.

Blake asked, "Do you mind if he records?"

"Not at all. What the heck do I have to hide?" She laughed with a jovial bellow. Laughter seemed to be her default reaction.

Blake sat down. The room became still as he reviewed a report. It had a long list of chemicals and trace percentages next to them. Andy knew this report well. It listed many carcinogens found in her body. This document was the secret behind the Blake Number. Blake's dark eyes softened with compassion as he looked at Gloria. Blake said, "Got your number back." He waved a document in front of his face.

Her legs wiggled with excitement. She said, "I get so nervous. It's like getting test results back!" She laughed with Andy as if they were old friends.

"Everything looks good. Your number even dropped from last year." Gloria stood up and did a little dance, reaching for Blake's arm. The doctor whirled around with her. Andy had never seen the doctor so jovial.

Blake handed her the printout and said, "And diet and supplements..."

Gloria insisted, "All the time."

"You weren't just well-behaved this month because you knew you were coming here?" Blake asked.

"No, Dad..." Gloria sarcastically said like a disciplined child.

"Seriously, Gloria."

She shifted immediately. "Seriously. Joking aside. I have been meticulous, following every last detail. Super smoothies in the morning with super greens, enzymes and probiotics. Veggies, veggies, veggies. Mainly vegetarian. Cheating on very rare occasions. Which is funny, it makes cheating so much better when you do it so infrequently."

Andy nodded in agreement.

"I used to eat burgers and drink regularly. I didn't even realize how much I appreciated eating burgers with a cold beer when I did it all the time. But now, whenever I'm allowed to cheat during some rare occasion," Gloria explained. "It's like the gates of heaven opened up just for me. Every bite. Every sip. So good to be alive!"

Blake echoed, "Exactly."

Andy asked, "So you can cheat?"

"On rare occasions. Big social events, vacation. You can completely cheat," Gloria said as she watched Blake for a reaction.

"Really?" Andy asked.

Blake responded, "We're not robots here."

"How much?" Andy asked. "I don't think my mom knew that."

"She does," Blake abruptly stated. He seemed slightly uncomfortable with the conversation. "Once a month your dad gets her fast food."

Gloria asked Andy, "You've heard of the 80/20 rule?"

"Yeah, do you mean that you follow the Blake diet 80% of the time and cheat 20%?"

Gloria said, "Yeah, but it's more like 95/5. I even like to say 97/3."

"Very little cheating."

"Okay. Everything looks great," Blake said as he rose to his feet. "Still doing yoga?"

"Five days a week. It's changed my life," Gloria said as she stretched her back.

Blake turned to Andy and said, "Yoga can be very beneficial for early-stage lymphoma patients. I want you to imagine a healthy functioning body as a stream with several systems flowing within this stream. Nervous, bloodstream, hormonal, reproductive and lymphatic. Each layer serves a critical purpose. When cells in our body are damaged – from toxins, sunburns or whatever – they are cut off from the flowing stream. You know those muddy cesspools that often form just beyond the reach of a flowing river?"

"Yeah. All mossy where mosquitoes live," Andy said as he shifted in his chair.

"Precisely," Blake answered. Gloria nodded as well. Blake continued, "That is exactly what happens when a group of cells is damaged. The systems of the body cannot reach them. They become a low-oxygen, toxic waste area."

"You were talking about the lymphatic system before," Andy pressed.

Blake explained, "The lymphatic system remains one of the greatest mysteries in western medicine. Cancer spreads through the lymph nodes to some organs and not others in ways that no doctors or scientists can fully understand. Other cultures make great efforts to activate the lymph nodes. Yoga is very effective in targeting certain lymphatic points and activating the system. I believe there is a hierarchy of systems in our body, the highest and most critical being the lymphatic, the lowest being the reproductive system. I believe the reproductive portions of the body get the trash from all the others, which could explain the reason for so much cancer in our reproductive systems. Cancer and its connection to the lymph nodes is one of the great mysteries that must be understood and discovered in the coming decades."

"It happened with my mom."

"That's right. It traveled through her lymphatic system. To her bones, her liver, her intestines," Blake said.

The room suddenly fell silent. Blake move toward the door. He asked Gloria, "Do you mind if Andy asks you a question or two?"

"Not at all."

"I'll leave you two alone," Blake said as he slipped out the door. "Andy, you can catch up with me in a couple minutes."

Andy looked at his notes. He knew what he wanted to ask but just needed a moment to muster the courage. "So you still have cancer? You're still fighting cancer?"

Gloria nodded, "I live with cancer. I don't fight it. I don't want to kill it. I'm not looking for a magic cure for it. It's a part of me." Her bright eyes blazed with energy and focus.

"How long have you been coming here?" Andy focused on his questions. He directed his voice recorder toward her mouth.

She answered, "Four years." Andy pushed the voice recorder extremely close to her face. Gloria leaned away from it.

"Sorry." He pulled the microphone back. "I'm a little excited to be interviewing people again." Gloria waved off his apology. Andy asked, "What's the secret? How do you reverse this disease?"

"I've thought about this a lot," she said. Her tone shifted. "And it's very hard to talk about cancer and not address death. Death could be right around the corner. But I'm not afraid of death."

"That's the key?" Andy asked. "Accepting death?"

"That, but more important is releasing fear."

"Fear."

Gloria held up her hands and said, "First off, let me say that all cancers and all bodies are different. I learned that from Doctor Blake. So it's hard to say what works for one will work for all. I may just be partly lucky. But another key is to release the fear. Fear plays a huge role in dealing with cancer. Fear closes us up; it restricts us. Body, mind and spirit shut down with fear. It's like a car engine without oil. The whole system just locks up. But releasing fear is key. Fear of cancer, fear of death. All of it. The key is to be brave and move forward into the great unknown without fear. It's very difficult to do. It takes great bravery to let go of fear when you have cancer. And regular hospitals only enhance that fear for most people."

Gloria reached for her glass of water. She wiped her mouth. "In this place, there's no fear."

She shrugged her shoulders and smiled, "And humor."

"Humor," Andy echoed. He switched the recorder to his other hand as he jotted down notes with his left hand.

"It's the most underrated remedy in the history of medicine." Gloria nodded with resolution. "Laughter is medicine."

"I feel like I should say something funny right now," Andy quipped.

"Think about the pressure on me! I said it." Her eyes squinted so much from laughter that Andy wasn't sure she could see.

"So, basically, if you learn anything from talking to me, fear bad, humor good. Me no talk so good," Gloria said.

Andy nodded. "Thank you so much, Gloria. I've got to get back to the doctor."

"Thanks, blue eyes."

Andy approached a nurse in the hall. She had red hair and fair skin. He asked, "People come here all the way from New York?"

The nurse looked at him with a confused smirk. "From all over the country. Practically every day. You didn't know that?"

Andy peeked into the next room. A woman in her sixties sat in a recliner. Her bald head was wrapped in an orange scarf. Blake looked up at Andy with dark, impatient eyes. Andy slowly pulled his slender frame back out of the room.

"It's okay. He can come in," she announced.

Andy sat in the corner. He didn't record. He just listened.

Blake said, "We're going to give the injections another month. But I have to tell you, Ava, I may recommend more conventional treatment, if the cancer remains resistant. Chemo may be your best option."

She said, "If that's our last chance."

"Let's not say that yet. You have a very stubborn form of breast cancer. It means that recovery is more difficult. But it also means that you're very strong for fighting it for so long. I want you two to think about the possibilities moving forward," Blake explained. "Doctor Reynolds will be in soon. He'll go over all of the options."

Ava nodded as her lips pressed tightly. Her husband reached for her hand. His touch unleashed a stream of tears. Blake got down on his knees and hugged her.

"We're here for you, Ava. We're here."

As Blake led Andy toward the reception area, he said, "These patients like Ava. They're so brave. They stare death in the face every day. And they remain so strong. For their families and friends. They amaze me."

Andy pulled his shirt away from his chest several times in an effort to ventilate. "Where are we going?" Andy's tall, slender body moved with long strides through the hall.

"House call," Blake said.

"You do that?" Andy asked as he fumbled with his voice recorder.

Blake breezed through the waiting room. "She's family."

Blake tapped the large man at the door and said, "Jerry."

"You ready?" Jerry asked the doctor. "Let's go."

Edna kissed Jerry on the cheek. She said, "Love you, baby."

Jerry marched ahead of them. Andy whispered to the doctor, "I didn't know Jerry worked for you. I thought he was just coincidentally hanging around whenever I came here. What does he do?"

"My driver," Blake answered. "He's helping me out with a few different things right now."

Andy chuckled as they walked out the front door. "Driver? He looks more like a bodyguard."

"Yeah."

They walked outside. Jerry was first. He eclipsed the two of them. His dense hair flared out from his head. His thick brown neck was budding with drips of perspiration. Jerry looked like a pro football lineman. Blake followed close behind, looking down at the ground.

Andy followed. The summer sun was blinding. He shriveled from the glare like a reclusive vampire. He wasn't expecting a road trip.

A man with short gray hair and a stained t-shirt ran toward them from his navy F-150 pickup truck. "Doctor Blake!"

Jerry looked at the doctor, who abruptly shook his head at the sight of the strange man. Blake quickly walked in the opposite direction. He threw a hasty wave toward the man.

"Doctor Blake!"

Jerry reached into his coat where a holster would be. He said to the strange man, "Sir, sir. Slow down. He can't talk right now. We're late for a patient. Sorry, you can schedule an appointment with him."

"I just wanted to thank the doctor," he said as he tried to elude Jerry. It didn't work. In a surprisingly agile move, Jerry mirrored the man's evasive maneuver and held out his arm. He explained, "Okay, he's got to go right now. Are you a patient?"

The man answered, "No, my wife. He saved her life. I just wanted to tell him." He seemed devastated by the snub.

Jerry said, "I'll tell him. I promise."

The strange man walked back to his truck.

Moments later, their car sped away with Jerry behind the wheel. Andy and Blake sat in the back.

"What the hell was that?" Andy asked. He pointed to Jerry. "Why do you have a bodyguard? Why did I just feel like I was part of the Secret Service?"

Blake looked at the road speeding behind them. No one was following. He said, "This is confidential. Not even your mom can know this. I've been receiving some threatening phone calls lately."

"What?" Andy asked with a chuckle of disbelief. "What are they saying?"

"Shut down, or bad things will happen to you and your family." Andy nervously looked out the window. Blake continued, "Threats are a part of the deal. It's part of the risk of going public with my treatment. I'm not worried. Once this all comes out, the issue will be over."

"If you're not concerned, why is Jerry driving you around?"

"Better to be safe right now."

Half an hour later, the city of Madison faded into the rolling hills of western Wisconsin. Dairy farms spanned the undulating terrain. Yellow dandelions dotted the grasslands. A group of bikers in colorful spandex pumped the pedals of their aerodynamic bikes.

Jerry checked his GPS. "Is this it?" He asked Blake pointing to a gravel drive that led uphill through a thick canopy of trees.

"That's it."

Their black Cadillac sped up the dusty drive.

Andy asked, "Who is this?" He flipped on his camera and recorder.

"My mother's sister," Blake answered as he gazed up at the green foliage with a familiar grin.

The path leveled off as they drove through an open field. Black and white cows grazed. Long reeds outlined a stream that winded through the middle of the field. At the end of the drive stood a two-story white house. A three-car garage faced the house. Half of a crumbling barn remained on the other side of the field. A vast green lawn surrounded the white house. Adirondack chairs lined a broad porch that wrapped around most of the house.

Blake said, "I used to love spending time over here when I was a kid."

"How old is she?" Andy asked.

"Ninety-two. She has lung cancer. Smoked for a lot of her life."

Andy mumbled, "Smoking."

"It still amazes me that anyone who smoked for so much of their lives ever lives past fifty," Blake said. "The human body is astoundingly resilient."

Ellie stood on her walker at the front door. A round nurse stood behind her. Ellie looked like someone propped her up just for the introduction. She had frazzled white hair, a round face, and puppy-dog eyes. She actually looked a little like Albert Einstein.

"You're going to treat her?" Andy asked as the parked the car. "You think you can save her?"

"No. We're here to comfort her. Suggest some remedies and supplements that might ease her pain and symptoms," Blake explained. "There's a point where the care shifts from reviving to easing the passing. This is one of the most difficult issues in health care today. The high costs of unnecessary drugs and procedures during the last year of life. If you could do a half-million-dollar procedure for a loved one to live another month, would it be worth it? I know that's a terrible question. It's very difficult to put a price tag on these procedures, but there has to be a limit. These surgeries at the end of life are exorbitantly costly and marginally helpful. Sometimes we spend too much money fighting death, when we should be accepting it. Everyone can feel when this shift happens."

"That doesn't seem right," Andy said. He thought about his mother and emotions rose to the surface. "I mean, what if they don't think it's time to give up?"

They walked along a gravel path up to the front door. "It's different. I can't explain it. But there's a shift that happens when we start to detach from the living world. And we turn our heads and first glimpse into the expansive unknown of death. Ellie has made the turn. Now she's waiting. Instead of being invaded with more surgery and medication that will only create complications and discomfort for the rest of her days, she has decided to die gracefully and accept the process. And the process of dying is often easier and more natural if we don't fight it."

Blake walked up to the house. He reached for her frail hand. "How are you, Ellie?"

"Oh, Richie," Ellie exclaimed.

Andy whispered, "Richie?"

Ellie slowly made her way back to her bed. It was a hospital bed temporarily occupying a sunroom. Blake asked, "How are you feeling, my dear?"

"I'm okay." She groaned as she fell back into her bed with the help of her nurse.

Blake asked, "Is that pain medication working for you?"

Ellie reached for knitting needles and a piece of cloth that looked like the start of a pink scarf. "Yes, yes," she insisted.

Blake reached into his bag. "You're not in pain?" He pulled out a couple of vials of aromatherapy. The two small bottles were labeled Tranquility and Heart.

"No, I feel just fine. Just fine, Richie," Ellie answered.

Blake smiled at Andy. "Well, I wanted to stop by and see how you were doing."

"Oh, you're such a good boy," Ellie said as she reached for his hand. "I always liked you."

"Thanks, Aunt Ellie."

"I'll tell you a secret." She leaned in closer.

"What's that?" Blake asked.

"I always liked you the most out of all my nieces and nephews."

"Ellie! You can't say that," Blake said as he leaned back in his chair with an embarrassed laugh.

"Well, why the heck not?" Ellie asked. She dropped her knitting project onto her lap. "I can say whatever I want right now. I loved you all, but you were always my favorite. All you boys used to run through the garden playing hide-and-go-seek. Your mother used to get so upset because you kids would get so dirty."

Blake said, "Your garden was amazing. It was like a garden labyrinth. Big ripe tomatoes. Juicy strawberries. Sweet corn."

"We used to eat that corn raw," Ellie said with a smile. She gazed up at the ceiling. "You know, Richie, I can see the garden again. Lately, in my dreams. But it looks as real as you standing here right now, I tell you. In the dream, I'm younger. My legs are strong and limber. It's always a bright summer evening. Bugs hover over the land and the sky is painted with colors. My garden. I can see my garden. You still helping people with cancer?"

"As best I can, Aunt Ellie. As best I can."

Andy and Doctor Blake visited with his Aunt Ellie for the next hour. They talked about the old days between breaks of silence. Death was near.

Everyone around Ellie knew it. They didn't resist it. Andy sensed a curious comfort in Ellie's situation. The uncertainty was gone.

On the way back to the office, Blake sat quietly. He stared out the window. The car meandered along a winding country road. Jerry kept his distance behind a slow delivery truck in front of him. The truck finally turned into a driveway, narrowly missing a mailbox. Andy leaned toward Blake several times, seemingly ready to ask something. He retreated back to his side of the car each time.

Blake turned. "What is it? What do you want to ask me?" The car bounced around on the rough, rural road leading back to Madison.

"Over the last few months, you've shown me so much. You've explained so much. I feel like I know your process, like I can tell your story. And I do believe that you have a dramatically better way to treat cancer. Personalized and comprehensive."

"I'll take that as a compliment, my friend."

"But one thing remains. One question that you haven't answered."

Blake asked flatly, "What is that?"

"The injections." The car came to a stop at a red light. Jerry adjusted his wide frame in the front seat. The tan leather creaked from the friction.

Blake answered, "Ah yes, the injections."

"What are they?" Andy asked.

Blake pointed to the voice recorder. "Andy, shut it off." He whispered in disbelief, "You really don't know?"

"Of course not," Andy insisted. The car accelerated onto the ramp leading to a highway. "No one at the center says a word about the injections whenever I bring it up. My mom has no idea. I know it isn't a cure, but it certainly seems like a lynchpin."

"You could say that." A large truck emerged alongside of them. Jerry raced ahead and barely pulled ahead of it before their lane merged.

"What are you injecting, Doctor Blake?"

Jerry poked his head backwards. He wanted to hear.

Blake asked, "Have you ever heard of the trophoblastic theory of cancer?"

"Never."

"Let me paint a picture for you." Blake turned and faced Andy. Andy almost felt unworthy of his presence when he faced him. His eyes constantly shifted out the window. Cars pulling boats and jet skis raced up

139

the road. Another summer weekend was upon them. "The term trophoblast is just another word for a cluster of cancer cells. Imagine cells connecting to a new tissue in the body. They attach and invade the previously healthy tissue as they multiply rapidly, digging deeper and deeper into this tissue. Sound at all familiar?"

Andy answered, "Not really." Jerry raced past a semi on their right.

"I'll give you a hint. The initial cluster of cells drops down from a tube and attach to the tissue in a woman..." Blake looked at Andy. He waited for a response.

"Fallopian?" Andy asked. The buildings in central Madison began to rise ahead of them.

Blake encouraged him, "You're right! A cluster of cancer cells is exactly the same as embryonic cells. An embryo drops into the uterus, attaches to its wall and rapidly eats away at the tissue while multiplying in a way that is identical to cancer. The conundrum with the exterior embryonic cells eating away at the uterus is that, normally, the immune system would attack a foreign object invading healthy tissue. But embryos, thankfully, possess a signal that tells the immune system not to attack."

"Otherwise the immune system would kill every embryo," Andy said.

"That's right. No more babies."

Andy's eyebrows rose as he sarcastically responded, "That would be bad."

Blake continued, "Cancer cells mimic this signal, keeping the immune system unaware of its rapid invasion. Our immune systems are usually capable of destroying cancer cells, but they're fooled into thinking that the cancer cells aren't a threat. But at a certain point in the early stages of pregnancy, this cluster of invasive embryonic cells shuts off. They stop eating away at the uterus wall."

"What makes the cells stop?" Andy asked.

"This is the right question. The body secretes an enzyme that tells the immune system that the trophoblast is no longer allowed to invade the tissue of the uterus. The cells slow their invasion and the immune system is back in control."

"We use these same enzymes injected into cancerous areas."

"That's what you've been injecting?"

"That's right."

"Were you the first to do this?"

"The process was given its big chance long ago and failed miserably. One doctor injected the enzyme with little success. He failed to successfully replicate the critical active assets of the enzyme. A second doctor discovered this method over fifty years ago. Unfortunately, the injections killed all cancer cells at once, creating a toxic shock to the body that resulted in a quicker death. Plaxin and a couple other drug companies tried to test the enzymes in the past as well. But all of them considered it to be a dead end and moved on to other remedies. It was abandoned altogether. They stood on the edge of discovery and turned around."

"These enzyme injections are the key," Andy stated.

"The enzyme injections work like a kill switch, shutting off all power to the electrical grid of cancer cells in the body," Blake affirmed.

"That's what Jennifer said to me."

Blake asked, "She told you about the injections?"

"No, she just said you guys discovered a cancer kill switch. She wouldn't tell me what it was."

Blake raised his eyebrow. "Once the cancer cells go dormant, we have time for the body to recover. So when the injections are over, tumors and metastasized cancer are easier to treat. The system of the body can once again control the disease."

"Why not keep the kill switch on?"

"I wish it were that simple, but it never is. Cancer is agile, adaptable. We've found that cancer cells adapt and eventually strengthen," Blake explained. "The injections only buy time, as mysterious and exciting as they may be. It's nutrition, supplements, liquid gold, along with conventional medicine that help the body recover during that time. This is the problem with cancer patients. Their bodies are so battered by the treatment, that they're never able to regain control of the internal environment. Cancer almost always wins. But the injections change that, if only for months. They give us time to treat the patient, to strengthen them. In addition to the enzymes, we're exploring many other treatments that may also weaken or temporarily disable cancer. There isn't just one path to reversing this disease."

"Like what?"

"Sound waves, heat therapy, light waves," Blake explained as he waved his hand over a ray of light that illuminated part of the back seat. "Treatments that only seemed plausible in science fiction movies are now becoming very real possibilities."

"Unbelievable."

"It's not unbelievable, really. It's about time. Ask any one of my cancer patients," Blake explained. "A revolution in cancer treatment will be a great catalyst for the future of health care. Because cancer has no fixed point, no consistent drug that works for all forms, it will require us to rethink our entire paradigm of treatment and healing. The lessons we learn from cancer will ripple out to all diseases. It will reaffirm the importance of all cultures and their medicines working in conjunction. And it will remind us that mutations in our food create mutations in our bodies. Cancer has come to the forefront to teach us how to live better lives, to teach us that we have lost our way. Mindless expansion, insatiable appetite, detachment from its surroundings. Cancer is the disease of our time."

They finally pulled into the Blake Center parking lot. Andy asked, "Are these injections illegal?"

"They're not approved by the FDA in a conventional way, but I've been carefully testing for years," Blake explained as he checked his phone.

"Experimenting on terminal patients?" Andy asked.

"In a way, yes, but I knew they were ineffective in small doses and very harmful in large ones. So I carefully tested them over decades, just as a drug company would. These enzymes exist in a kind of legal middle ground. That's why I'm reaching out to someone I trust at Plaxin Pharmaceuticals about drug approval. I don't know what to do. I have no idea how to make my treatment available on a larger scale."

Andy asked, "Do they know how?"

"We'll see," Blake answered. He walked toward his office. "See you in a bit."

"It's a hell of a risk," Andy said as he rose from the back seat of the car. The sun was blinding. "Letting a drug company know about your treatment."

Blake turned and squinted his eyes. "I know, Andy."

Andy returned to his mother's side. She sat up in her chair. She no longer needed a hospital bed when she visited. A woman gently massaged her feet. His mother faced the ceiling, her eyes closed. She looked better and stronger. On the table next to her, she had a laptop. She was constantly online, keeping up with friends and family. A notepad displayed scribbled notes and lists. All of these clues were promising to Andy.

An hour later, Doctor Blake entered. "Haven't seen you in a while," he sarcastically said to Andy. The casual statement sounded kind of awkward coming out of the doctor's mouth.

He walked in with a small silver tray. A needle filled with clear fluid rested on top. *Injections.* His mother asked Andy, "Did he tell you yet?"

Andy looked up at the doctor. He nodded. Andy nodded back to his mother.

"About damn time," she said with a laugh. "Are you going to tell me? It's been driving me crazy."

She rolled up her sleeve and wrapped a rubber tube around her upper arm. Andy thought his feisty mother might even grab the syringe from the doctor. She moved with a renewed energy. She was improving, and the emotions rising within Andy were seductive.

Blake said to her. "Embryonic enzymes."

"That was one of my guesses," she said with a hint of disappointment. Before Blake could even say it, she insisted, "I won't tell anyone. I assume it's not completely on the up and up."

As Doctor Blake told Andy's mother more about the mysterious cancer kill switch, Andy drifted away from the room and deep into thought.

Andy Stone didn't know if there was an ultimate meaning to life. He didn't know if he would look back at his life and it would all make sense. He wasn't sure whether his mother's illness would fit into some grander narrative of existence. He didn't know if there was a God or whether God cared about him. But he did know that, through all of the pain and uncertainty, there had always been hope. He believed that hope was his veiled understanding that there was a purpose for his chaotic life. He didn't know if this was true, but he knew that through all his days, hope never died. It was the product of a bottomless well that blossomed within. He figured he would never know until he could move beyond his final breath, but he hoped it was true. And the hope gave him strength.

The doctor was gone, and his mother had fallen asleep. Andy unfolded a blanket and draped it over her. The injection usually made her tired. Her eyes were closed, face looking up at the ceiling. Her mouth was open, as if she was stuck at the peak of a big yawn. She sucked in precious inhales. Her chest stopped during a slight delay between breaths, until she finally exhaled. Andy looked at his mother and remembered something he had been meaning to ask the doctor all day. He was nervous to ask, but the sight of his mother's strained breaths gave him courage.

Andy rushed outside his mother's room. He scanned the office for the doctor. He ran to the waiting room and asked Edna, "Did he leave?"

"Just walked outside."

"Doctor Blake! Doctor Blake!" Andy yelled as he ran toward the doctor walking to his car. For a moment, Jerry turned in defense. He rolled his eyes when he saw Andy.

"Sorry, Jerry," Andy announced as he ran up to the doctor. He panted for air.

"What is it?" Blake asked. His forehead was beading with sweat.

Andy eventually stood up straight as his breaths slowed. He asked, "How many more injections?"

Blake asked, "For your mother?"

"Yes," Andy pleaded.

"Two."

"Can't you go longer? Give her another month. She just needs to be a little stronger. All she wants is to get back down to Key West again this winter. It's her favorite place in the world. She hasn't gone down there for three years."

Blake answered, "I know. Your father mentioned Key West."

Andy replied, "She's so happy down there. She's been dreaming about getting back down to the island. Can't we keep the injections going for a little longer?"

"We've taken it as far as we can with your mother," Blake said. He carefully placed his strong hand on Andy's shoulder. "Soon, the switch will turn back on. If we treat her with more injections, the cancer will become very resistant. It will expand even further throughout her body. And she will most certainly die."

"Is she gonna be okay?" Andy stood with his naked emotions in the middle of the parking lot. The sun baked his slender frame. He was pleading for an answer, searching for something he could grab onto. His eyes welled up.

The doctor locked eyes with him. "I don't know."

CHAPTER ELEVEN

Pale gray coals glowed bright orange and then faded in a dance of pulsing heat. Andy stood with his dad on an unseasonably warm September evening over a smoking grill. Sweet corn husks browned and burgers dripped onto the glowing coals below. Grease drippings hung, suspended in a semi-cooked state over the coals. Andy and his father both held beers on the newly finished stone patio. On the perimeter of the patio, ripe vegetables dangled from tall plants. Fully bloomed roses began to wilt. The edge of their pastel leaves had turned dry and brown. Andy held a ripe tomato.

The log house in which Jamie and Andy had grown up stood tall behind them. The thick horizontal logs were dark and glossy. They had received a new coat of chocolate-colored oil stain in the spring. Vines retreated from their August peak along the walls of the house. Three broad sliding doors behind them faced south. The windows allowed heat to drench the house during the cold Midwestern months. But during this hot evening at the end of summer, the house was wide open. Fans hummed in the living room above a rug which dogs had pooped and peed on way more times than any family member would admit.

A quaint sunroom was filled with projects that Andy's mother had abandoned. An intricate dollhouse, stained glass and acrylic paintings. The family continued to encourage her to paint. But the room only collected dust. Various discarded water filters were stacked next to her desk. The filtration systems were signs of a family trying to mitigate potential cancer catalysts. The sunroom also had stacks of books about cancer treatments. It was filled with alternative health remedies, books and supplements for Andy's mother and friends of the family. Above all things, his mother was a healer. She surrounded herself with energy therapists, massage specialists, and alternative healers of all kinds. She sifted through the newest techniques and figured out which ones were actually beneficial. She needed no one else to tell her what was good. Andy's mother could always tell.

Behind the sunroom, the office glowed with warm, golden light. Andy's mother was sitting up on her bed. The first-floor room was converted to a temporary bedroom. She could no longer make it up the stairs. So the converted office had become her home. She watched a cooking show while actively taking notes on a pad of paper. A pale blue laptop screen glowed next to her on the bed. Despite the appearance of stability, her health had become severely unstable. A bad fall in the middle of the night had left her bed-ridden for a week. Family friends began coming in shifts to watch her. Andy's mother had become too weak to be alone. She was having difficulty performing the most fundamental tasks – going to the bathroom, getting a drink of water, watering plants, doing laundry. She was having trouble absorbing the concentrated array of supplements critical to the Blake treatment.

But her spirits remained high, primarily fueled by Richard Blake. The doctor understood what propelled cancer patients to persevere. It was hope. Andy's mother needed it now more than ever. It was the reason she kept hanging on to the ledge and clawing her way back up whenever she slipped lower. The loss of hope meant that she would let go. Her fountain of hope was the reason why she had always been looking ahead to holistic treatments, alternatives to conventional medicine, and finally the Blake Treatment Center. All of them gave her a new focal point on the horizon; all of them kept her believing that there was something else out there. Andy's mother continued to focus her eyes on the faint glimmer of light on the horizon that promised to be what she had been seeking for the last twenty years of her life – a cure to cancer.

Andy and his father absorbed a gorgeous fall evening outside. September was Andy's favorite month in the Midwest. The regular barking of rambunctious dogs echoed from the vast, fenced-in back yard. Various gas-powered machines buzzed on and off throughout the spacious, wooded subdivision. Neighbors were committed to weekend yard work before the harsh cold fronts from Canada would descend in the coming months.

Andy's father said, "You know, there are a lot of people who deal with illness in the family around the world every day, and a lot of them don't have the support system that we do."

"Yeah," Andy agreed. He bit into the ripe baby tomato in his hand.

"It's been good to have you back, Andy." His father's voice shook and his eyes glossed. "Having you guys around, I've been crying like crazy this summer."

"How are you?" Andy asked.

"Pretty good. I'm doing pretty good right now. We've strung some good days together in a row lately."

The two shared a common goal now and small talk just seemed kind of small. It was enough for Andy and his father to just share a beer and soak in the pastel landscape of the dimming sky above. Andy focused on what his mother's friend called "holding the space." This meant that Andy remained positive, steady and strong as he came into their home, their space. A visitor's mental state and thoughts carried more weight around his mother than words. Some visitors didn't need to say anything. The ones who could hold the space. His father had been holding the space for years. He made his wife laugh and massaged her head during the bad nights. To be fearful or negative around his mother wasn't holding the space. The answer was to be focused on the moment, to resist the desire to conclude and cut through the pervasive uncertainty.

"Come here," his father said. He waved Andy over to the new porch, which was recently built along with the stone patio. It was promising for Andy to see his parents making home improvements. It was a subtle sign of hope. Andy followed his father into the newly-constructed porch. Wicker furniture surrounded the room. Tall screens shielded the room from bugs. The vaulted ceiling rose from two sides to a peak in the middle.

"Whoa," Andy said, looking up toward the vaulted ceiling. Rows of track lighting illuminated stunning glass sculptures.

His father agreed, "I know."

Three five-foot-long glass pieces hovered above them. A slim metal rod discretely bolted to the ceiling suspended them. It latched onto the pieces with two arms that reached around them. The glass looked like elongated, vivid blades of grass from a sci-fi movie. They hung horizontally above the room, each curving and undulating in seductive frozen motion, yet geometrical simplicity. Andy had watched his brother make similar pieces.

"Wow, I knew what he was doing, but I had no idea it would look like this," Andy said in awe. Bewildering depth of design streamed from one end to the other in each piece. Within the clear glass were intricate strands of color that ran the entire length of the sculpture. The patterns looked like pastel-colored cirrus clouds encased in clear glass. Sections of the pieces had speckles of color, spirals and random patterns. Andy marveled, "When did Jamie put this up?"

"Monday," his father said with pride. "He wanted to get it done for Mom."

"She can see it from the office?" Andy gazed into their makeshift bedroom. He couldn't tell if his mother was awake or sleeping.

"Yeah, she loves it," his father said, "I talked to Jamie a lot on Monday. That big art show is going to be his debut of this series."

Andy ran his fingers along the middle sculpture suspended above him. It displayed mystifying, interwoven plumes of color.

"SOFA," Andy said. "The massive art show on Navy Pier."

His father asked, "What does SOFA stand for again?"

"Sculptures, Objects and Functional Art? I think," Andy said.

"Mom really wants to go," his father said. He looked back at the office. "I really hope we can. Apparently, some of the organizers saw Jamie's recent work, and they're giving him one of the big display areas," his father explained. "When is it again?"

"A couple months. Just after Thanksgiving."

"I think he's getting really excited." His father gazed up at Jamie's installation. "Jamie also told me about Mya. It sounds pretty serious. He told me he was in love with her. I've never heard Jamie use love to describe a relationship."

"Pretty amazing. He just moved in with her. I'm living in his old place with a friend of his now," Andy said. He trailed off at the end. They walked back outside. Andy hastily flipped the burgers and rotated the corn on the perimeter of the grill.

His father asked, "So he already moved in with this woman?"

"Yup."

"How are you?" His father watched Andy react to this question out of the corner of his eye.

"I'm good," Andy said. He took an awkward sip of beer. His parents could always see him so clearly and nakedly, and he could feel it happening now.

"You've been spending a lot of time with us lately," his father said. "We've all made sacrifices during this time. But I worry how much moving back here has changed your life. You can't sacrifice your life and your dreams forever."

"I'm not sacrificing my life," Andy said. He steadily shook his head. He rolled a couple of browned cornhusks around on the grill. The stringy ends were catching fire.

"I know you aren't happy bartending. I know you miss Colorado. Jamie even told me about a girl you met?" His father asked.

"There's no girl," Andy said abruptly. "There was, but I screwed it up."

His father put his beer down and adjusted the deck chairs on the patio. The painful directness of the conversation seemed to require partial attention on a peripheral chore. He continued, "Jamie said you really liked her. You lost her number or something?"

"I liked her. A lot. It's kind of hard to understand. How you could meet someone who seems so perfect for you. She was so amazing, intoxicating. And then you lose her number and that's it. I guess it just wasn't meant to be. I mean, even if I had found her number, what were we going to do? Date long distance between San Francisco and Chicago? While my mom was sick? Maybe the whole thing was just too much of a dream."

"Maybe she'll reach out to you still," his hopeful father said.

"Maybe."

"Your life isn't here, Andy." His dad looked up at the clear sky above. "Your life is in Colorado. You have connections out there. I know how important it is for you to work in journalism. And I know how easy it is for journalists to get derailed."

The words cut into Andy. His dad had a way of illuminating reality in a way that cut to his core.

"It's just been hard to break into any news outlets here. I've had some success, but nothing like Colorado. And you're right, Dad, it does scare me. I can feel the fear creeping in every day I work behind that bar. That I'm losing touch with my career, that the boat is floating away without me. And every day I wait, I'll have to swim harder and harder to catch up. But I can't leave you guys. Not now, not yet. Not at this critical point in Mom's recovery."

"Every point is critical these days, Bubba."

"I know," Andy said. "But I'm not going anywhere right now. Not yet."

Their neighbor meandered into her yard. She looked around, assessing the damage from another day of her children playing in the grass.

"Hey, Kelly," his father yelled as he waved to his neighbor in her sprawling yard.

She walked over. "It's like a tornado comes through when these kids play out here," she yelled from across the yard. Toys were scattered around the neighboring yard, increasing in density as they neared the door to the back porch. She dropped a plastic truck and walked over. Her shoulder-length hair was dyed an unnatural auburn color. It framed her warm green eyes and a sweet smile.

"How are you guys doing?" Kelly asked with a tone of compassion. Her voice echoed through the open house.

Andy's father answered, "We're good."

"Sorry about the mess over here."

"Are you kidding me? We love the action," his father said. "It's been fun to have a young family around here."

Kelly asked, "How's Sarah doing?"

A dull tapping noise made Andy turn around. His mother stood with her aluminum walker on the other side of the sliding door. She struggled to get the door open. Her skinny hands shook. Andy pulled it open, and she walked onto the porch. She wore yellow pajamas with faded, recurring floral patterns and a robe slung around her torso. Her short hair was covered with a pastel pink wrap.

She threw a wave to her neighbor Kelly as she navigated the two shallow steps that led outside. It was only the third time she had been outside since she fell.

Kelly asked, "Sarah, how are you? I haven't seen you guys in months."

Andy's father helped his mother onto the patio. Once she felt comfortable, she stubbornly batted her husband's arms away. Andy observed Kelly as she watched his mother emerge from the house. Kelly was kind and thoughtful. Her grandparents used to live in the neighboring house. After they died, she and her husband decided to make the home their own. They had two kids with a third on the way. She was a lively woman, the glue of her family. She worked as a nurse in a nearby hospital. The parallels to his mother were striking. They always got along well. Perhaps that was the reason why Kelly's expression after seeing his mother was so difficult for Andy. She tried to hide it, but Kelly was heartbroken. She looked with pain and despair. Since she hadn't seen Andy's mother in months, she could see the broader downward trajectory that the Stone family could not.

Even though her posture was slumped, Andy's mother shuffled around the large, half-oval patio with brief and surprising bursts of quickness. Despite a significantly dimming evening sky, she still squinted.

"Hey, Kelly. You're getting closer. What are you, six months?" Andy's mother asked. She gazed down at her neighbor's protruding belly.

She liked Kelly.

"Almost six months to the day, Sarah." Kelly's voice rang out again through the neighborhood.

As she chatted with Andy's mother, curtains and garage doors opened. Other neighbors came outside. One woman watered one spot of her lawn as she continually glimpsed over at the Stone house. Andy's mother threw a sarcastic wave at her nosy neighbors.

His mother asked, "Why it was so important for them to dig into other people's lives?" Her voice squeaked. She pointed at the houses with people peeking over at her. "It's like they're trying to take something from me. I don't know what, but something."

Kelly retreated from the situation. It wasn't hard to see that Andy's mother wasn't in the best mood. "You guys look like it's almost time for dinner. I should get back." She waved as she walked back to her toy debris field.

Andy said, "Let me help you with those toys, Kelly."

"Oh, no, really. It's fine."

"I'm happy to," Andy said as he ignored her refusals. The two had known each other since early childhood.

Andy asked her, "How is it to live in your grandparents' old house?"

"I love it," she answered. She looked into her house with a warm smile. "We love it."

She paused from picking up various plastic toys and whispered, "How is your mom doing?" She flipped her amber hair away from her eyes.

"She's doing decent, but worse lately. It's hard to ever tell how she's doing. There are so many moving parts. It's really hard to explain," Andy whispered back. He twisted as he grabbed two more toys with wheels and bright colors. "She has good days and bad ones. She's hanging on. She's making lists for Thanksgiving."

"Looking forward is good," Kelly said with genuine hope.

"Always. But it's tough. We see her every day. So I don't think we see the overall decline like someone who sees her more sporadically," Andy explained. "She's got a lot of problems, but she's still very strong willed."

"I know that." She looked over at the Stone house.

Andy said, "And the will to live, the love of her husband and family are very powerful forces." He looked back at his parents' home. It looked different, and he wished he could figure out why.

"Yes, they are," Kelly agreed.

"But I know she doesn't look good. We know she's not doing great. I've been trying to think of a metaphor for this time in my mother's life.

Because dealing with advanced cancer is complicated, with all kinds of moving parts," Andy said. He plopped two toy cars into a bin on his neighbor's porch. "It's almost like she's an old airplane flying high up in the sky, and she's been badly damaged. Part of one wing is torn off. The engine is sputtering. Part of the fuselage has been ripped away. The gauges are malfunctioning, but the plane is still flying. Repairs are being made in-flight. But the old plane could fall apart at any moment. It could keep flying for a while, or it could fall out of the sky..." Andy stopped himself and said, "I know that's a little dramatic."

"Is it?" She asked.

"I guess not." Andy tossed two neon hula hoops over a patio chair. They eventually wobbled to rest.

When Andy returned to the patio, his father brought the food inside. Andy plopped onto the long deck chair next to his mom. The nylon cushions felt warm. Robins swooped down to the bird feeder. Every time his mother adjusted her position on the other lawn chair, the birds darted away to the thick canopy of nearby trees.

Andy prodded, "I was looking around in the sunroom over there. Lots of new packages from Blake. Have you been taking any of those supplements lately?" Andy pointed to boxes stacked up near the sliding door. The neighbor's reaction to his mother's condition had shaken him. It sent him searching for anything that could help his mother.

"Yeah, not as many. Don't ask me that. It makes me feel guilty, like I should be doing more," his mother snapped.

"Mom, I didn't mean to make you feel bad, I just..."

"It's okay."

In recent years, his mother blamed herself for not doing enough to combat her disease. He saw his mother experience unfounded guilt due to cancer. This burden of personal blame weighed on her with great force, and he wondered how someone so kind and loving could have such dislike for herself at times. Her guilt was a voice that grew with cancer. It was a cancer of her mind. During her bouts with cancer, this voice would be louder and he could see the pain registered in her expression.

This trait scared her son, because he could see it developing within himself. He found it easy to be kind and accept others, but he always had trouble accepting his own path. He blamed himself for the makeshift career he had carved out, working as a part-time reporter and hustling at the bar. It was why he had trouble with men his age in suits. He figured everyone had their sensitive demographics, resulting from that insecure voice within that said they should be more. *More something.* Young professionals were Andy's weakness. He saw their steady careers. He imagined cushy savings accounts and nice cars. He imagined them having everything that he didn't. Somewhere within him a seed began to grow, or rather a voice. It was a voice that told him he was failing at his career, that freelance journalist wasn't good enough, that real men needed to go out and work in the real world. The prospect of his thirties was daunting. There was a point in his thirties where all those things you wanted to accomplish in your career began to become unrealistic. He feared he would dislike himself for bartending forever. He already did. He tried to rationalize it. It was the means to an end. It was an honest living. But he could see himself slipping into a pattern that imprisoned his mother, self-loathing for the things he wasn't, for the person he should have been, for the life he should have lived. He could see this pattern's broader trajectory. It was a ridiculous battle, but he had trouble fighting it. For there was nothing more naive than a man constantly blaming himself for his faults. They actually weren't even faults. They were handpicked, arbitrary faults that he saw in himself through his own warped, subjective lens. How many ways could you blame yourself? How many reasons could you find to dislike yourself? They were endless and infinite, and they were all bullshit.

After dinner, Andy's mother walked with her son's assistance back out onto the patio. The house was hot from a humid week. The cool evening air refreshed her aching joints. Andy propped a sun chair up two clicks so she could look onto the yard where lightning bugs had gathered. Their luminescent yellow glow faded in and out. They speckled the nearby atmosphere, like little moving radioactive stars in the neighbor's yard.

"Normal life is so amazing," she said. She leaned back on her sun chair, and rolled her head toward her son.

"What do you mean?"

"Imagine you never saw lightning bugs before. Imagine we never knew that bugs could create a bright glowing light. Then we woke up one day, and they were here."

"They would seem pretty crazy, I guess."

His mother nodded at this. "It would be a miracle."

When he sat with his mom, the world became as magical as it had been when he was a little boy. Milky clusters of stars twinkled in the heavens and lightning bugs saturated their vision down here on Earth. She had a way of making everyday life seem extraordinary.

After a few minutes of the steady chirp of crickets, she raised her right arm toward the stars in the western sky. "Have I ever told you about the Pleiades?"

"No."

She had described to Andy the special way to see the Pleiades constellation out of his peripheral vision many times, but he didn't want to stop his mother. As his parents got older, this became a growing issue. He had heard their old stories a million freaking times and for some reason they could never recall whether they told their children about *that one time*. He thought about how many times he heard about his dad running a marathon, their legendary parties, and how Andy was a serious little child. He knew the stories by heart, but rarely had the heart to remind his parents. At times like this, he just let it go.

"You can always see the Pleiades by facing the Big Dipper and looking for the small cluster of stars to your right." Andy never really understood why she felt so connected to a random group of stars.

"The Pleiades are a cluster of stars over there." She pointed.

"Oh yeah, I see it now. That's really cool, Mom."

"It's my home. The Pleiades," she said, as she gazed upon the distant cluster of stars.

Andy didn't really know what this meant. He had never heard her call the Pleiades her home. But he knew that it was significant to his mom. He recalled some new age books that she had read about Pleiadeans being these wise aliens who guided earthlings through space or something like that. It didn't matter. All that mattered was the shared moment. So he went along with his mother's words, squeezed her hand, and held the space.

CHAPTER TWELVE

Ashley Markum sat on a park bench just north of Michigan Ave. Cars crawled along on Lake Shore Drive behind her. The Drake Hotel stood nestled between downtown high-rises to her south. Sporadic pedestrians passed her on the bike path in front of an unusually turbulent Lake Michigan. Winter was coming. She could feel the change in the air. She wasn't usually a cold weather person, but the lakefront had a peaceful majesty to it after the beaches emptied. Ashley looked out over the water. She wore slim black gloves and clutched a cup of coffee. Steam rose from the narrow opening on the coffee cup's plastic top. Determined runners and bikers whizzed by in black spandex outfits. Waves slammed into the concrete wall and spewed whitewash ten feet high. How different the world could look a mere two blocks from her civilized loft.

On the shores of the lake, Ashley thought about her own place. The wave was the final act of momentum. It was the manifestation of multiple undercurrents; it was the tipping point when the unforeseeable became reality. These currents were not visible from above, but they were the force that drove everything on the surface. Momentum was everything, and now Ashley Markum was riding a wave underneath the surface. She wondered when it would explode to the shore and thunder across Lake Shore Drive to the offices downtown.

Since Mike's ex-wife slammed into a concrete wall and tragically perished, it was widely whispered that he was in a terrible state of denial. Most of the time, he refused to acknowledge the incident. He rejected counselors and friends who reached out. He stopped dating any of the beautiful, promising women in the company's ranks, as had been his modus operandi in the past. He overcompensated for the tragedy with a curious, almost euphoric enthusiasm. He worked with great energy and vigor. The energy was unsustainable, even for Mike.

Ashley was emerging as the perfect person to lead a shift in a new direction. The whispers of her supporters grew louder. Ashley's rise began decades ago – in the way she lived, the way she thought, and the way she treated people. As she watched the rumbling waters of the lake, she understood that every single thought, every word and every action was represented in the woman she was on this day. Nothing was lost. This momentum had been building for decades, but now it was exploding to the surface. Ashley was the answer, and everyone around her knew it.

"Man, the lakeshore can be freezing!" Tanji said. His boisterous voice cut through the strong lake breeze. He joined Ashley on the bench as a determined rollerblader cruised passed them. He wore a skimpy gray rain jacket with the collar pinched together over his clenched lips.

"That's like a spring jacket, Tanji." Ashley laughed.

Tanji replied, "I didn't think it would be this cold! It's a whole lot warmer in the suburbs at the main office. I swear the difference is like fifteen degrees."

"You want to go inside somewhere?"

"No, no, I'll be fine. Besides, I like talking out here." Tanji pulled out a thin, blue folder. It was labeled "Blake Center." He handed it to Ashley and said, "I've been spending lots of time at one of our research branches up near Minneapolis. For the last three months, we've been intensely researching Doctor Richard Blake and his treatment center. And, Ashley, I have to tell you, it's impressive. We never could've found this."

"Why not?" She asked. She took another sip of her coffee. A little tuft of steam rose from the little opening on the lid.

Tanji explained, "Well, we tried with this series of enzymes many years ago. We began development in 1984. The enzymes showed promise in pre-clinicals, but once they got to trials, the results were unpredictable; they were extremely volatile."

Ashley shook her head. "Volatile?"

Tanji nodded. His black hair waved in the breeze – like a wheat field on a windy day. He explained, "The enzyme injections over the long term, over extensive trials are useless on their own."

"Useless on their own?" Ashley asked. "I thought this was the key to the whole treatment."

Tanji held out his hands in an effort to halt hasty conclusions. His skinny hands were trembling in the cold air. He explained, "Over the last few months, we've conducted tests with the Blake Center enzyme injections on rodents with cancer. Basically, three groups. A control, one with the injections alone, and one with injections and something the Blake Center calls liquid gold. The third group also followed nutrition and supplemental regimens that mirrored the Blake Center, as best we could."

Ashley answered, "I heard about liquid gold. Doctor Blake told me about it, but he never told me exactly what was in it."

Tanji explained, "Liquid gold is a concentrated combination of supplements and remedies. The fluid is given intravenously. It's highly alkalizing to the body. It contains antioxidants, amino acids. The list of ingredients is astounding. It truly is liquid gold." A powerful wave slammed into the adjacent concrete wall. The mist sprayed across the lakeshore bike path.

"We used accelerated testing techniques. In the simulations, the results were..." He tapered off.

"What?" Ashley pleaded. She opened the blue folder in her hands.

Tanji explained, "We estimate the one-year survival rate of the rodents getting injections alone to be at 30%."

Ashley looked down at the numbers. Her soft brown eyes scanned the complex data in moments. "Not surprising," she answered.

"That's basically a little lower rate than chemotherapy," Tanji agreed. "No real gain. Hence one of the reasons we abandoned the treatment. Of course, these are very preliminary projections and estimates."

Ashley flipped through the pages, until she stopped at one spreadsheet. The information blew her back on the bench. Her slender hands clutched the pages as a gust of wind blew their corners up. Tanji nodded, "But the third group. With liquid gold regularly administered to the rodents, we estimate that 74% will survive. That number will almost certainly go up whenever we incorporate more of the doctor's supplements and treatments."

Ashley looked out to the churning, gray waters of Lake Michigan. Her long hair gently waved in the wind. She said, "I can't believe it."

"The rodents aren't cancer-free," Tanji clarified. "But something amazing happened with the third group. Their bodies regained control of the tumors. They shrank. It's like nothing I've ever seen before. The disease isn't eradicated, but its advance is completely reversed."

"I don't know what to say. I knew this doctor had something special, but to see the data in my hands..." Ashley squinted her eyes and looked back down at the numbers. "I just can't believe it."

"Ashley, we never could have found this," Tanji said as he turned to her. "Doctor Blake's treatment has shown me that our research method is tragically incomplete and insufficient when it comes to cancer."

"What do you mean?"

Tanji explained, "Like I said, our testing procedures plowed right through these enzymes around 1984. The embryonic injections alone aren't the answer. Every part matters. Blake makes adjustments as needed. No patient receives the exact same care, but it's everything working together. Synergy, as they say. All of it matters – the injections, the liquid gold, change in diet, massage therapists, everything they do at the Blake Center. It's all connected; it's all a part of the comprehensive care. We could have isolated proteins and simulated them with other isolated compounds for centuries and never discovered what this man has found."

Ashley continued to flip through the pages. "Together, these pieces create a powerful new treatment."

Tanji added, "But separately, they look like nothing. And all we do in our experiments is isolation. One-to-one relationships."

"We've been working in isolation," Ashley said. "Like cancer."

"Yes. Just like cancer."

"But the Blake Center is different."

"The doctor has opened up three decades of research and clinical treatments to me," Tanji said. "I've barely been sleeping, just diving into the data."

Ashley turned toward him with an intense stare. "What did you find?"

"So much. Most of his data comes from terminal patients. For years, he was only able to treat people with advanced cancer. Among this group, his five-year survival rate is about 60%. Depending on the type of cancer, conventional treatment's five-year stands at about 8%. In the late nineties, he began working with younger patients with a non-lethal cancer diagnosis. He has reversed almost all of their diseases. Although he has only worked with about two hundred non-terminal patients, his success of reversing their disease is double the average."

"That's not a lot of patients," Ashley said.

"No, it isn't. His data with terminal patients is much more comprehensive. But with early stage cancer, this treatment needs a lot more research. I can see why he came to you. He's stuck. He needs FDA approval." Tanji rubbed his hands together. His slight frame bounced up and down on the bench, hoping to create some kinetic heat. He continued, "Doctor Blake knows that a reputable drug company with advanced research facilities can help him."

Ashley said, "He needs us."

Tanji agreed, "This treatment needs a lot more research. It needs years of testing. But this is the most promising thing I've ever seen. And because it's about balancing the system of the human body as a whole, it may be applicable to many more diseases."

"But approval?" Ashley asked. A biker in spandex covered with blue pastel designs pedaled past.

"Approval is a huge question."

Ashley stated, "You realize the risks if we take this road."

"I don't care. I can't deny what he has discovered. With most diseases, the conventional, big pharma-discovery process was our best option. But Doctor Blake has convinced me that it isn't the answer when it comes to cancer. My mission has always been to find the best treatment. We've found it. It's our job to test it, to make it reliable, stable and beneficial, to make it safe, to somehow get this treatment approved, and bring it to the market on a mass scale so it can help the most patients possible. That's what we do best, and that's why Doctor Blake came to us."

"I wish it were that easy," Ashley said.

"It hasn't been before. But it is now. This man has created something revolutionary, something that could potentially reshape the landscape of cancer care. It *is* that easy now. To hell with anyone who wants to make it difficult," Tanji said. "Have you talked to Mike about this yet?"

"No." She shook her head and looked down at her empty coffee cup. "Soon. Not yet."

Tanji and Ashley gazed out at the water, as the waves that had been building in the depths of the lake crashed to shore. Momentum shaped the world.

CHAPTER THIRTEEN

Ashley Markum weaved through traffic. Her silver Audi A6 darted north on Lake Shore Drive. She drove in silence. Her chest regularly seized up, and she had to remind herself to breathe. She gripped the steering wheel tightly. She'd called Mike Landis and requested that they meet tonight. She zipped up the freshly-paved road that ran between the spacious parks along the lakeshore and the rows of North Side high-rises to her left. Christmas lights framed condos in the lake front high-rises. It was less than a week before Thanksgiving.

After speeding through Evanston, Ashley finally pulled up to Mike's waterfront home. Large, pale stones stacked three stories high. The grounds descended behind the house down to Lake Michigan. Sparse lights dotted the sprawling mansion. A circle drive was empty. The vast entryway was dark. The house looked vacant. The lawn was brown and unkempt.

Ashley sat in her car as she texted Tanji, "Where are you?"

"Ten minutes," he replied.

She started her car. She decided to drive around for a bit. Ashley had no intentions of engaging Landis alone.

Just a she shifted the car into drive, a loud thump, thump, thump reverberated through the car. Mike Landis stood outside of the passenger side door looking at Ashley.

"Hey," he said in a disturbingly casual way. "Where are you going?"

"Mike, how are you?" Ashley asked. She breezed past his question. She pulled her wool gray pea coat tight around her neck, even though it wasn't that cold.

"I'm good," he said. The words felt hollow to Ashley. "So what's so urgent that you and Tanji need to come all the way up to the North Shore on a night like this? Where's Tanji?"

"We can wait for him."

"Fine with me," Mike said. He waved Ashley into the house. "Come on."

"This should be quick. Let's just wait out here."

Mike's broad shoulders slumped ever so slightly. He looked up at her with an endearing smile. For a second, she remembered her attraction. He requested, "Really? Ashley, you're *that* worried about me?"

Ashley insisted, "No, it's not that. I just..."

"Let's go inside." Mike motioned for her to follow as he walked toward the house. "It's cold out here."

The dense front door popped open. The house looked more like a museum, like no one had lived there for years, and the home had been perfectly maintained by a curator. Mike led Ashley into his study. He walked behind a small bar area.

"A drink?" He asked.

"I'm driving. Can't," Ashley said. She smiled politely. Her cheeks formed a delicate grin.

"Just one?" He poured a very tall glass of scotch for himself. He plopped three square ice cubes into the glass. For a moment, he focused on Ashley's face. She was the most beautiful woman he had ever seen. He hadn't been this close to her in months. He felt the unfamiliar sting of unfulfilled desire.

"No," Ashley insisted. Her slender, yet gracefully curved frame clashed with the clunky, leather chair upon which she sat. "I don't need anything."

He swirled his glass. "You know, they say you're not supposed to drink scotch this good with ice, but I don't care. I like my drinks cold. To hell with them." He took a large gulp that enveloped almost half of the liquor in the glass.

"Easy, Mike," Ashley said. She sat on the edge of the lounge chair. She checked her watch.

"Easy?" He asked.

They sat in silence for a few moments. Ashley looked straight ahead. The television chattered in the next room. Mike's phone buzzed to life on the mahogany bar.

Mike lifted his iPhone. He took another sip of his drink and laid it down next to his iPad. His 70-inch television glowed in the adjacent room. He said, "All these devices now. All these ads and marketing. You can't escape it anymore. It's everywhere. P and L statements, thousands and thousands of compound simulations are happening every day. I get two hundred emails a day. *Two hundred.* Screens everywhere. A bunch of screens that promise us more speed and efficiency at work. Then I go home to more screens, more tentacles grabbing for every ounce of independent thought that I have left. It's all a dream, created by this layer of screens that reaches out and tangles us with noise, like the tentacles of some giant monster. It wraps around us, suffocates and ensnares us until we can't think for ourselves anymore. I'm tired of screens." He gazed into his glass of scotch as he shook his head.

Ashley changed the subject. "How are you doing?" Her left eyebrow was uncharacteristically raised with concern. She spoke with monotone caution.

"What do you care?" Mike snapped. "What does it matter?"

"I still care about you, Mike. I'm worried about you. Lots of people are," she explained.

"Lots of people are worried?" Mike chuckled. "*About me?*"

"Ophelia has always been..." Ashley hesitated. She saw Mike's reaction to his former wife's name.

"Don't you talk about my wife. It isn't any..." Mike was interrupted by a dull thumping sound.

The front door popped open and Tanji's voice echoed through the halls. "Hello? Is anybody here?"

Ashley bounced to her feet and headed for the front door. The thump of her heels resonated through the cavernous home.

In his left hand, Tanji held the familiar blue folder labeled, "Blake Treatment Center." To Ashley, it seemed to glow like some sort of Holy Grail.

"Let's step outside." Mike flipped on the rear floodlights. "It's hot in here."

They walked outside. A narrow lap pool stood at the top of crested land in the middle of the back yard. Ornate stone benches and walkways framed the empty pool. Bare plots of rectangular dirt hinted at elaborate landscaping, which had been shut down for the winter. Slivers of a dense forest divided the estate from its neighbors. Tall trees framed the land. Branches divided, twisted and reached for the sky. A few remaining leaves clung to the skinnier fingers of the trees. Everything about Mike's residence seemed to be withering and siphoning from the rest of the world.

Ashley thought, "This place is dead."

Ashley, Tanji and Mike Landis sat at a solitary set of patio furniture. It stood at the top of the rise in the back yard that descended to the shore of Lake Michigan. Tanji slid the blue folder over to Mike. As he quickly skimmed the pages, Ashley told him everything. She told him about the results, the Blake Center, and its patients. She told him about her vision. Mike listened as he drank the last of his scotch. He tossed the folder onto the patio table as if it were a newspaper from last month.

"Tanji, you agree?" Mike asked. "You think this could be a revolution in cancer treatment?"

"It's incredibly promising. I've never seen anything like it," Tanji said. He spoke slowly. He chose his words carefully. "The man is a visionary and somehow we were lucky enough that he came to us. I believe this treatment could potentially reverse cancer in most patients, but we need the full resources of Plaxin before we know for sure. The results are still very preliminary."

Mike stood up and looked out at the unusually tranquil surface of Lake Michigan. He laughed. Ashley and Tanji both stood up. They took a couple steps back. Mike's right arm began to tremble slightly. He took one last sip of scotch, and he threw the empty glass into the woods. It bounced a couple times then shattered. Tanji and Ashley both took another step backwards, rethinking their decision to tell him at his home, at night.

Mike turned and looked at his guests. His eyes were bloodshot. He looked up at a window in the attic. "She used to spend all her time up there. Ophelia did. My wife did." He pointed. "Drinking. From morning till night some days, she just drank. Maybe she wrote a little. I'm not sure, but she was in a prison. It was my fault."

"Mike," Ashley said.

"How did it get to this point? How could it have gotten this far? There had to be signs along the way. What's wrong with me?" He asked.

Tanji said, "Mike." He reached his slender hand out to Mike.

"Yeah?" Mike asked. His drooping eyes temporarily perked up.

"The Blake Center. This is the direction we want to go," Tanji bravely said. "We feel that we can test and perhaps patent the Blake treatment. We believe that we can work together with him. A partnership."

Mike asked, "Who's been working on this so far?" He returned to the conversation at hand.

"Just the two of us," Ashley replied. "No one else knows, as of now."

"Mike, we need to do this," Tanji said.

Mike laughed and shook his head. His distant eyes returned. He came closer, his intense energy refocused. "You both think this should be the new direction of the company?"

"Yes," Ashley stated.

"Tanji?" Mike asked.

Tanji answered, "I think so."

"Have you both lost your fucking minds?" Mike threw a chair off the patio. It tumbled down the hill. "What are we going to patent? You realize this company needs patents to survive? Without patents, we have nothing!"

"We're definitely not sure about approval," Ashley said. Her voice grew louder. She didn't back down. "But we believe that a co-branding with Blake, and testing with us will create cancer centers that could expand throughout the world. Even without the patents, this could be our future."

Mike yelled, "That's not what we do!"

"But we could," Ashley insisted, "It's still about testing, research and development, which is exactly what we do."

Mike whirled toward her. "Our cancer drugs account for about half of our revenue. What you two are proposing, if it works, would effectively kill that revenue stream. And your proposal is to replace that with a treatment that you're not even sure we can patent?"

Tanji insisted, "It's not that..."

"What you two are proposing is to gut this company," Mike announced, as if the empty backyard were filled with shareholders. He raised his arms into the air. His thick arms flexed with anger.

"Listen," Ashley said.

"From the inside!" Mike continued. "You're messengers of death. Here to destroy our business, to destroy the careers of honest, hardworking people."

Ashley rose to her feet. She walked toward Mike. She argued, "Don't play that saving jobs line. It's bullshit, Mike! Innovation saves jobs, not clinging to a dying treatment."

Mike continued, "You will gut this company from the inside out."

"We're not gutting anything!" Ashley yelled. "Our chemo drug was dead anyway. Sales are falling. Its days are numbered."

"It's still the top-selling cancer drug in the world," Mike answered.

"Not for long," Ashley said.

"So you think." Mike's head twisted with disgust. "Many people have promised the next great cure for cancer. They've all been wrong, and so will you."

"You're wrong. This place is different, and we can help him," Ashley said. She took a step closer to Mike. "His treatment is better.

There's no debate here. Cancer treatment has to be personalized, using a combination of methods. Why can't you believe that? This is the future, whether you buy into it or not."

"It isn't. You have a treatment that's untested. And utterly fucking unpatentable! What are you two thinking? Have you lost your minds?" Mike pleaded.

Ashley stepped in front of Tanji, who seemed to be in shock about the entire exchange. She said, "Don't talk to us like that."

"You're at my house," Mike walked closer to them. He wobbled slightly. The effects of the scotch appeared to be taking hold. "I'll talk to you however I want."

"We're not going to sit here and let you treat us like this." Ashley stood her ground as the beast of a man approached.

"I'll tell you this," Mike said. His eyes began to glaze over. "As long as I run this company, this is going nowhere. Nowhere." He spoke with repressed rage. "You're going to tear this company apart."

"We're not going to stop," Tanji said.

"You do whatever you want," Mike waved at Tanji. He planted his feet wider in an effort to stop swaying. It worked. "But I can assure you, this Blake thing is going nowhere, as long as I'm here."

"Mike. This is the answer. We've been searching for this for decades. Now that it's right in front of us, you want to deny it?" Ashley asked.

"It's a dead end," he said, cutting her off.

Tanji laid the blue folder on the patio table. "We'll leave this with you."

"Don't. I don't fucking want it," Mike bellowed. "Take your hippie crystal and incense doctor with you."

"You should take a look at this," Ashley insisted, pointing to the folder.

Mike walked up to her. They stood within a couple feet. He pointed at her and whispered, "You should be careful."

"Excuse me?" Ashley asked. She grabbed the folder off the table.

Mike's eyebrows rose as he said, "What you're trying to do. This can be a very dangerous road. Watch out." He chuckled. It was a disturbing chuckle. A slight laugh on the surface that showed signs of torment underneath.

Tanji tried to pull Ashley away. She ripped her arm out of his grip and looked Mike in the eyes. "Is that a threat?" She asked.

"For everyone involved, I think you should forget about this road," Mike explained. "Turn around."

Ashley stated, "I think we're done here." She motioned to Tanji.

"Yeah, you're definitely done here, Ashley. Done with me. Done with everything. You're done," Mike yelled. Tanji and Ashley quickly marched around the house. "Done!"

They got in their cars and sped away.

CHAPTER FOURTEEN

As winter drew near, Andy Stone continued to serve drinks in Lincoln Park as his primary income, working at a neighborhood restaurant across from the Lincoln Park Zoo. It attracted suburbanites to the bar stools during the summer months and holidays. They would sip Blue Moon and muse about the old days living on the North Side before they succumbed to the land of Applebees and Pier One Imports. During the slow times, he would fill martini glasses and serve oversized burgers in woven baskets to the locals who lived in the lakeshore high-rises. They would discuss Obama, their jobs, and why they never wanted children.

"Hey, bro," Andy's friend, Jake, grabbed his shoulder. "Saw your story in the *Tribune*. Nice work." Andy was closing up the bar. It was the night before Thanksgiving.

"Thanks, man," Andy said with a modest smile.

Jake insisted, "It's impressive. I'm kind of surprised you still work here."

"Stories like that don't pay the bills alone," Andy explained.

"You working on anything else right now?"

"I am," Andy answered. "I'm sitting on the biggest story of my life, but I can't do anything yet."

"Why not?"

"I need permission to write the story, from the *subject* of the story," Andy said slightly cryptically. "It's driving me crazy. I've never put in so much work researching for something that I had to wait to tell. I'm handcuffed right now. It's a story that could change my career. But for now, I'm just a bartender. Just a guy who writes the occasional feature story." Andy shook his head. He thought about the Blake Center as he counted singles in his drawer.

The restaurant was packed earlier in the evening. It was an easy place to work. He made steady money and got out early. Andy walked with his cash drawer and a wobbly garbage can downstairs. Attractive younger ladies who were moonlighting as servers – when not teaching or doing something closer to their college majors – counted cash and sorted through thin white receipts in the office. Short, chubby Mexican kitchen

167

guys rushed into the dry storage room, breezing by with blue towels and plastic containers. There was something pleasant about this ritual, something reassuring, even if it did drive Andy crazy to still be bartending. "What else do you do?" Patrons would often ask, implying that this career wasn't enough. The question cut into him. He had spent the last six months researching the Blake Center. He now thoroughly understood the treatment from its inception to its current state. Andy understood the potential implications of the story. He also respected Richard Blake's demand that he only do the story when the time was right. So Andy was stuck in a holding pattern, waiting for clearance to land. Waiting was always the toughest part. He found himself back in the space of uncertainty, wondering if the most important story of his life would ever reach an audience.

He was out by ten on this November evening. He walked out of the revolving doors and felt a shocking blast of cold wind that tunneled through the vaulted condo buildings. The stop signs rattled back and forth in the wind. As Andy forgot where he had parked on Clark Street, he looked around and appeared momentarily lost. Taxis slowed as drivers watched him and tapped their horns in solicitation.

As he angled onto the Kennedy Expressway toward Rockford from North Avenue, his phone hummed and glowed to life. He didn't recognize the number.

"Andy?" A woman's voice clearly enunciated on the other end.

"Yeah, hi." Andy spoke bluntly.

"It's Emma." These words took his breath away. His chest froze, and he almost swerved into a car speeding past on his left.

"Emma?"

Her voice softened. "You remember, don't you? From the bar."

"Of course I remember. I just can't believe I'm talking to you," Andy insisted. An ocean of latent emotions rushed to the surface.

Emma asked, "What do you mean?"

"I thought I blew my chance. What happened?"

"I finally read your email, about your move and your mom. I'm so sorry."

"You did?"

"Yes."

Andy asked, "But I don't understand, why call me now?"

"Well, I just got a little scared when you got my email, and work number."

"It was just a Google search. I didn't mean to scare you. I lost your number on the flight home. With my mom and everything. I guess that could have been seen as coming on too strong." His words rambled on with horribly masked excitement.

Emma explained, "There was something else. I might have been dating someone when I met you. Nothing serious. In fact, I never really liked him, but it just didn't feel right to call you behind his back."

"I thought we had a pretty strong connection that night, was I imagining that?"

A long pause. "No. It wasn't just your imagination." Emma opened up and her voice shuddered, "You were just a little intimidating. I mean, you're bartending and all of those girls are around, talking to you. It's hard to believe you would want any long distance...interests."

"I've never met anyone like you at my bar, believe me."

Emma asked, "Why didn't you tell me you were moving?" He could tell this question had been lingering in her mind for a long time.

Andy said, "I don't know. I didn't want to scare you. I was dealing with some pretty heavy stuff during that time."

"How's she doing now?"

"She's okay," Andy said. His voice deflated as he continued, "She had a bad fall recently. She's kind of been stuck in bed lately. But her mind is still sharp. Her heart is strong. Cancer can't get to her heart."

Emma said, "The reason why I'm calling you is that I have a meeting in Chicago in three weeks. I was wondering if you wanted to hang out. Maybe you could show me your city."

"Three weeks?" Andy asked.

"Yes."

"That sounds absolutely great. Awesome. I can't wait." He tried to act calm. "I'm sorry. I'm still just a little shocked that I'm talking to you."

"I know."

They talked for an hour, all the way to the edge of Rockford. When they finally said goodbye, he checked his cell phone four times to make sure the call had ended, and then yelled with excitement at the road in front of him. Two women in a green Toyota laughed at this display as they passed.

But the next sight sent a chill down Andy's spine. On the exit around Rockford, emergency lights illuminated the adjacent neighborhoods. A semi had pulled to the side, and an SUV was on its side in the middle of the road. Black and metallic shrapnel and chunks of the bumper created a wake behind the vehicle, evidence of a violent crash. Someone was dead. Andy could feel it, and the feeling jolted him. He imagined someone casually driving on the highway, perhaps someone just like him was taking a mundane exit one moment, then they were gone.

A friend once talked to Andy only months after losing his father to a heart attack. He felt a strong desire to see his dad's body right after he had passed. He believed this viewing would provide a powerful sense of closure. There would be no room for delusion or denial. There his father would rest, dead on the table. Andy's friend imagined that the realization of death would come instantly – like a light switch flipping off. The cold touch of his father's hand would help him to fully understand.

But his actual experience was much different. In the days and months that followed, he still felt like his father was alive, somewhere. Of course, on the surface he knew that he was gone, but somewhere in his vast spectrum of awareness he had been living with his father's energy for so long. This feeling didn't just vanish. Something deep within took much longer to accept death than did his eyes as they gazed upon a pale corpse, or his hands as they touched cold skin. His friend compared the feeling to recent amputees who still felt an itching sensation on their now-missing appendage. Of course, they knew the arm was gone, but a part of their awareness wasn't ready to let it go.

Jamie sat at the desktop computer in the Stone family's former office, which had become his mother's permanent residence. She was still sleeping behind him. It was early. The neighborhood was quiet. Snowflakes meandered from murky clouds above down to the cold, wet grass outside. It was the morning of Thanksgiving. He sat at their desk and stared into a computer screen. His mother rustled behind him. He looked at her from the corner of his eyes. She was disoriented. She slowly awoke from a rough night. She was experiencing a growing pain in her abdomen. She was coughing regularly. She was also dealing with a host of infections in her mouth and throat. Eating and drinking became painful. It was a cruel symptom on Thanksgiving. Jamie shut off the computer and turned to his mother. He lifted his legs onto the bed and scratched their dog's insistent head. Jamie's mother reached for a ring that was resting on a high heel ring holder. The inside of the shoe had rows of foamy cloth and little slivers where various rings were placed. She wiggled her arms and legs. Jamie watched as his mother seemed to be assessing her own symptoms and level of pain. She opened a drawer on her bedside table, pulled out two medicine bottles out of the twenty that rattled in the drawer, and popped a couple pills into her mouth. She slowly rocked up to a sitting position.

"Happy Thanksgiving," Jamie said. His voice was steady and cautious.

His mother smiled. "You too, sweetie."

"Dad sounds energetic," Jamie said, pointing to the ceiling. Above them, the steady drumbeat of footsteps made the house crack and flex.

"Is that another Dylan album?" Jamie asked.

His mother nodded. She did her impression of Bob Dylan. She bellowed out several sarcastic "eehs" and "aays" in an unintelligible garble of rising, wheezing sounds. Her joke made Jamie feel better about her current state.

She reached down to the port in her chest. A small plastic piece shaped like the top of an oversized pen dug under her skin. A short clear tube ran up to her wrist where it divided into two receptors for intravenous fluids. A long cord was clamped onto one of the receptors. Her intestines were not functioning properly. This was one of the reasons for her adverse reactions to supplements. For months, she had been receiving total parenteral nutrition, also known as TPN, which was a bag of highly concentrated nutrients pumped directly into her bloodstream through the port every night. Jamie rushed over to her side. He pulled the blue medical backpack out from under the bed. It contained the TPN bag and a small, powerful pump. He shut off the pump. A clear cord connected the empty bag to the pump.

"Are you ready?" His mother asked him. She expertly twisted apart the tube from her port. She impatiently held out her hand, waiting for her son to grab her medical supplies. Jamie rushed to keep up with his mother's expert hands. Even in her weakened state, almost completely bed-ridden, she could perform medical tasks common to nursing.

"Am I ready for today?" Jamie asked, sarcastically. "It's just Thanksgiving. I think I'll be okay." He grabbed rubber gloves, sterile alcohol pads, and clamps.

"For your opening." His mother slapped him on the head with a pair of rubber gloves.

Jamie laughed and asked, "What?"

His mother said, "For your big show. The day you unveil your beautiful creations for the entire world to see. This weekend."

"Yeah. I'm ready. I've made more than I ever dreamed I could. I'm ready."

His mother grabbed a sterile pad and wiped her fingers. She looked down at her frail hands as if she didn't recognize them anymore. She asked, "Do you have buyers yet? Commissions?" She checked the TPN bag. It was empty. She had been pumped full of concentrated nutrition for another night.

"Nothing yet," Jamie calmly stated. He held out another sterile pad as his mother twisted the plastic lock that connected the thin, clear tube between the bag of nutrition and her port. Jamie explained, "We're telling any potential buyers or dealers to wait for the show."

"We?" His mother asked with rising curiosity. She expertly unhooked the long cord. Jamie grabbed it from her and carefully wrapped it around the blue bag that contained the pump. He zipped up the bag and slid it underneath the bed.

Jamie explained, "I'm finally working with an agent. She's been great. Helping me sell the pieces more."

"It's never been your strong point," his mother said with candor.

Jamie agreed, "I know. And I'm tired of fighting that. So, yeah, basically my agent is taking care of all of the business. From what I can tell, there's a lot of interest. Which is good, because I'm running out of money."

"Do you need some help?"

"I'll be okay. I just need to sell some pieces."

Jamie's mother kept her eyes locked on the port as she told her son, "I'm not sure I'll be able to make it to your show." Her squeaky voice cracked with emotion. "I really wanted to make it, Jamie."

"It's okay, Mom," Jamie looked over at the porch where his new sculptures hung in clear sight of his mother's bed. "That's why I put in the installation on the porch for you guys."

His mother held a sterile alcohol pad up to her face.

"No booze yet, Mom," Jamie joked.

"Your dad doesn't like me changing the TPN bags on my own anymore, but I love it. The sound of the rubber gloves, the smell of rubbing alcohol, the dull sound of the fluid pump. It reminds me of nursing, of working in hospice. I miss it. I wish I could still do it." Her voice broke up. As she dropped the used medical supplies into the garbage, a thin stream of tears ran down her cheek. She said, "I'm sorry."

"For what?"

"For this." She pointed to her body, as if she were apologizing for crashing an old car. "For causing our family so much pain."

She cried.

Jamie Stone searched his heart for the right words. The ones that would appease her, that would assure her that her guilt was misguided, that she should never blame herself for such a terrible affliction. But he could feel that this emotion lived in the deep caverns of her awareness, in a part of herself that few were allowed to see. He could find no words that mattered, or aptly expressed such unwavering love from a son.

He held her head next to his. He held her and prayed with all of his energy that she could find the courage to forgive herself, and come to the understanding that cancer was not her fault. She had been the most wonderful mother in the world. She stood suspended in his eyes, as a beautiful image of the kind of person he wanted to be.

"There's nothing to be sorry about, Mom."

Mya, Andy and their father eventually descended from the bedrooms upstairs. Andy and Jamie sat with their mother and devised a cooking plan. Their mother directed the cooking from her bed. She assured them that she would be able to get out to the kitchen in a little bit. Relatives began to filter into the house. An hour later, the house was jammed with family and friends, and others who had no other option for the holiday. Shrimp appetizers, platters of cheese, mediocre wine covered the dining room table. Their mother never made it to the kitchen to cook. Dirty dishes steadily rose next to the kitchen sink. When it was finally time to eat, Jamie plopped his mother into a wheelchair and pulled her up to the main table. She didn't speak much, only rarely forcing a slight smile. Halfway through the meal, she requested to go back to bed.

After dinner, the older generation beached on the couches and sipped coffee. Plates clanked in the kitchen. Jamie, Andy and their father put up Christmas lights on the four-story pine tree in the front yard. A friend of their father's joined them with his cherry picker. The brothers lined up long strands of colored LED lights across the front yard and followed the cherry picker around the tree.

After an hour of casual labor, the brothers stood with their father on the street. They basked in the successful lighting of a tree sure to be seen for miles. The cherry picker rumbled up the hill.

"I'm going to help with the garbage," their father said. He walked into the garage.

"We might have overdone it this year," Jamie noted.

"That's a lot of lights," Andy agreed.

"We should turn them off."

Andy asked, "You don't think we should leave them on tonight? Kind of festive?"

Jamie explained, "It's too bright for Mom and Dad to sleep. I'm going inside."

Andy stood in the front yard alone. Small flecks of white fell from the dark sky above. He walked out to the street and looked at the bulging evergreen. It was losing branches on the back, but the tree was still massive. He walked over to the silver electrical box next to the house, pulled out two green extension cords, and the outside world went black. He looked into his parents' converted bedroom and saw his mom propped up by a complex system of pillows. Her gaze startled him. She appeared to be looking right at him. But as he took a few steps back into the darkness, he realized that she was lost in her thoughts. Andy stood in the silent front yard, staring nakedly at his unsuspecting mother. He watched her take steady, slow breaths. She increasingly jolted and shifted with uncontrollable expressions of pain. Something was wrong.

Andy rushed inside. "Something's wrong with Mom," he announced to his family in the living room and kitchen. People rushed into the converted bedroom to find Andy's mother on her side, moaning. Andy's father didn't hesitate. He directed various orders to certain family members. Get the car warmed up, put blankets in the back seat, take care of the dogs.

"Can you get her overnight bag?" Andy's father asked him. Andy ran upstairs and grabbed the red leather bag that he had grown to hate. It always meant his mother was headed back to the emergency room.

They rushed her to the hospital. She spent two hours in the emergency room. She was too weak for any surgery. Her abdominal pain was diagnosed as severe acid reflux. After she got comfortable in yet another hospital room, Andy reached into his computer bag and pulled out a touch screen computer, similar to an iPad. "The newest thing for Blake," Andy tapped a password into the touch screen. "He's trying it out with us and a handful of other patients."

Andy's father asked, "What does it do? Scan her body or something?"

"No. Give me a second." The tablet booted up and started an application called "Diagnostics."

After a couple of phone calls and some hospital wireless difficulties, the doctor's voice echoed through the room, "Hello, Stone family." Andy held the small screen facing the room. Richard Blake's face filled the screen. He was wearing rectangular glasses and a tattered blue t-shirt.

"How do you do that?" Andy's father asked. He was baffled.

"This is a video chat, Dad. It's a way to meet with Doctor Blake even when we can't physically meet with him. See this panel over here." Andy pointed to a complex column of graphs and spaces. "Eventually, we'll be able to scan everything into this tablet, and the doctor can see it on the other side. X-rays, charts, you name it. The doctor also records these chats. He'll have a video record of all of these meetings with his patients," Andy explained to his father, whose eyes began to glaze over with more technical information than he was ready to absorb.

"It's darn close to me being there. About as close as we can get." The sound of the doctor's voice made everyone relax. Andy's mother was in a deep sleep.

"Also, when families are forced to go to the emergency room away from Doctor Blake, he can check on his patients," Andy explained. His hand began to tremble as he held up the tablet displaying the doctor's face. He switched hands and shook out his tired left arm. "He can be there as an active participant."

"How's she doing?" Blake asked. Andy held the tablet over his mother. Blake assessed his patient. Andy's father told him everything they were doing. He grabbed the chart from outside of the room. Blake read the diagnosis.

After a long, careful examination from the screen of a tablet computer, Blake seemed satisfied with his patient's situation. "She can rest for now. They've done everything they should have." As always, he expressed his unique ability to be realistic and hopeful.

Blake said, "Well, I guess I'll let you guys get some sleep."

"Actually," Andy interrupted. "Can we talk for a second?"

"Sure," Blake answered.

Andy walked down the hall to a vacant waiting room. Black metal chairs surrounded a central circle of couches. Vending machines glowed near the front of the room. The world outside of the windows was pale and dark. The snow had stopped. A murky gray haze descended upon the landscape. Andy looked back down at the face of Richard Blake on the touch screen.

"What's up, Andy?"

As much as he wanted to, he resisted the urge to press the doctor about the story. He asked, "How are you doing? Have there been any more...threats?"

Blake rustled and lifted his tablet. He hastily carried it onto his back porch. "Careful. I don't want my wife to hear about any of that."

"Sorry."

"I don't know. I keep getting calls," Blake said. "They seem to be dying down a bit. I know you're wondering when you can do the story, but it's not time, not yet..."

"Okay, I just..."

"What was that?" Blake asked. He looked up above the computer into his yard.

"What?" Andy asked.

"Something outside here."

Doctor Blake turned his tablet away from his face. He used it like a flashlight. It illuminated a limited area of his vast, wooded back yard. Another crack of a stick made the doctor jolt. Even though Andy stood in the safety of a hospital waiting room, he remained silent and still. He watched the stagnant wooded scene in front of him. On the screen, he saw a dark forest. He could see the condensation from Blake's quickening breaths billow across the screen.

Andy heard dry leaves rustle. The doctor walked closer to the woods. He called, "Hello?"

Andy whispered, "Get out of there. What are you doing?"

"Shh," Blake insisted. He whipped the glowing screen around toward the house. Nothing. Andy was displayed on the screen, watching the same thing Blake was. Leaves dragged again as Blake quickly walked around one side of the house. A mother deer and her doe jolted at the sight of him. Andy yelled in the waiting room. The deer bounded into the dark forest.

"Just a deer," Blake said with a deep sigh.

Andy said, "Holy crap."

"Get some sleep. We'll talk about the story more when I come to see you guys."

"When are you coming down here?" Andy asked.

"Early next week," the doctor responded as he waved. "I'll talk to you then." The screen went black.

Andy returned to the hospital room and tried to sleep. He watched his mother, and his heart burned with energy. His heart was a finite space.

His capacity to love was a barometer for his condition. His heart was filled with a wealth of friends and family. Some connections intensified with time; others faded. Deep in the center of this space was his mother. He felt great energy and emotion in his chest whenever he looked at his mother now. As she gave him unwavering love, he was able to give love and receive it from others. He could feel that great expanse in his heart, so deeply cultivated by his mother, quietly receding like a falling evening tide. His mother was his heart. If she were to die, the core of his heart would be ripped out of him. Andy could never fully quantify or articulate this pain. His connection to his mother felt tenuous now. He held onto the hope that she could survive another harsh winter because, without his mother, he didn't know what he would do.

The next day Andy's mother was discharged from the hospital. There were no plans for surgery, no battle plan for recovery. She wasn't going to see Jamie's opening at the famed SOFA show this weekend. Family and friends continued to stay with her. Andy's mother agreed to home health care. Only five years ago, she was the nurse coming into the homes of terminal patients as they transitioned out of life. She resisted hospice because she knew what it meant. But this time she didn't fight it. She accepted the suggestion for hospice care, as tears fell from her hardened hazel eyes.

CHAPTER FIFTEEN

Jamie Stone lifted the two layers of down blankets that were wedged between himself and Mya. She was turned away from him, naked. She always slept naked. He reached his hands along her rounded hips and over to her tight stomach. He pulled his cool body against her warm back. She moaned. He began to move her body toward him and away, toward and away.

"What are you doing?" She requested with a drowsy grin. "Didn't you have your way with me last night?" The evening rushed back to him. A little work at the studio, dinner with friends, and drinks at a local dive. Later in the night, Jamie grabbed Mya and told him they needed to leave. His passion was intoxicating to her. He took her home, stripped off her clothes, and spent hours under the covers.

"I did, but I just thought..." He trailed off as he grabbed her waist again.

"Jamie Stone," Mya said like a disapproving mother. "I want to sleep. I love you."

"I love you too. I can't sleep. I've been staring at the ceiling for an hour."

"What time is it?" She asked.

Jamie checked his watch on the side table. "Early."

"Are you excited?" She asked with a sensual moan.

"Yeah. Can't sleep," Jamie answered, as he threw off the covers. "I might go to the studio."

She looked up at him with her warm, light brown eyes. Her thick brown curls splayed across beige pillowcases.

Jamie stood up. He looked back down at his lovely Argentinean girlfriend. "This is the biggest day of my life as an artist. What if it doesn't go well? What if I don't sell anything? All this work."

Mya grabbed his chin and directed a calming, grounding smile at him.

"You're right," Jamie replied to her smile. "I might go to the studio." He jumped up. "I'm also just worried."

"About your mom," Mya wisely said.

"Yeah." Jamie threw an old hoodie over his head. His thick abdominal muscles flexed from the motion. "I feel like I should be there right now."

"You've been planning for this show for a year. You know how terrible your mother would feel if you missed it."

"You're right." Jamie nodded. He wrapped his black leather watch around his thick wrist. He pulled on some green fatigue-like pants with more pockets than anyone would ever need. Jamie kissed Mya and asked, "No chance for morning sex?"

"No. Get out of here. You'll feel better after you go to the studio. Everything's gonna be fine."

"Love you. I'll be back before I head over to the show."

The city was still quiet. A group of people staggered along the street. They were formally dressed, obviously wrapping up a very late night; ties were draped over wrinkled dress shirts; short skirts were stretched over chilly knees. Jamie popped the door open to the studio. He walked over to his empty storage space. Everything was ready for SOFA. It was opening day. And there was something freeing and wonderful about being done with the series of sculptures. He felt unbridled. But there was something else. There was a growing fear that he was losing that well of creation that had been bubbling up for the last months. He didn't feel the same.

Jamie Stone plugged his music player into a stereo. Mellow hip-hop thumped throughout the empty studio. It was his morning mix. He grabbed a cool metal blow rod. It felt familiar in his hands. Other blow rods clanked together. Vents hummed above him. Sparks rose as he rolled orbs of glass back and forth, shaping them with wooden molds that looked like a cup sliced in half and attached to a handle. The glass contorted to the force of his grasp. For the first time in months, his hands weren't sore.

Jamie spent hours dipping blow rods into molten glass. He heated some orbs until they drooped and spilled onto a heated steel sheet. The streaming glass curved and stretched. Some of it cracked; some of the shapes showed promise. For the first time in almost a year, Jamie was unbridled by preconceived forms. He had no piece to finish or refined technique to follow. Ironically, after the seed of profound creation, he had to be quite methodical and disciplined. He watched how the glass reacted as he clipped it with metal sheers. He examined the breaking points when he let streams of molten glass spill to the floor. He felt a distant, yet rising pressure to come up with his next series.

Other artists entered and exited with some last-minute pieces for the big show. Every time they walked into the studio, Jamie felt a wave of tension. He was tired of people watching him work. Two kinds of people visited Jamie during his creative months. People visited who respected his equilibrium and sought to watch with appreciation and support. Then there were those who desired to take some of his well of internal energy. Jamie became hypersensitive to the people who entered his space. Some were welcome to stay for hours. Others were asked to leave from the moment they let out a seemingly innocuous, "Hello." Jamie knew the difference.

It was a subtle technique of staying in the space of creation, the delicate balance within, where Jamie stood bravely at the center of uncertainty, accepting all that came his way. Some people wanted to knock him off this equilibrium and take something for themselves. He didn't know exactly what they were looking to take from him, but he could feel this phenomenon. It was the same thing his mom felt when she went out in public. The deeper he got into the beautiful act of creation, the more people wanted to invade his energy.

Jamie cringed whenever anyone wanted to ask questions about his work. What it meant, what it symbolized, what he was feeling when he was making it. Any summary was mental and mechanical. The crude words could never encompass the arc of experience and emotion that went into each piece. Every time he answered questions about his art or his intensive work over the past six months, he felt like a little piece of him was being splintered off and was lost. Just as Native Americans were rumored to feel that a portion of their soul was divided up every time someone took a picture of them.

But today everyone left Jamie to his work. He felt revived. Mya was right. The front door popped open once again at 9:30 in the morning. Jamie had been playing with glass for three hours.

"There he is." The studio owner pointed to Jamie.

Jamie stopped twisting a small, orange ball of malleable glass. "You're looking for me?" He studied the man in front of him. He had long curly hair. He wore jeans and a sweatshirt. His brown curls fell down over rectangular glasses.

The strange man answered, "Yes. I tried to call you. Talked to a nice lady named Mya. She told me I could find you here."

"What happened? Did something happen to my space? My sculptures?"

"No, no. Nothing like that. My name is Marcell." Jamie noticed his thick Italian accent. Italy was the home of modern glassblowing. It was the birthplace of many of the most prominent glassblowers of the last century. An Italian accent alone could almost launch a glassblower into prominence. He had Jamie's full attention. "I got a chance to check out your work late last night. So did Giovani."

Marcell sat down in the metal-framed chair next to Jamie's workspace. He motioned for Jamie to keep working. Jamie lifted his protective sunglasses and said, "You can't be talking about Giovani Tomba." Jamie caught a whiff of an exotic, understated spice of cologne. He smelled the way Jamie imagined an Italian man should smell.

"Yes."

"Giovani checked out *my* work?" Jamie asked. He was shaking his head in disbelief.

"I work for Mr. Tomba. I'm his manager and one of his glass assistants. Yes, he was very impressed. He said you were doing some of the most inspired work he has seen in a long time."

Jamie stopped rotating the blow rod. He tilted his head and gave this strange man a close look. "Are you messing with me right now?"

"No." Marcell laughed. "That's why I was looking for you this morning. One of our current apprentices will be leaving in the summer. We saw your work, and we would like to offer you an apprenticeship."

"Giovani Tomba wants to offer me an apprenticeship?" Jamie stood up. The blow rod dramatically fell to the ground.

"I assume you understand what that means, how few are offered the position, and who has taken this prestigious position in the past."

"In Italy?" Jamie asked.

"Yes, he lives in Italy," Marcell said.

"Are you kidding me?" Jamie asked. His upper body trembled a little as his eyes scanned the rafters. Questions flooded his mind. "Why this morning? Why did you come out to my studio?"

"This weekend is a whirlwind for us, as I'm sure it is for you as well. Our schedules are already very busy for the next few days. And we really wanted to tell you. I know this is a big deal. I know it means great changes to your life. Once we choose to work with you, we are somewhat flexible about the time you come over. You can always refuse..." Marcell trailed off. He grabbed a blow rod. He continued, "No one has ever refused."

"I don't believe it." Jamie's chest quickly rose and fell. His fair-skinned forehead beaded up with sweat. "I can't believe it."

His energy shifted. He thought about the beautiful woman he left in bed earlier. "How long do these things last?"

"Depends. Some run as short as a year. Others work with him for almost five years."

"Italy," Jamie stated with apprehensive excitement.

"That's right, Jamie. Italy."

"It's a once in a lifetime opportunity."

"That's right," Marcell agreed.

"Wow."

"That's right." Marcell stood up and shook Jamie's outstretched hand. Jamie hugged him. "I'm sorry. I know I just met you, but I feel like I have to give you a hug."

"I understand. I was in your position too, a while ago. It's a good thing. It means you'll be able to do what you love for a long time."

Jamie shook his head. "Tomba."

Marcell explained, "Look, I know this is a big day for you. I know you've poured your heart and soul into those pieces. So I'll leave you alone. But please let us know by the end of the weekend." He handed him a folder. It had contact numbers, schedules and travel information. Clipped to the folder was a letter. It said congratulations. The acceptance was assumed. Jamie thought about Mya.

"Okay. I will." Jamie anxiously picked at the hardened wax on the workstation.

Marcell turned back and waved. "Good luck today. Stop by and see us."

"Thanks. I will."

After he left, Jamie pulled the tattered hood of his sweatshirt over his head and yelled into the fabric. He jumped up and down. He whispered, "One of the biggest artists in the world wants me to work for him." The statement would need to be repeated many times before it absorbed.

Jamie Stone walked into Navy Pier around noon. He wore a pressed black shirt. His sleeves were rolled up, showing his bulging forearms and strong, delicate hands. His hair was cut short and brushed toward the front. His face had a uniform beard of reddish scruff. His soft brown eyes gleamed. He wore gray dress pants with unconventional pockets. He looked like an artist. As he entered the convention hall, people looked. Jamie Stone walked with gravitational pull.

His agent requested that he arrive late. He was supposed to drop in and out, glad-handing like a grateful diplomat, letting his agent do all of the work.

Tall banners framed the broad entrance to the Navy Pier art show. The banner read, "Welcome to SOFA. Sculptures, Objects & Functional Art." The sprawling convention hall looked like it could easily shelter two of Boeing's largest aircraft. Steel girders spanned the vaulted ceilings. A thin blue carpet covered the floor. A sea of sectioned artist galleries and intricate track lighting arrangements stretched as far as Jamie could see in both directions. White walls connected and intersected creating a labyrinth of galleries and nooks for artists of all profiles and collections from the smallest to vast displays. Various pedestals, stepped tables, and modern shelving fixtures added to the depth of each gallery space. The steady hum of thousands of people was almost absorbed by the enormity of the space.

Jamie walked past the gallery of Giovani Tomba. Pictures flashed. Local television correspondents were illuminated by intense, pale lights emanating from television cameras. Women in professional suits held microphones up to their mouths, spoke into the cameras, and pointed at Tomba's gallery. The cameras looked like a firing squad about to blow up the legendary glassblower's ethereal shapes. Art students examined pieces and jotted down thoughts on notepads. One series of sculptures reached toward the ceiling with understated elegance. The stretched vases resembled the female figure bending and reaching to the sky. Jamie's chest fluttered as Giovani Tomba entered the gallery. His hands trembled. He wondered if he should talk to him, but a flood of fans, buyers and media descended upon the famed Italian artist before Jamie could approach him.

Jamie turned and headed away from the crowd. He couldn't take it anymore. He had to see his space. He darted through various galleries. He briefly stopped to see metallic sculptures of a dog and man with shockingly realistic features and intricate designs. The pieces looked ready to run off their pedestals and star in a futuristic movie. A ceramic sculptor stood by her curious pots. They were four feet high, perfectly symmetrical at their core. But they had been coated with reckless globs of clay that looked like acid had melted and eaten through these stunning pieces. Jamie gave the artist a nod of approval. In another gallery, pristine pyramids of vibrant blues and yellows jutted out of a rocky base. As he hastily scanned above the crowd for his gallery section, he bumped into a slight lady with a handful of flyers.

"I'm so sorry," Jamie said, reaching down and grabbing the flyers for her.

"Watch where you're going," she said with sass. Jamie let out a nervous chuckle.

He finally reached his gallery. His agent, Monica, stood talking to an older couple. They smiled as Monica pointed out some of the fine details of the sculptures. They were the only people in his area. That was it. His gaze drooped toward the floor. He slinked into his gallery. Fear rushed into his mind. A brief wave of insecurity joined the fear. He examined his pieces up close. He wondered if he was crazy. Was he any good?

"Jamie, could you come over here and talk to the Jacobsens?" Monica asked. Her black dreadlocks were neatly pulled back into a ponytail. She reached her hand out to Jamie. Monica stood next to the older couple. She was composed and confident. Her chestnut skin glowed, and her dark green eyes beamed today.

"Of course," Jamie answered.

"The Jacobsens were just talking to me about a commission piece," Monica explained. Her voice was bubbly. Her excitement didn't seem to match the empty gallery space.

"We love your work," the older man said. He must have been in his seventies. He was wearing a three-piece suit and matching hat. He stood propped up by a cane. His wife nodded emphatically. She reached for Jamie's hand and said, "You must be so excited. What a day!"

Jamie quietly replied, "Well, hopefully we can do all right..."

Monica cut him off. She said to Jamie, "The Jacobsens loved the three wall fixtures. The elongated blades that you so delicately and intricately produced. They were devastated to find out that all of them had already been sold this morning." Jamie's face fell motionless, frozen in an expressionless stupor. Another wave of onlookers walked into Jamie's gallery section. A large group of college students were directed to his pieces by an older man with a tweed jacket and brown elbow patches.

Monica continued, "They would like you to do a commission for them."

"We know it wouldn't be exactly the same, but we would like something similar. Of course, we're happy to give you some freedom too," Mr. Jacobsen explained. "But something along these lines would be stunning in our entryway."

Mrs. Jacobsen announced, "I just love it. Would you do this for us, Jamie Stone? We need to catch you before you're all booked up."

"I would love to," Jamie said. He was still in disbelief.

Monica took over. "Jamie enjoys commissions. He can make a fixture that still embodies the spirit of the original pieces, but is built with your home in mind."

"Great!"

Monica explained, "We can talk about the details on Monday. We only have one other commission right now."

"Another one?" Jamie quickly tried to do the math. All three of the blades of grass installations were sold. Two commissions. His mind wouldn't let his emotions rise to their desired levels.

"But you guys will be next in line." Monica hugged the jubilant Jacobsens.

Within minutes, Jamie's gallery space was full. A group of four older women with reading glasses and colorful sweaters examined his bulbous vessels along the south wall. The vessels had diagonal tiger stripes that stretched up to a very narrow neck that looked like the nose of a sailfish. They rose five feet into the air. Some of the necks twisted and curled. A row of twelve vessels lined the wall. Jamie couldn't believe how beautiful they looked in the gallery. Two bored children played on their hand-held video games and wandered dangerously close to the installations in the middle of the gallery space until their mother finally grabbed them. Four-foot-tall, sci-fi-looking pieces of frozen blades of grass jutted out from the wall. Silver clamps connected them. They spanned almost from the floor vertically above the heads of an expanding sea of interested faces. Their vibrant, bewildering depth of color had entranced a couple of the students taking notes. The north wall displayed a variety of abstract shapes. They shared similar designs as the other pieces, but they were a more complex combination of the elegant vessels on the south wall. Every sculpture possessed stunning grace and drama. They demanded the attention of most of the pedestrians sauntering by the gallery.

The Jacobsens waved to Jamie. "So nice to meet you."

"You too," Jamie said. His eyes were fixated on his agent.

Jamie grabbed Monica and nudged her over to the side. "Are you messing with me right now?"

"What?"

"You sold all three of the blades of grass installations?"

"Yeah." She scoffed. "In like an hour. The first one, I actually had two buyers almost get into a fight over it."

Jamie asked, "How much have you sold?"

"Ten pieces. Three commissions."

"Ten plus three commissions?"

Monica nodded with satisfaction. "Ten, but it gets better."

"What?"

"You were selected as one of the Best in Show. I think they just officially announced it." Monica looked around at the rapidly multiplying crowd. "That may be the reason why so many people are crowding into your gallery right now."

Jamie fell to the ground shaking his head. A group of older tourist-looking people with bags and cameras walked into Jamie's gallery. Monica nudged Jamie. "Get up. Get up." Monica motioned over to a television crew. They asked for an interview.

Monica mainly spoke. Jamie stood with a blissful smile. An audience gathered around the news camera. They looked like they came to SOFA together. They all had nametags and matching red folders. Their nametags read, "Iowa Art Collective."

More voice recorders emerged at the front of the crowd.

Jamie talked about his work. He looked into a sea of faces. *I just made three hundred thousand dollars.* He kept saying to himself. The crowd grew. People in the back stood on their toes to catch a glimpse of Jamie. Over to the corner, peeking up over two rows of onlookers, he saw Michael Donald trying to catch a glimpse of his former assistant. Jamie smiled and waved.

Michael mouthed the words, "Holy shit."

Jamie mouthed back, "I know." He shook his head. Adrenaline pulsed through his body. His hands throbbed with energy. His strong frame stood rigid in front of the cameras.

A question was finally directed at Jamie. "What were you thinking when you made these pieces?" For a moment, he paused and looked around the crowd.

Jamie looked up to the camera and said, "Glassblowing is a dance. It's a celebration of life, of the wild experience that is life. It's an intricate process of creation and focus over the course of many months, even years. My thoughts, the themes of this work could never be grouped into a nice little box. But I can tell you that every ounce of myself, of my passion and emotion is represented in each hardened final act of creation. I could never explain all of the themes that led to these shapes. But they're in clear view in the finished product."

After hours of interviews and discussions, his space finally fell almost silent. A young art student talked to Jamie. She was breathtaking, with a slender body and short, blond hair that framed her large oval eyes and thick lips.

Andy Stone walked in right when she was leaning suggestively forward. He had promised his brother he would make it to the show tonight, despite their mother's condition.

Jamie continued his discussion with the young lady. "This is an exchange of energy. All art is an exchange of energy."

"You're giving me your energy?" She reached for his arm.

Jamie answered, "That's the beauty of all art. It's the free exchange of raw emotion. You get to see and feel the deepest parts of myself. In these pieces, I give my heart and soul. Because the canvas, or the blank page, or the cask of molten glass is neutral, I can express the deepest places within, and no one can invade my energy. If I opened up to another person right now and nakedly expressed the deepest parts of myself, there's a risk that they will suck my energy. But not with art. All of the pieces in this convention hall are naked emotions, thoughts and feelings crystallized through a medium. Within these media, we can connect with the most intimate, personal parts of the artists themselves in an exchange of energy that is clean and beneficial to both sides. That's the beauty of art – the safe exchange of raw humanity without the issues of energetic manipulation that happen when people engage directly."

She said to Jamie, "The canvas is like a mediator." Her eyes were wide and bright. Jamie gazed deeply into them.

"Yes, it's the safety net," Jamie said. "Without it, I could never express such naked emotions without someone using these openings to suck my energy."

"I would never do that to you," she whispered to the newly successful artist.

"Brother!" Jamie exclaimed as he saw Andy checking out his abstract sculptures. Jamie looked back at the petite woman who was in the middle of throwing herself at him. "Listen, it was great to meet you. Stop by tomorrow and we can talk more."

Andy walked up to his brother. Jamie pointed to a SOFA ribbon near his artist sign. Andy exclaimed, "I heard!"

Jamie said, "I was voted one of the top in the show. At *SOFA*."

Andy looked around. His lanky frame matched some of his brother's slender sculptures. He meandered through the gallery with his skinny hands on his waist. Jamie followed his brother. Andy asked, "It's crazy around here. How much have you sold?"

Jamie laughed. He put his strong arm on his brother's shoulder. "You don't even want to know."

"How much?"

"So far, twelve pieces."

Andy looked at the price tag of one of the abstract sculptures. It almost looked like a single vessel that had divided in half – like a mutating blob of dynamic fluid. Intricate streams of magenta and bright green ran contiguously through the piece. He finally saw the selling price. "Are you kidding me? They're selling for this?" Andy scoffed. He shook his head. He looked down at the floor. "I need a drink," he said.

"Thanks for the support, brother," Jamie sarcastically replied. Monica calmly waved him over. "Crap, I need to talk to these people," Jamie said to his brother.

"That's fine. They sell beer over there, right?" Jealousy oozed through every syllable out of Andy's mouth.

After another discussion with yet another potential buyer, Jamie's phone hummed to life in his pocket. "Hey."

Mya answered, "Hey, how's it going?"

"You wouldn't believe it if I told you." Jamie covered his ear to silence the steady chatter in the convention hall.

"I bet I would."

Jamie looked up at the steel girders that lined the ceiling. His eyes were slightly glossy. "Really, really good."

Mya asked, "You sure you don't want me to be there today?"

"It's okay. How's work?"

"Good."

Jamie remembered his meeting from the morning. His chest burned with nervous energy. He said to Mya, "We need to talk."

"Something bad?"

"No, good. I think."

"Jamie!" His agent yelled for him once again.

Jamie said, "Listen, I have to go. But we'll talk tonight."

Andy returned with two beers in small, clear plastic cups. He handed one to his brother with his head facing down. Jamie toasted with his brother and said, "I'm only marginally helpful. Monica told me to get out of here for today. Wanna dump these drinks and grab a proper one before you need to head back to Rockford?"

The brothers eventually settled in a nearby bar. Andy looked at his brother and said, "Sorry about that back there. The numbers were just a bit astonishing."

Jamie unbuttoned a couple notches of his pressed black shirt. "It's okay, brother."

"My own issues coming out." Andy examined himself in the mirror behind the bar. "The amount of money just dug into me for a moment there. But don't mistake my childish reaction, Jamie. I'm really happy for you, and really proud of you. Have you called Mom and Dad yet?"

"Not yet. I still can't quite believe it myself."

Andy asked with a fatherly sense of pride, "How many pieces have you sold today?"

Jamie looked up from his Jack Daniels on the rocks and answered with a suppressed smile, "By the end of the day, probably fifteen pieces, not counting commissions." He had barely taken a sip of his drink, but sucked down two pints of water.

Jamie asked, "How many do you have out?"

"Twenty-five. There's still tomorrow," Jamie said.

Andy wondered, "How much money is that?"

"About four hundred thousand."

"Four hundred thousand?"

Jamie took a sip of his drink. He quietly said, "Not counting commissions. I got three commission gigs."

Andy's head drooped. He looked at his brother dumbfounded.

"I know. I know. It's crazy, man," Jamie said with jovial loopiness. "*What just happened?*"

"I don't feel like I even know you anymore," Andy said with a proud smile. It was an expression that only a truly proud brother could convey. "It's like you just won the lottery. A smaller lottery, but the lottery. I can't find a job in my profession to pay the rent and now you're making thousands of dollars every time you touch glass."

Jamie turned to his brother and explained, "I can see how you would see it that way, but it really isn't. I've been blowing glass for over ten years now. I don't get a salary. I don't get paid at all to work. I only make money when I sell pieces. You see me now, and I can crank out one of those ten thousand dollar pieces in about three hours. And you think, holy crap, that's a ridiculous amount of money, but it really isn't. That piece doesn't just represent three hours of work. It represents all of the years of working in a studio. Every piece, every good day and bad day, all of the times I have been blocked, and all of the times I have been creating are all represented in that one piece. The whole collection of moments that make up my life as a glassblower are all represented in that little act of creation. So I don't think it's crazy at all. It's back pay for years of unpaid labor. Will I make pieces that everyone wants forever? I hope, but you never know."

Andy said, "I've never heard an artist explain it like that."

"I know it's easy to get caught up in the numbers of this weekend. I'm trying not to. It feels like some sort of artificial validation. Obviously, I won't have to worry about paying bills as much. But this is the ritual after the fact," Jamie explained. He wound the crank on his rectangular silver watch. He held the watch up to his ear.

"What?" Andy asked.

"It's merely the ceremony honoring the act of creation. I mean, it's nice to have money, but this is just the ceremony. It's the actual moment of creation that matters. That's what they're drawn to. That's what no artist can fake. That raw moment of creation is what I care about most. It's all that I want. To once again experience that seed of light that materializes somewhere within. It's everything," Jamie said to his brother. He took another small sip of his drink as his brother ordered another bottle of beer. "Now, everything I do will be to get that back. That reminds me." Jamie pulled out some information about Giovani Tomba. Jamie told his brother about his meeting with Marcell in the morning.

Andy asked, "What about Mya?"

Jamie shook his head. For some reason, the name made Jamie think of the stunning art student who was flirting with him just before his brother arrived. "I don't know if it's going to work out."

"You always do that." Andy shook his head and stared into his brother's intense eyes.

Jamie asked, "What?"

"You always find a reason to run."

"Run? I'm not running," Jamie answered. "This is a dream opportunity. It changes my career."

"I'm just saying, don't give up on this one so quickly. She's an amazing girl. I don't know how someone could deal with your tormented soul on a daily basis, but she does. The woman is a saint."

"We'll see. How is Mom?"

"Not good," Andy told his brother. "Stable. But not good."

"Have you heard anything else from Dad?" Jamie asked.

Andy explained, "I talked to him just before I met you. He's upset. They're trying to come up with a plan for recovery, but they don't know what to do. She's so weak right now, and she's in so much pain."

"Doctor Blake is coming to the house on Wednesday, right?"

"Yeah."

Jamie asked, "When's he going to let you tell his story?"

"Don't know," Andy answered.

"Why is he waiting?"

"I ask that question all the time. I think he's working with a drug company. Maybe they want to keep it a secret until they can test it more. Don't know. It'll work out. Forget about me. I still can't believe you just did so well. My brother was talking to the news!"

"I know. Crazy."

Andy looked at his brother with a smile and asked, "How did you do this?"

Jamie replied, "What do you mean?" He took a small sip from his barely-touched drink. Ice cubes rattled against the glass.

"Well, you've been blocked for years. And this work, it's amazing," Andy answered. "How did it happen?"

Jamie asked, "You really need me to explain this?"

Andy was confused. His brother sounded shocked. "What do you mean?"

"You, of all people, brother, should know exactly how this happens. It comes from the place between the two extremes, the place within. Relative to nowhere." Jamie said, as if this term explained everything.

Andy asked, "Relative to nowhere?"

"It's what you've been talking about whenever we have a few too many beers and you let your guard down and start talking to me about things you actually think about inside of that head of yours. Sometimes you're a lot like our mother. Closed and constantly pontificating. You talked to me about life in relation. Life relative to others," Jamie said.

Andy could feel red blood rushing to his cheeks. He didn't really know why he felt embarrassed. "I talked to you about that?"

"Like five times! You don't remember?"

Andy insisted, "I do. I do. I think. At the Carlyle Brewery once?"

"Yeah, like three times at the Carlyle. You kept going on and on about living in relativity." Jamie explained, "I've got to tell you, bro. It's defined my life lately. I was living in reaction, in response to everyone around me when I was blocked and couldn't create any quality pieces. Then I woke up in Mya's bed one morning and a glass shape was born from within. It wasn't a reaction to other artists; it wasn't a reaction to anything else out there in the art world; it was a spontaneous creation born in a place within myself that's relative to nothing."

"For years my pieces had been copies of artists that I liked or rejections of artists that I didn't like."

Andy agreed, "Creation in relation to others."

Jamie pulled out a white piece of paper. It was tattered and looked identical to the pages from the mini-notebook Andy always carried around. Jamie showed his brother the paper. It was filled with random notes and thoughts.

Jamie explained, "You left this the last time we went to the Carlyle. I kept it for myself. Hope you don't mind." He cleared his throat, and then he spoke Andy's words back to him. "In the dawn of time, one became two. Thus began the life between two polarities, the life relative to somewhere, the life within. Cold is only cold relative to hot; good is only good relative to bad. And so too was our existence. We had to fight the seductive pull to live relative to others, to feel better, superior or inferior because of the car we drive, or the job we have, or the cell phone we use, or the house we buy, or the brand of jeans we wear. But all great things, all meaningful things in life and indeed all things that have the power to shape, and create, and transform our world come from a place relative to nowhere, the tenuous space within the polarities."

Jamie folded the paper and handed it to his brother and said, "For me, it was the birth of several glass shapes."

Andy added, "For Doctor Blake it was a brand new way to treat cancer."

Jamie concluded, "No matter who it is, they receive a vision or hear a voice from within that is relative to nothing outside of them. What you're talking about is a connection that is almost beyond relativity…"

"Exactly, it's post-relativity."

Jamie explained to his brother, "In the place that is relative to nowhere, I know God."

After two drinks, Jamie was exhausted. Andy hugged his brother, told him how proud he was, and drove back to be with their mother. Jamie would return to her side the next night after the show. He got on the Red Line train heading north, got out at the Fullerton stop, and waited for the Brown Line. A snowfall earlier in the day had created a thin white blanket over the city. The train stop glistened in the snow. The dissipating flurries rejuvenated him. It was tranquil, delicate, and cleansing. He leaned over the bright blue rubber mats that lined the platform. He gazed south searching for an oncoming train. He saw nothing. The swirling snow glittered under the lights. Certain gusts shot flurries down the back of his neck.

The city glowed pale orange from the streetlights above. The sidewalks were empty. The platform had a few people scattered around. The snow blanketed the city with a thin film of white powder – like whipped cream that was aerated to a state of angelic weightlessness. It outlined the branches of the trees and coated the roofs. Cars carefully navigated the roads, the snow beneath beginning to stain black from exhaust.

The DePaul University soccer field was vacant and quiet just beyond the El platform. The field cut a perfect rectangle through the imperfect city. It was a pristine field of snow. There were no steps, no marks, just a delicate block of snow. It was an empty vessel, a place where the creation was whatever the observer brought to it. The field was clean and pure. It reminded Jamie of his conversation with his brother.

When one became two, the universe became a dance in polarity and the spectrum of life in between. Human existence was predicated upon uncertainty, and it was precisely this uncertainty that made life relative to somewhere so seductive. But it was the place in the middle, the awakened person in the moment, free of existence in relation who could truly live. In the space that was relative to nowhere, was the place of God. The place within.

The dull round lights of the Purple Line broke him out of this window. *Wrong train.* Jamie stood practically alone on the platform with his thoughts. He thought about his mom, and he thought about Mya. Another pair of dull lights appeared above the tracks to the south. The brown sign in front of the train meant that he was headed home. His focus shifted from the perfect soccer field to the dreaded tracks ahead. The moment was gone.

His family had been living with the threat of cancer for decades. Jamie still remembered the first day that he became aware of this disease.

During a chilly spring day in Rockford, his soccer team practiced in the faculty parking lot of his school. Jamie was leading sprint drills. He initially felt embarrassed by the sight of his family's mini-van. The large black conversion van looked like a relative of the old A-Team vehicle. It slowly rolled into the parking lot. Jamie was getting a ride home from a friend. He didn't understand. His father emerged from the vehicle. His dad talked to the coach and put his broad arm around Jamie's shoulder. He climbed in the back of the van, confused. His brother was curled up in the back. He was crying. His father told him that his beloved mother had cancer.

Jamie walked into Mya's place. She was lying in bed. She dropped a book right when Jamie came in. "What do you want to talk about?"

Jamie flopped down next to her. "Someone visited me in the studio today."

"Who?" Mya sat up in bed and ran her hands through his short hair.

Jamie said, "Someone who works for Giovani Tomba." He averted his eyes as hers desperately tried to lock onto his.

Mya asked, "Why do I know that name?"

"He's one of the biggest glassblowers in the world, if not *the* biggest," Jamie explained. "The one you like so much. The most high-profile artist at SOFA."

"What did he want?"

Jamie took a deep breath. He turned. "He offered me an apprenticeship."

"In Chicago?" She asked.

"Italy."

"Italy? Jamie?" Mya's voice shook. "What does that mean?"

"Mya, I've been dreaming about working with a glassblower like Tomba as long as I've been making glass," Jamie said. Dramatic arm movements matched his emphatic words.

"When? How long?" Mya's voice became quiet and soft.

"Don't know yet," Jamie said. His chest quickly rose and fell.

"Probably would begin in a year. After my commissions were done. It would take anywhere from one to five years." Jamie carefully watched his girlfriend react.

Mya looked deflated. "Are you considering it?"

Jamie nodded rapidly.

"What does that mean for us?" She shook her head as she sat up. She drank a large gulp of water from the glass next to her lovely, naked shoulder.

"I don't know," Jamie answered. "You could come with me. There are hospitals in Italy too."

"I don't know," she said. Her head was shaking in disbelief. She gazed deep into the white comforter on the bed. She asked, "Can we talk more about this?"

"Not now. I love you." Jamie grabbed a blanket and shuffled into the living room.

"Are you leaving?" Mya pleaded.

Jamie looked at his girlfriend through narrow eyes. His muscular shoulders slumped. "No, I'm not leaving, just exhausted, Mya. Can we talk about this tomorrow?"

Mya said, "I'm not just picking up and moving to Italy. I have a life here. I love my job. I can't leave, Jamie."

"Please just tell me you'll think about it. I won't be going for a while. Lots of commissions to do before I go anywhere. Maybe the apprenticeship can be on the shorter end. More like a year," Jamie said.

"Jamie," Mya said. "Please."

"There's nothing else to say right now," Jamie said. His tone was almost casual. Jamie dispassionately wandered into the living room and fell asleep.

Mya buried her head into the pillow.

CHAPTER SIXTEEN

Richard Blake slid his feet into some cozy hiking boots. The rugged, roughed-up liner felt familiar to him. He slipped a silver linked chain around his Saint Bernard, Max. All his life he had been working to get people to consume less sugar and fewer refined carbs, but his dog had swelled from an addiction to them. The dog would regularly steal entire loaves of bread from the counter. So he was walking him more now. It was Sunday night. The end of a calming Thanksgiving weekend for the doctor and his family. He looked out the window at the clear, black sky and decided to add another layer to his coat. A frigid cold front had descended from the north. It would be a short walk today.

"C'mon, buddy," he said to Max.

His dog trotted in front of him as he noticed a silver Lexus parked on the street. It was churning out white exhaust smoke. Modern blue dashboard lights illuminated the dark silhouette of a man in the driver's seat. As Blake walked closer to the car, the door popped open and Mike Landis stepped out.

The doctor stopped at the edge of the driveway and looked down at the next crack in the concrete, as if another step would drop him off a cliff. The normally reserved Max was expressing steady, tired bellows at the tall man with black leather shoes clomping on the street toward them.

Blake said nothing. For the first time in his memory, he was thrown off by the mere presence of another man. They both smiled at the importance of the moment. Two opposing forces had finally come together.

Mike Landis casually asked, "I thought I was due to pay you a visit. Do you know who I am?"

Blake looked into his eyes. "Yes."

"I've been trying to contact you lately." Mike raised his right hand to his right ear. "Trouble with your communication?"

"No trouble."

Mike grabbed his shoulder and turned him around. "Let's go inside."

"No, I'd like to stay right here." Blake began to lisp as his lips got numb.

Mike sounded perfectly normal. He seemed impervious to the cold. "I know that you've been working with Tanji and Ashley, but they did not represent the company when they made commitments to you. I control this company, not Ashley Markum. I'm going to give you an offer. Shut down the Blake Center and you won't go to prison for using illegal medication. I have powerful friends everywhere. You and your treatment will go away. That is a certainty. Now how this happens, that's up to you."

Blake coldly stated, "You have no power over me or my treatment center."

"That's really what you think?" Mike let out a loud bellow.

"I've received your offers, along with your threats. I'm a doctor with an experimental treatment. You think it's the first time someone has threatened to shut me down? You think this is the first time I have had some executive in a pressed suit show up on my doorstep?" Actually, it was the first time.

"I'm not just some guy," said Mike.

"You might as well be to me." Blake said the line and knew it was a bit brash. He wished he could retract it.

Mike moved closer and peered into his eyes with the fiery stare. Mike grabbed his arm and smiled, yet his eyes continued to bore into Blake's. "Listen, Richard, I really wish you would consider this."

Blake pulled his arms away and buried his hands into his pockets as he shivered. "There's nothing to consider. I'm not shutting down. You will not make me. Now let me walk my fucking dog." His voice rose with a surprising amount of intensity.

"All right, sir. But I don't think I can hold off the FDA any longer if you keep going this direction."

"You can't stop this. You know what I've discovered, and your biggest drug is about to become obsolete. This is the reality, and you know it. Your old model is incomplete for cancer. Everyone knows it. Ashley knows it."

Mike explained, "Ashley doesn't know anything. You think you have a better treatment. That's far from certain, but I will tell you what is certain. If you continue down this path, if you continue to use this treatment method, you will be stopped. There will be no treatment centers, no books, no more talk of enzyme therapy. You will shut down. Now. If you keep going, you will regret this night, and you will regret refusing my offer."

"The FDA can do what they want. Do you know how many countries I can go to? You can't get to me."

Mike Landis leaned in closer. The breeze from his words stung Richard Blake more than the cold. "It's not the FDA you should worry about, my friend. I have many ways of stopping you, and let me assure you, you can leave this mess quietly, or things will get very scary for you. You have no idea what you're walking into. Do you want to die for this cause?"

"What did you say?"

"Not just you. You're gone first. But your wife, your friends in Plaxin, and anyone else who may know too much about your treatment. I'll say it again, so there's no confusion. Do you want to die for this cause?"

"Goodbye, Mr. Landis."

Blake walked down the block until the Lexus sped away. His chest pounded, and he wondered whether he should tell his wife. He walked into his house. His hands shook as he poured himself a small shot of whiskey. He peeked out his front door. The neighborhood was silent once again. He closed the door and activated his house alarm, which felt disturbingly inadequate. He grabbed a golf club out of his front closet and went to bed. He kissed his wife, rolled over, and clutched the golf club the whole night. He jolted awake at every creak of the house and blast of air from the heater. It was the longest night of his life.

part three
RELEASE

CHAPTER SEVENTEEN

Richard Blake walked into the Stone house on the West Side of Rockford. It was Wednesday. The thin layer of snow from the holiday weekend had almost completely melted. It was early evening and the last glow of sunlight was descending into the western sky. Thanksgiving decorations were still scattered in the living room. The wood floors creaked from the weight of his steps. Family and friends congregated under the warm light of the kitchen. They tried to sneak a glance at the revolutionary doctor. Andy Stone waved to Blake. The doctor knocked on the door to the converted first-floor bedroom.

"Come in."

"Hey, Sarah," Blake said. His voice was quiet. He walked into the converted downstairs bedroom with a small leather bag.

"How are you doing?" Blake asked. Somehow this question sounded thoughtful when he asked. His dark eyes focused on his patient. He rolled a desk chair over to her side.

She said, "Okay. The usual issues. I'm okay. Acid reflux." She coughed through the words.

He opened his bag and pulled out some small glass jars with eyedroppers as caps. "This will help you with excess acid in your stomach." He placed a few drops under her tongue. Blake said, "I know you're not really one for small talk, and I don't have much time so I think I'll just tell you..."

"What?" She asked. She sat up in her bed with budding curiosity.

"The Blake Center is shut down," the doctor said as he looked around the room. It had become a shrine to the Stone family and their vacation spot in the Keys. Paintings of old white Victorian homes surrounded by thick foliage hung from the walls, as well as wooden painted signs for the Conch Republic and the Key West International Airport. He remembered how important it was for the Stones to get their mother back down to the island of bikers, shellfish and acceptance of the abnormal.

"We've been shut down, Sarah," Blake repeated.

She asked, "For good?" She stubbornly shook her head.

"Don't know." Blake leaned back on the chair and gazed into a crystal that hung from the window. A floor lamp gleamed next to it. The crystal spouted off all colors of the spectrum onto nearby surfaces.

"Who did this?" She asked.

Blake let out a forced breath that sounded like a sarcastic laugh. He said, "FDA, Plaxin. It's a mess right now." He examined her arm. He checked her port.

"It makes me so mad," she grumbled.

"We might be setting up a practice in Germany," Blake explained. "There's a doctor who's very interested in my treatment there. I hope we will be able to return here when all of this is sorted out."

"In Germany?" She asked. She pushed her chest into the air as she looked up at the ceiling.

"It should be temporary. Until our treatment is tested a little more. I'm sorry." His voice shook as he tried to explain, "They have a center set up, and I wouldn't go to prison for treating cancer. But I feel like I'm abandoning my patients. I feel like I'm abandoning you."

She looked at the door and listened for any family members. She heard nothing. She told Blake, "My body is done. My cancer is too strong, but you can help other people. Somewhere out there is a young mother in her forties. Just like I was. And she will be looking for an answer, looking for you. I can't ask you to stay. You could risk everything, and you and I both know that my chances of remission are very low. For much of my adult life, I've lived alongside cancer. Sometimes I was afraid of it, but I've always been searching for a better way to treat it. Now here I am, sitting next to the man I've been searching for my whole life, and that makes me happy, even if it's too late for me."

"I have to go," Blake said as he hastily rose to his feet. He left several supplements and more pain medication on the table next to his patient. "Some refills."

"You're leaving now? So soon?"

A car drove past. The lights temporarily illuminated the windows. "I have to keep moving now," Blake said as he peered through the window.

"What? What about my son? Is he safe?"

"No one else knows about Andy's connection to me. I've made sure of that."

Someone fumbled with the lock on the bathroom door and the two paused the private discussion for a moment. When the room was quiet again, Blake insisted, "This will work out. I have some powerful allies now fighting for me. But for now, I have to leave. How is hospice treating you?"

"Fine," she said. "I feel okay."

"Not too much pain?" Blake asked. He had come to know how little she liked to burden others with her own suffering. She shrugged.

"I guess I'm not going to make it to Key West this year," she said to lighten the mood.

Richard Blake smiled softly, until he said, "Maybe you should go."

"Seriously?" She asked.

He grabbed her hand. "Wouldn't you rather be down there?" Blake looked around at the room enshrined to Key West. He recalled her days at his treatment center. She often talked about her beloved island atop the iridescent Caribbean. She didn't go the last few years, and it was a devastating blow. Most of the recovery plans this past year were centered on a return to the island.

"I think you guys should go, Sarah," Blake insisted.

"When?"

"As soon as possible."

She asked, "Do you think I could make it?"

"You will make it."

"It's a one-way trip," she said, her voice rising with curiosity. But she knew the answer to this. She always knew the answers. She just wanted to hear it from Blake.

"Yes. I can talk to the hospital and hospice for you and get everything arranged." Blake peered out the front window again. "I really have to go. You've been a wonderful advocate for my treatment, and you're an incredible person. I'm very happy that I got to know you," Blake said. He hugged her. "This is goodbye, Sarah Stone."

"The big goodbye. The final one."

"I wish I could do more for you, Sarah."

"You've been incredible. It's been a pleasure getting to know you. I feel lucky to have found you. Keep going. Keep fighting. Get your treatment to other people. My son will be able to help, when the time is right. Thank you, Doctor Blake." They embraced.

"I'm so sorry, Sarah," he said. His voice shook.

She said, "You have nothing to be sorry about. No regrets."

Blake waved to the people in the kitchen. He grabbed Andy and pulled him away from the group. "Come back here." He led Andy deep into the back yard. Thick woods surrounded them. Thin, smoky clouds raced across the cold, dark sky. Stars glistened across the deep canopy of space. The back yard was silent and still.

"We have to talk," Blake said. His words left his mouth with thick puffs of condensation that quickly rose and dispersed. He looked up at the shimmering stars. He tried to gain some composure. Andy had never seen him so frantic.

"Why are you here?" Andy asked.

"I told your mom first. The Blake Center has been shut down."

"What? Who?"

"The short answer is the FDA," Blake said. He checked his watch. Its aqua light temporarily illuminated his tan face and tense neck muscles. "But the complete answer is one that I'm only beginning to uncover."

"I can't believe it," Andy said. He looked back into the house and thought about his mother.

Blake grabbed Andy's shoulder. "I need you to focus right now. I don't have much time. There's more. I received a visit on Sunday night."

"From who?"

"Mike Landis," Blake answered.

Andy asked, "Why do I know that name?"

"He's the CEO of Plaxin. And, according to my connections in the company, he's spinning out of control. I'm worried about what he might do," Blake explained. He checked his watch again, then hastily tucked the glowing light under his coat.

"Just let me do the story," Andy insisted. "All of these threats will go away."

"I will. I just need to get the labs back from the Plaxin tests. I need their approval, their validation," Blake said. "Then it will be ready."

Andy shook his head. "This doesn't make any sense. How are you going to get results back from them if they're shutting you down?"

Blake answered, "I have allies in the company. People working against Mike Landis. He will likely be out of the company soon. We have to wait for the lab results. Until then, we have to be very careful."

"What are you going to do?" Andy rubbed his numb hands together in an effort to warm up.

"For now, my wife and I are going away. Until everything calms down."

"So this is it? This is goodbye?"

Blake nodded. He looked down at the ground. "For now. I've got to get out of here," he said between deep, strained breaths. "I fear I'm putting you in danger every moment I'm here."

"Once we get the lab results for the enzymes, is the story ready?" Andy asked. His voice rose with hope.

"Almost. There's something else. One last thing about my treatment, and about who I am and what I believe. Have you ever heard of Rasa?" A thin branch snapped in the dark forest. It made both of them turn for a moment and step back from the woods. They gazed into the darkness in silence, until the faint steps of a small rodent could be discerned through the stillness.

"Rasa," Blake repeated.

"No, never," Andy said.

"It's born out of India and Sanskrit. The word's purest definition is life juice or life essence." Blake checked his watch again. He peered into the woods again. Nothing.

"Life juice?" Andy said. It would have sounded like a joke had Blake not been so tense.

"In Indian culture, Rasa is often used in art to explain the feelings and emotions expressed in creating artwork or the feelings and emotions evoked in the observer. But I believe the true meaning of this term goes much deeper. Rasa is more than life essence. It's the need to embrace and cultivate our own signature and fingerprint in our lives. In each and every human being born on this planet, there is a one-of-a-kind internal essence. It's the source of personal power that springs from within. Humanity has always struggled to define it. We call it our soul, awareness, consciousness, personality, whatever. But more accurately I believe it's our Rasa. To live a life in line with one's Rasa is to live a truly blessed life. Much of our modern world seeks to rip it away. This is the problem with a drug company like Plaxin and their cancer treatment. The antidote to cancer is personalized treatment. Each person, each cancer is unique. The treatment must be just as customized. The drug development process and conventional medicine cannot treat unique individuals. They are handcuffed by protocols, rigid development procedures, and the fear of litigation. They will never discover a treatment like mine. Ever. Until they are willing to change and respect the vital need for personalized care."

Blake scanned the back yard. "I have to go."

"Why?"

"The man who runs Plaxin has threatened me." Richard Blake pulled his keys out of his pocket. He grabbed Andy's arm and said, "Be ready, my friend. I'll need you soon."

"But I don't understand, why don't you..."

"I've got to go." Blake's breaths quickened. "Be ready. You guys may be taking a trip very soon."

"What are you talking about? Wait!" Andy stood dumbfounded as the doctor raced toward the front of the house. "Wait a second," Andy called.

"I can't," Doctor Richard Blake yelled back. His silhouette quickly vanished into darkness.

CHAPTER EIGHTEEN

On the next Tuesday, Andy Stone sat next to his father in the front seat of a rental car. They were headed down Highway One in the Florida Keys. His mother slept on top of an elaborate combination of blankets, pillows and medical devices.

"I can't believe we're doing this," Andy said to his father as they raced south.

"It was Blake's idea. Blake and your mother," his father explained. He watched the road ahead with intense focus. "They cleared her to fly. The hospital and hospice are all arranged down here."

"But still. This was crazy."

"You know what kept your mother going for the last year. The dream that she could make it back down to Key West this year," his father said.

They cruised by a rusty pickup truck. Oncoming traffic raced toward them. He quickly whipped back into their lane. "It kept her going. You know how much she loves it." The rental car passed old ships that made their graves in the shallow everglades. The road felt unstable like it could sink into the endless marshes and developing Keys.

"She'll be so happy to get down here. Even if it's a one-way trip," his father said as he watched for his son's response. Andy's mother had been sleeping the majority of the drive down. Andy would occasionally steady his head against his seat and look back at her chest to make sure it was still rising and falling, rising and falling. He caught his father doing the same thing.

Andy asked, "It is, right? A one-way trip?"

"Yes," his father answered. "We don't know how long, but she'll probably never return home. They passed through the portal where the mainland crumbled into little plots of land scattered atop the sapphire blue of the Caribbean.

Andy and his parents arrived in Key West two hours later. Two-story homes lined the streets. They looked like a mix between Southern mansions, Victorian cottages, and tropical bed and breakfasts. The houses were saturated with light blues, soft greens, and brilliant pale yellows. Tall white shutters were swung open. Most houses were fronted by spacious wood-plank porches and wicker furniture. Front yards were thick with tropical vegetation. Some had well-manicured wooden signs for hotels, law offices or nautical museums.

As the rental car crawled down the crowded main drag called Duval Street, Andy's mother lifted her head up from the pillows in the back seat. She watched the world on the other side of the car window continue to move. She observed a man sitting at his wooden stand who carved names into seashells, and a little girl tugging at her mom's skirt for attention. She looked into a bar where a bigger couple sang a country tune at a karaoke bar. She faintly smiled. Andy fought back the tears as he felt he was looking at the closest person in his life accepting her death. It hurt him more than he could ever explain.

They pulled into the Banyan Resort. Flat, black cobblestones lined the driveway. Snaking paths meandered through lush, tropical foliage. Fountains trickled into pools of water. Vivid orange and red flowers opened up to the warm December sun. Victorian houses checkered the grounds. They were surrounded by porches with patio furniture and chubby tourists from northern states. A gray cat sprawled out on the porch next to the front office. Mopeds whizzed past on the street in front of the resort. Rambunctious couples with plastic bags from t-shirt shops stopped to pose for pictures in front of the banyan tree that towered over the resort. Its trunk twisted and contorted into the pale blue sky above. Its thick canopy housed a choir of singing birds. Vines dangled down from the tree's complex web of branches and trunks. Some vines had anchored into the ground, creating yet another tree trunk.

Andy's father checked in. They were staying in two units. Andy, and eventually Jamie, were staying in unit 506. It was the condo where their parents usually stayed, perched on the second floor with a breathtaking porch overlooking a bustling, entertaining Key West street. Their parents were staying in a first-floor unit, but Andy knew his mother loved unit 506. She would spend any time she could up there. When his father returned, he told Andy, "I thought of everything but the fact that our unit is on the second floor. Hospice is all set up. Her hospital bed is ready in the lower unit, but you know your mother will want to sit on the porch up there. What do we do?"

"Carry her," Andy stated. "We got this far."

Andy and his father carefully walked upstairs with his frail mother in between them. He worried he might break a bone just by lifting her out of the car. She was disoriented. Her skin hung loosely from her arms. Her head brushed against the thick foliage next to the stairs. A little lizard ran across the warm gray steps. The island tour ride, known as the Conch Train, rolled past with the muffled sound of a tour guide speaking through a microphone. Andy and his father tried to ignore the tourists who watched them carry their mother's limp body up the stairs.

They entered the condo and laid Andy's mother onto the bed. "We made it, sweetie," his father whispered.

A faint smile rose on his mother's face.

Jamie arrived on Wednesday. Hospice nurses came regularly. They gave her pain medication and changed her fluids. For the first couple days, she mainly slept. The boys began to wonder if she would ever wake up. By Thursday night, she woke with renewed strength. The boys rolled her onto her beloved second-floor porch. She sat in a wheelchair with blankets wrapped around her fragile body. She watched the thick atmosphere of Key West race past her on the street below.

By Friday morning, she felt even better. The family embarked on one last trip. Their blue Mustang rental car pulled up to Simonton Beach. The public beach was less than half a city block wide. It was normally crowded with homeless men lying next to empty liquor bottles. It was the beach that most of the island had forgotten, but Andy's mother loved it. It was next to the Coast Guard and tucked behind a hotel. She had hoped to step into the emerald saltwater of the Caribbean for years, but couldn't make her annual vacation trek to the island. She believed in the cleansing power of immersing her tired body in the sea.

Andy and Jamie carried her out of the car. The boys carried her to the edge of the water, past the line of broken seashells and coral, and down to the hard, wet sand. She reached for her husband's hand as she walked into the water. She walked with uncertain feet. Her stiff, weakened body masked a lifetime of coordination. She carefully waded into knee-high water and fell backwards. Her little body plunged into the sea, and Andy's father caught her. She emerged lying on her back, gazing up at the wisps of light clouds high in the atmosphere. The boys stood on the beach. They watched their mother's tired body hover on top of the emerald and light blue tinted water. Jamie fell to the ground. Andy dropped down next to him and put his arm around his brother.

Back on the second-floor porch, Andy sat with his mother. They absorbed the sights and sounds of the island. His mother waved to a walking ghost tour. A group of about twenty people followed a man in a black cape with a lantern. The building next to them was rumored to have an old woman from the early 1900s living in the attic.

Andy asked his mother, "Are you afraid to die?"

"No," she calmly stated. "I don't think so."

Andy reached for his mother's hand under the blanket. He laid his head on the clump of blankets surrounding her shoulder.

His mother said, "I worry more about leaving all you guys behind, than me dying. Take care of Jamie, okay? He has a propensity for inflicting torture upon himself."

"I will." Andy nodded, rubbing his head closer to her shoulder.

A man with frazzled hair, wearing a silver jumpsuit rode his three-wheel bicycle wrapped in Christmas lights. He rolled up the street, blaring music from a stereo on the back of the bike.

"I love you, Mom."

"I love you too, Buzzie."

They sat in silence as pedestrians, mopeds and cabs raced up and down the street.

A voice from the front office below shouted, "Hey, Sarah!" Andy snapped out of his thoughts.

He hesitantly called over the railing, "She's up here!" He wasn't sure how the resort's staff felt about his dying mother staying there.

"Is Andy your son?"

Andy leaned over the glossy white railing. "Yeah, that's me!"

"There's a delivery here for you," a man in a green Banyan t-shirt said, waving him down.

"A delivery? Now?"

"You have to sign for it and it's marked urgent." Andy heard the word "urgent" as he gazed down at the resort's pet – a white and tan striped cat – lazily stretching its front legs as it was splayed out on a black bench facing the front office. "What could be urgent down here?" Andy wondered. He looked at the box. It had no return address and looked as though it had been packed today. One could fit two slender laptops in it. Andy thanked the FedEx guy and waved up to his mom with the curious package as he brushed by a few towering ferns. His flip-flops clacked up the wooden stairs.

"What is it?" His mom's voice squeaked.

Andy plopped back down in the chair. "Don't know. I'm a little scared to open it." He ripped the plastic strip out of the side. He pulled out a stack of documents and a handwritten letter on the top with the distinct swooping "R" and "B" signature of Richard Blake. The letter said to call Blake immediately when he received it.

Andy looked down in disbelief at stacks of documents with the Plaxin letterhead. He flipped through dozens, even hundreds of internal emails, letters and reports from Plaxin R&D to Mike Landis. He saw emails to the FDA itself, discussing the shutdown of the Blake Treatment Center. At the bottom of the stack was a blue folder labeled "Blake Center."

The letter read, "Andy, I had a surprising visit on Wednesday. A man named Tanji, the head of North American Research at Plaxin gave me this information. These are the lab results I was waiting for, but there's much more. It's proof of corruption and deception in Plaxin. It's time you told the story. No one else knows about this, so keep it quiet, and get the story out there as soon as possible."

Andy's heart thumped as he flipped through the documents, he flopped many of them onto the table in front of his mother. A small audiotape fell out of the bottom of the box. It was the kind of tape from the recorder that Richard Blake always kept in his pocket for memos and random thoughts. He always had the tape recorder, especially when he came up with things while he went running, driving up a scenic road, or walking his dog. "Don't lose the audio tape," said the letter.

His mother's eyes went wide with shock as she scanned the pages. She kept saying, "Those bastards!" She said it so loud once that it startled a Banyan employee walking along the path in the front garden. The pages told a story of deception and attack by Mike Landis and his allies. As Andy passed the pages over to his mother, who lifted them to her face with a shaking right hand, the two began to realize that a bomb had been placed in his hands. He shivered with adrenaline.

Jamie and his father returned from dinner and plopped half a key lime pie on the glass porch table. Jamie asked his brother, "Want some?" He tossed a white plastic fork onto the table.

Andy jumped up from his chair and said, "I've got to go." His eyes were glossy and distant. He grabbed the stack of papers and rushed down the stairs.

"Was it something I said?" Jamie yelled down. His father laughed.

Andy rushed into the Walgreens on Duval Street. He stuck his credit card into the copier and began photocopying the pages. He wanted to make eight copies and hide them all over the place. His excitement gave way to anger as he thought about his mother, and all of the cancer patients who were desperately searching for a different treatment. He looked around at a drunken couple holding beers in hand, thumbing through Key West postcards. Another patron sifted through his pocket for change to pay for his "pack a Marbie Reds."

The vibration from his phone made his vision go white for a moment. The phone's display read, "Richard Blake Cell."

"Hello? Is this you, Andy?" The pace of the voice on the other end confused him at first. "Andy, I can't talk long, but you must listen to me very carefully. I fear that I've put you in great danger. We both are. I don't know how, but someone knows I received that information." Blake's signal was full of static, and he sounded terrified. Andy could hear the fluctuations in wind noise in Blake's cell phone, as if he was constantly turning to look behind him.

"Are you serious?" Andy asked. He wasn't ready for such a frantic tone from the normally composed doctor.

Blake paused until he finally whispered, "I am absolutely serious. They knew about Tanji; they knew about me; and you must assume that they'll know you got that package."

"You think I'm in danger? Like violent danger?" The combination of the words sounded redundant and awkward in Andy's head.

"Do you realize what you have in your hands?" Blake pleaded.

Andy's voice shook. "Yes, of course I do."

"The man who gave me that information, named Tanji," Blake stated. "He's in a coma. I just found out. He was severely beaten just outside of his house. The assailants didn't take his wallet or his phone. They took his briefcase and his laptop. A neighbor saw it happening. It's the only reason he's alive right now. Everyone connected to my treatment center is running right now."

"Seriously? Are you sure his beating had to do with us?" Andy asked. The last statement didn't sound real. It took him a while to process the information.

"It's possible that the assault is a coincidence, but I don't think so. And neither does Ashley."

"Who's Ashley?"

"Don't worry about that now. The people who want to suppress this information are very powerful, and the news of my cancer treatment and its success could be potentially devastating to Plaxin."

"But how did they?"

Blake said, "I don't know, but I have to get off my phone. I have to get out of here."

Andy's chest burned. He felt like throwing up. He had to brace himself with a rack of sunglasses. "Holy shit," he whispered. "Where are you going?" Andy asked. The question was met with a distant pause that made Andy check his phone to see if they had been disconnected.

Blake said, "Get the story out, immediately."

"Blake, wait!"

"I've got to go. Get it out!"

The phone went dead as he looked down at the flashing screen that signaled the ended call. It lasted for 1 minute and 58 seconds.

Andy scrambled to arrange the pages. He had the original, one copy, and half of another. He spilled papers as he looked down the aisles of the drug store for any sign of danger. He scanned the checkout for any indication of someone paying attention to him.

Andy had no idea what to do. He was at the very end of a skinny strip of islands off the southern tip of Florida. The Key West paper shut down three years ago. He could email the pages, or fax them, but this was *his* story. He had to see it through. Besides, who would follow him down here?

His phone rang again. The caller ID read, "Unavailable." His thumb hovered over the button until he concluded that it was probably Blake and answered.

There was a pause and then a deep, raspy voice slurred the question, "Is this Andy Stone?"

Instincts kicked in before he could think. "Yes, who is this?"

The call was lost. He thought about all the calls he had been making to Blake in the last week and all of the references to the Banyan and his family's travel plans. Andy looked down at his phone. He had just made a terrible mistake.

CHAPTER NINETEEN

Ashley walked into Chicago's Union Station wearing a long winter coat. Her slender boots clomped on the stone tiles. A gray hood veiled her trademark hair. She climbed onto the northbound train to Kenosha without a specific destination in mind. The station was quiet. A couple dozen people boarded with her. Most looked like typical professionals commuting back to their homes in the suburbs. She scanned black computer bags and men dressed in suits, refusing to wear coats, hats or gloves in the frigid weather. Their ears were red and burned from the harsh wind. She constantly checked behind her for any suspicious movement. She saw nothing. Ashley climbed the steep stairs to the second level.

Two hours earlier, she received a call from Tanji's wife about his savage beating. She decided to get away. She called Doctor Blake and headed for the train station.

Ashley pulled her hood further over her head. The fake fur at its perimeter shielded her radiant face. She counted the stops. *Ravenswood, Rogers Park, Wilmette.* Commuters filtered out. About ten remained on the passenger car. She tried to casually flip through a newspaper, but had trouble focusing on anything other than Tanji. She wanted to see him, but knew it wasn't a good idea. Not right now. Questions swirled. Her eyes scanned the rapidly passing Illinois landscape, searching for an answer. She had to get out of the city. She was in danger.

The train raced through northern Chicago. It precariously rattled along the tracks. The passenger car was warm. Ashley's head began to sweat. As a few more commuters left at the Kenilworth stop, she breathed easier and shed her insulated hood. She noticed a middle-aged man facing backwards on the train look up from his magazine. He carefully analyzed Ashley's unique face. She looked out the window, trying to bury her head in the collar of her winter coat. He kept staring.

"What do I do?" She whispered.

She stood up and walked downstairs next to the exit door away from the strange man. No one else seemed to notice. Ashley checked the stops. She debated getting out at the next one, but the strange man stood up as the train slowed. His thick hand wrapped around the silver vertical railing. He peeked back at Ashley.

Her chest pounded. The train slowed. The doors wedged open. Yellow lights illuminated the empty platform. She watched the strange man. He watched her. The doors quickly closed again. Neither one of them left. The train picked up speed. Ashley stood up and walked over to the doors leading to the next passenger car. Her hands slipped several times as she tried to pull the lever. The strange man sat back down. He had advanced several rows closer.

"You're not supposed to open that," a young woman said to Ashley.

Ashley ripped the door leading to another passenger car open and rushed into the next one. The train began to slow down once again. She stood next to the doors. She watched as the platform for Winnetka rushed past. Two people stood outside on the platform. She leaned over to see if the strange man moved to the door once again, but pulled her head back fearing he would see her.

The doors opened. Steam rose from the beneath the train. She peeked outside on the platform. She saw nothing. Just before the doors slammed shut, she jumped onto the platform. Her right shoe grazed the closing door. She fell to the ground as the train started moving away. She looked around. She was alone.

Ashley Markum walked two blocks with her hood drawn. Rapid clouds of condensed breath rose from under her furry lining. She finally saw a cab, waved it down, got into the back, and raced to the north. She had to hide.

CHAPTER TWENTY

Andy ran down Duval Street past lazy patrons spilling out of the Margaritaville bar, past a few hippies on a Mexican rug making bowls and hats out of green palm tree reeds. He ran by the Tropical Cinema. His heart thumped as he looked up at the banyan tree illuminated by blue and green floodlights. Tourists were snapping photos next to the sprawling tree and his brother stood at the foot of the stairs with a drink in his hand.

Jamie asked as he took a big sip, "How you doing, bro?"

Andy clutched his side. He held up one finger to his brother.

"Let's go out tonight," Jamie casually said. "Grab a few drinks. Mom's doing okay."

"I've got to go," Andy said. He gasped for breath.

Jamie asked, "Where are you going?"

"Up Highway One to Miami."

"Those documents. What exactly did Doctor Blake send you?" Jamie asked. His tone and posture straightened with the intensity of the conversation.

"A man in R&D at Plaxin – the drug maker that produces the main chemo drug – gave Blake a stack of evidence that basically proves that his enzyme therapy and other treatments used together can reverse many forms of cancer." A younger couple wrapped in green and white striped towels slinked past them on their way to the hot tub. Once they were safely out of audible range, Andy continued, "And it shows the CEO tried to suppress Blake's treatment, even though he knew it worked."

"You found a whistleblower from inside the company?"

"Yeah, *the* whistleblower."

Jamie pointed to the stack of papers. "That's what you have in your hand right there?"

"Yes." Pale blue lights illuminated the water fountain in the front garden. Copper pennies shimmered in the rippling water.

Jamie asked, "I don't understand. Why Miami? Why can't you do the story here?" He swirled the drink in his hand.

Andy looked around before he whispered into his brother's ear, "Because I fear that I may be in danger."

"What?" Jamie took another large gulp with a chuckle.

"The man who gave Blake this information is in critical condition." Andy pulled his brother behind one of the stairwells. He spoke so quietly and carefully that Jamie could barely decipher the words over the bubbling hot tub in the distance. "He was almost beaten to death."

"Are you fucking kidding me?" Jamie's joking tone turned deadly serious. "So email it or fax it to somebody you trust."

Andy stubbornly shook his head. His spiky hair twisted and turned with the shaking motion. "No, this is my story to tell. I'm the one who completely understands Blake and his treatment. It's about Mom, everything. Don't you see? I can't give up this story to anyone. I've got to get out of here. I'm afraid I'm putting you all in danger."

"Do you think someone might be after you?" Jamie's voice dropped.

"Blake does. I've got to go," Andy said.

The brothers looked nervously at a man in jeans and a black leather jacket heading into the resort. He stopped and stared at Jamie and Andy. Andy tucked the evidence behind him. Jamie moved forward. The man said to the brothers, "You guys should have some fun." His words were a slurred mess of vowels. "Go have fun."

"Thanks, bye," Jamie curtly stated. The drunken man stumbled toward his condo, fumbled with a lighter, and eventually slammed the French doors behind him.

"Why don't you email it? Get it out there now," Jamie repeated.

Andy said, "Don't you see? This is the story that Blake has been preparing me for. This is the answer to Mom's searches. It's the answer for other people like Mom. This is the story I came home to write. It is the reason why I have become so close with this doctor. No second-hand journalist is qualified to tell this story. It can't be just handed off, and I need to find shelter, away from the family. I need the protection that can only be found in a major newsroom. There, I can write the story with the help I need, away from our family, and protected. I need to get to the *Miami Herald*."

Jamie looked around. He stood tensely scanning their surroundings like a paranoid guard dog. "When are you leaving?" He asked.

"Now."

"I'm going with you."

"Jamie, no, not here. You don't understand how serious this is. Besides, you need to stay with Mom and Dad." For a second, he wished that he had slipped away before the family had any idea.

"I'm coming with you. Don't play this game. I am your brother, and I'm coming with you."

Andy had a powerful urge to down his brother's drink. He replied, "Fine. We'll go together. What do we tell them?"

"The truth. Tell them the truth."

By one in the morning, they had successfully moved their parents to a neighboring hotel. Andy paid with cash and made the owner promise not to give out any names. His mother was asleep. They moved her without complications. He had been carrying her up and down stairs all week.

"I'm sorry, Dad. I can't let you guys stay back there," Andy said to his exhausted father. "This will all be over soon."

"When can we go back? How serious is this?"

"Tomorrow. I promise you by tomorrow, when the story is out. Everything will be fine. I just want to be totally careful," Andy assured his father with a calming tone that was a lie. "Don't go back to that room. I love you guys very much." The brothers rushed out of the room.

They climbed into their Mustang rental car. The car gurgled with repressed power as they rolled away from the Banyan under the cover of night. They came to a stoplight a few blocks away. Locals and tourists swelled beyond the walls of the legendary bar called the Green Parrot. A guitarist with frazzled hair and curiously sexual facial expressions was barely visible. He was elevated above the crowd in the back corner. Andy watched behind their car as headlights stacked one after the other. Mopeds pulled away from the bar.

A skinny, bronzed man riding a beach cruiser ran into the side of their car. The thump made Andy and Jamie jump. Andy checked the locks. "Crap," he said with rising tension. "I might be a little jumpy."

The drunken biker walked toward the driver's side window. He peered into the car. Andy continued to face forward, afraid to lock eyes with anyone outside of the car. His body sat tense. His muscles twitched. "Sorry," the biker mumbled with a half-hearted wave.

Jamie said, "No problem. Bye." The light turned green, and they sped away from Duval Street. They watched the lights of Key West sink in the rear view. The road felt more like a faint strip of civilization in the vast, open and wild Caribbean than a stable highway. Stars dusted the sky, and Andy felt death lurking in the darkness of the world around them.

Andy drove the blue Mustang as it darted up the lone highway surrounded by saltwater. He slowed through towns and signs of civilization, then quickly accelerated whenever the road in front of him was primarily black and empty. Andy had to jam the breaks as they neared Sugarloaf Key. A large semi crawled up a bridge in front of them. Andy whipped the car to the left as he scanned for oncoming traffic. He couldn't see anything as the road curved in front of them. Highway One was a two-lane road that spanned from the end of Key West through Miami. The road stretched from island to island via long bridges over the Caribbean Sea. The highway ran through small towns and clusters of civilization on its way up north. It was a narrow road. Passing slower vehicles was practically impossible along certain stretches. Although the distance from Key West to Miami was less than two hundred miles, a drive up Highway One could be incredibly slow.

After Jamie and Andy finally passed the large truck, Andy looked around inside of their car and said, "Let's think about this. How could anyone know where we were?"

"The GPS," Jamie offered. He sounded tired.

"Phones." Andy looked at his brother and said, "I think we need to toss them over the bridge."

Jamie asked, "Can't we just hide them in a bush or something so we can get them back?"

"No, we have to toss them."

"Andy, my iPhone?" Jamie whined. "I love that thing. It's got the directions on there."

"I printed out directions." Andy tapped some printed pages under his left leg.

Jamie asked, "You seriously think someone is following us by our phones?"

"I think it's possible, yes," Andy stated. "Listen to me. This isn't a joke, Jamie. We need to dump the phones. I'll buy you a new one after all of this."

"Seriously," Jamie said, not believing his brother would actually do it.

"I'll buy you a new phone."

"Give me your phone. I'll toss them," Jamie insisted as he lowered his window. The cool evening breeze rushed into the car.

Jamie asked one last time as they neared the center of the next bridge, "You really want me to do this?"

"Absolutely."

Jamie opened the windows at the next bridge and threw the rental GPS and his brother's cell phone into the water below. He quickly tucked his iPhone under the seat without Andy seeing it.

Numbers on the green mile markers climbed higher. Andy kept looking into his rear-view mirror for any signs of oncoming cars racing after them. He saw nothing but the lights of trucks they had passed. Every few miles, they had to negotiate the dangerous pass of a semi along the meandering, undulating highway. Andy began banging on the steering wheel with frustration whenever another truck would come into view in front of them. His lane changes became more reckless. He slammed onto the gas pedal with rising tension.

"What's up with all these damn semis?" Andy yelled at the rear of yet another large truck. The red brake lights illuminated his scrunched eyebrows. "It's past two in the morning."

Jamie said with a yawn, "Maybe they do this drive at night because it's supposed to be a lot faster. It usually takes a lot longer during the day."

"For them maybe. But they aren't helping us out."

For every mile that the car accelerated up to seventy, they were stuck for two miles behind a semi. Andy slowed to twenty-five miles per hour behind a bread company delivery truck. It was the sixth sluggish vehicle they had encountered in fifty miles.

"Cars coming up behind us," Jamie said as he peered into the side mirror.

"I know. We've got to get around this damn truck."

Three sets of vehicle lights quickly closed the gap. They were directly behind the Mustang. Jamie focused his intense gaze behind them. "A Ford pickup truck, gray Nissan, and I can't tell what the last car is." A pair of halogen lights whipped into the left lane and accelerated past the Mustang and delivery truck.

Andy followed. He swerved into the left lane and pushed on the gas. The car roared to life. Andy looked back as the gray Nissan Maxima followed close behind. By the time Andy turned back around, the car in front of him had quickly maneuvered back into the right lane. Andy was staring down the headlights of a truck barreling toward them in oncoming traffic.

"Hey, Andy!" Jamie yelled.

It was too late. They had drifted too far to the left and couldn't make it back to their lane in time. Andy swerved to the left, slammed the brakes, and the car spun onto the shoulder. The two braced for impact. They braced for a tree, a car, a house that never came. Gravel battered the exterior, as if they were caught in a strong hailstorm. The blue Mustang came to rest in a cloud of dust.

Andy buried his head in his hands. Jamie said, "Brother, I know you're worried right now. I know you're wound up. But you're going to kill us before we even make it to Miami."

"Sorry," Andy said, shaking his head.

"It's okay." Jamie slid his seat belt across his chest. "Let's get there fast, but alive."

"You're right."

"Good." Jamie tapped his brother's arched back.

Andy said, "We need gas."

"You really want to stop right now?" Jamie asked.

"We have to."

Their dusty Mustang gurgled to a stop at a gas station. The gas pumps and convenience store were brightly illuminated with pale fluorescence that cut into the muggy Florida night. "I need some coffee," Jamie said, as he walked past his brother filling up the tank. Excitement was giving way to fatigue. Coffee sounded good to Andy. He grabbed the duffel bag into which he had stowed all of the evidence and headed inside. Moments later, a gray Nissan Maxima slowed and turned into the gas station. It came to a stop on the side of the gas station. Its lights shut off. It sat in silence just out of reach of the gas station lights. Andy peered outside. He saw a faint silhouette rush from the shadows over toward the cars at the pumps. The lights inside the convenience store were so bright he had to squint his eyes.

"Did you see that?" Andy asked his brother.

"No." Jamie lifted his heavy eyelids as he filled a cup of coffee. "What?"

"I thought I saw something," Andy said as he walked over to the window.

Moments later, two white vans rolled into the gas station. About a dozen party people in a blur of sunglasses, feather boas, and glowing cell phones stumbled out of the vans in clouds of smoke.

"What was it?" Jamie asked. "What did you see?"

"Nothing, I guess."

As the brothers walked back to their Mustang, a car sped away kicking up gravel in its wake.

Jamie ran behind the car. He tried to see the license plate, but it was completely obscured by the dust.

Andy asked, "What kind of car was that?"

"It was a gray Maxima," Jamie said as he looked around the gas station.

"The same car as before?"

"I don't know. I don't know." Jamie reached for the passenger door. His powerful hands yanked it open. "Let's get out of here."

They sped away.

The next fifty miles went fast. They breezed past the northern Keys, occasionally taking random detours in case any of the distant cars in the rear-view mirror were following them. They watched for the mysterious Maxima. They finally turned directly north as the sporadic islands turned into solid marshland. The world outside was still black and silent.

"I think we made it, brother," Jamie said. "I can show you now." He reached under his seat and pulled out his iPhone.

"What the hell?" Andy yelled out.

"I couldn't dump the thing," Jamie said. His voice echoed a combination of guilt and indignation.

"I can't believe you..."

"Wait." Jamie held up his finger as the white iPhone screen came to life. "Wait a second."

"What?" Andy pleaded. "What is it?"

"Oh shit," Jamie said as he looked out the window. Distant house lights blurred past his vision.

"What?" Andy grabbed his brother's arm in a way that made him jolt.

Jamie asked his brother, "You didn't touch this phone?" His eyes peered into Andy's searching for the truth.

"I didn't know it was there," Andy said. He threw up his hands. The car started to drift to the right. It ran over the warning rivets on the shoulder. The sound only added to the tension in the car.

Jamie looked at his phone as if he had never seen it before. "Are you messing with me right now?"

"No. Do you think I'd be messing with you now?" Andy said, easing off the gas.

"It's like somebody was using my phone," Jamie said in disbelief. "I powered it off."

"Are you sure?" Andy looked at his brother like a disbelieving parent.

"I'm positive. And the map is up. Our directions from Key West to the *Herald*."

"What? Are you kidding me?" Andy asked.

"Some GPS function has been enabled." Jamie punched the screen.

Headlights emerged in the rear-view mirror.

Andy asked, "What kind of car is that?"

"I can't tell," Jamie squinted into the rear-view mirror then jumped around and looked backwards.

"Is it a Maxima?" Andy asked his brother.

"I don't know," Jamie said. He clutched the door with his left hand and leaned further back. "Kind of looks like it."

"What do we do?" Andy pleaded.

"Go," Jamie motioned ahead. He threw his iPhone out the window.

Andy hit the accelerator and they raced ahead. The car behind them faded in the background. They accelerated more. Suddenly, it began catching up with them.

"What do we do?" Andy crouched over the steering wheel trying to anticipate every turn slightly quicker.

Jamie pointed ahead. "There's a turn coming up here. Slow down after the curve and try to turn off somewhere secluded. There are all these dirt roads on the left."

As they raced around the corner, Andy tapped the brakes. Headlights were just about to emerge on the horizon behind them.

"There!" Jamie yelled.

Andy slammed the brakes and whipped the car to the left. It bounced, and the brothers jostled along a violently choppy dirt road surrounded by tall reeds.

"Stop! Kill the car!" Jamie yelled.

They sat in silence in the middle of the Florida Everglades.

"If he saw us and turns..."

Jamie peered into his brother's eyes with razor-sharp intensity. "Don't even think about it."

They could barely see the two-lane highway through a narrow sliver between the overgrown reeds. Headlights grew brighter. Andy cocked the keys in the ignition. Jamie's chest rose and fell with deep, uncontrollable gasps.

A sedan rushed by in a blur.

"What was that?" Jamie asked.

"Don't know," Andy answered. "Couldn't tell."

"What should we do?"

Andy looked at his watch. "Give it five minutes, then get to the freaking newspaper."

It was six in the morning by the time Jamie and Andy finally reached the city of Miami. Andy thought about calling the police. He thought about slowing to a crawl, laying on his horn, and flashing his bright lights for all to see, but he didn't. He still partially believed this ominous, foreboding feeling was a delusion. He didn't want to complicate the matter. Daylight broke over the eastern sky. They passed the Miami airport on their left. Planes shot into the sky out over the Atlantic Ocean and banked left toward the north. They descended an exit ramp that led to the waterfront of the city. Orange lights flashed. A homeless man buried his head in a round garbage bin. The downtown streets were practically empty.

"Something's wrong," Andy said. He jiggled his head in an effort to stay awake. His hair was now wildly spiked. He felt the end of the journey had been too easy, as if they were being pushed into something that was destined to happen, a cataclysmic event that was no longer burdened by red lights, pedestrians or traffic. They passed delivery trucks with flashing lights, joggers in black spandex and white headphones, and men and women in suits and uniforms at bus stops.

A straight row of palm trees lined the street leading to the *Herald*. A vast parking lot on the right had only a few cars. The building looked like a crappy six-story office building with dim rectangular windows and yellow panels below them. Cars streamed along a road on the right side of the building. The entrance looked like a fortress with tall, cold concrete pillars. Above the entrance was a track for an elevated train. Its thick round supports ran from left to right along the front of the building. Andy could see delivery trucks in the warehouse on the left side of the building. The familiar font of the *Miami Herald* sign glowed a brilliant light blue. It illuminated the streets below.

Andy rolled to a stop one block away from the building. He had hoped for a large, secure entrance with dozens of security guards, but he was caught off guard by the layout of the paper. The main entrance was dark, desolate and kind of peripheral to the building.

Andy asked, "How do you turn the lights off?"

"I don't know. Just turn the car off."

"What if we need to get away?" Andy wondered.

Jamie looked at his brother and said, "I don't know."

CHAPTER TWENTY-ONE

They killed the car and sat in silence, looking out at the concrete pillars that marked the entrance to the building. Papers were being loaded in the yellow light of the delivery truck docks. Music was blaring.

Andy slowly opened his door. The sound made his brother jump. Andy said, "All right. I'm going."

"No, wait. Let me go first. Is that the half copy with blank pages?" Jamie asked.

"Yeah."

Jamie said, "I'll take that. I'll go before you."

Andy insisted, "No, absolutely not."

"Wait, who is that?" Jamie pointed along the street next to the entrance of the *Herald*.

Andy said, "It's a homeless guy. He's looking at us."

"Stop moving."

The man started walking toward the car.

Andy explained, "Listen, I'm going to drive backwards."

"No." Jamie opened the passenger door. "I'm going. If he comes after me, I'll run away. If I make it to the front door, come after me with the original copy."

"Jamie, that makes no sense!"

Jamie ran out the door and walked toward the entrance before Andy could stop his brother. Andy slid out from the driver's side and quickly ran along the fence on the other side of the street. His heart pounded.

He saw Jamie in flashes through the breaks in the bushes, as he carefully ran undercover across the street from the newspaper entrance. The homeless man was walking away from Jamie, seemingly disinterested. Andy stopped behind a large round column that supported the elevated tracks. He clutched the sandy finish of the paint with his sweaty, pulsing fingers. The homeless man looked over at the round column. Andy froze and carefully slid to the other side. He thought about running back to the car.

Suddenly, cutting through the music in the warehouse and the steady hum of traffic, Andy heard a dull thump and the sound of a folder hitting the ground. He peeked around the pillar to see his brother lying against the curb at the entrance and a man with a rifle running toward him.

Andy inhaled and exhaled in short, panicked bursts. His mind raced. He looked again at the man standing over his brother with the long butt of a rifle pointed at his head and the blue folder in his hands. The sniper thumbed through the pages. He was compact with a neck that appeared wider than his head. He was dressed in black. His hair was short and dark. His eyes gazed upon the morning scene with powerful intensity.

Andy closed his eyes and tried to slow his frantic, shallow breaths. He wasn't quite sure why he was going to make his next move. He didn't weigh any other options. He didn't think about the rational thing to do. With his brother involved, it was instinct. He briefly looked up to the heavens and prayed that one of them would make it alive, that the majority of their family wouldn't evaporate in a matter of days.

"Wait! Please!" Andy's voice shuddered as he emerged from behind the round column and walked briskly toward the man with the gun.

"This is what you want." Andy held his hands in the air and looked up at a folder in his left one. "They're the originals. It's what you're looking for. Please don't kill my brother. He has nothing to do with this. Please!"

The man briefly looked down at Jamie who was clutching his right leg. Then he turned the barrel of the rifle at Andy.

Andy always thought he would be more confident facing the barrel of a gun, like his mother bravely staring death in the face, but it wasn't like that. He trembled furiously, and his voice trembled as well.

"Throw the pages on the ground and turn the fuck around!"

Andy explained, "Those are the originals. It's what you want. Please."

"No more talking."

Andy looked up at the murky sky. It glowed a dull yellow from the Miami street lights. He listened to the man behind him thumbing through the pages.

"Get on your knees."

Andy fell to the ground and energy pulsed through his body. His arms and legs tingled with a numbing sensation. His vision began to narrow and fade. What could he do? How could he get out of this? Suddenly, the halogen lights of a car turned onto the street lined with palm

226

trees leading to the paper. Andy felt a violent force impact the back of his head, and the world went black.

CHAPTER TWENTY-TWO

Andy didn't really know what he believed would happen after he died. If he did experience existence after death, he imagined waking up on a mountain peak and looking through amber goggle lenses at two feet of fresh, pristine powder and an endless ski run of cliffs, chutes, and expansive powder fields. He definitely wasn't expecting the afterlife to look like a drab parking lot with lots of emergency personnel and the foggy Miami skyline in the background.

"Where am I?" Andy mumbled to himself. An EMT in her short white-collared shirt flashed a light in his eyes. She looked like a very strong woman. She had a brown ponytail and compassionate eyes. Her shirt had the familiar red patch of an emergency worker.

"What's going on?" He pleaded to the medic. She appeared very far away, as if Andy were watching the scene from deep within the ground below looking up at this surreal scene.

"Try to remain calm, Mr. Stone. Everything's going to be all right," a man said standing next to the medic. He was wearing a Miami Police uniform. Andy looked around at all of the people watching over him. His body jolted to life with long, unsteady breaths. He clutched his head.

"How's your head?" The strong woman asked.

He felt a sharp sting at the back of his skull. The sounds of sirens and chatter of security guards, police, emergency workers, and reporters didn't help his condition. The air smelled foul. It smelled like Bourbon Street on a Sunday morning.

He tried to get up.

"No." The medic placed her hand on his shoulder.

"Where is my brother?" Andy pleaded to her.

"Don't worry about that now."

"Where is my brother?" He pushed the woman's hand away.

"He's okay. He went to the hospital. He got shot in the leg. He's going to be okay. Now, stay down."

"Am I okay? Am I going to live?"

"You had a pretty bad gash on your head. You bled out a little, but you'll be all right. Probably a concussion. Relax. Everything's okay now."

Andy sat up. Policemen circled and asked him questions. What did he look like? Did you see a car? What was he after? And, of course, the more obvious question: Why were you and your brother almost killed trying to get into the *Miami Herald* at six in the morning?

Andy tried to stand up and almost fell over. He looked over at the car.

He looked at the emergency worker and explained, "The reason why I'm here is in the trunk of my car. That blue Mustang. If you lift up the carpet in the trunk, there should be a stack of papers in a folder in the spare tire, unless he got it. Can you please check for me? *Please?*"

She grabbed the keys from his trembling hand. "As long as you promise to stay there." He nodded, and she marched toward the rental car.

"What happened to my brother?" Andy repeated, temporarily forgetting that he already asked the question.

"Your brother will be fine. I've seen injuries like his before. He'll probably be in a cast for a couple months. He'll need some rehab, but he will be fine," the police officer standing above him said.

Andy Stone watched the medic walking back toward him with her head pointed down to the ground. He saw keys in her left hand, and finally caught a glance through the crowd of a thick blue folder in her right hand. The mystery man didn't take it. Andy made one and a half copies of the original documents. Jamie took half of one. Andy made a run for it with the second copy. He used an old trick he learned from wannabe drug dealers in high school who used to wrap a twenty-dollar bill around a wad of one-dollar bills to create the initial illusion of a wad of twenties. He grabbed a few originals from the documents and placed them on the front of the folder. It worked. Andy looked at the real evidence walking toward him. She even waved a small black tape at him.

Over the next two days, Andy spoke to his family regularly and stayed with Jamie in the hospital during the day. They watched old Seinfeld episodes and ate lemon popsicles. But mostly, Andy sat at a desk in the newsroom of the *Miami Herald*. He told the story of his family, the Blake Treatment Center, and Plaxin. He gave the editors stories that were to run consecutively on the front page. After the third day, he quietly shut down his computer, collected his notes, sat with his eyes closed, and listened to the hum of the newsroom.

Andy stepped out of the *Miami Herald* with a stack of newspapers. The sky blazed a deep blue that reminded him of Colorado. He looked over at the spot where he thought he was going to die. The confrontation still didn't feel real to him. It was a dream, and he wondered when it would feel different. Two reporters popped out of a cab and congratulated him on his work. Then they raced back inside, most likely to finish a story on deadline. Andy grabbed his newly-purchased disposable cell phone and dialed Richard Blake.

"Hey there. It's all over now."

"How's your brother doing?" Blake asked.

"He's okay. Lots of rehab, but he's going to be okay. We're heading back down to Key West today."

Blake wondered, "You driving?"

"No, we're flying. I don't need to see the mile markers of the Keys for a while," Andy explained.

"I bet."

"Well, I need to get my brother, but I just wanted to tell you that it's all over. The story is out."

"Thank you, Andy," the doctor said. "Sorry I almost got you killed."

"See you soon."

Jamie and Andy Stone boarded American Airlines flight 2560 down to Key West. It was Thursday morning in the middle of December. Thick gray clouds rolled over the airport. The dark propellers spun furiously. The tension of the chase released with the flight and the newspaper that Andy held in his hands. It told the story of a Plaxin cover-up and a CEO who fought to suppress a revolutionary new treatment. A newlywed sitting in front of Jamie read her husband page after page of *Men are from Mars, Women are from Venus.* When Jamie got up to go to the bathroom and came back to hear her still reading, he conveniently bumped his cast into her chair. The move sent the bride's book flying. Andy tried to restrain his laughter.

When Jamie and Andy returned to the Banyan, their mother was on the other side of the worst night she ever had. Three hospice nurses were packing medication and equipment. An ambulance backed into the cobblestone driveway to the resort. Andy's mother was sound asleep through all of the movement. Their father was talking on his phone. He hung up when he saw Jamie and Andy in the doorway. He walked over with arms spread and hugged his boys.

Andy told his father, "It's over."

"The story's out?"

"Yes, and we're here," Jamie said. He leaned on an aluminum crutch. "For good."

"Good. I need you guys," their father said.

Andy asked, "What's going on?" He peered into the condo. His eyes gleamed particularly crystal blue. Andy saw his mother lying on the bed.

"We have a change of plans. Last night was bad," their father explained. "Mom was moaning a lot from the pain. She's okay now, but we have to leave the Banyan."

"Another hospital?" Jamie shook his head. He wiped sweat from his forehead with his gray shirt, exposing his tight stomach. "I'm so sick of hospital rooms."

"No, we found something better," their father said. He hesitated telling them.

Two men stood at the door with a stretcher. They wore the dark blue pants and white shirts of EMTs. It was a uniform that Andy had become disturbingly familiar with over the last week. "We're ready," one of them announced.

"Let's go." Their father motioned.

"Where are we going?" Andy asked. He reached for his mother's nearly bald head. She didn't react to his touch.

"You'll see."

The ambulance quietly drove out of Key West. The brothers and hospice nurses followed in a large van. After a few stoplights off the main island, the ambulance turned right and headed south onto the neighboring Key. A few more turns led them to a quiet residential street. The pavement crumbled into gravel. Two-story homes transformed into ranch-style cottages. Andy peeked through the yards to see boats bobbing next to long piers, then the expanse of the sea. The yards were thick with lush green plants. Three cottages away from the end of the street, the ambulance pulled into a driveway. A small white cabin stood warmly illuminated from the inside. Ferns surrounded the broad porch. It was a classic Key West home – an elegant combination of Victorian and Caribbean architecture. Long white shutters over the windows were cracked open at the bottom.

"What is this place?" Jamie asked his father.

"Clients of mine own this place. I've managed their money for a long time," their father explained. He stretched his tall, tired body. His arms reached for the sky. His black wavy hair was particularly curly. He explained, "When they had a good financial cushion, they started talking about retirement. They both wanted a place in Florida, but didn't want to move to any of those stuffy communities on the Gulf. Kind of like us. I suggested Key West. They came down several years ago and loved it. During the housing collapse, they bought this nice little cottage that opens up to the Caribbean in its backyard. The husband's still working. He didn't fully retire yet. They won't be back down for a couple months. They offered us the cottage for as long as we needed it."

Andy whispered to his father, "Your clients really don't mind if we go to their vacation home so Mom can die?" Andy's slender face scrunched on the right side. His head tilted with skepticism.

"No, they love your mother. The wife had breast cancer too. Your mother spent months with her. She cared for her and offered guidance. Mom did what she had always done without asking for anything in return. They were always really grateful."

Jamie asked, "But still. Do they know Mom's reaching the end?"

Their father explained, "They said they would be honored if Mom were to haunt their Key West home." The boys laughed.

Emergency workers walked inside the house. Hospice nurses carried bags and medical devices out of the van. The brothers and their father waited outside.

Jamie asked, "What can we do to help?" He paced along the front lawn.

"Nothing," their father answered. "They told me to stay out of the way until she's in her bed."

Jamie and Andy remained outside as the bedroom was prepped for their mother. The two hospice nurses continued to rush back and forth from the van like a pair of wedding coordinators. One of the nurses was older. She had frizzy brown and gray hair. She wore scrubs and clean white sneakers. Their father had gotten to know her over the last week of visits to the Banyan. She had a background in alternative medicine, just like their mother. Andy's father encouraged her to do anything to make the house more "cosmic," as he put it. She lit a packed cylindrical bunch of herbs just outside of the house. The tip of the cylinder glowed a deep orange and white smoke rose into the atmosphere. The smell of sage quickly filled the air. The hospice nurse walked around the exterior of the house, waving the sage stick all around.

Once their mother had been successfully transferred to the bed, Andy followed his brother inside the house. Smoky light gray tiles lined the floor. An abrupt front hallway opened up to a surprisingly large kitchen to the left and a sunken living room to the right. Copper-coated pans hung above a modern kitchen island. Stainless appliances were interspersed between birch cabinets. His father grabbed a tall glass of water from the kitchen sink.

Beyond the living room, the main bedroom was bustling with activity behind a door that was cracked open. Andy walked over to the main bedroom. He peeked inside. Through the commotion, Andy could see his mother lying asleep on a hospital bed. Her arms twitched as her pale, naked, unconscious body rested upon clean blue linens. The hospice nurses hurried to change her sheets and clothes. Andy's immediate reaction was to turn away, but he didn't. He looked over his mother's battle-scarred torso through the crack in the door. She had lost two-thirds of her small intestine, had terminal cancer in her liver, lost her left breast, had reconstructive surgery on her right one. She had scars from multiple incisions – evidence of fleeting attempts to fix her broken core. And through all of this, his mother held on. She acted gracefully and courageously. Andy eventually joined his brother and father waiting in the kitchen.

The cosmic hospice nurse finally waved Andy's father into the bedroom. She opened the door. She had been visiting the family ever since they got to the Banyan Resort last week.

She waved to the brothers as well. "You boys should come in here for this."

"Her feet are probably getting colder." The second hospice nurse laid an additional warm blanket over their mother's feet. The nurse was younger with straight brown her. She was short and confident. She expressed an aura of faith and stability. Her strong, dark eyes were framed by purple glasses coated with a metallic glitter. She stood at the foot of the bed and told Andy, his brother and father, "You want to make sure Sarah seems comfortable. If she starts moving around a lot, if she looks agitated, you can give her more pain medicine. The important thing now is that she's comfortable. This is a good time to be alone with your mother and talk to her. To say goodbye."

"How much time do you think?" Jamie asked.

The two hospice nurses looked at each other. The cosmic nurse with long, frazzled hair inspected his mother's arm. "A few days at most."

"You just know that?" Andy asked.

"This is a pretty predictable process," she explained. "Her body has begun to shut down."

Jamie asked, "Why did you look at her arm?" He leaned closer to his mother.

The nurse with glittery glasses explained, "It's the beginning of the body's process of shutting down. Her extremities will shut down first. Her hands and feet will turn a light purplish hue. You'll know when you see it. The discoloration will gradually climb up her arms and legs. Then, when it's time, she will go."

Andy asked, "You think she might live another few days even with her breathing like that? With those long gaps in between?"

"That's very normal. The delays between breaths are only a couple of seconds," the nurse with glittery glasses explained.

"That seems like a long time to me," Andy said. "How long can they go?"

"I've seen patients have delays between breaths up to forty-five seconds," cosmic nurse explained. She dabbed some aromatherapy oil into a diffuser. Ethereal steam billowed toward the ceiling. The potent smell of rose oil filled the room.

"Will she ever wake up?" Jamie asked. "Or will she just stay sleeping like that?"

"She might, or she might wake up for a little bit. It often happens that they will have a brief space of alertness very close to the end."

"Okay." Their father nodded. He sat with wide eyes looking at his soul mate.

The nurses grabbed their things. "I think you guys are all set."

"Thank you so much," their father said. "You two have been incredible."

"We're here. Whenever you guys need us, we can be right over." The younger nurse with glittery glasses expressed a contented smile. It was a smile that came from the noble job of seeing humans off to the afterlife. Andy remembered how much his mother used to enjoy working for hospice. She especially loved comforting families during the death calls.

After everyone left, Andy's father quickly fell asleep on the bed next to his mother. Jamie curled up on the couch in the living room. Jamie regularly got up and peeked into the bedroom, wondering if he would ever see his mother alive again. Andy slept in the second bedroom. His head still ached from the gash from his mysterious assailant.

Brilliant rays of sunlight warmed Andy's face on Friday morning. He gazed through the sliding glass windows in the bedroom to see a tropical ocean setting more beautiful than he imagined under the cover of darkness last night. His head felt better. He tried to get up, but found the task daunting. He was afraid to look in the next bedroom. His bedroom was furnished with bamboo dressers and tables. A small patio with a dark metal table and chairs overlooked the turquoise sea. He had fallen asleep atop a yellow blanket with tropical flowers. A small, hotel-like soap, shampoo and conditioner sat next to clean white towels above the dresser. Andy finally rose to his feet and walked outside of his room. Jamie was asleep. His dense frame was sprawled out on a white velvet couch.

Andy watched his father making coffee in the kitchen. He was wearing his old plaid robe. His round black spectacles sat above his scruffy cheeks. Andy searched for some sign of closure in his father's actions.

He saw Andy and said, "Mom's awake."

"Really?"

"You should go in there. Don't know how long she'll stay awake."

"Mom," Andy said as he peeked into the room.

"Yes?" His mother answered through a forced whisper. "Hey, Buzzie," she said as he walked up to the bed. It would be the last time she ever called him that.

Andy explained, "It's over. The story's out. Doctor Blake is safe." His mother faintly nodded.

"Is he still shut down?" She asked. Her right leg twitched in a regular rhythm.

"No," Andy answered. "The Blake Center will reopen. The enzyme injections will take longer to get cleared. That topic is still a little gray, but for now, he's using something else."

"What?" She asked.

"Not sure. Might be another Blake mystery to solve," Andy said. "The injections will return soon. Apparently, they don't need to go through a very complicated approval process."

"Good." She carefully nodded during a long blink of her tired eyes. "I'm so proud of you, Andy."

Jamie walked into the room.

She reached out her other arm. Jamie clutched her hand. She said, "I'm so proud of both of you. You've grown up to be so strong."

Jamie sat next to her on the bed. He said, "We love you, Mom."

"I love you too. Take care of your father. This will be hard for him."

"We know," Jamie answered.

Andy echoed, "We will."

"It's so beautiful here," she said. She looked out the window at the shimmering water.

Andy looked outside. A sailboat drifted from west to east on the horizon. Jet skis whizzed around in a neighboring bay. They kicked up watery spray into the air. Green grass and tropical foliage in the back yard soaked in the late morning rays. When he turned back around, his mother was back asleep.

By Friday night, her condition had stabilized. The eerie purple discoloration had temporarily halted at her hands and feet. Jamie and Andy sat on the patio. They peeled the skin away from pink shrimp brought to shore that day. They both sipped bottles of Corona and regularly glanced back at their mother's bedroom.

"What happened with Emma?" Jamie asked his brother. He laid his head back on the patio chair and looked up at the tropical sky.

Andy shook his head. He popped another shrimp into his mouth. "We were going to get together in Chicago. She was coming to town. Then we decided to go to Key West. I still haven't seen her. I had to postpone our meeting, but we've been talking on the phone quite a bit."

"She's still talking to you?" Jamie asked through squinting eyes. His broad forehead had a growing red spot from the intense Caribbean sun.

"As of yesterday, yes, she's still talking to me," Andy answered. His slender frame hunched over a plate of shrimp shells. "I think she understands. I hope." Andy asked his brother, "How about Mya? How's she taking this whole apprenticeship thing?"

"I don't know," Jamie shook his head. "For us, it's not very good. I don't know if our relationship will last. She's happy in Chicago."

"You're going to do this for sure?"

Jamie answered, "Andy, it's the biggest opportunity of my life. It will change my life. I have to go. Nothing will stop that. Nothing. Glass is my life. If I can fit a relationship in with my art, I will. But I won't sacrifice my work. Not for anything, not anymore. I'm going. No matter what. I'm going. Beyond that, it doesn't matter."

"Mya's a great girl, Jamie. She's special, and she loves you." Andy spoke carefully to his brother.

"I know." Jamie nodded. "I want it to work out. I do. But we'll have to see. I actually need to call her. Give her an update." Jamie reached into his pocket for his phone. Just as Jamie rose from his chair, Andy said, "Don't get up. I want to check on them."

Andy walked into the kitchen and grabbed a couple more beers from the lonely six-pack in the fridge. The older hospice nurse with frizzy gray hair walked out of the bedroom. She stopped by for a routine check-in. She motioned Andy toward the bedroom. Andy heard conversation in the bedroom and quietly walked over to the door. He peeked through the crack. His parents embraced.

"How are you, sweetie?" His father's voice broke up.

"Okay," she said. She was struggling to breathe.

"I love you so much, Sarah."

"I love you too, my husband."

"Are you in pain?" He asked.

"No, not anymore. Listen to me." Her voice strained. "You've been the most wonderful, caring husband through all of this. There's nothing that I would have changed. You've been so loving and supportive to me. You're a good man, and you have nothing to feel sorry about. Live your life. Keep living, my darling. Don't feel sorry."

"Okay," Andy's father whispered back.

"No guilt," she said.

"No guilt."

Andy quietly slipped into the room. The nurse joined him.

"I'm just going to miss you so much," his father said.

"I know. You will always have me in your heart."

"I know."

Andy's mother winced. The cosmic hospice nurse rushed over to the bed. "Do you need a little more pain medication?"

She nodded through scrunched eyes. Andy's father nodded in approval. The nurse grabbed a small, plastic vial and dropped a clear fluid into his mother's mouth. Her eyes quickly closed.

On Saturday, the boys sat with their mother in shifts. Their father barely left her side. During one of Andy's shifts, he tried to read with little success. He noticed that the round catheter bag dangling from the dull copper metal frame of the bed was practically empty. It had been empty for two days. Catheters drained a patient's bladder and the bags were usually filled with urine, but a few blood-red ounces were the only fluid in the bag. The rest of the clear tube was dry. She had no more waste and was consuming no more fluid.

In the early afternoon, Jamie had pleaded with the hospice nurse to try to give her more water, but the nurse told him that it would only accelerate the dying process by flooding her lungs.

Andy realized that the tide had turned. She no longer opened her eyes. Her breathing became more strained. Her fingers and toes began to turn a cold blue, with sedentary veins that grew purple stretching further up her limbs.

Overcast skies brought occasional rain on this lazy Saturday afternoon. Small drops pattered the roof of the cottage. All Andy could do was to wait and hold the space, and count down the invariable breaths until she succumbed. Sometimes it was therapeutic, sometimes it was depressing, and sometimes it made the world feel like it could just crumble on top of Andy at any time. But most of all, it made him want to live his life the best he could, the way his mother taught him, and the way she would have wanted.

As the sun fell below the horizon to the west and the rain clouds moved to the east, her shoulders flexed and lurched with pain, as if her body had become a straightjacket. Her arms raised and lowered, raised and lowered. Her feet would twitch in phases, and her breathing slowed. Her breaths would be the toughest part about sitting awake with Andy's unconscious mother. They didn't slow in the way that a Buddhist monk's might in deep, tranquil meditation. Rather she exhaled and inhaled rapidly, with her whole upper body jerking at the stress of each breath. Her dry, open mouth pointed up, calling out to the Pleiades above for each gasp of oxygen. As she exhaled, there was a delay before she began the next breath. The delays expanded to a few seconds. Andy watched her body sit completely still until it was jolted back to life for another gasp of air. Whenever the delays were longer than a few seconds, Andy found himself tapping his mother's cold, purple-tinted wrist in an effort to wake her. He didn't know why he did this. It was just instinct.

The nurse with glittery glasses visited on Saturday evening.

"It will be soon," she told the Stone family as she examined their mother's cold, discolored feet and hands. The strange discoloration was now aggressively climbing up to her thighs and upper arms.

Andy, Jamie and their father gathered in the bedroom. By ten at night, the delays between her breaths grew longer. They were so long that

Andy decided to grab his watch and count the seconds. Her arm movements had subsided. Her face looked free of pain. Andy counted the pauses between his mother's breaths. They were five seconds, which wasn't a very long delay by hospice standards.

Sometimes he felt relieved that she would no longer be in pain. But on other breaths he felt hollow inside, as if someone was ripping out a part of his soul. The woman who was so central to his life – in morality and meaning, in love and trust – was about to leave him.

He checked his watch and the five-second breaks in between breaths had quickly expanded to seven seconds within minutes.

Andy also thought about life. He never wanted to be a victim. Everyone was going to die. Many families went through death and loss every day. It was up to him to carry on the light of his mother. He promised to remember the good things. He promised to remember his mother in her better days. He thought about the woman who loved to laugh with her husband and learn from her children.

Eight seconds. Her chest shocked back to life with each new inhale.

As he squeezed her cold hand, he promised to carry on her search for a better way to treat cancer and to keep the flame of the Blake Center alive. He knew that there were other families out there who were struggling to deal with the pain of cancer and many who were searching for a better treatment.

Ten seconds between breaths.

He finally promised to live in her light, always seeking meaning and reveling in the thrilling, imperfect process of life.

She took two breaths with fifteen-second breaks. Then Andy and his family watched their mother exhale for the last time. Her body was still and silent. Fifty-eight years of breaths had finally come to an end, and his mother released from her torturous body.

Andy clutched his brother. They cried as they hugged. Their father sat at the side of the bed. He asked his boys, "Is that it? Is she gone?" He searched for another miraculous breath to follow the long delay. It never came.

Jamie hugged his father. He whispered, "She's gone, Dad." Jamie grabbed the phone and walked outside of the bedroom. "I'll call the nurse."

Andy sat in silence at the foot of the bed. He looked through tear-filled eyes at an empty shell of flesh and bones that used to be his mom. She died at 10:10 on a Saturday night. *My mother is dead. My mother is dead.* He repeated the statement multiple times. The body in front of him alone wasn't enough for the reality to sink in. *My mother is dead.*

A few minutes later, an ambulance rolled into the gravel drive. Andy heard no sirens. Two men exited the ambulance and walked into the illuminated house. They talked with Andy's father and the hospice nurse with glittery glasses. From the darkness outside, Andy could see his brother knelt down next to his mother's hospital bed. Jamie clutched his mother's hand.

The scene was overwhelming for Andy. He turned to the beach and looked out over the black sea. Stars shimmered above him. Waves, whose force had been dispersed out on the reef to the south, quietly washed ashore. Palm trees stretched into the bewildering night sky above. Their fern-like leaves gently rustled in the cool evening breeze. Andy looked up at the galaxies above. He found the Big Dipper and looked out of his peripheral vision until he saw the constellation known as the Pleiades. The dense cluster of stars made him think of his mother. He couldn't believe she was gone.

The moon rose above the horizon. As his mother's body was taken away, Andy hoped that she would still be with him. Somewhere. Through all of the pain and all of the uncertainty, she would be watching over him. His mother would always be there. These things he believed.

Andy had gotten used to the shadow of a body that encased his mother. A part of him hoped that her weakened body could continue to strengthen, day-by-day, week-by-week. The whole family did. They weren't delusional. They still understood the reality and the statistics, but statistics didn't mean anything when it was your mom. Andy always lived in this space with the hope that she could get a little better, that the mother who had every answer could still be there for her children. He imagined a woman who could stand at the kitchen island again cutting fresh herbs and tossing them into a steaming pot with arms that regained the strength they had lost from the drugs. He imagined his mother's voice returning for the first time in years, a mother who could impart more of her vast knowledge. He imagined a mom who would have time to mentor more people, even if they only met her for a day or an hour. He thought about the scores of individuals who couldn't talk to anyone else about their cancer and health problems who found shelter, comfort and guidance from her soothing voice. She tried to find what was right, best and just for the people around her. And he wanted her back. He wanted his mom to be around. He dreamed of a mom who could beat this disease and live on with her husband. And they could grow old and enjoy the fruits of their working days in the lazy twilight of their lives, and wave to their kids – as old and gray grandparents – from the porch of unit 506 at the Banyan Resort on Whitehead Street. He hoped these things. And he hoped them until her final days.

CHAPTER TWENTY-THREE

Ashley Markum, Andy Stone and Doctor Richard Blake stood together in Ashley's downtown Chicago office. They didn't speak. There was nothing more to say. The decisions had been made. The course set. The three of them had been meeting and planning for a month. They all shared a common goal now. Andy's work was almost done. He would soon board a plane heading west.

Richard Blake never went to Germany. Ashley and Blake were beginning a vital partnership. The evidence sat in front of them on a broad oval conference table. Above the table, encased in glass stood an initial architectural model. A modern main building was surrounded by smaller ones. The elegant structures displayed stunning, angular roofs and broad sides of shimmering glass panels. The model looked like part of a futuristic campus. It was a modern complex of spacious gardens, patient rooms, kitchens, and offices. Broad glass panels along two sides of the main building marked fifty patient rooms. *Fifty.* Rows of large, comfortable and welcoming patient rooms stretched along the east side of the building. An extensive research facility and laboratory occupied the expansive southwest wing of the complex. The front of the model displayed the name of this proposed center to be erected in western Madison, "The Blake Treatment Center." This line was no surprise, but beneath it, an equally large line read, "in Partnership with Plaxin Pharmaceuticals." It was to be the first facility of its kind – incorporating Blake's revolutionary treatment with the stable, reliable research and development of Plaxin. Doctor Richard Blake retained total control of his treatment. But he would have a talented research team dedicated to stabilizing and replicating his methods. If successful, many more centers would be built.

Blake looked down at the model of the proposed treatment center with a smile. His brilliant eyes illuminated the room with intense energy. He looked at Ashley and said, "I never could have imagined."

She answered, "Neither could we." She put her arm around her friend. "Not without you, Doctor Blake."

"This is the answer," Blake said.

Ashley nodded. "Yes."

Moments later, the voice of Ashley's assistant cut through the potent silence. "Miss Markum."

"Yes," Ashley answered with resolve.

"It's time."

Blake and Andy nodded. Ashley smiled back. "I'll see you after," she said as she grabbed a folder on her desk and breezed out the door with her blond locks waving behind her.

She took a series of elevators, descended stairs, and walked through dark hallways until she came to the dark side of a broad, flat curtain. Ashley could see just a sliver of the piercing light from television cameras.

"Five minutes," Mallory, Plaxin's PR director, told Ashley as she handed the new CEO a bottle of water.

Ashley stood alone. The loneliness was difficult at times, but she had a new mission. Days after Andy Stone's stories broke, Mike Landis resigned from his position as CEO. He was facing criminal charges, but a high-priced legal team was assembling to defend him. Plaxin was dragged through the mud. Rumors echoed on Wall Street that it wouldn't survive the recent storm. The board was desperate to find a dramatically new direction for the company. None of Mike's handpicked successors were viable options for the board. They needed someone new, someone known to have differences with Mike Landis. Ashley was the only choice. She was given great freedom and encouragement to seek a new direction.

On this day, she began to repair the damage done during the previous years under Mike Landis. Many of Plaxin's darkest secrets had surfaced in the series of stories in the *Miami Herald*. Ashley rubbed her palms with her fingers, checking for sweat. She had been nervous all day, but now she felt a soothing calm wash over her. Listening to the fervent buzz from the press conference, she finally felt the gravity of her new position.

Mallory reached for Ashley's water bottle. She whispered to her new boss, "It's time. I'm happy to be working for you, Miss Markum." Mallory added, "I'm sure you already know, but Tanji was released from the hospital today."

Ashley Markum stood at the podium at an impromptu shareholders' meeting. She took a deep breath and thought about the advice that her father always told her, "When you're nervous about speaking, take a moment to touch your chest, and speak from the heart." And she did. She closed a black binder with a carefully manicured speech, and she spoke from the heart.

"As has been widely reported, I will be taking over as the Chief Executive Officer for Plaxin," Ashley said. "It's quite a profound coincidence that I stand before you today because of the suppression of a new cancer treatment. As anyone knows who kept up with Andy Stone's powerful stories, he lost his mother to the disease only weeks ago. It generates within me and my fellow employees great remorse that our company would ever do anything to limit the treatment options for someone like Andy's mother. I can assure you that all of the people who work for Plaxin seek a common goal – to find cures to modern ailments for the benefit of humanity. It may seem strange for me to reaffirm such a seemingly obvious statement, but it would appear necessary following the disturbing actions of our former leadership.

"Doctor Blake and Plaxin have been working together in recent months. In conjunction with the head of our research department, Plaxin has been testing some of Doctor Blake's remedies. The initial results have been nothing short of astounding.

"I feel it is very important to emphasize that the gross actions connected to Plaxin were the result of one man. This is not a systematic indication of the people in this company. I'm pleased to say that many believed this change in direction was long overdue. Many have argued, that there had to be a better way for cancer treatment.

"The Blake Treatment Center and Plaxin have formed a strong partnership. Doctor Blake's groundbreaking treatment will now have access to the largest, most reliable cancer research and testing facilities in the world. We are extremely excited to be a part of the Blake Center. Doctor Blake will retain all control of his treatment, and we have established a partnership that will show promise in realizing a stable, replicable new way to reverse cancer.

"On a personal note, I am very pleased to call Doctor Blake my friend. In recent days, the doctor and I have discussed the cancer cell. He claims that cancer is not something to be eradicated, but reversed and controlled. Although the cancer cell is often viewed as merely a faceless replicating machine, these cells also serve a vital function in our bodies. But sometimes the system fails to control cancer cells and they're allowed to invade other parts of the body.

"Grow, invade, replicate, and repeat. Expand invariably. Grow for the sake of growth. The modern corporation is the cancer cell of our democracy. When held in check by human rationale and conscience, the modern corporation is a functioning aspect of a healthy system. But left to its own volition, the unbridled corporation is a dangerous cancer, and it has invaded in ways that are detrimental to the democratic system as a whole. The unchecked company will expand indefinitely, seeking to grow profits forever. The corporate model has invaded every aspect of our country, including our democracy. This is the greatest single problem facing our country moving forward. The will of the unbridled corporation, like the will of the cancer cell, has taken control of our society, and convinced everyone that what is good for the cancer is good for all.

"I come to you today ready to lead Plaxin into a new era as a responsible, efficient tool, aware of its uses and limitations, and fully ready to benefit the system, even if the means it comes at the expense of the company. This is my pledge to you today. Plaxin will be a place of integrity, an example of a new way to do business for a new era."

Ashley stopped and took a sip of water. The cool fluid felt like it almost evaporated in her burning throat before it even made its way to her stomach.

She hoped this speech made sense, as she was filled with emotion, but remained focused as she continued, "Cancer is a vacancy of awareness. It's a vacancy of personality, humanity, and responsibility. Cancer is the great American illness, and cancer has been spreading for decades.

"We have the power to change course. The beautiful, elegant systems of the human body and of democracy can flourish in the ways initially imagined by their creators. It's time for this change. It's a change that has been building for decades, and it will happen here at Plaxin from this day forward. These things I promise to each and every person listening to me today. The decisions that I make for this company – and I know many won't be easy – will be of the greatest benefit to the most people, not just the greatest benefit to our short-term stock price. This, I promise with everything that I am, because it is all that I have to give you. Plaxin's future is intertwined with my own, and I plan to live my life with integrity and honesty. Thank you."

CHAPTER TWENTY-FOUR

On the flight to Denver from Chicago, Andy flipped down his tray table when the flight attendant handed him a Coke. Words were scribbled into the gray table just below the little drink indentation. They said, "An old Scandinavian proverb: Heaven is a place between too little and too much." As he looked out the window, he felt content with his life. The waves of emotion from his mother continued to rise with little warning, but he was happy to be alive, and felt very lucky for such abundance in his life. He was right in the space that he wanted to be – a place between too little and too much. He hoped that he could find this space a little more as the days moved forward. He always had everything he needed. He was a lucky man.

After Key West, the family returned to Rockford for the visitation and funeral service for Andy's mother. Her body was cremated. Her ashes were displayed in a pastel blue vessel at the services. Tropical flowers surrounded her ashes. The Stones were overwhelmed by the hundreds of people who came out to pay their respects.

Andy didn't speak at the funeral. He could think of no words that could ever do his mother justice. She was the center of his world; she was his guide. And now he held the light of his mother inside of him. A part of his heart died with his mother, but his love for her only strengthened. And the emptiness of losing her was a pain that he would carry for the rest of his life. She was his heart, and now she was gone. He missed her in ways that only his brother and father would ever understand. He missed her to the molecular level of his body, to the deepest layers of his emotions. In the core of his heart, there was a vacancy now, a wound that would never completely heal.

The pain of losing his mother left anger, despair and confusion at times. Like an amputee, the missing part of him took a while to fully comprehend, but he eventually saw light again. His heart was a changing, flowing current. It was never meant to be stagnant. Love expanded and contracted, and expanded again. In Andy's heart was where life began – in the space of true pain and sorrow, joy and love. The place within. The family stayed with their dad, cared for him, and watched out for him in the coming months. After hastily ending his relationship with Mya, Jamie moved back to Rockford for a year before his apprenticeship in Italy. He built a glassblowing studio and worked feverishly on a groundswell of commission requests.

Before Andy's return to Denver, he received constant phone calls from other cancer patients who wanted him to tell their story. His dream of becoming a freelance investigative journalist was coming true.

The day after he returned to Colorado, he found himself back on a chairlift rising to the top of Blue Sky Basin in Vail. A strong storm left two feet of snow in the mountains, so Andy returned to his little slice of heaven.

"Yeah!" His friend, Dan, exclaimed as a skier cruised under the lift, turned sharply to the right, and launched off the cornice known as Lover's Leap. He landed in a cloud of white powder, as if an old battleship cannon had been fired out of the side of the slope.

The mountain was almost silent. Only the sporadic ski edge grinding against the narrow groomed portion of the run, the occasional elated skier shouting random exclamations from the thick evergreens, or the steady hum from the twisted metal lift line broke the stillness.

As the lift sped up to the peak, Andy turned around and looked back at empty chairs. Snow-capped peaks crowded the horizon. Out there, somewhere in those hills, was his religion.

As they rode off the lift, Dan slapped his goggles over his eyes and looked at Andy. With a subtle lean to the right, Andy knew exactly what he meant and nodded. He followed as Dan shuffled along the packed snow on his telemark skis. Andy skated behind on his snowboard. They rode along the ropes that marked the ski boundary and slipped through a gate that read "Warning-Experts Only."

Andy – his black Never Summer board under his feet – raced down the tight, snaking path through the alpine forest along the gradual ridge of the mountain. His body was relaxed and flowed with the turns and undulations. He popped off a bump and whipped his board around 180 degrees riding out smooth on his backside. His sharp metal edges cut into the packed snow with the sound of a shovel scooping up snow and scraping against pavement. He flipped the board back to his front side and accelerated down the trail. The turns came quicker, the bumps rougher as his heart thumped from the slight loss of control. The space narrowed as he ducked in an attempt to avoid a few low-lying branches. They smacked his helmet.

They came to an abrupt stop at the top of a vast, steep face of pristine white powder, cliffs, and pine trees whose branches sagged from the weight of clumps of snow. If silence could be deafening, it certainly was in the back runs of Vail. Specks of skiers angled down the adjacent slopes of the sprawling resort. He heard his friend clip into his bindings. The sound was muted. It was absorbed by two feet of fresh powder like a soundproof room. The sounds dropped to the snow and fell flat.

Dan looked over at his friend. "What time is she getting into town tonight?"

"Emma said she would be at her friend's house by about seven," Andy answered as he ratcheted his bindings tighter.

"You're finally going to see her again."

"Finally," Andy echoed. His chest thumped at the thought of seeing Emma again.

Andy said, "After you." He motioned for his friend to drop into the steep powder field.

"No way. I'm not taking your tracks. Not today," Dan insisted.

"It's okay. I just want to sit up here for a few moments. I'll meet you at the end of the traverse."

"All right, man," Dan said, as a broad smile showed through his rough beard. He gracefully dropped into the run. His skis danced through the trees. Dan charged through the snow, paused for a moment, and then flew off a fifteen-foot cliff, landing in a white cloud below.

"Yeah!" Dan yelled from below. He cruised down the hill onto the single trail. He waved a ski pole back at Andy before he vanished into the woods below.

Andy looked out over the Rocky Mountains and smiled. He thought about his incredible journey since the last time he stood on a snowboard. He looked up at the blue sky above and thought about his mother. His eyes welled up. The pain of her death came in waves of emotion. He eventually refocused on the steep slope of powder. Andy flexed his thighs. They burned from the unfamiliar motions of snowboarding. He angled his board downhill. The nose of the board cut through the deep powder. The mountain steepened as he carved around stoic pine trees. Riding through pristine powder wasn't merely a sport. It was a spontaneous act of creation. Andy danced with the mountain. He constantly shifted his line in unison with the slope in front of him. His turns were an expression of art, as if he were carving out his name in a form of snowboard calligraphy. He slowed and steadied his board and rode onto a massive downed tree. It was smooth and level with a thick band of snow running along the top. He skidded above the tree as long as his balance would allow and landed in the familiar cloud of powder. He was home.

As the last arcs of purple faded into the western sky later that evening, Andy Stone walked up to the gates of a set of modern condo buildings west of downtown Denver. He buzzed #302.

Emma answered, "I'll be right down." He heard the soft, sweet voice that had become so familiar to him. Months of extensive phone calls had brought the two of them close.

Even though he wasn't aware of it before Emma, Andy felt like she was always there. She had always been waiting for him. He believed their paths were supposed to meet not as random particles that happened to collide, but more like gravitational poles, invariably drawn to each other on a dimension deeper than space and time. It wasn't destiny; it was just magnetism. It was physics of a fourth dimension, a magnetism that made him search the eyes of so many women, craving one in particular and resisting others, because somehow he knew, somehow he could feel a stronger pull. So this meeting wasn't chance or random. It was the inevitable unity of two forces that had always been living in connection with each other.

Emma performed a combination run-skip across the lawn. Andy could see her bright smile; he could feel her magnetic energy. It felt like so long ago, that he met this entrancing woman. After many conversations on the phone, they were back together again. He was nervous to see her. He wasn't scared, just shivering with anticipation.

"Hello, Emma," he said.

"Hi, Andy." She tilted her head with an irresistibly alluring smile as she spoke.

She let him inside the black metal gate, and they embraced. He inhaled the sweet smell of her hair, the sound of her soothing voice. They walked back toward the condos where they were to have dinner with Emma's friends. Emma led him to the front door, but Andy reached for her hand and turned her toward him at the front steps.

Andy said, "I've never felt this way about anyone. I know this has been a lot to deal with, my mother and the whole Florida thing. But I never forgot about you, or the way you made me feel that night, or how I feel when we talk on the phone. You feel like home."

Emma reached for his face. She touched him gently on the cheeks. Her hands fell to his shoulders. She spoke with a combination of joy and relief. "I feel the same way, Andy."

In these moments, the energy center that was his heart, which was fading after his mother's death, returned and expanded in a different form.

Andy Stone's heart was reborn.

In loving memory of my mother

Although he is a fictional character, I am hopeful that a doctor like Richard Blake will become a reality. This is not the story of cancer treatment as it exists today, but rather a vision of what it could be. Many doctors and practitioners are making dramatic advances in the way we treat and think about cancer. Their discoveries are often restricted because of the big business of health care and the expense of drug development. But the advances will continue. A cancer revolution has begun.

Made in the USA
Lexington, KY
11 July 2012